To the Lighthouse

OTHER VIRGINIA WOOLF TITLES
AVAILABLE IN ANNOTATED EDITIONS

Mrs. Dalloway

A Room of One's Own

To the
Lighthouse

VIRGINIA
WOOLF

Annotated and with an introduction
by Mark Hussey

Mark Hussey, General Editor

A Harvest Book • Harcourt, Inc.
Orlando Austin New York San Diego London

www.HarcourtBooks.com

Library of Congress Cataloging-in-Publication Data
Woolf, Virginia, 1882–1941.
To the lighthouse/Virginia Woolf; annotated and with an introduction by Mark Hussey;
Mark Hussey, general editor.—1st Harvest ed.
p.   cm.—(A Harvest Book)
Includes bibliographical references.
1. Skye, Island of (Scotland)—Fiction.   2. English—Scotland—Fiction.
3. Loss (Psychology)—Fiction.   4. Mothers—Death—Fiction.
5. Summer resorts—Fiction.   6. Married people—Fiction.   7. Lighthouses—Fiction.
8. Widowers—Fiction.   I. Hussey, Mark, 1956–   II. Title.   III. Series.
PR6045.O72T6   2005
823'.912—dc22   2005004201
ISBN 978-0-15-603047-2

Text set in Garamond MT
Designed by Cathy Riggs

Printed in the United States of America

First edition
G I K M N L J H

CONTENTS

To the Lighthouse

Virginia Woolf

VIRGINIA WOOLF was born into what she once described as "a very communicative, literate, letter writing, visiting, articulate, late nineteenth century world." Her parents, Leslie and Julia Stephen, both previously widowed, began their marriage in 1878 with four young children: Laura (1870–1945), the daughter of Leslie Stephen and his first wife, Harriet Thackeray (1840–1875); and George (1868–1934), Gerald (1870–1937), and Stella Duckworth (1869–1897), the children of Julia Prinsep (1846–1895) and Herbert Duckworth (1833–1870). In the first five years of their marriage, the Stephens had four more children. Their third child, Virginia, was born in 1882, the year her father began work on the monumental *Dictionary of National Biography* that would earn him a knighthood in 1902. Virginia, her sister, Vanessa (1879–1961), and brothers, Thoby (1880–1906) and Adrian (1883–1948), all were born in the tall house at 22 Hyde Park Gate in London where the eight children lived with numerous servants, their eminent and irascible father, and their beautiful mother, who, in Woolf's words, was "in the very centre of that great Cathedral space that was childhood."

Woolf's parents knew many of the intellectual luminaries of the late Victorian era well, counting among their close friends novelists such as George Meredith, Thomas Hardy, and Henry James. Woolf's great-aunt Julia Margaret Cameron was a pioneering photographer who made portraits of the poets Alfred

Tennyson and Robert Browning, of the naturalist Charles Darwin, and of the philosopher and historian Thomas Carlyle, among many others. Beginning in the year Woolf was born, the entire Stephen family moved to Talland House in St. Ives, Cornwall, for the summer. There the younger children would spend their days playing cricket in the garden, frolicking on the beach, or taking walks along the coast, from where they could look out across the bay to the Godrevy lighthouse.

The early years of Woolf's life were marred by traumatic events. When she was thirteen, her mother, exhausted by a punishing schedule of charitable visits among the sick and poor, died from a bout of influenza. Woolf's half sister Stella took over the household responsibilities and bore the brunt of their self-pitying father's sorrow until she escaped into marriage in 1897 with Jack Hills, a young man who had been a favorite of Julia's. Within three months, Stella (who was pregnant) was dead, most likely from peritonitis. In this year, which she called "the first really *lived* year of my life," Woolf began a diary. Over the next twelve years, she would record in its pages her voracious reading, her impressions of people and places, feelings about her siblings, and events in the daily life of the large household.[1]

In addition to the premature deaths of her mother and half sister, there were other miseries in Woolf's childhood. In autobiographical writings and letters, Woolf referred to the sexual abuse she suffered at the hands of her two older half brothers, George and Gerald Duckworth. George, in one instance, explained his behavior to a family doctor as his effort to comfort his half sister for the fatal illness of their father. Sir Leslie died

---

[1]Woolf's early diary is published as *A Passionate Apprentice: The Early Journals, 1897–1909,* edited by Mitchell A. Leaska. A 1909 notebook discovered in 2002 has been published as *Carlyle's House and Other Sketches,* edited by David Bradshaw (London: Hesperus, 2003).

from cancer in 1904, and shortly thereafter the four Stephen children—Vanessa, Virginia, Thoby, and Adrian—moved together to the then-unfashionable London neighborhood of Bloomsbury. When Thoby Stephen began to bring his Cambridge University friends to the house on Thursday evenings, what would later become famous as the "Bloomsbury Group" began to form.

In an article marking the centenary of her father's birth, Woolf recalled his "allowing a girl of fifteen the free run of a large and quite unexpurgated library"—an unusual opportunity for a Victorian young woman, and evidence of the high regard Sir Leslie had for his daughter's intellectual talents. In her diary, she recorded the many different kinds of books her father recommended to her—biographies and memoirs, philosophy, history, and poetry. Although he believed that women should be "as well educated as men," Woolf's mother held that "to serve is the fulfilment of women's highest nature." The young Stephen children were first taught at home by their mother and father, with little success. Woolf herself received no formal education beyond some classes in Greek and Latin in the Ladies' Department of King's College in London, beginning in the fall of 1897. In 1899 she began lessons in Greek with Clara Pater, sister of the renowned Victorian critic Walter Pater, and in 1902 she was tutored in the classics by Janet Case (who also later involved her in work for women's suffrage). Such homeschooling was a source of some bitterness later in her life, as she recognized the advantages that derived from the expensive educations her brothers and half brothers received at private schools and university. Yet she also realized that her father's encouragement of her obviously keen intellect had given her an eclectic foundation. In the early years of Bloomsbury, she reveled in the opportunity to discuss ideas with her brother Thoby and his friends, among whom were Lytton Strachey, Clive Bell, and

E. M. Forster. From them, she heard, too, about an intense young man named Leonard Woolf, whom she had met briefly when visiting Thoby at Cambridge, and also in 1904 when he came to dinner at Gordon Square just before leaving for Ceylon (now called Sri Lanka), where he was to administer a far-flung outpost of the British Empire.

Virginia Woolf's first publications were unsigned reviews and essays in an Anglo-Catholic newspaper called the *Guardian*, beginning in December 1904. In the fall of 1906, she and Vanessa went with a family friend, Violet Dickinson, to meet their brothers in Greece. The trip was spoiled by Vanessa's falling ill, and when she returned to London, Virginia found both her brother Thoby—who had returned earlier—and her sister seriously ill. After a misdiagnosis by his doctors, Thoby died from typhoid fever on November 20, leaving Virginia to maintain a cheerful front while her sister and Violet Dickinson recovered from their own illnesses. Two days after Thoby's death, Vanessa agreed to marry his close friend Clive Bell.

While living in Bloomsbury, Woolf had begun to write a novel that would go through many drafts before it was published in 1915 as *The Voyage Out*. In these early years of independence, her social circle widened. She became close to the art critic Roger Fry, organizer of the First Post-Impressionist Exhibition in London in 1910, and also entered the orbit of the famed literary hostess Lady Ottoline Morrell (cruelly caricatured as Hermione Roddice in D. H. Lawrence's 1920 novel *Women in Love*). Her political consciousness also began to emerge. In 1910 she volunteered for the movement for women's suffrage. She also participated that February in a daring hoax that embarrassed the British Navy and led to questions being asked in the House of Commons: She and her brother Adrian, together with some other Cambridge friends, gained access to a secret warship by dressing up and posing as the Emperor of Abyssinia and his retinue. The "Dreadnought Hoax" was front-page news, complete with photographs of the phony Ethiopians with flowing robes, blackened faces, and false beards.

To the British establishment, one of the most embarrassing aspects of the Dreadnought affair was that a woman had taken part in the hoax. Vanessa Bell was concerned at what might have happened to her sister had she been discovered on the ship. She was also increasingly worried about Virginia's erratic health, and by the early summer 1910 had discussed with Dr. George Savage, one of the family's doctors, the debilitating headaches her sister suffered; Dr. Savage prescribed several weeks in a nursing home. Another element in Vanessa's concern was that Virginia was twenty-eight and still unmarried. Clive Bell and Virginia had, in fact, engaged in a hurtful flirtation soon after the birth of Vanessa's first child in 1908. Although she had been proposed to twice in 1909 and once in 1911, Virginia had not taken these offers very seriously.

Dropping by Vanessa's house on a July evening in 1911, Virginia met Leonard Woolf, recently back on leave from Ceylon. Soon after this, Leonard became a lodger at the house Virginia shared with Adrian, the economist John Maynard Keynes, and the painter Duncan Grant. Leonard decided to resign from the Colonial Service, hoping that Virginia would agree to marry him. After some considerable hesitation, she did, and they married in August 1912.

By the end of that year, Woolf was again suffering from the tremendous headaches that afflicted her throughout her life, and in 1913 she was again sent to a nursing home for what was then called a "rest cure." In September of that year, she took an overdose of a sleeping drug and was under care until the following spring. In early 1915 she suffered a severe breakdown and was ill throughout most of the year in which her first novel was published.

Despite this difficult beginning, Virginia and Leonard Woolf's marriage eventually settled into a pattern of immense productivity and mutual support. Leonard worked for a time for the Women's Cooperative Guild, and became increasingly involved with advising the Labour Party and writing on international politics, as well as editing several periodicals. Virginia began to establish herself as an important novelist and influential critic. In 1917 the Woolfs set up their own publishing house, the Hogarth Press, in their home in Richmond. Their first publication was *Two Stories*—Leonard's "Three Jews" and Virginia's experimental "The Mark on the Wall." They had decided to make their livings by writing, and in 1919, a few months before Woolf's second novel, *Night and Day,* was published, they bought a cottage in the village of Rodmell in Sussex. After moving back into London from Richmond in 1923, Woolf would spend summers at Monk's House, returning to the social whirl of the city in the fall.

"The Mark on the Wall" was one of a number of what Woolf called "sketches" that she began to write around the time she and Leonard bought their printing press. *Night and Day* was the last of her books to be published in England by another press. In 1919 Hogarth published her short story *Kew Gardens,* with two woodcuts by Vanessa Bell, and two years later came *Monday or Tuesday,* the only collection of her short fiction published in Woolf's lifetime. Her next novel was *Jacob's Room* (1922), a slim elegy to the generation of 1914, and to her beloved brother Thoby, whose life of great promise had also been cut short so suddenly. Woolf had written to her friend Margaret Llewelyn Davies in 1916 that the Great War, as it was then called, was a "preposterous masculine fiction" that made her "steadily more feminist," and in her fiction and nonfiction she began to articulate and illuminate the connections between the patriarchal status quo, the relatively subordinate position of

women, and war making. Thinking about a novel she was calling "The Hours," Woolf wrote in her diary in 1923 that she
wanted to criticize "the social system." Her inclusion in the
novel of a shell-shocked war veteran named Septimus Warren
Smith would confuse many of the early reviewers of her fourth
novel, *Mrs. Dalloway* (1925), but others recognized that Woolf
was breaking new ground in the way she rendered consciousness and her understanding of human subjectivity.

By the time she wrote *Mrs. Dalloway,* Woolf was also a sought-
after essayist and reviewer who, like many of her celebrated
contemporaries, was staking out her own particular piece of
modernist territory. The Hogarth Press published radical young
writers like Katherine Mansfield, T. S. Eliot, and Gertrude Stein.
Approached by Harriet Shaw Weaver with part of the manuscript of James Joyce's *Ulysses* in 1918, the Woolfs turned it down.
Their own small press could not cope with the long and complex manuscript, nor could Leonard Woolf find a commercial
printer willing to risk prosecution for obscenity by producing it.
In 1924 the Hogarth Press became the official English publisher
of the works of Sigmund Freud, translated by Lytton Strachey's
brother James. Woolf's own literary criticism was collected in a
volume published in 1925, *The Common Reader*—a title signaling
her distrust of academics and love of broad, eclectic reading.

The staggering range of Woolf's reading is reflected in the
more than five hundred essays and reviews she published during her lifetime. Her critical writing is concerned not only with
the canonical works of English literature from Chaucer to her
contemporaries, but also ranges widely through lives of the obscure, memoirs, diaries, letters, and biographies. Models of the
form, her essays comprise a body of work that has only recently
begun to attract the kind of recognition her fiction has received.

In 1922 Woolf met "the lovely and gifted aristocrat" Vita
Sackville-West, already a well-known poet and novelist. Their

close friendship slowly turned into a love affair, glowing most intensely from about 1925 to 1928, before modulating into friendship once more in the 1930s. The period of their intimacy was extremely creative for both writers, Woolf publishing essays such as "Mr. Bennett and Mrs. Brown" and "Letter to a Young Poet," as well as three very different novels: *To the Lighthouse* (1927), which evoked her own childhood and had at its center the figure of a modernist woman artist, Lily Briscoe; *Orlando* (1928), a fantastic biography inspired by Vita's own remarkable family history; and *The Waves* (1931), a mystical and profoundly meditative work that pushed Woolf's concept of novel form to its limit. Woolf also published a second *Common Reader* in 1932, and the "biography" of *Flush,* Elizabeth Barrett Browning's dog (1933). She went with Sackville-West to Cambridge in the fall of 1928 to deliver the second of the two lectures on which her great feminist essay *A Room of One's Own* (1929) is based.

As the political situation in Europe in the 1930s moved inexorably to its crisis in 1939, Woolf began to collect newspaper clippings about the relations between the sexes in England, France, Germany, and Italy. The scrapbooks she made became the matrix from which developed the perspectives of her penultimate novel, *The Years* (1937), and the arguments of her pacifist-feminist polemic *Three Guineas* (1938). In 1937 Vanessa's eldest son, Julian Bell, was killed serving as an ambulance driver in the Spanish Civil War. Woolf later wrote to Vanessa that she had written *Three Guineas* partly as an argument with Julian. Her work on *The Years* was grindingly slow and difficult. Ironically, given Woolf's reputation as a highbrow, it became a bestseller in the United States, even being published in an Armed Services edition. While she labored over the novel in 1934, the news came of the death of Roger Fry, one of her oldest and closest friends and the former lover of her sister, Vanessa. Reluctantly, given her distaste for the conventions of biography, Woolf agreed to write his life, which was published in 1940.

In 1939, to relieve the strain of writing Fry's biography, Woolf began to write a memoir, "A Sketch of the Past," which remained unpublished until 1976, when the manuscripts were edited by Jeanne Schulkind for a collection of Woolf's autobiographical writings, *Moments of Being*. Withdrawing with Leonard to Monk's House in Sussex, where they could see the German airplanes flying low overhead on their way to bomb London, Woolf continued to write for peace and correspond with antiwar activists in Europe and the United States. She began to write her last novel, *Between the Acts,* in the spring of 1938, but by early 1941 was dissatisfied with it. Before completing her final revisions, Woolf ended her own life, walking into the River Ouse on the morning of March 28, 1941. To her sister, Vanessa, she wrote, "I can hardly think clearly any more. If I could I would tell you what you and the children have meant to me. I think you know." In her last note to Leonard, she told him he had given her "complete happiness," and asked him to destroy all her papers.

By THE END of the twentieth century, Virginia Woolf had become an iconic figure, a touchstone for the feminism that revived in the 1960s as well as for the conservative backlash of the 1980s. Hailed by many as a radical writer of genius, she has also been dismissed as a narrowly focused snob. Her image adorns T-shirts, postcards, and even a beer advertisement, while phrases from her writings occur in all kinds of contexts, from peace-march slogans to highbrow book reviews. That Woolf is one of those figures upon whom the myriad competing narratives of twentieth- and twenty-first-century Western culture inscribe themselves is testified to by the enormous number of biographical works about her published in the decades since her nephew Quentin Bell broke the ground in 1972 with his two-volume biography of his aunt.

Argument continues about the work and life of Virginia Woolf: about her experience of incest, her madness, her class attitudes, her sexuality, the difficulty of her prose, her politics, her feminism, and her legacy. Perhaps, though, these words from her essay "How Should One Read a Book?" are our best guide: "The only advice, indeed, that one person can give another about reading is to take no advice, to follow your own instincts, to use your own reason, to come to your own conclusions."

—Mark Hussey, General Editor

CHRONOLOGY

Information is arranged in this order: 1. Virginia Woolf's family and her works; 2. Cultural and political events; 3. Significant publications and works of art.

1878   Marriage of Woolf's parents, Leslie Stephen (1832–1904) and Julia Prinsep Duckworth (née Jackson) (1846–1895). Leslie Stephen publishes *Samuel Johnson*, first volume in the English Men of Letters series.
England at war in Afghanistan.

1879   Vanessa Stephen (Bell) born (d. 1961). Edward Burne-Jones paints Julia Stephen as the Virgin Mary in *The Annunciation*. Leslie Stephen, *Hours in a Library*, 3rd series.
Somerville and Lady Margaret Hall Colleges for women founded at Oxford University.
Anglo-Zulu war in South Africa.

1880   Thoby Stephen born (d. 1906).
William Gladstone becomes prime minister for second time. First Boer War begins (1880–81). Deaths of Gustave Flaubert (b. 1821) and George Eliot (b. 1819). Lytton Strachey born (d. 1932).
Fyodor Dostoyevsky, *The Brothers Karamazov*.

1881 Leslie Stephen buys lease of Talland House, St. Ives, Cornwall.

Cambridge University Tripos exams opened to women. Henrik Ibsen, *Ghosts;* Henry James, *The Portrait of a Lady, Washington Square;* Christina Rossetti, *A Pageant and Other Poems;* D. G. Rossetti, *Ballads and Sonnets;* Oscar Wilde, *Poems.*

1882 Adeline Virginia Stephen (Virginia Woolf) born January 25. Leslie Stephen begins work as editor of the *Dictionary of National Biography* (*DNB*); publishes *The Science of Ethics.* The Stephen family spends its first summer at Talland House.

Married Women's Property Act enables women to buy, sell, and own property and keep their own earnings. Triple Alliance between Germany, Italy, and Austria. Phoenix Park murders of British officials in Dublin, Ireland. James Joyce born (d. 1941). Death of Charles Darwin (b. 1809).

1883 Adrian Leslie Stephen born (d. 1948). Julia Stephen's *Notes from Sick Rooms* published.

Olive Schreiner, *The Story of an African Farm;* Robert Louis Stevenson, *Treasure Island.*

1884 Leslie Stephen delivers the Clark Lectures at Cambridge University.

Third Reform Act extends the franchise in England. Friedrich Engels, *The Origin of the Family, Private Property and the State;* John Ruskin, *The Storm-Cloud of the Nineteenth Century;* Mark Twain, *The Adventures of Huckleberry Finn.*

1885   First volume of Leslie Stephen's *Dictionary of National Biography* published.
Redistribution Act further extends the franchise in England. Ezra Pound born (d. 1972); D. H. Lawrence born (d. 1930).
George Meredith, *Diana of the Crossways;* Émile Zola, *Germinal.*

1887   Queen Victoria's Golden Jubilee.
Arthur Conan Doyle, *A Study in Scarlet;* H. Rider Haggard, *She;* Thomas Hardy, *The Woodlanders.*

1891   Leslie Stephen gives up the *DNB* editorship. Laura Stephen (1870–1945) is placed in an asylum.
William Gladstone elected prime minister of England a fourth time.
Thomas Hardy, *Tess of the D'Urbervilles;* Oscar Wilde, *The Picture of Dorian Gray.*

1895   Death of Julia Stephen.
Armenian Massacres in Turkey. Discovery of X-rays by William Röntgen; Guglielmo Marconi discovers radio; invention of the cinematograph. Trials of Oscar Wilde.
Thomas Hardy, *Jude the Obscure;* H. G. Wells, *The Time Machine;* Oscar Wilde, *The Importance of Being Earnest.*

1896   Vanessa Stephen begins drawing classes three afternoons a week.
Death of William Morris (b. 1834); F. Scott Fitzgerald born (d. 1940).
Anton Chekhov, *The Seagull.*

1897 Woolf attends Greek and history classes at King's College, London, and begins to keep a regular diary. Vanessa, Virginia, and Thoby watch Queen Victoria's Diamond Jubilee procession. Stella Duckworth (b. 1869) marries Jack Hills in April, but dies in July. Gerald Duckworth (1870–1937) establishes a publishing house.
Paul Gauguin, *Where Do We Come From? What Are We? Where Are We Going?;* Bram Stoker, *Dracula*.

1898 Spanish-American War (1898–99). Marie Curie discovers radium. Death of Stéphane Mallarmé (b. 1842).
H. G. Wells, *The War of the Worlds;* Oscar Wilde, *The Ballad of Reading Gaol*.

1899 Woolf begins Latin and Greek lessons with Clara Pater. Thoby Stephen goes up to Trinity College, Cambridge University, entering with Lytton Strachey, Leonard Woolf (1880–1969), and Clive Bell (1881–1964).
The Second Boer War begins (1899–1902) in South Africa. Ernest Hemingway born (d. 1961).

1900 Woolf and Vanessa attend the Trinity College Ball at Cambridge University.
Deaths of Friedrich Nietzsche (b. 1844), John Ruskin (b. 1819), and Oscar Wilde (b. 1854).
Sigmund Freud, *The Interpretation of Dreams*.

1901 Vanessa enters Royal Academy Schools.
Queen Victoria dies January 22. Edward VII becomes king. Marconi sends messages by wireless telegraphy from Cornwall to Newfoundland.

1902   Woolf begins classics lessons with Janet Case. Adrian
        Stephen enters Trinity College, Cambridge University.
        Leslie Stephen is knighted.
        Joseph Conrad, *Heart of Darkness;* Henry James, *The
        Wings of the Dove;* William James, *The Varieties of Religious
        Experience.*

1903   The Wright Brothers fly a biplane 852 feet. Women's
        Social and Political Union founded in England by Em-
        meline Pankhurst.

1904   Sir Leslie Stephen dies. George Duckworth (1868–
        1934) marries Lady Margaret Herbert. The Stephen
        children—Vanessa, Virginia, Thoby, and Adrian—move
        to 46 Gordon Square, in the Bloomsbury district of
        London. Woolf contributes to F. W. Maitland's biogra-
        phy of her father. Leonard Woolf comes to dine before
        sailing for Ceylon. Woolf travels in Italy and France.
        Her first publication is an unsigned review in the
        Guardian, a church weekly.
        "Empire Day" inaugurated in London and in Britain's
        colonies.
        Anton Chekhov, *The Cherry Orchard;* Henry James, *The
        Golden Bowl.*

1905   Woolf begins teaching weekly adult education classes at
        Morley College. Thoby invites Cambridge friends to
        their home for "Thursday Evenings"—the beginnings
        of the Bloomsbury Group. Woolf travels with Adrian to
        Portugal and Spain. The Stephens visit Cornwall for the
        first time since their mother's death.
        Revolution in Russia.

Albert Einstein, *Special Theory of Relativity;* E. M. Forster, *Where Angels Fear to Tread;* Sigmund Freud, *Essays in the Theory of Sexuality;* Edith Wharton, *The House of Mirth;* Oscar Wilde, *De Profundis.*

1906   The Stephens travel to Greece. Vanessa and Thoby fall ill. Thoby dies November 20; on November 22, Vanessa agrees to marry Clive Bell.

Deaths of Paul Cézanne (b. 1839) and Henrik Ibsen (b. 1828). Samuel Beckett born (d. 1989).

1907   Woolf moves with her brother Adrian to Fitzroy Square. Vanessa marries Clive Bell.

First Cubist exhibition in Paris. W. H. Auden born (d. 1973).

Joseph Conrad, *The Secret Agent;* E. M. Forster, *The Longest Journey;* Edmund Gosse, *Father and Son;* Pablo Picasso, *Demoiselles d'Avignon.*

1908   Birth of Vanessa Bell's first child, Julian. Woolf travels to Italy with Vanessa and Clive Bell.

Herbert Asquith becomes prime minister.

E. M. Forster, *A Room with a View;* Gertrude Stein, *Three Lives.*

1909   Woolf receives a legacy of £2,500 on the death of her Quaker aunt, Caroline Emelia Stephen. Lytton Strachey proposes marriage to Woolf, but they both quickly realize this would be a mistake. Woolf meets Lady Ottoline Morrell for the first time. She travels to the Wagner festival in Bayreuth.

Chancellor of the Exchequer David Lloyd George (1863–1945) introduces a "People's Budget," taxing wealth to pay for social reforms. A constitutional crisis ensues when the House of Lords rejects it. Death of George Meredith (b. 1828).

Filippo Marinetti, "The Founding and Manifesto of Futurism"; Henri Matisse, *Dance*.

1910 Woolf participates in the Dreadnought Hoax. She volunteers for the cause of women's suffrage. Birth of Vanessa Bell's second child, Quentin (d. 1996).

First Post-Impressionist Exhibition ("Manet and the Post-Impressionists") organized by Roger Fry (1866–1934) at the Grafton Galleries in London. Edward VII dies May 6. George V becomes king. Death of Leo Tolstoy (b. 1828).

E. M. Forster, *Howards End;* Igor Stravinsky, *The Firebird.*

1911 Woolf rents Little Talland House in Sussex. Leonard Woolf returns from Ceylon; in November, he, Adrian Stephen, John Maynard Keynes (1883–1946), Woolf, and Duncan Grant (1885–1978) share a house together at Brunswick Square in London.

Ernest Rutherford makes first model of atomic structure. Rupert Brooke, *Poems;* Joseph Conrad, *Under Western Eyes;* D. H. Lawrence, *The White Peacock;* Katherine Mansfield, *In a German Pension;* Ezra Pound, *Canzoni;* Edith Wharton, *Ethan Frome.*

1912 Woolf leases Asheham House in Sussex. Marries Leonard on August 10; they move to Clifford's Inn, London.

Captain Robert Scott's expedition reaches the South Pole, but he and his companions die on the return

journey. The *Titanic* sinks. Second Post-Impressionist Exhibition, for which Leonard Woolf serves as
secretary.

Marcel Duchamp, *Nude Descending a Staircase;* Wassily
Kandinsky, *Concerning the Spiritual in Art;* Thomas
Mann, *Death in Venice;* George Bernard Shaw, *Pygmalion.*

1913 *The Voyage Out* manuscript delivered to Gerald Duckworth. Woolf enters a nursing home in July; in September, she attempts suicide.
Roger Fry founds the Omega Workshops.
Sigmund Freud, *Totem and Taboo;* D. H. Lawrence, *Sons
and Lovers;* Marcel Proust, *Du côté de chez Swann;* Igor
Stravinsky, *Le Sacre du printemps.*

1914 Leonard Woolf, *The Wise Virgins;* he reviews Freud's
The Psychopathology of Everyday Life.
World War I ("The Great War") begins in August.
Home Rule Bill for Ireland passed.
Clive Bell, *Art;* James Joyce, *Dubliners;* Wyndham Lewis
et al., "Vorticist Manifesto" (in *Blast*); Gertrude Stein,
Tender Buttons.

1915 *The Voyage Out,* Woolf's first novel, published by Duck-
worth. In April the Woolfs move to Hogarth House in
Richmond. Woolf begins again to keep a regular diary.
First Zeppelin attack on London. Death of Rupert
Brooke (b. 1887).
Joseph Conrad, *Victory;* Ford Madox Ford, *The Good Sol-
dier;* D. H. Lawrence, *The Rainbow;* Dorothy Richardson,
Pointed Roofs.

1916   Woolf discovers Charleston, where her sister, Vanessa (no longer living with her husband, Clive), moves in October with her sons, Julian and Quentin, and Duncan Grant (with whom she is in love) and David Garnett (with whom Duncan is in love).
Easter Rising in Dublin. Death of Henry James (b. 1843).
Albert Einstein, *General Theory of Relativity;* James Joyce, *A Portrait of the Artist as a Young Man;* Dorothy Richardson, *Backwater.*

1917   The Hogarth Press established by Leonard and Virginia Woolf in Richmond. Their first publication is their own *Two Stories,* with woodcuts by Dora Carrington (1893–1932).
Russian Bolshevik Revolution destroys the rule of the czar. The United States enters the European war.
T. S. Eliot, *Prufrock and Other Observations;* Sigmund Freud, *Introduction to Psychoanalysis;* Carl Jung, *The Unconscious;* Dorothy Richardson, *Honeycomb;* W. B. Yeats, *The Wild Swans at Coole.*

1918   Woolf meets T. S. Eliot (1888–1965). Harriet Shaw Weaver comes to tea with the manuscript of James Joyce's *Ulysses.* Vanessa Bell and Duncan Grant's daughter, Angelica Garnett, born; her paternity is kept secret from all but a very few intimates.
Armistice signed November 11; Parliamentary Reform Act gives votes in Britain to women of thirty and older and to all men.
G. M. Hopkins, *Poems;* James Joyce, *Exiles;* Katherine Mansfield, *Prelude* (Hogarth Press); Marcel Proust, *À*

l'ombre des jeunes filles en fleurs; Lytton Strachey, *Eminent Victorians;* Rebecca West, *The Return of the Soldier.*

1919   The Woolfs buy Monk's House in Sussex. Woolf's second novel, *Night and Day,* is published by Duckworth. Her essay "Modern Novels" (republished in 1925 as "Modern Fiction") appears in the *Times Literary Supplement; Kew Gardens* published by Hogarth Press.

Bauhaus founded by Walter Gropius in Weimar. Sex Disqualification (Removal) Act opens many professions and public offices to women. Election of first woman member of parliament, Nancy Astor. Treaty of Versailles imposes harsh conditions on postwar Germany, opposed by John Maynard Keynes, who writes *The Economic Consequences of the Peace.* League of Nations created. T. S. Eliot, "Tradition and the Individual Talent," *Poems;* Dorothy Richardson, *The Tunnel, Interim;* Robert Wiene, *The Cabinet of Dr. Caligari* (film).

1920   The Memoir Club, comprising thirteen original members of the Bloomsbury Group, meets for the first time. *The Voyage Out* and *Night and Day* are published in the United States by George H. Doran.

Mohandas Gandhi initiates mass passive resistance against British rule in India.

T. S. Eliot, *The Sacred Wood;* Sigmund Freud, *Beyond the Pleasure Principle;* Roger Fry, *Vision and Design;* D. H. Lawrence, *Women in Love;* Katherine Mansfield, *Bliss and Other Stories;* Ezra Pound, *Hugh Selwyn Mauberley;* Marcel Proust, *Le Côté de Guermantes I;* Edith Wharton, *The Age of Innocence.*

1921   Woolf's short story collection *Monday or Tuesday* published by Hogarth Press, which will from this time publish all her books in England. The book is also published in the United States by Harcourt Brace, which from now on is her American publisher.

Aldous Huxley, *Crome Yellow;* Pablo Picasso, *Three Musicians;* Luigi Pirandello, *Six Characters in Search of an Author;* Marcel Proust, *Le Côté de Guermantes II, Sodome et Gomorrhe I;* Dorothy Richardson, *Deadlock;* Lytton Strachey, *Queen Victoria.*

1922   *Jacob's Room* published. Woolf meets Vita Sackville-West (1892–1962) for the first time.

Bonar Law elected prime minister. Mussolini comes to power in Italy. Irish Free State established. British Broadcasting Company (BBC) formed. Discovery of Tutankhamen's tomb in Egypt. Death of Marcel Proust (b. 1871).

T. S. Eliot, *The Waste Land;* James Joyce, *Ulysses;* Katherine Mansfield, *The Garden Party;* Marcel Proust, *Sodome et Gomorrhe II;* Ludwig Wittgenstein, *Tractatus Logico-Philosophicus.*

1923   The Woolfs travel to Spain, stopping in Paris on the way home. Hogarth Press publishes *The Waste Land.*

Stanley Baldwin succeeds Bonar Law as prime minister. Death of Katherine Mansfield (b. 1888).

Mina Loy, *Lunar Baedeker;* Marcel Proust, *La Prisonnière;* Dorothy Richardson, *Revolving Lights;* Rainer Maria Rilke, *Duino Elegies.*

1924   The Woolfs move to Tavistock Square. Woolf lectures on "Character in Fiction" to the Heretics Society at Cambridge University.

The Labour Party takes office for the first time under

the leadership of Ramsay MacDonald but is voted out within the year. Death of Joseph Conrad (b. 1857). E. M. Forster, *A Passage to India;* Thomas Mann, *The Magic Mountain.*

1925 *Mrs. Dalloway* and *The Common Reader* published. Woolf stays with Vita Sackville-West at her house, Long Barn, for the first time.

Nancy Cunard, *Parallax;* F. Scott Fitzgerald, *The Great Gatsby;* Ernest Hemingway, *In Our Time;* Adolf Hitler, *Mein Kampf;* Franz Kafka, *The Trial;* Alain Locke, ed., *The New Negro;* Marcel Proust, *Albertine disparue;* Dorothy Richardson, *The Trap;* Gertrude Stein, *The Making of Americans.*

1926 Woolf lectures on "How Should One Read a Book?" at Hayes Court School. "Cinema" published in *Arts* (New York), "Impassioned Prose" in *Times Literary Supplement,* and "On Being Ill" in *New Criterion.* Meets Gertrude Stein (1874–1946).

The General Strike in support of mine workers in England lasts nearly two weeks.

Ernest Hemingway, *The Sun Also Rises;* Langston Hughes, *The Weary Blues;* Franz Kafka, *The Castle;* A. A. Milne, *Winnie-the-Pooh.*

1927 *To the Lighthouse,* "The Art of Fiction," "Poetry, Fiction and the Future," and "Street Haunting" published. The Woolfs travel with Vita Sackville-West and her husband, Harold Nicolson, to Yorkshire to see the total eclipse of the sun. They buy their first car.

Charles Lindbergh flies the Atlantic solo.

E. M. Forster, *Aspects of the Novel;* Ernest Hemingway, *Men without Women;* Franz Kafka, *Amerika;* Marcel

Proust, *Le Temps retrouvé;* Gertrude Stein, *Four Saints in Three Acts.*

1928   *Orlando: A Biography* published. In October, Woolf delivers two lectures at Cambridge on which she will base *A Room of One's Own.* Femina-Vie Heureuse prize awarded to *To the Lighthouse.*
The Equal Franchise Act gives the vote to all women over twenty-one. Sound films introduced. Death of Thomas Hardy (b. 1840).
Djuna Barnes, *Ladies Almanack;* Radclyffe Hall, *The Well of Loneliness;* D. H. Lawrence, *Lady Chatterley's Lover;* Evelyn Waugh, *Decline and Fall;* W. B. Yeats, *The Tower.*

1929   *A Room of One's Own* published. "Women and Fiction" in *The Forum* (New York).
Labour Party returned to power under Prime Minister MacDonald. Discovery of penicillin. Museum of Modern Art opens in New York. Wall Street crash.
William Faulkner, *The Sound and the Fury;* Ernest Hemingway, *A Farewell to Arms;* Nella Larsen, *Passing.*

1930   Woolf meets the pioneering composer, writer, and suffragette Ethel Smyth (1858–1944), with whom she forms a close friendship.
Death of D. H. Lawrence (b. 1885).
W. H. Auden, *Poems;* T. S. Eliot, *Ash Wednesday;* William Faulkner, *As I Lay Dying;* Sigmund Freud, *Civilisation and Its Discontents.*

1931   *The Waves* is published. First of six articles by Woolf about London published in *Good Housekeeping;* "Introductory Letter" to *Life As We Have Known It.* Lectures to London branch of National Society for Women's Service on "Professions for Women." Meets John Lehmann (1907–1987), who will become a partner in the Hogarth Press.

Growing financial crisis throughout Europe and beginning of the Great Depression.

1932   *The Common Reader, Second Series* and "Letter to a Young Poet" published. Woolf invited to give the 1933 Clark Lectures at Cambridge, which she declines.

Death of Lytton Strachey (b. 1880).

Aldous Huxley, *Brave New World*.

1933   *Flush: A Biography,* published. The Woolfs travel by car to Italy.

Adolf Hitler becomes chancellor of Germany, establishing the totalitarian dictatorship of his National Socialist (Nazi) Party.

T. S. Eliot, *The Use of Poetry and the Use of Criticism;* George Orwell, *Down and Out in Paris and London;* Gertrude Stein, *The Autobiography of Alice B. Toklas;* Nathanael West, *Miss Lonelyhearts;* W. B. Yeats, *The Collected Poems.*

1934   Woolf meets W. B. Yeats at Ottoline Morrell's house. Writes "Walter Sickert: A Conversation."

George Duckworth dies. Roger Fry dies.

Samuel Beckett, *More Pricks Than Kicks;* Nancy Cunard, ed., *Negro: An Anthology;* F. Scott Fitzgerald, *Tender Is the Night;* Wyndham Lewis, *Men Without Art;* Henry Miller, *Tropic of Cancer;* Ezra Pound, *ABC of Reading;* Evelyn Waugh, *A Handful of Dust.*

1935 The Woolfs travel to Germany, where they accidentally get caught up in a parade for Göring. They return to England via Italy and France.

1936 Woolf reads "Am I a Snob?" to the Memoir Club, and publishes "Why Art Today Follows Politics" in the *Daily Worker.*
Death of George V, who is succeeded by Edward VIII, who then abdicates to marry Wallis Simpson. George VI becomes king. Spanish Civil War (1936–38) begins when General Franco, assisted by Germany and Italy, attacks the Republican government. BBC television begins.
Djuna Barnes, *Nightwood;* Charlie Chaplin, *Modern Times* (film); Aldous Huxley, *Eyeless in Gaza;* J. M. Keynes, *The General Theory of Employment, Interest and Money;* Rose Macaulay, *Personal Pleasures;* Margaret Mitchell, *Gone with the Wind.*

1937 *The Years* published. Woolf's nephew Julian Bell killed in the Spanish Civil War.
Neville Chamberlain becomes prime minister.
Zora Neale Hurston, *Their Eyes Were Watching God;* David Jones, *In Parenthesis;* Pablo Picasso, *Guernica;* John Steinbeck, *Of Mice and Men;* J. R. R. Tolkien, *The Hobbit.*

1938 *Three Guineas* published.
Germany annexes Austria. Chamberlain negotiates the Munich Agreement ("Peace in our time"), ceding Czech territory to Hitler.
Samuel Beckett, *Murphy;* Elizabeth Bowen, *The Death of the Heart;* Jean-Paul Sartre, *La Nausée.*

1939 The Woolfs visit Sigmund Freud, living in exile in London having fled the Nazis. They move to Mecklenburgh Square.

Germany occupies Czechoslovakia; Italy occupies Albania; Russia makes a nonaggression pact with Germany. Germany invades Poland and war is declared by Britain and France on Germany, September 3. Deaths of W. B. Yeats (b. 1865), Sigmund Freud (b. 1856), and Ford Madox Ford (b. 1873).

James Joyce, *Finnegans Wake;* John Steinbeck, *The Grapes of Wrath;* Nathanael West, *The Day of the Locust.*

1940 *Roger Fry: A Biography* published. "Thoughts on Peace in an Air Raid" in the *New Republic.* Woolf lectures on "The Leaning Tower" to the Workers Educational Association in Brighton.

The Battle of Britain leads to German night bombings of English cities. The Woolfs' house at Mecklenburgh Square is severely damaged, as is their former house at Tavistock Square. Hogarth Press is moved out of London.

Ernest Hemingway, *For Whom the Bell Tolls;* Christina Stead, *The Man Who Loved Children.*

1941 Woolf drowns herself, March 28, in the River Ouse in Sussex. *Between the Acts* published in July.

Death of James Joyce (b. 1882).

Rebecca West, *Black Lamb and Grey Falcon.*

INTRODUCTION
BY MARK HUSSEY

CHRONOLOGICALLY AND thematically, *To the Lighthouse* (1927) stands at the center of Virginia Woolf's works. It has attracted more critical commentary than her other novels, earning the praise even of those typically hostile to her art. In 1930 the influential Cambridge professor and critic F. R. Leavis, for example, made an exception to his habitual distaste for Woolf's writing and placed *To the Lighthouse* alongside James Joyce's *Ulysses* and T. S. Eliot's *The Waste Land* as an expression of the finest consciousness of its time.

To the Lighthouse deals with the experience of time and the function of memory, drawing on Woolf's own family history to model the recent history of her culture. Through that narrative, Woolf criticizes the ideology of the late Victorian world in which she grew up and that seemed to many at the time to have been shattered by the First World War. Her critique is concentrated in the portrait of an artist, Lily Briscoe, who struggles against the patriarchal injunction to marry and against the belief that "Women can't paint, women can't write..." (51). Through Lily's painting, Woolf engages with issues of form that preoccupied many of her artist contemporaries, most significantly Roger Fry. *To the Lighthouse* itself is a masterpiece that captures in its unique design what Woolf had termed in an early literary manifesto the "flickerings of that innermost flame" of consciousness ("Modern Fiction" 151).

In this introduction, we will follow the account Woolf gives in her diary, letters, and notebooks of writing *To the Lighthouse;* then, we will look at the biographical sources on which it draws; next, we will examine the issues of form and aesthetics that concerned Woolf as she wrote the novel; lastly, we will take a very brief look at the response *To the Lighthouse* has evoked. Explanations of historical, geographical, and literary allusions will be found in the notes to this edition.

Writing *To the Lighthouse*

What I thought was this: if art is based on thought, what is the transmuting process?

Virginia Woolf, *Diary* 3: 102

In May 1925, the month that Virginia Woolf's fourth novel, *Mrs. Dalloway,* was published, she made notes for a project that would "consist of the stories of people at Mrs. D's party. . . . My idea is that these sketches will be a corridor . . . leading from Mrs. Dalloway to a new book." Woolf wanted to continue thinking about "the party consciousness, the frock consciousness," something she had mused on as she sat, wearing one of her mother's Victorian dresses, in the studio of *Vogue*'s chief photographers on April 27.[1] That studio had been built in 1861 by a Pre-Raphaelite sculptor named Thomas Woolner, who, Woolf recalled, had wanted to marry her mother, Julia (*Diary* 3: 12). The lines of emotion and themes persisting after she had finished *Mrs. Dalloway* had to do not only with the heightened emotions of people at parties, but also with the relation of the present to the past.

In "Ancestors," one of the brief stories she drafted at this time, a Mrs. Vallance feels alienated from the young people at Mrs. Dalloway's party and begins to recall her enchanted childhood in Scotland, and the beautiful figures of her parents, John Ellis Rattray and Catherine Macdonald. Glimpses, then, could already be seen of *To the Lighthouse* at the end of that "corridor" she described in her writing notebook. In *To the Lighthouse*, Woolf would resituate the memories of her childhood summers in St. Ives on the coast of England's Cornwall, to the remote Isle of Skye off the coast of Scotland hundreds of miles to the north.

On the day *Mrs. Dalloway* was published, Woolf jotted a synopsis of her next novel in her diary:

> This is going to be fairly short: to have father's character done complete in it; & mother's; & St Ives; & childhood; & all the usual things I try to put in—life, death &c. But the centre is father's character, sitting in a boat, reciting We perished, each alone, while he crushes a dying mackerel—However, I must refrain. I must write a few little stories first, & let the Lighthouse simmer, adding to it between tea & dinner till it is complete for writing out. (*Diary* 3: 18–19)

An image of her father, Sir Leslie Stephen, had impinged on her consciousness several months earlier. In October 1924 Woolf wrote, "I see already The Old Man" (*Diary* 2: 317), and at the start of 1925 she brought this vision into sharper focus as she thought of various stories and scenes, "for instance The Old Man (a character of L. S.)" (*Diary* 3: 3). She would later tell her sister, Vanessa, that she had made up the *Lighthouse* all at once, in a walk around Tavistock Square, where she lived in London.

In a memoir that she began in 1939, Woolf also remembered how she had made the book up "in a great, apparently involuntary, rush. One thing burst into another . . ." ("A Sketch of the Past" 81).

Before she had even begun to write it, Woolf worried about the subject matter of her new work. Autobiographical fiction was certainly nothing unusual for a modernist writer—James Joyce, D. H. Lawrence, Katherine Mansfield, Marcel Proust, and Dorothy Richardson all wrote works that drew directly on their own lives. But Woolf had long been dubious about the relations between fiction and autobiography, wondering in 1920 whether "I too, deal thus openly in autobiography & call it fiction" (*Diary* 2: 7), and recording her wariness of "the damned egotistical self; which ruins Joyce & Richardson to my mind" (*Diary* 2: 14). In her first novel, *The Voyage Out* (1915), a character complains that people only read novels "to see what sort of a person the writer is, and, if you know him, which of his friends he's put in." Clear from the start about what she wanted to achieve in *To the Lighthouse* and that it would draw on her own memories, Woolf wondered whether it could really be called a "novel": "I have an idea that I will invent a new name for my books to supplant 'novel'. A new —— by Virginia Woolf. But what? Elegy?" (*Diary* 3: 34).

Elegy ran the risk of nostalgia and, what was worse in Woolf's view, sentimentality. Her close friend Lytton Strachey, the iconoclastic biographer whose *Eminent Victorians* (1918) and *Queen Victoria* (1921) had been cited by Woolf in her 1924 essay "Mr. Bennett and Mrs. Brown" as examples of a new generation's rebellion against the art and ideologies of their predecessors (116), had praised *The Voyage Out* as "very, very unvictorian." That the generation she named the "Edwardians" had made their mark in part by sweeping away lugubrious Victorian emotions gave Woolf pause as she contemplated a novel that would return to the world of her own Victorian parents. A particularly nasty review of *Mrs. Dalloway* in the July 1925 *Calendar of Modern Letters* had accused her of sentimentality, a word that "sticks in my gizzard," she wrote as she contemplated beginning *To the Lighthouse* at Monk's House, her country home:

> But this theme may be sentimental; father & mother & child in the garden: the death; the sail to the lighthouse. . . . It might contain all characters boiled down; & childhood; & then this impersonal thing, which I'm dared to by my friends, the flight of time, & the consequent break of unity in my design. (*Diary* 3: 36)

Her conception was quickly broadening, however, moving away from the central figure of her father to become "a far wider slower book" (*Diary* 3: 37). At Monk's House, on August 6, 1925, Woolf made a plan for the novel that shows how remarkably present to her many of its elements were from the start: It would be in three parts; there would be "a sense of waiting, of expectation: the child waiting to go to the Lighthouse: the woman awaiting the return of the couple" (*Holograph* 2). Dividing the book, and joining its first and third parts, would be "an interesting experiment . . . giving the sense of ten years passing" (*Holograph* 2). The "dominating impression" now was to be the character of Mrs. Ramsay. In the small notebook she had labeled "Notes for writing," Woolf made a visual representation of her new work as "Two blocks joined by a corridor" (*Holograph* Appendix A):

Woolf also planned to write this book differently than she had her previous novel. She wanted "to find a unit . . . for the

sentence which shall be less emphatic & intense than that in
Mrs D: an everyday sentence for carrying on the narrative easily" (*Holograph* 2). Seven months later, she remarked that "I am
writing exactly oppositely from my other books: very loosely at
first; not tight at first . . . Also at perhaps 3 times the speed"
(*Holograph* 3). Susan Dick, who transcribed the first draft of *To
the Lighthouse*, has said that it gives "the impression that at times
her mind was working more swiftly than her pen and that she
was able only to jot down fragments of her thoughts before
these were crowded out by others" (*Holograph* 15). Dick also
points out that in revising her draft Woolf muted the elements
that linked the novel most directly to her own family history
(*Holograph* 21).

Later that August of 1925, Woolf fainted at her nephew
Quentin's fifteenth birthday party and for some time afterward
was ill. Although she made a "flourishing attack" on her novel
in September, by the end of the year she was feeling dejected
about it: "What theme have I? Shan't I be held up for personal
reasons? It will be too like father, or mother: & oddly, I know
so little of my own powers" (*Diary* 3: 49). But she was also writing in the glow of her love affair with Vita Sackville-West, which
had begun when she stayed with Vita at her house, Long Barn,
for three nights beginning December 17. In the last entry in her
diary that year, Woolf described Vita's womanliness and the
"maternal protection" she felt Vita lavished on her, "which, for
some reason, is what I have always most wished from everyone"
(*Diary* 3: 52). At the beginning of 1925, Woolf had commented
on "the lovely *womans* eyes" of the teenage daughter of a friend,
and made a note to herself that she wanted "to begin to describe
my own sex" (*Diary* 3: 3). The intense feelings of one woman
for another would also become an important element of *To the
Lighthouse* as Lily Briscoe worked out her complicated emotions
toward Mrs. Ramsay.

Returning to work on her novel in January 1926, Woolf felt invigorated by both her art and by Vita, and the writing went fast and fluently. In her letters to Vita, she reported on her progress, and also shared with her thoughts on her process:

> Style is a very simple matter; it is all rhythm. Once you get that, you can't use the wrong words. . . . Now this is very profound, what rhythm is, and goes far deeper than words. A sight, an emotion, creates this wave in the mind, long before it makes words to fit it; and in writing (such is my present belief) one has to recapture this, and set this working (which has nothing apparently to do with words) and then, as it breaks and tumbles in the mind, it makes words to fit it. (*Letters* 3: 247)

As most readers of *To the Lighthouse* have understood, Lily Briscoe's efforts to create a painting while staying with the Ramsays are analogous to Virginia Woolf's own efforts to create her novel. Woolf and her artist character are simultaneously involved in "making of the moment something permanent" (165), mixing memory and desire in the effort to embody in a sharable form deeply personal emotions. Like Woolf, Lily Briscoe depends upon a particular rhythm to discover how to realize her conception on the canvas. When she paints, her brush falls into a rhythm "which was dictated to her . . . by what she saw, so that while her hand quivered with life, this rhythm was strong enough to bear her along with it on its current" (163).

To achieve this rhythm, Lily must step back from life, "drawn out of gossip, out of living, out of community with people" (162). Woolf complained to Vita that trying to write in London was like "nailing a flag to the top of a mast in a raging gale" (*Letters* 3: 244) because she was constantly interrupted. After making a start on Part III in June 1926, she put her novel aside until she could resume it in the peace of Monk's House, in late July. Once there, Woolf mused about "the greatest book in the world," a book made "solely & with integrity of one's thoughts" caught before they became "works of art" (*Diary* 3: 102). But this, she knew, was a fantasy: "the process of language is slow and deluding. One must stop to find a word; then, there is the form of the sentence, soliciting one to fill it" (*Diary* 3: 102).

Discussions about form in painting were common among members of Woolf's Bloomsbury circle, initiated by Roger Fry's "An Essay in Aesthetics" (1909). In his essay, Fry identified several "emotional elements of design" that produce the "order and variety" necessary to a work of art: the rhythm of the line, mass, space, light and shade, and color (33–34). Woolf became particularly interested, as we will see below, in how the term "form" might be applied to a literary work. Echoing her description of the "slow and deluding" process of finding the right words for the "form of the sentence," Lily Briscoe struggles to "fill" her blank canvas: "She could see it all so clearly, so commandingly, when she looked: it was when she took her brush in her hand that the whole thing changed" (22). The problem still faces Lily when she returns after a ten-year absence to the Ramsays' house: "But there was all the difference in the world between this planning airily away from the canvas, and actually taking her brush and making the first mark" (161).

For a painter, Woolf implies, the "uncompromising white stare" of the canvas (160) is equivalent to "the form of the sentence, soliciting one to fill it." After visiting an exhibition in June 1926 in which her sister, Vanessa, showed four paintings, Woolf wrote to her: "I expect the problem of empty spaces, and how to model them, has rather baffled you. There are flat passages, so that the design is not completely comprehended" (*Letters* 3: 270–71). The aesthetics of *To the Lighthouse* have often been discussed in relation to the theories of Roger Fry, but Diane Gillespie has explained how Lily Briscoe's experiences as a woman artist also bear close comparison with those of Vanessa Bell (*The Sisters' Arts* 195–203). In a draft of the passage in which Lily attempts to explain her painting to William Bankes (179–80), probably written around the time of Woolf's letter to Vanessa about empty spaces, Lily tells William that "faces . . . can be left blank" in paintings (*Holograph* 273). Many of Vanessa Bell's portraits, including several of Woolf herself, have blank or obscure faces. (In the introduction to a 1973 show of Bell's paintings, Richard Morphet commented on her "obsession with verticals," remarking that she would "seize any opportunity that reasonably presented itself of introducing a vertical line into a painting.")

Woolf was anxious about Vanessa's reaction to the image of their childhood embodied in *To the Lighthouse,* but she also prepared herself for adverse opinions about her representation of a visual artist. Vanessa Bell and her partner, Duncan Grant, another accomplished and successful painter, would surely "laugh at the painting bits in the Lighthouse!" she wrote to Vanessa a few days after the book was published (*Letters* 3: 372). On the contrary, Vanessa was impressed by Woolf's insights into her own art form, remarking that "surely Lily Briscoe must have been rather a good painter" (Bell, *Letters* 318).

THE CENTRAL PART of *To the Lighthouse,* "Time Passes," posed a unique challenge to Woolf: "I have to give an empty house, no people's characters, the passage of time, all eyeless & featureless with nothing to cling to" (*Diary* 3: 76). Woolf was writing this part during the General Strike of May 1926, and recorded in her diary how difficult it was in the absence of external routines to remember the day of the week. Called by the Trades Union Congress in support of British mine workers, who had been in dispute with management since 1925, the strike interrupted many essential services in early May 1926. There was a general sense of torpor, of openness; "It feels," Woolf wrote, "like a deadlock, on both sides; as if we could keep fixed like this for weeks" (*Diary* 3: 78). Critics, such as Kate Flint, have shown how it is possible to connect the movement of "Time Passes" to Woolf's preoccupations at this time; Woolf kept what she described as "an exact diary" during the strike (*Diary* 3: 77). In an undated plan for the middle section of her novel, Woolf outlined its ten "chapters" that were to convey the "gradual dissolution of everything . . . contrasted with the permanence of— what?" (*Holograph* Appendix A). Shortly after *To the Lighthouse* was published, Woolf wrote Vita Sackville-West that she was "doubtful" about "Time Passes." It had been written "in the gloom of the Strike" and she had thought it "impossible as prose" (*Letters* 3: 373).

Woolf permitted an early version of "Time Passes" to be translated into French by Charles Mauron, a friend of Roger Fry's, for publication in the winter 1926 issue of *Commerce,* a journal based in Paris. Fry was not impressed, writing to Mauron's wife, Alice, that he felt Woolf "poeticizes just a little bit" in her descriptions of inanimate objects. His opinion evidently was communicated to Woolf, who noted in February 1927 that "Roger, it is clear, did not like Time Passes" (*Diary* 3: 127).[2] Jane Marcus has speculated that Woolf took this unique step of allowing a part of one of her novels to be published separately to "place herself as a writer in relation to the powerful community of women artists in Paris in the twenties" (5). Whatever her reasons, Woolf does seem to have regarded "Time Passes" as an especially significant development of her art. The published version is very different from the typescript translated by Charles Mauron, as Woolf continued to work on what she had called "the most difficult abstract piece of writing" (*Diary* 3: 76).

The most startling innovation of this section of the novel is Woolf's use of bracketed passages that continue the narrative begun in Part I but isolate it from the ascription of meaning. The stark and sudden fact of Mrs. Ramsay's death is shocking on a first reading, as are the deaths of Prue and Andrew, stripped of sentiment as they are. The brackets are bulletins from a world far away, reporting only a kind of generalized gossip ("people said"; "they said"), signifying the erasure of subjective response in the modern public world where news of death has become routine and impersonal. Roger Poole has convincingly related Woolf's use of brackets to the kind of telegraphic and "objective" journalism that emerged from the period of the First World War (Poole 83–87). Memory itself, in consequence, becomes impersonal. As Poole points out, Mrs. McNab is not even sure who has died: "Some said he was dead; some said she was dead. Which was it? Mrs. Bast didn't know for certain either. The young gentleman was dead. That she was sure. She had read his name in the papers" (144). Life and death become only news items.

BY THE SUMMER of 1926 Woolf had progressed to Part III, "The Lighthouse." That July, the Hogarth Press was preparing to publish a book of the photographs of Woolf's great-aunt Julia Margaret Cameron. Woolf was going through Cameron's photographs of *Famous Men and Fair Women*—as the book was called—from the era of her parents' youth. She wrote to ask Vanessa whether she had any "Aunt Julia letters" to help her research one of two introductions for the book (the other was written by Roger Fry). At this time Woolf had in her possession a photograph album that her father had compiled after the death in 1895 of Julia Stephen, while he was writing *The Mausoleum Book*. Although Leslie Stephen described this work as a "letter" to Julia's children in which he wanted "simply to talk about your mother" (3), in the family it was always referred to as "the Mausoleum Book." It seems most likely that Woolf did not consult this document while she was writing *To the Light-house,* but she certainly looked at the photographs in her father's album: Several images of her mother are included in the Cameron book published by the Hogarth Press. Jane de Gay has argued that Woolf specifically drew on the photographs in her father's album "as ways of remembering the dead" (15–16), and it is possible to see specific photographs almost as illustrations to the novel.[3]

At the end of July, Woolf visited the novelist and poet Thomas Hardy, now eighty-six, who spoke to Woolf about her mother and father, whom he had known very well. He recalled her mother "coming in & out when I was talking to your father" (*Diary* 3: 99). The visit led Woolf to think about the "transmuting process" by which life experienced is made into art (*Diary* 3: 102), the very process in which she was at the time engaged.

By the fall she was "casting about for an end," and facing another technical problem: how to convey a sense of simultaneity as Lily finished her painting and Mr. Ramsay reached the Lighthouse: "Could I do it in a parenthesis? so that one had the sense of reading the two things at the same time?" (*Diary* 3: 106). She felt confident about her method, feeling it "proved, I think, that what I have to say is to be said in this manner" (*Diary* 3: 106). But still, she worried about the charge of sentimentality, and that the "stock criticism" would be that her novel was "Victorian." As always, her first reader was Leonard, her husband. He read it in January 1927 and pronounced it a masterpiece, a "psychological poem" (*Diary* 3: 123). Woolf set to work reading the whole book through, revising her manuscript, seeing the book into print, and then correcting the proofs. Given that she corrected separate proofs differently for the English and American editions of her novels, *To the Lighthouse* exists in significantly different versions on each side of the Atlantic.[4] It was published in England and in the United States on May 5, 1927, the thirty-second anniversary of her mother's death. By July, the book had sold so well the Woolfs were able to buy their first car, an event Woolf described as "a great opening in our lives" (*Diary* 3: 147).

The Ramsays and the Stephens

> One begins to wonder whether, if one knew the very hour and moment of De Foe's birth, the colour of his complexion and hair . . . one would suck an ounce of additional pleasure from *Robinson Crusoe,* or read it one whit more intelligently.
>
> Virginia Woolf, "Robinson Crusoe" (1926)

IN A REMINISCENCE written several years after her sister's death, Vanessa Bell recalled an evening from their early childhood when Virginia asked whom she liked best, their mother or their father. Vanessa answered with little hesitation that she preferred their mother. Virginia, on the other hand,

> went on to explain why she, on the whole, preferred my father. I don't think, however, her preference was quite as sure and simple as mine. She had considered both critically and had more or less analysed her feelings for them which I, at any rate consciously, had never attempted. This seemed to begin an age of much freer speech between us. If one could criticize one's parents, what or whom could one not criticize? Dimly some freedom of thought and speech seemed born, created by her question. (*Notes on Virginia's Childhood*)

When Vanessa read *To the Lighthouse* in May 1927, she wrote to her sister that perhaps she was the only person in the world who could have the feelings it evoked:

> ... in the first part of the book you have given a portrait of mother which is more like her to me than anything I could ever have conceived possible. It is almost painful to have her so raised from the dead. (Bell, *Letters* 317)

Woolf had briefly pondered whether this novel should more properly be called an elegy, and certainly *To the Lighthouse* is haunted by the ghosts of her parents. But as Vanessa Bell discerned even as a child, Woolf's view of their parents was complicated by critical analysis, an impersonal appraisal that, as Suzanne Nalbantian has put it, makes the autobiographical ingredients "less than the sum total of the aesthetic product" (156). Although Leslie and Julia Stephen are clearly the models for Mr. and Mrs. Ramsay, Woolf, like Lily Briscoe, is an artist who "made no attempt at likeness"; "the picture was not of them, she said" (52).

Woolf herself commented several times on how writing *To the Lighthouse* had laid her parents to rest in her mind. She wrote in "A Sketch of the Past" about how she had once been obsessed by the presence of her mother: "I could hear her voice, see her, imagine what she would do or say as I went about my day's doings" (80). But after writing *To the Lighthouse,* "I ceased to be obsessed by my mother. I no longer hear her voice; I do not see her" (80). She described also how, until she "wrote it out" in her novel, she would "find my lips moving; I would be arguing with [my father]; raging against him; saying to myself all that I never said to him" (108). Yet, despite this close association of the novel with memories of her parents, Woolf grew to resent readings that simply identified Mr. and Mrs. Ramsay as

Leslie and Julia Stephen. In 1941, for example, she told her friend Shena Simon that she did not like "being exposed as a novelist and told my people are my mother and father, when, being in a novel, they're not" (*Letters* 6: 464).

As Woolf's life and those of her family and friends have been explored in ever greater detail during the past few decades, it has become clearer that the Ramsays are less a portrait of Leslie and Julia Stephen than what Jane Lilienfeld has described as "fictional constructs based on the idea of the late-Victorian father and mother" ("[The Critic]" 152). The Ramsays recall several characteristics of the Stephens, but there are also many differences between them. Just as Woolf transported the Cornwall setting of her childhood summer holidays in St. Ives to the remote Isle of Skye in the Hebrides (apparently irritating some readers, who wrote to tell her of errors in the novel's flora and fauna), so she transmuted the complex characters of her parents into the somewhat more monolithic figures of the Ramsays. Differences between Mr. Ramsay and Leslie Stephen have been described in detail in John Bicknell's "Mr. Ramsay Was Young Once," and by Alex Zwerdling ("Domestic Politics"), among others. Furthermore, the sense of Leslie Stephen and Woolf's relations with him to be gleaned from her writings as a whole is more nuanced than that offered by *To the Lighthouse*. Mr. Ramsay is a rather remote figure who seems to interact with his children hardly at all, whereas there is plenty of evidence that Sir Leslie was often an attentive and loving parent, for all his gloom and egotism.

Woolf identified as "ambivalence" the feelings of alternating rage and love she had for her father, and noted in "A Sketch of the Past" that by writing *To the Lighthouse* she had done what psychoanalysts, she supposed, do for their patients: "expressed some very long felt and deeply felt emotion" (81). In 1934 she recalled that upon completing the novel she had been "nearer suicide, seriously, than since 1913" (*Diary* 4: 253), and although she claimed that the book had laid her emotions about her parents "to rest," her subsequent references to them somewhat belie this. In one often-quoted diary entry on what would have been her father's ninety-sixth birthday, in 1928, she imagined what would have happened had he still been alive: "His life would have entirely ended mine. . . . No writing, no books;— inconceivable" (*Diary* 3: 208). In creating her portrait of a couple who were *not* like her parents in several respects, but who did represent the prevailing ideology of the Victorian middle class particularly with regard to gender roles, Woolf looked forward to what would be the focus of her intellectual life over the next decade—the effects of patriarchal culture on women, with particular attention to women artists.

In Lily Briscoe, Woolf creates the "daughter" who must resist Mrs. Ramsay's ideology, which offers only marriage as her proper vocation. Although the personal ambivalence toward her father is distributed by Woolf across the characters of James and Cam Ramsay, especially in those sections of Part III that follow their journey to the lighthouse, Woolf embodied a broader critique of her culture in Lily's ambivalent feelings about Mrs. Ramsay. We might even see her great feminist essay, *A Room of One's Own* (1929), as an explicit response to the centuries of denial and oppression summed up in Charles Tansley's misogynist phrase, "Women can't paint, women can't write . . ." (51).

Critics have disagreed about the relatively positive or negative influence on her of Woolf's father, but their subject never laid claim to any such definitive view. That Mrs. Ramsay should have evoked so powerful a sense of their mother was a "psychological mystery," Woolf wrote to Vanessa, given that she had been only thirteen when Julia died (*Letters* 3: 383), yet the mother's central presence in Woolf's fiction has often been remarked. Furthermore, as Elizabeth Abel has explained, Woolf's novel can be connected to the debates in anthropology of the 1920s over whether culture's origins are matrilineal or patrilineal, and to the opposition between the patricentric developmental theories of Freud and the matricentric ones of Melanie Klein. Woolf would certainly have been well aware of these arguments as her brother Adrian (the model for James Ramsay) was not only one of the first British psychoanalysts but had hosted Klein's lectures on object relations theory at his house in Bloomsbury in 1925.

A week after the book was published, Woolf told her sister that she had particularly refrained from reading her parents' letters or "father's life," and was very pleased that Vanessa found Mrs. Ramsay "so like mother" (*Letters* 3: 383). There is some doubt as to what "life" she was referring to (*Letters* 3: 379); it could be the authorized biography of Leslie Stephen by Frederic Maitland (1906), to which Woolf had anonymously contributed a brief reminiscence, or it could be to Stephen's own *Mausoleum Book*. One record from the past that Woolf does appear to have referred to, however, is the diary of a trip to their old summer haunts in Cornwall that she made with her sister, Vanessa, and their two brothers, Thoby and Adrian, in August 1905. She wrote to Vita on January 7, 1926, that she had "left a rain coat, a crystal ruler, a diary for the year 1905, a brooch, and a hot water bottle somewhere—either Long Barn or Charleston [Vanessa's house]" (*Letters* 3: 227); it seems highly unlikely she would have been carrying this particular journal around with her in 1926 by chance. The soft cover notebook with a label reading "Diary/Cornwall/1905" pasted to its cover is included in *A Passionate Apprentice* (Virginia Woolf's early journals).

The 1905 diary begins with her feeling of "enchantment" as she and her siblings, now all in their twenties, board the train that will return them to the scene of their happiest memories.

At first—with a significance only apparent after one has read *To the Lighthouse*—she refers to the "ten years" that have passed since their last visit. Within a couple of paragraphs she has corrected herself as it was, in fact, eleven years since their last visit, in 1894, the summer before their mother's death. Once in Cornwall, the Stephens spend time with the fishermen, hiring a boat one day and inducing the boatman to "discourse of the sea." He tells them of how he once capsized and was miraculously rescued, clinging to the keel.

One rainy day, Virginia and Adrian take refuge in an old parish church and fall into conversation with the caretaker. When this elderly woman learns whose children they are, her tears "start at the thought of all the beauty & charity that are recalled by a name" (285). Woolf was moved by "those humble words of the love that one woman felt for another," and their evidence of the powerful effect her mother had had upon the community in St. Ives. Unlike Mrs. Ramsay, whose husband and children laugh at her concern to improve dairy hygiene (105), the efficacy of Julia Stephen's charitable work was realized in the Julia Prinsep Stephen Nursing Association in St. Ives. Julia's professional approach to healthcare is exemplified in her *Notes from Sick Rooms*, a manual for the care of the ill that was published in 1883.[5]

Woolf remarked in the 1905 diary on the operation of memory, employing a photographic metaphor that seems to prefigure the way she re-created her childhood's atmosphere in Part I of *To the Lighthouse*. Visiting a woman who once had done laundry for the family, the Stephens claim never to have forgotten her: "Indeed, we were not guilty of insincerity; her portrait had been lying unexposed in some dim recess of our brains, & at the first sight of her face the old picture became clear again, & with it a multitude of slighter impressions which seem to cluster round it. I could see her once more trudging up the drive with her basket of clean clothes . . ." (*Passionate Apprentice* 287). The laundry woman is recalled by the figure of Mrs. McNab in *To the Lighthouse,* who remembers Mrs. Ramsay: "She could see her, as she came up the drive with the washing, stooping over her flowers . . . she could see her with one of the children by her in that grey cloak" (139–40).

In the manuscript of *To the Lighthouse,* Woolf wrote, "There need be no specification of date" (*Holograph* 2), and there are, indeed, very few clear indications in the novel of precisely when its several parts are taking place. Jane Lilienfeld, nevertheless, has provided a convincing rationale for the novel's chronology:

> Part III takes place in 1919 as the Great War has ended; in it Mr Ramsay tells Macalister that he is seventy-one. Since Mr. Ramsay was over sixty in Part I, we know that Part II covers ten years, making Part I occur in 1909. Since Prue is eighteen in Part I, the Ramsays must have been married at least nineteen years, having married about 1889 or earlier. Thus we can argue that the Ramsays had been raised in the England of the 1860s, a time of momentous intellectual turmoil. ("Where the Spear Plants Grew" 150)

The three-part structure of *To the Lighthouse,* therefore, reflects that movement from the coherent but oppressive world of the late Victorian middle class through the trauma of the First World War to the realities of the postwar world. In *A Room of One's Own,* Woolf would figure this movement as the replacement of illusion by truth (15). Although the experience of that historic shift in consciousness was available to her in the trajectory of her own life, that biography provided only some elements of her vision in *To the Lighthouse,* not the whole of its imaginative truth.

In considering the relations between *To the Lighthouse* and Woolf's own past, it is helpful to remember that she took her place in a long family tradition of life-writing, following in the footsteps of her father and his forebears, who all had written a great deal about themselves and other relatives. That tradition was explicitly questioned by Woolf, who wrote extensively about the limitations and possibilities of the biographical genre. Her own autobiographical projects extend from the chronicling of her own and her siblings' exploits in a family newspaper begun in the 1880s, the *Hyde Park Gate News,* through memoirs addressed to her own circle of friends (some of which are published in *Moments of Being*), to the fragments of a more formal autobiography she began in 1939, "A Sketch of the Past."

One of Woolf's earliest attempts to write about her mother is found in an untitled "life" of Vanessa Bell that Woolf began in 1907, ostensibly addressed to the as-yet unborn first child of her sister and Clive Bell (Julian, born 1908). The first chapter of "Reminiscences" (under which title it was published in *Moments of Being*) begins with Woolf's memories of Vanessa as a child, but quickly moves to a rather stilted portrait of their mother, ending with her death in 1895. "Reminiscences" is one aspect of the genealogy of *To the Lighthouse,* adding another angle of vision to a complex of memories that Woolf returned to throughout her life. In "A Sketch of the Past," she emphasizes the creative character of memory: "This past is much affected by the present moment. What I write today I should not write in a year's time" (75). In any case, *To the Lighthouse* is the creation of a writer who had thought long and deeply about the relations between "fact" and "fiction," and specifically about the dubious nature of claims to veracity made by the traditional form of biography. In an essay published a few months after *To the Lighthouse,* Woolf opined that "it would seem that the life which is increasingly real to us is the fictitious life" ("The New Biography" 478).

Rather than the truth of biographical fact, *To the Lighthouse* expresses the "truth" of creative memory. On the brink of beginning to write the novel in June 1925, Woolf had discussed the possibility of candor in autobiography with Jack Hills, who had been married to her half sister Stella Duckworth; Stella's untimely death in 1897, three months into their marriage, is recalled by the sudden death of Prue Ramsay in *To the Lighthouse* (132).[6] As she recorded in her diary Jack's questions, " 'But could one tell the truth? About one's affairs with women? About one's parents? . . .' " (*Diary* 3: 34), Woolf found that she was simultaneously hearing the rhythms of her nascent fiction: "(But while I try to write, I am making up 'To the Lighthouse'—the sea is to be heard all through it. . . .)" (*Diary* 3: 34). Her most important memory, she wrote in "A Sketch of the Past," was of lying in bed in the nursery at St. Ives on summer vacations and hearing the waves break on the shore below. It is the emotional truth of Woolf's re-created past that *To the Lighthouse* significantly embodies, more than any linear correspondence to the lived history of the Stephen family.

Form

> The dinner party the best thing I ever wrote: the one thing that I think justifies my faults as a writer: This damned 'method'. Because I don't think one could have reached those particular emotions in any other way.
>
> Virginia Woolf to Vita Sackville-West, May 13, 1927

THE FORM of Woolf's fiction, both at the level of the individual sentence and of the work as a whole, has typically been the greatest challenge for readers opening one of her books for the first time. Woolf eschews what she described in 1928 as "this appalling narrative business of the realist: getting on from lunch to dinner: it is false, unreal, merely conventional" (*Diary* 3: 209). In her early literary manifesto "Modern Novels," written for the *Times Literary Supplement* in 1919 and revised as "Modern Fiction" for her 1925 *Common Reader,* Woolf argued that reality itself had come to mean something very different for her generation than it had for the pre–First World War Edwardians or for the Victorians. In that essay she identified James Joyce, excerpts of whose *Ulysses* had been published in 1918 in the *Little Review,* as an exemplar of the kind of "spiritual" writing that would "reveal the flickerings of that innermost flame which flashes its messages through the brain" ("Modern Fiction" 151) and contrasted this with the "materialism" of writers of the preceding generation, such as H. G. Wells, Arnold Bennett, and John Galsworthy. For Woolf and her peers, interest lay not in the description of externals but in "the dark places of psychology" (152).

When Woolf wrote her third novel, *Jacob's Room* (1922), she built upon the experimental short fictions she had written between 1917 and 1921, wondering if she could extend her methods to the length of a novel. The bestselling writer Arnold Bennett used *Jacob's Room* as an example of what he believed to be the decay of the novel in an article published in March 1923: "I have seldom read a cleverer book than Virginia Woolf's *Jacob's Room,*" Bennett wrote; "But the characters do not vitally survive in the mind because the author has been obsessed by details of originality and cleverness" (Majumdar 113). In the 1920s debate raged in the pages of literary periodicals about what constituted the successful creation of character in fiction. Quite frequently, the debate was carried in public exchanges between Bennett and Woolf.

In one of her most significant contributions to this argument, Woolf invents the figure of "Mrs. Brown" to represent the human nature that novelists attempt to describe ("Mr. Bennett and Mrs. Brown" [1924]). By the 1920s, the understanding of that nature and the reality it inhabits had been dramatically transformed, for example by the revolution in physics brought about by the propositions of Einstein, Bohr, and Heisenberg, and by the theories of Sigmund Freud. The literary techniques of the previous generation, Woolf argued, would be "death" for the art of her own. It is in "Mr. Bennett and Mrs. Brown" that Woolf made her famous pronouncement that "on or about December, 1910, human character changed" (96). Although the date is significant in a number of ways (King Edward VII unexpectedly died that May), many have noted that it was in this year that Woolf's close friend Roger Fry organized "Manet and the Post-Impressionists," or, as it came to be known more familiarly, the First Post-Impressionist Exhibition, at the Grafton Galleries in London. The show created an uproar when the British public saw for the first time paintings by Cézanne, Gauguin, Manet, Picasso, Seurat, Signac, van Gogh and others, confronting them with radically new ideas about representation and the meaning of art.

Fry was a restless proselytizer of the new art movements of the early twentieth century, a member of the original Bloomsbury Group, the lover of Vanessa Bell between 1911 and 1913, and was described by Woolf at his death in 1934 as having changed the way people looked at art. Fry's theories about the visual arts were at the heart of aesthetic theorizing among those in Woolf's Bloomsbury circle in the years just before the First World War and in the following decade. Woolf had engaged with Fry's ideas, at least implicitly, in the early experimental short fiction she published in *Monday or Tuesday* (1921), work that Fry had praised. Woolf did not, however, agree with many of Fry's ideas about form (in sharp contrast to her brother-in-law Clive Bell's wholesale acceptance of a rigid formalism in his 1914 book *Art*). In *To the Lighthouse,* with its painter protagonist, Woolf made her dialogue with Fry more visible.

Returning the proof of Fry's lecture "The Artist and Psychoanalysis" (published by the Hogarth Press in 1924), Woolf remarked to him that she had been making notes on *The Craft of Fiction* by Percy Lubbock (1921) and "trying to make out what I mean by form in fiction. I say it is emotion put into the right relations; and has nothing to do with form as used of painting" (*Letters* 3: 133). Woolf had already addressed the arguments of Lubbock's book in "On Re-Reading Novels" in 1922, but she continued for several years to revise this article after its first appearance in the *Times Literary Supplement,* and to think about the issues it raised for her. The question of what "form" meant in literature was clearly fundamental to an artist whose aim was to create new forms of fiction.

In "The Artist and Psychoanalysis," Fry argued that there are two kinds of art. Art that appeals to emotions associated with objects is likely to be popular but the pleasures it offers will not often survive the context in which it was made. Art that is detached from "the instinctive life" and that arouses, in those few viewers sensitive enough to appreciate it, an emotion derived from the "contemplation of formal relations," is more mature, more "pure," and likely to persist through the ages. In her biography of Fry, Frances Spalding notes of this address to the British Society of Psychoanalysts that it is Fry's "most severe formalist statement" (253). Although Woolf found much of interest and even of use in Fry's formalism, her reference to Lubbock in her letter to him indirectly indicates the point at which she would take issue with Fry. In "On Re-Reading Novels," she maintained that "both in writing and in reading it is the emotion that must come first" (161). For Lubbock, "the book itself is equivalent to its form," but Woolf disagreed:

the "book itself" is not form which you see, but emotion which you feel, and the more intense the writer's feeling the more exact without slip or chink its expression in words. And whenever Mr Lubbock talks of form it is as if something were interposed between us and the book as we know it. We feel the presence of an alien substance which requires to be visualized imposing itself upon emotions which we feel naturally, and name simply, and range in final order by feeling their right relations to each other. (160)

As she noted in this essay, the term *form* came from the visual arts, and she was uncomfortable applying the terminology of visual art criticism to literature. The debate, however, was not entirely cerebral. Woolf and her sister, Vanessa Bell, participated from childhood in an intimate rivalry, usually couched in ironic terms that mocked the failure of one to understand the other's particular branch of the arts. Diane Gillespie points out that over the years, Woolf "made many condescending remarks about the visual arts. She generalized repeatedly about the differences between writers and painters, usually to the advantage of writers" (46). With Lily Briscoe, Woolf was boldly trespassing onto her sister's territory, as well as implicitly arguing with Fry about formalism. Christopher Reed, in a detailed account of Woolf's relationship to formalism, argues that *To the Lighthouse* is Woolf's "most eloquent investigation of the connections between formalism and feminism" (24).

Woolf presents in great subjective detail the struggles of Lily Briscoe to paint the reality she experiences. For Lily, Mrs. Ramsay is "an august shape; the shape of a dome" (55), and it is this, she attempts to explain to Mr. Bankes, that she wishes to paint, rather than anything that "looks like" her. Fry wrote that "no one who has a real understanding of the art of painting attaches any importance to what we call the subject of a picture—what is represented" ("Artist" 16), but although Woolf acknowledges in her novel the movement away from realism in contemporary art, she also emphasizes through Lily's experiences with her painting that emotion is a significant aspect of the work. When Lily returns to the Ramsays' house in Part III, she faces formal problems similar to those she had identified in Part I: "The question was of some relation between those masses. She had borne it in her mind all these years" (151). But before Lily can achieve her vision, she must also come to terms with the emotions aroused in her by the Ramsays, and by Mrs. Ramsay in particular.

Fry had offered a hypothesis in his 1924 lecture that might have encouraged Woolf in her creation of Lily Briscoe. He suggested that "art really calls up, as it were, the residual traces left on the spirit by the different emotions of life, without however recalling the actual experiences, so that we get an echo of the emotion without the limitation and particular direction which it had in experience" (19–20). As Woolf herself would write in "A Sketch of the Past," "is it not possible—I often wonder—that things we have felt with great intensity have an existence independent of our minds; are in fact still in existence. . . . I feel that strong emotion must leave its trace" (67).

Three weeks after *To the Lighthouse* was published, Woolf wrote to Fry,

> I meant *nothing* by The Lighthouse. One has to have a central line down the middle of the book to hold the design together. I saw that all sorts of feelings would accrue to this, but I refused to think them out, and trusted that people would make it the deposit for their own emotions—which they have done, one thinking it means one thing another another. I can't manage Symbolism except in this vague, generalised way. Whether its right or wrong I don't know, but directly I'm told what a thing means, it becomes hateful to me. (*Letters* 3: 385)

Her somewhat defensive tone might be explained in part by what Fry had had to say about symbols:

> Since most people are unable to perceive the meaning of purely formal relations ... they always look for some meaning that can be attached to the values of actual life, they always hope to translate a work of art into terms of *ideas* with which they are familiar. None the less in proportion as an artist is pure he is opposed to all symbolism. (16)

As Reed explains, Woolf took what she needed from Fry, but was not entirely convinced by his doctrine, which in any case Fry was continually revising. In "An Essay in Aesthetics," first published in 1909 but brought to a wide audience when it was republished in Fry's very popular 1920 book *Vision and Design,* he stressed the importance of unity in a work of art and wrote that in a painting unity "is due to a balancing of the attractions of the eye about the central line of the picture" (31). This thesis is clearly echoed in Woolf's own "line there, in the centre," both the one painted by Lily at the end of the novel (211), and the one that divides Parts I and III, "Time Passes."

To the Lighthouse is a triptych whose central "panel" simultaneously divides and unites the other two parts. Woolf's earliest ideas about the novel were expressed in terms that could as easily apply to the formal patterning and relations of a work of graphic or plastic art (and that, of course, also describe what Lily Briscoe works toward). The careful design of *To the Lighthouse* is expressed at the "macrotextual" level in the relations of its three parts to one another, and of the individual sections within those three parts. At the "microtextual" level, a similar patterning is embodied in the structure of individual sentences, where parenthetic interruptions frequently mimic the larger design of the novel's two parts interrupted by the central passage, "Time Passes." This "interruption" is further present at the thematic level, where the sudden deaths of family members and the cataclysm of global war interrupt both individual and world-historical human experience. Lily's painting, like Woolf's novel itself, is not simply "of" the Ramsays; it is also "the deposit of each day's living mixed with something more secret than she had ever spoken or shown in the course of all those days" (55). The subject and shape of Woolf's fifth novel richly exemplify what she had concluded in the 1920s about form: "when we speak of form we mean that certain emotions have been placed in the right relations to each other" ("On Re-Reading Novels" 165). Or, as Lily Briscoe puts it, "A light here required a shadow there" (56).

Responses

... if we try to follow the writer in his experiment from the first word to the last, without imposing our design upon him, then we shall have a good chance of getting hold of the right end of the string.

  Virginia Woolf, "How Should One Read a Book?" (1926)

WOOLF'S FIRST REVIEWS always came from her friends and family. As we have already seen, her husband, Leonard, believed *To the Lighthouse* to be a "psychological poem," a masterpiece. In the weeks immediately following its publication, Woolf began to hear from the people whose opinion she most cared about. Vanessa Bell assured her that aside from her obvious personal interest in the book's subject matter, she would not "have been moved as I was if it hadn't moved me impersonally too" (Bell, *Letters* 317). Vita Sackville-West wrote to say she was "dazzled and bewitched," as well as "afraid" of Woolf's genius. She agreed with Woolf that it was "perfectly ridiculous to call it a novel." Roger Fry, to whom Woolf wished she had dedicated the book, thought it "the best thing you've done," and better than *Mrs. Dalloway*. When the novelist E. M. Forster added his praise ("it stirs me much more to questions of whether and why than anything else you have written"), Woolf felt she could now put the book behind her and move on.

Anticipating but also contradicting the lament of many more recent readers of *To the Lighthouse,* the Scottish poet Rachel A. Taylor wrote in the May 1927 *Spectator* that "Nothing happens, and everything happens" (Majumdar 199). Another poet, Conrad Aiken, writing two months later in the American journal *Dial,* echoed Taylor when he wrote, "Nothing happens . . . and yet all of life happens" (208). Even Arnold Bennett allowed that "Mrs. Ramsay almost amounts to a complete person" (Majumdar 200), but by 1927 Woolf was not roused to respond to him in particular.

In his review, Aiken raised the issue of Woolf's subject matter, arguing that although she was in style as radical and adventurous as Joyce or Dorothy Richardson (though "highly feminine"), Woolf remained " 'old-fashioned' " in terms of the content of her novels. His reservation about Woolf identifies succinctly what long prevented a majority of critics accepting her as the equal of most of the male modernists; it was not until American feminist writers in the late 1960s and early 1970s began to provide a more illuminating context in which to read her works that the bias inherent in this view was exposed. Woolf herself commented on this gendered aspect of reading in *A Room of One's Own:*

Speaking crudely, football and sport are "important"; the worship of fashion, the buying of clothes "trivial." And these values are inevitably transferred from life to fiction. This is an important book, the critic assumes, because it deals with war. This is an insignificant book because it deals with the feelings of women in a drawing-room. (73)

In "Modern Fiction," too, she had cautioned readers not to "take it for granted that life exists more fully in what is commonly thought big than in what is commonly thought small" (150).

The significance of Woolf's attention to apparently trivial details received an influential reading in Erich Auerbach's magisterial survey of the representation of reality in western literature, *Mimesis*. First published in German in 1946, *Mimesis* was translated into English in 1953 and remains an important landmark in the study of fiction. Auerbach begins his book with Homer's *Odyssey*, and concludes it with a close analysis of the entire fifth section of Part I of *To the Lighthouse*, in a chapter titled "The Brown Stocking." Posing the question, "Who is speaking?" he minutely examines Woolf's narrative technique and concludes that in her attention to "trivial" matters like knitting and the furnishings of a house, readers can discover "nothing less than the wealth of reality and depth of life in every moment to which we surrender ourselves without prejudice" (552). Lily Briscoe herself articulates just such an idea near the end of *To the Lighthouse:*

One wanted, she thought, dipping her brush deliberately, to be on a level with ordinary experience, to feel simply that's a chair, that's a table, and yet at the same time, It's a miracle, it's an ecstasy. (204)

More has been written about *To the Lighthouse* than about any of Woolf's other books. The vast terrain of scholarship on the novel is daunting. From early works that examined its structure and form, through to contemporary studies of Woolf's anti-imperialism and radical politics, critics have generated a rich and diverse body of commentary. In addition to those works cited in this introduction, I have provided in the Suggestions for Further Reading some ways into this terrain that will serve both beginning readers of Woolf and those already familiar with *To the Lighthouse*. From these suggestions, pathways extend that follow the tracks of aesthetics, androgyny, class, family systems theory, mythology, ideology, language, lesbianism, narrative, psychoanalysis, war, and many other emphases in the past eight decades of critical analysis of *To the Lighthouse*.

Despite the differences of interpretation that fuel literary criticism, there has been almost unanimity about the extraordinary achievement of *To the Lighthouse* in extending the possibilities of the novel form. In her account of having tea with Thomas Hardy in July 1926, Woolf recorded the elderly novelist saying to her, "They've changed everything now.... We used to think there was a beginning & a middle & an end. We believed in the Aristotelian theory" (*Diary* 3: 101). Virginia Woolf's art did "change everything," both in itself and as part of that turbulent and diverse movement called Modernism. Drafting a talk she gave at a private school for girls in January 1926, Woolf wrote, "The same book is different to different generations. Your grandmothers read Pride & Prejudice, & so do you; but you are reading different books.... Each generation must read everything over again for itself" (Daugherty 127). The *To the Lighthouse* of future generations remains to be read.

NOTES

[1]A photograph from this session is reproduced in Nicola Luckhurst, *Bloomsbury in Vogue* (London: Cecil Woolf, 1998).

[2]The typescript translated by Mauron has been published by James Haule in *Twentieth Century Literature* 29.3 (Fall 1983): 267–311. See also Haule in the suggestions for further reading.

[3]Images from this album, now in the Mortimer Rare Book Room at the Neilson Library, Smith College, may be viewed at www.smith.edu/libraries/libs/rarebook/exhibitions/stephen/.

[4]The notes to this edition identify salient differences between versions of the novel. Readers interested in more detail about textual matters may refer to articles in the suggestions for further reading, and to the list in Kirkpatrick (54). Susan Dick's edition of the novel for the Shakespeare Head Press (1992) is based on the only known existing corrected proof, which is in the Mortimer Rare Book Room at Smith College.

[5]See *Julia Duckworth Stephen: Stories for Children, Essays for Adults,* edited by Diane F. Gillespie and Elizabeth Steele (Syracuse, NY: Syracuse University Press, 1987).

[6]For Woolf's account of Stella's illness and death, see *A Passionate Apprentice,* 94–118. Louise DeSalvo has argued that *To the Lighthouse* "explores the emotional confluence of the events of 1897" (*Virginia Woolf: The Impact of Childhood Sexual Abuse on Her Life and Work,* 222 [Boston: Beacon, 1989]).

For their assistance with and suggestions for this edition, I am deeply grateful to Jane Goldman, Susan Gubar, Karen Kukil, Evelyn B. Leong, Helane Levine-Keating, Shirley Lord, Vara Neverow, Bonnie Kime Scott, Carmen Königsreuther Socknat, and Alexandra Truitt.

WORKS CITED

Auerbach, Erich. "The Brown Stocking." In *Mimesis: The Representation of Reality in Western Literature.* Translated by Willard R. Trask. Princeton: Princeton University Press, 1968.

Bell, Vanessa. *Notes on Virginia's Childhood.* Edited by Richard Schaubeck, Jr. New York: Frank Hallman, 1974.

————. *Selected Letters of Vanessa Bell*. Edited by Regina Marler. New York: Pantheon, 1993.

Daugherty, Beth Rigel. "Virginia Woolf's 'How Should One Read a Book?'" *Woolf Studies Annual* 4 (1998): 123–85.

de Gay, Jane. "Behind the Purple Triangle: Art and Iconography in *To the Lighthouse*." *Woolf Studies Annual* 5 (1999): 1–23.

Fry, Roger. "The Artist and Psycho-Analysis." Hogarth Essays, First Series, No. 2. London: Hogarth Press, 1924.

————. "An Essay in Aesthetics." In *Vision and Design*. London: Chatto & Windus, 1920.

Gillespie, Diane. *The Sisters' Arts: The Writing and Painting of Virginia Woolf and Vanessa Bell*. Syracuse, NY: Syracuse University Press, 1988.

Lilienfeld, Jane. "The [Critic] Can't Say That, Can She?: Naming Co-dependence and Family Dysfunction in *To the Lighthouse*." In *Virginia Woolf: Emerging Perspectives*. Edited by Mark Hussey and Vara Neverow, 151–56. New York: Pace University Press, 1994.

————. "Where the Spear Plants Grew: The Ramsays' Marriage in *To the Lighthouse*." In *New Feminist Essays on Virginia Woolf*. Edited by Jane Marcus, 148–69. Lincoln: University of Nebraska Press, 1981.

Majumdar, Robin, and Allen McLaurin, eds. *Virgina Woolf: The Critical Heritage*. London: Routledge, 1975.

Marcus, Jane. *Virginia Woolf and the Languages of Patriarchy*. Bloomington: Indiana University Press, 1987.

Morphet, Richard. "The Art of Vanessa Bell." In *Vanessa Bell, Paintings and Drawings*. London: Anthony D'Offay, 1973.

Nalbantian, Suzanne. *Aesthetic Autobiography: From Life to Art in Marcel Proust, James Joyce, Virginia Woolf, and Anaïs Nin*. New York: St. Martin's, 1994.

Poole, Roger. " 'We all put up with you, Virginia': Irreceivable Wisdom About War." In *Virginia Woolf and War: Fiction, Reality, and Myth*. Edited by Mark Hussey, 79–100. Syracuse, NY: Syracuse University Press, 1991.

Reed, Christopher. "Through Formalism: Feminism and Virginia Woolf's Relation to Bloomsbury Aesthetics." In *The Multiple Muses of Virginia Woolf*. Edited by Diane F. Gillespie, 11–35. Columbia: University of Missouri Press, 1993.

Spalding, Frances. *Roger Fry: Art and Life*. Berkeley: University of California Press, 1980.

Stephen, Leslie. *Sir Leslie Stephen's Mausoleum Book*. Edited by Alan Bell. Oxford: Clarendon, 1977.

Woolf, Virginia. "Modern Fiction." In *The Common Reader*. Edited by Andrew McNeillie. San Diego: Harcourt, 1984. Originally published in 1925.

————. "Mr. Bennett and Mrs. Brown." In *The Captain's Death Bed and Other Essays.* New York: Harcourt Brace Jovanovich, 1950.

————. "The New Biography." In *The Essays of Virginia Woolf.* Vol. 4. Edited by Andrew McNeillie, 473–80. London: Hogarth Press, 1994.

————. "On Re-Reading Novels." In *The Moment and Other Essays.* New York: Harcourt Brace Jovanovich, 1974. Originally published in 1948.

————. "A Sketch of the Past." In *Moments of Being.* Edited by Jeanne Schulkind. San Diego: Harcourt Brace Jovanovich, 1985.

————. To the Lighthouse. *The Original Holograph Draft.* Transcribed and edited by Susan Dick. Toronto: University of Toronto Press, 1982.

To the Lighthouse

Contents

THE WINDOW

"YES, OF COURSE, if it's fine tomorrow," said Mrs. Ramsay. "But you'll have to be up with the lark," she added.

To her son these words conveyed an extraordinary joy, as if it were settled, the expedition were bound to take place, and the wonder to which he had looked forward, for years and years it seemed, was, after a night's darkness and a day's sail, within touch. Since he belonged, even at the age of six, to that great clan which cannot keep this feeling separate from that, but must let future prospects, with their joys and sorrows, cloud what is actually at hand, since to such people even in earliest childhood any turn in the wheel of sensation has the power to crystallise and transfix the moment upon which its gloom or radiance rests, James Ramsay, sitting on the floor cutting out pictures from the illustrated catalogue of the Army and Navy Stores, endowed the picture of a refrigerator, as his mother spoke, with heavenly bliss. It was fringed with joy. The wheelbarrow, the lawnmower, the sound of poplar trees, leaves whitening before rain, rooks cawing, brooms knocking, dresses rustling—all these were so coloured and distinguished in his mind that he had already his private code, his secret language, though he appeared the image of stark and uncompromising severity, with his high forehead and his fierce blue eyes, impeccably candid and pure, frowning slightly at the sight of human frailty, so that

his mother, watching him guide his scissors neatly round the refrigerator, imagined him all red and ermine on the Bench or directing a stern and momentous enterprise in some crisis of
public affairs.

"But," said his father, stopping in front of the drawing-
room window, "it won't be fine."

Had there been an axe handy, or a poker, any weapon that
would have gashed a hole in his father's breast and killed him,
there and then, James would have seized it. Such were the ex-
tremes of emotion that Mr. Ramsay excited in his children's
breasts by his mere presence; standing, as now, lean as a knife,
narrow as the blade of one, grinning sarcastically, not only with
the pleasure of disillusioning his son and casting ridicule upon
his wife, who was ten thousand times better in every way than
he was (James thought), but also with some secret conceit at his
own accuracy of judgement. What he said was true. It was always true. He was incapable of untruth; never tampered with
a fact; never altered a disagreeable word to suit the pleasure
or convenience of any mortal being, least of all of his own
children, who, sprung from his loins, should be aware from
childhood that life is difficult; facts uncompromising; and the
passage to that fabled land where our brightest hopes are extinguished, our frail barks founder in darkness (here Mr. Ramsay
would straighten his back and narrow his little blue eyes upon
the horizon), one that needs, above all, courage, truth, and the
power to endure.

"But it may be fine—I expect it will be fine," said Mrs.
Ramsay, making some little twist of the reddish-brown stocking
she was knitting, impatiently. If she finished it tonight, if they
did go to the Lighthouse after all, it was to be given to the
Lighthouse keeper for his little boy, who was threatened with a
tuberculous hip; together with a pile of old magazines, and
some tobacco, indeed, whatever she could find lying about, not

really wanted, but only littering the room, to give those poor fellows, who must be bored to death sitting all day with nothing to do but polish the lamp and trim the wick and rake about on their scrap of garden, something to amuse them. For how would you like to be shut up for a whole month at a time, and possibly more in stormy weather, upon a rock the size of a tennis lawn? she would ask; and to have no letters or newspapers, and to see nobody; if you were married, not to see your wife, not to know how your children were,—if they were ill, if they had fallen down and broken their legs or arms; to see the same dreary waves breaking week after week, and then a dreadful storm coming, and the windows covered with spray, and birds dashed against the lamp, and the whole place rocking, and not be able to put your nose out of doors for fear of being swept into the sea? How would you like that? she asked, addressing herself particularly to her daughters. So she added, rather differently, one must take them whatever comforts one can.

"It's due west," said the atheist Tansley, holding his bony fingers spread so that the wind blew through them, for he was sharing Mr. Ramsay's evening walk up and down, up and down the terrace. That is to say, the wind blew from the worst possible direction for landing at the Lighthouse. Yes, he did say disagreeable things, Mrs. Ramsay admitted; it was odious of him to rub this in, and make James still more disappointed; but at the same time, she would not let them laugh at him. "The atheist," they called him; "the little atheist." Rose mocked him; Prue mocked him; Andrew, Jasper, Roger mocked him; even old Badger without a tooth in his head had bit him, for being (as Nancy put it) the hundred and tenth young man to chase them all the way up to the Hebrides when it was ever so much nicer to be alone.

"Nonsense," said Mrs. Ramsay, with great severity. Apart from the habit of exaggeration which they had from her, and from the implication (which was true) that she asked too many people to stay, and had to lodge some in the town, she could not bear incivility to her guests, to young men in particular, who were poor as church mice, "exceptionally able," her husband said, his great admirers, and come there for a holiday. Indeed, she had the whole of the other sex under her protection; for reasons she could not explain, for their chivalry and valour, for the fact that they negotiated treaties, ruled India, controlled finance; finally for an attitude towards herself which no woman could fail to feel or to find agreeable, something trustful, childlike, reverential; which an old woman could take from a young man without loss of dignity, and woe betide the girl—pray Heaven it was none of her daughters!—who did not feel the worth of it, and all that it implied, to the marrow of her bones!

She turned with severity upon Nancy. He had not chased them, she said. He had been asked.

They must find a way out of it all. There might be some simpler way, some less laborious way, she sighed. When she looked in the glass and saw her hair grey, her cheek sunk, at fifty, she thought, possibly she might have managed things better—her husband; money; his books. But for her own part she would never for a single second regret her decision, evade difficulties, or slur over duties. She was now formidable to behold, and it was only in silence, looking up from their plates, after she had spoken so severely about Charles Tansley, that her daughters, Prue, Nancy, Rose—could sport with infidel ideas which they had brewed for themselves of a life different from hers; in Paris, perhaps; a wilder life; not always taking care of some man or other; for there was in all their minds a mute questioning of deference and chivalry, of the Bank of England and the Indian Empire, of ringed fingers and lace, though to them all there was something in this of the essence of beauty, which called out the manliness in their girlish hearts, and made them, as they sat at table beneath their mother's eyes, honour her strange severity, her extreme courtesy, like a Queen's raising from the mud to wash a beggar's dirty foot, when she thus admonished them so very severely about that wretched atheist who had chased them—or, speaking accurately, been invited to stay with them—in the Isles of Skye.

"There'll be no landing at the Lighthouse tomorrow," said Charles Tansley, clapping his hands together as he stood at the window with her husband. Surely, he had said enough. She wished they would both leave her and James alone and go on talking. She looked at him. He was such a miserable specimen, the children said, all humps and hollows. He couldn't play cricket; he poked; he shuffled. He was a sarcastic brute, Andrew said. They knew what he liked best—to be for ever walking up and down, up and down, with Mr. Ramsay, and saying who had won this, who had won that, who was a "first-rate man" at Latin verses, who was "brilliant but I think fundamentally unsound," who was undoubtedly the "ablest fellow in Balliol," who had buried his light temporarily at Bristol or Bedford, but was bound to be heard of later when his Prolegomena, of which Mr. Tansley had the first pages in proof with him if Mr. Ramsay would like to see them, to some branch of mathematics or philosophy saw the light of day. That was what they talked about.

She could not help laughing herself sometimes. She said, the other day, something about "waves mountains high." Yes, said Charles Tansley, it was a little rough. "Aren't you drenched to the skin?" she had said. "Damp, not wet through," said Mr. Tansley, pinching his sleeve, feeling his socks.

But it was not that they minded, the children said. It was not his face; it was not his manners. It was him—his point of view. When they talked about something interesting, people, music, history, anything, even said it was a fine evening so why not sit out of doors, then what they complained of about

Charles Tansley was that until he had turned the whole thing round and made it somehow reflect himself and disparage them—he was not satisfied. And he would go to picture galleries they said and he would ask one, did one like his tie? God knows, said Rose, one did not.

Disappearing as stealthily as stags from the dinner-table directly the meal was over, the eight sons and daughters of Mr. and Mrs. Ramsay sought their bedrooms, their fastnesses in a house where there was no other privacy to debate anything, everything; Tansley's tie; the passing of the Reform Bill; sea birds and butterflies; people; while the sun poured into those attics, which a plank alone separated from each other so that every footstep could be plainly heard and the Swiss girl sobbing for her father who was dying of cancer in a valley of the Grisons, and lit up bats, flannels, straw hats, ink-pots, paint-pots, beetles, and the skulls of small birds, while it drew from the long frilled strips of seaweed pinned to the wall a smell of salt and weeds, which was in the towels too, gritty with sand from bathing.

Strife, divisions, difference of opinion, prejudices twisted into the very fibre of being, oh, that they should begin so early, Mrs. Ramsay deplored. They were so critical, her children. They talked such nonsense. She went from the dining-room, holding James by the hand, since he would not go with the others. It seemed to her such nonsense—inventing differences, when people, heaven knows, were different enough without that. The real differences, she thought, standing by the drawing-room window, are enough, quite enough. She had in mind at the moment, rich and poor, high and low; the great in birth receiving from her, some half grudgingly, half respect, for had she not in her veins the blood of that very noble, if slightly mythical, Italian house, whose daughters, scattered about English drawing-rooms in the nineteenth century, had lisped so charmingly, had stormed so wildly, and all her wit and her bearing and her temper came from them, and not from the sluggish English, or the cold Scotch; but more profoundly, she ruminated the other problem, of rich and poor, and the things she saw with her own eyes, weekly, daily, here or in London, when she visited this widow, or that struggling wife in person with a bag on her arm, and a note-book and pencil with which she wrote down in columns carefully ruled for the purpose wages and spendings, employment and unemployment, in the hope that thus she would cease to be a private woman whose charity was half a sop to her own indignation, half a relief to her own curiosity, and become what with her untrained mind she greatly admired, an investigator, elucidating the social problem.

Insoluble questions they were, it seemed to her, standing there, holding James by the hand. He had followed her into the drawing-room, that young man they laughed at; he was standing by the table, fidgeting with something, awkwardly, feeling himself out of things, as she knew without looking round. They had all gone — the children; Minta Doyle and Paul Rayley; Augustus Carmichael; her husband — they had all gone. So she turned with a sigh and said, "Would it bore you to come with me, Mr. Tansley?"

She had a dull errand in the town; she had a letter or two to write; she would be ten minutes perhaps; she would put on her hat. And, with her basket and her parasol, there she was again, ten minutes later, giving out a sense of being ready, of being equipped for a jaunt, which, however, she must interrupt for a moment, as they passed the tennis lawn, to ask Mr. Carmichael, who was basking with his yellow cat's eyes ajar, so that like a cat's they seemed to reflect the branches moving or the clouds passing, but to give no inkling of any inner thoughts or emotion whatsoever, if he wanted anything.

For they were making the great expedition, she said, laughing. They were going to the town. "Stamps, writing-paper, tobacco?" she suggested, stopping by his side. But no, he wanted nothing. His hands clasped themselves over his capacious paunch, his eyes blinked, as if he would have liked to reply kindly to these blandishments (she was seductive but a little nervous) but could not, sunk as he was in a grey-green somnolence which embraced them all, without need of words, in a vast and benevolent lethargy of well-wishing; all the house; all the world; all the people in it, for he had slipped into his glass at lunch a few drops of something, which accounted, the children thought, for the vivid streak of canary-yellow in moustache and beard that were otherwise milk white. No, nothing, he murmured.

He should have been a great philosopher, said Mrs. Ramsay, as they went down the road to the fishing village, but he had made an unfortunate marriage. Holding her black parasol very erect, and moving with an indescribable air of expectation, as if she were going to meet some one round the corner, she told the story; an affair at Oxford with some girl; an early marriage; poverty; going to India; translating a little poetry "very beautifully, I believe," being willing to teach the boys Persian or Hindustanee, but what really was the use of that?—and then lying, as they saw him, on the lawn.

It flattered him; snubbed as he had been, it soothed him that Mrs. Ramsay should tell him this. Charles Tansley revived. Insinuating, too, as she did the greatness of man's intellect, even in its decay, the subjection of all wives—not that she blamed the girl, and the marriage had been happy enough, she believed—to their husband's labours, she made him feel better pleased with himself than he had done yet, and he would have liked, had they taken a cab, for example, to have paid for it. As for her little bag, might he not carry that? No, no, she said, she always carried *that* herself. She did too. Yes, he felt that in her. He felt many things, something in particular that excited him

and disturbed him for reasons which he could not give. He
would like her to see him, gowned and hooded, walking in a
procession. A fellowship, a professorship, he felt capable of anything and saw himself—but what was she looking at? At a man
pasting a bill. The vast flapping sheet flattened itself out, and
each shove of the brush revealed fresh legs, hoops, horses, glis-
tening reds and blues, beautifully smooth, until half the wall was
covered with the advertisement of a circus; a hundred horse-
men, twenty performing seals, lions, tigers ... Craning forwards,
for she was short-sighted, she read it out ... "will visit this
town," she read. It was terribly dangerous work for a one-armed
man, she exclaimed, to stand on top of a ladder like that—his
left arm had been cut off in a reaping machine two years ago.

"Let us all go!" she cried, moving on, as if all those riders
and horses had filled her with childlike exultation and made her
forget her pity.

"Let's go," he said, repeating her words, clicking them out,
however, with a self-consciousness that made her wince. "Let
us go to the circus." No. He could not say it right. He could
not feel it right. But why not? she wondered. What was wrong
with him then? She liked him warmly, at the moment. Had they
not been taken, she asked, to circuses when they were children?
Never, he answered, as if she asked the very thing he wanted;
had been longing all these days to say, how they did not go
to circuses. It was a large family, nine brothers and sisters, and
his father was a working man. "My father is a chemist, Mrs.
Ramsay. He keeps a shop." He himself had paid his own way
since he was thirteen. Often he went without a greatcoat in
winter. He could never "return hospitality" (those were his
parched stiff words) at college. He had to make things last
twice the time other people did; he smoked the cheapest tobacco; shag; the same the old men did in the quays. He worked
hard—seven hours a day; his subject was now the influence of

something upon somebody—they were walking on and Mrs. Ramsay did not quite catch the meaning, only the words, here and   there ... dissertation ... fellowship ... readership ... lectureship. She could not follow the ugly academic jargon, that rattled itself off so glibly, but said to herself that she saw now why going to the circus had knocked him off his perch, poor little man, and why he came out, instantly, with all that about his father and mother and brothers and sisters, and she would see to it that they didn't laugh at him any more; she would tell Prue about it. What he would have liked, she supposed, would have been to say how he had gone not to the circus but to Ibsen with the Ramsays. He was an awful prig—oh yes, an insufferable bore. For, though they had reached the town now and were in the main street, with carts grinding past on the cobbles, still he went on talking, about settlements, and teaching, and working men, and helping our own class, and lectures, till she gathered that he had got back entire self-confidence, had recovered from the circus, and was about (and now again she liked him warmly) to tell her—but here, the houses falling away on both sides, they came out on the quay, and the whole bay spread before them and Mrs. Ramsay could not help exclaiming, "Oh, how beautiful!" For the great plateful of blue water was before her; the hoary Lighthouse, distant, austere, in the midst; and on the right, as far as the eye could see, fading and falling, in soft low pleats, the green sand dunes with the wild flowing grasses on them, which always seemed to be running away into some moon country, uninhabited of men.

That was the view, she said, stopping, growing greyer-eyed, that her husband loved.

She paused a moment. But now, she said, artists had come here. There indeed, only a few paces off, stood one of them, in Panama hat and yellow boots, seriously, softly, absorbedly, for all that he was watched by ten little boys, with an air of profound contentment on his round red face gazing, and then, when he had gazed, dipping; imbuing the tip of his brush in some soft mound of green or pink. Since Mr. Paunceforte had been there, three years before, all the pictures were like that, she said, green and grey, with lemon-coloured sailing-boats, and pink women on the beach.

But her grandmother's friends, she said, glancing discreetly as they passed, took the greatest pains; first they mixed their own colours, and then they ground them, and then they put damp cloths to keep them moist.

So Mr. Tansley supposed she meant him to see that that man's picture was skimpy, was that what one said? The colours weren't solid? Was that what one said? Under the influence of that extraordinary emotion which had been growing all the walk, had begun in the garden when he had wanted to take her bag, had increased in the town when he had wanted to tell her everything about himself, he was coming to see himself, and everything he had ever known gone crooked a little. It was awfully strange.

There he stood in the parlour of the poky little house where she had taken him, waiting for her, while she went upstairs a moment to see a woman. He heard her quick step above; heard her voice cheerful, then low; looked at the mats, tea-caddies, glass shades; waited quite impatiently; looked forward eagerly to the walk home; determined to carry her bag; then heard her come out; shut a door; say they must keep the windows open and the doors shut, ask at the house for anything they wanted (she must be talking to a child) when, suddenly, in she came, stood for a moment silent (as if she had been pretending up there, and for a moment let herself be now), stood quite motionless for a moment against a picture of Queen Victoria wearing the blue ribbon of the Garter; when all at once he realised that it was this: it was this:—she was the most beautiful person he had ever seen.

With stars in her eyes and veils in her hair, with cyclamen and wild violets—what nonsense was he thinking? She was fifty at least; she had eight children. Stepping through fields of flowers and taking to her breast buds that had broken and lambs that had fallen; with the stars in her eyes and the wind in her hair— He took her bag.

"Good-bye, Elsie," she said, and they walked up the street, she holding her parasol erect and walking as if she expected to meet some one round the corner, while for the first time in his life Charles Tansley felt an extraordinary pride; a man digging in a drain stopped digging and looked at her, let his arm fall down and looked at her; for the first time in his life Charles Tansley felt an extraordinary pride; felt the wind and the cyclamen and the violets for he was walking with a beautiful woman. He had hold of her bag.

II

"No going to the Lighthouse, James," he said, as he stood by the window, speaking awkwardly, but trying in deference to Mrs. Ramsay to soften his voice into some semblance of geniality at least.

Odious little man, thought Mrs. Ramsay, why go on saying that?

III

"Perhaps you will wake up and find the sun shining and the birds singing," she said compassionately, smoothing the little boy's hair, for her husband, with his caustic saying that it would not be fine, had dashed his spirits she could see. This going to the Lighthouse was a passion of his, she saw, and then, as if her husband had not said enough, with his caustic saying that it would not be fine tomorrow, this odious little man went and rubbed it in all over again.

"Perhaps it will be fine tomorrow," she said, smoothing his hair.

All she could do now was to admire the refrigerator, and turn the pages of the Stores list in the hope that she might come upon something like a rake, or a mowing-machine, which, with its prongs and its handles, would need the greatest skill and care in cutting out. All these young men parodied her husband, she reflected; he said it would rain; they said it would be a positive tornado.

But here, as she turned the page, suddenly her search for the picture of a rake or a mowing-machine was interrupted. The gruff murmur, irregularly broken by the taking out of pipes and the putting in of pipes which had kept on assuring her, though she could not hear what was said (as she sat in the window which opened on the terrace), that the men were happily talking; this sound, which had lasted now half an hour and had taken its place soothingly in the scale of sounds pressing on top of her, such as the tap of balls upon bats, the sharp, sudden bark now and then, "How's that? How's that?" of the children playing cricket, had ceased; so that the monotonous fall of the waves on the beach, which for the most part beat a measured and soothing tattoo to her thoughts and seemed consolingly to repeat over and over again as she sat with the children the words of some old cradle song, murmured by nature, "I am guarding you—I am your support," but at other times suddenly and unexpectedly, especially when her mind raised itself slightly from the task actually in hand, had no such kindly meaning, but like a ghostly roll of drums remorselessly beat the measure of life, made one think of the destruction of the island and its engulfment in the sea, and warned her whose day had slipped past in one quick doing after another that it was all ephemeral as a rainbow—this sound which had been obscured and concealed under the other sounds suddenly thundered hollow in her ears and made her look up with an impulse of terror.

They had ceased to talk; that was the explanation. Falling in one second from the tension which had gripped her to the other extreme which, as if to recoup her for her unnecessary expense of emotion, was cool, amused, and even faintly malicious, she concluded that poor Charles Tansley had been shed. That was of little account to her. If her husband required sacrifices (and indeed he did) she cheerfully offered up to him Charles Tansley, who had snubbed her little boy.

One moment more, with her head raised, she listened, as if she waited for some habitual sound, some regular mechanical sound; and then, hearing something rhythmical, half said, half chanted, beginning in the garden, as her husband beat up and down the terrace, something between a croak and a song, she was soothed once more, assured again that all was well, and looking down at the book on her knee found the picture of a pocket knife with six blades which could only be cut out if James was very careful.

Suddenly a loud cry, as of a sleep-walker, half roused, something about

Stormed at with shot and shell

sung out with the utmost intensity in her ear, made her turn apprehensively to see if any one heard him. Only Lily Briscoe, she was glad to find; and that did not matter. But the sight of the girl standing on the edge of the lawn painting reminded her; she was supposed to be keeping her head as much in the same position as possible for Lily's picture. Lily's picture! Mrs. Ramsay smiled. With her little Chinese eyes and her puckered-up face, she would never marry; one could not take her painting very seriously; she was an independent little creature, and Mrs. Ramsay liked her for it; so, remembering her promise, she bent her head.

IV

INDEED, HE almost knocked her easel over, coming down upon her with his hands waving shouting out, "Boldly we rode and well," but, mercifully, he turned sharp, and rode off, to die gloriously she supposed upon the heights of Balaclava. Never was anybody at once so ridiculous and so alarming. But so long as he kept like that, waving, shouting, she was safe; he would not stand still and look at her picture. And that was what Lily Briscoe could not have endured. Even while she looked at the mass, at the line, at the colour, at Mrs. Ramsay sitting in the window with James, she kept a feeler on her surroundings lest some one should creep up, and suddenly she should find her picture looked at. But now, with all her senses quickened as they were, looking, straining, till the colour of the wall and the jacmanna beyond burnt into her eyes, she was aware of some one coming out of the house, coming towards her; but somehow divined, from the footfall, William Bankes, so that though her brush quivered, she did not, as she would have done had it been Mr. Tansley, Paul Rayley, Minta Doyle, or practically anybody else, turn her canvas upon the grass, but let it stand. William Bankes stood beside her.

They had rooms in the village, and so, walking in, walking out, parting late on door-mats, had said little things about the soup, about the children, about one thing and another which made them allies; so that when he stood beside her now in his judicial way (he was old enough to be her father too, a botanist, a widower, smelling of soap, very scrupulous and clean) she just stood there. He just stood there. Her shoes were excellent, he observed. They allowed the toes their natural expansion. Lodging in the same house with her, he had noticed too, how orderly she was, up before breakfast and off to paint, he believed, alone: poor, presumably, and without the complexion or the allurement of Miss Doyle certainly, but with a good sense which made her in his eyes superior to that young lady. Now, for instance, when Ramsay bore down on them, shouting, gesticulating, Miss Briscoe, he felt certain, understood.

"Some one had blundered."

Mr. Ramsay glared at them. He glared at them without seeming to see them. That did make them both vaguely uncomfortable. Together they had seen a thing they had not been meant to see. They had encroached upon a privacy. So, Lily thought, it was probably an excuse of his for moving, for getting out of earshot, that made Mr. Bankes almost immediately say something about its being chilly and suggest taking a stroll. She would come, yes. But it was with difficulty that she took her eyes off her picture.

The jacmanna was bright violet; the wall staring white. She would not have considered it honest to tamper with the bright violet and the staring white, since she saw them like that, fashionable though it was, since Mr. Paunceforte's visit, to see everything pale, elegant, semitransparent. Then beneath the colour there was the shape. She could see it all so clearly, so commandingly, when she looked: it was when she took her brush in hand that the whole thing changed. It was in that moment's flight between the picture and her canvas that the demons set on her who often brought her to the verge of tears and made this passage from conception to work as dreadful as any down a dark passage for a child. Such she often felt herself—struggling against terrific odds to maintain her courage; to say: "But this is what I see; this is what I see," and so to clasp some miserable remnant of her vision to her breast, which a thousand forces did their best to pluck from her. And it was then too, in that chill and windy way, as she began to paint, that there forced themselves upon her other things, her own inadequacy, her insignificance, keeping house for her father off the Brompton Road, and had much ado to control her impulse to fling herself (thank Heaven she had always resisted so far) at Mrs. Ramsay's knee and say to her—but what could one say to her? "I'm in love with you?" No, that was not true. "I'm in love with this all," waving her hand at the hedge, at the house, at the children. It was absurd, it was impossible. So now she laid her brushes neatly in the box, side by side, and said to William Bankes:

"It suddenly gets cold. The sun seems to give less heat," she said, looking about her, for it was bright enough, the grass still a soft deep green, the house starred in its greenery with purple passion flowers, and rooks dropping cool cries from the high blue. But something moved, flashed, turned a silver wing in the air. It was September after all, the middle of September, and past six in the evening. So off they strolled down the garden in the usual direction, past the tennis lawn, past the pampas grass, to that break in the thick hedge, guarded by red-hot pokers like brasiers of clear burning coal, between which the blue waters of the bay looked bluer than ever.

They came there regularly every evening drawn by some need. It was as if the water floated off and set sailing thoughts which had grown stagnant on dry land, and gave to their bodies even some sort of physical relief. First, the pulse of colour flooded the bay with blue, and the heart expanded with it and the body swam, only the next instant to be checked and chilled by the prickly blackness on the ruffled waves. Then, up behind the great black rock, almost every evening spurted irregularly, so that one had to watch for it and it was a delight when it came, a fountain of white water; and then, while one waited for that, one watched, on the pale semicircular beach, wave after wave shedding again and again smoothly, a film of mother of pearl.

They both smiled, standing there. They both felt a common hilarity, excited by the moving waves; and then by the swift cutting race of a sailing boat, which, having sliced a curve in the bay, stopped; shivered; let its sails drop down; and then, with a natural instinct to complete the picture, after this swift movement, both of them looked at the dunes far away, and instead of merriment felt come over them some sadness—because the thing was completed partly, and partly because distant views seem to outlast by a million years (Lily thought) the gazer and to be communing already with a sky which beholds an earth entirely at rest.

Looking at the far sand hills, William Bankes thought of Ramsay: thought of a road in Westmorland, thought of Ramsay striding along a road by himself hung round with that solitude which seemed to be his natural air. But this was suddenly interrupted, William Bankes remembered (and this must refer to some actual incident), by a hen, straddling her wings out in protection of a covey of little chicks, upon which Ramsay, stopping, pointed his stick and said "Pretty—pretty," an odd illumination in to his heart, Bankes had thought it, which showed his simplicity, his sympathy with humble things; but it seemed to him as if their friendship had ceased, there, on that stretch of road. After that, Ramsay had married. After that, what with one thing and another, the pulp had gone out of their friendship. Whose fault it was he could not say, only, after a time, repetition had taken the place of newness. It was to repeat that they met. But in this dumb colloquy with the sand dunes he maintained that his affection for Ramsay had in no way diminished; but there, like the body of a young man laid up in peat for a century, with the red fresh on his lips, was his friendship, in its acuteness and reality, laid up across the bay among the sandhills.

He was anxious for the sake of this friendship and perhaps too in order to clear himself in his own mind from the imputation of having dried and shrunk—for Ramsay lived in a welter of children, whereas Bankes was childless and a widower—he was anxious that Lily Briscoe should not disparage Ramsay (a great man in his own way) yet should understand how things stood between them. Begun long years ago, their friendship had petered out on a Westmorland road, where the hen spread her wings before her chicks; after which Ramsay had married, and their paths lying different ways, there had been, certainly for no one's fault, some tendency, when they met, to repeat.

Yes. That was it. He finished. He turned from the view. And, turning to walk back the other way, up the drive, Mr. Bankes was alive to things which would not have struck him had not those sandhills revealed to him the body of his friendship lying with the red on its lips laid up in peat—for instance, Cam, the little girl, Ramsay's youngest daughter. She was picking Sweet Alice on the bank. She was wild and fierce. She would not "give a flower to the gentleman" as the nursemaid told her. No! no! no! she would not! She clenched her fist. She stamped. And Mr. Bankes felt aged and saddened and somehow put into the wrong by her about his friendship. He must have dried and shrunk.

The Ramsays were not rich, and it was a wonder how they managed to contrive it all. Eight children! To feed eight children on philosophy! Here was another of them, Jasper this time, strolling past, to have a shot at a bird, he said, nonchalantly, swinging Lily's hand like a pump-handle as he passed, which

caused Mr. Bankes to say, bitterly, how *she* was a favourite. There
was education now to be considered (true, Mrs. Ramsay had
something of her own perhaps) let alone the daily wear and tear
of shoes and stockings which those "great fellows," all well
grown, angular, ruthless youngsters, must require. As for being
sure which was which, or in what order they came, that was beyond him. He called them privately after the Kings and Queens
of England; Cam the Wicked, James the Ruthless, Andrew the
Just, Prue the Fair—for Prue would have beauty, he thought,
how could she help it?—and Andrew brains. While he walked
up the drive and Lily Briscoe said yes and no and capped his
comments (for she was in love with them all, in love with this
world) he weighed Ramsay's case, commiserated him, envied
him, as if he had seen him divest himself of all those glories of
isolation and austerity which crowned him in youth to cumber
himself definitely with fluttering wings and clucking domestici-
ties. They gave him something—William Bankes acknowledged
that; it would have been pleasant if Cam had stuck a flower in
his coat or clambered over his shoulder, to look at a picture of
Vesuvius in eruption; but they had also, his old friends could
not but feel, destroyed something. What would a stranger think
now? What did this Lily Briscoe think? Could one help noticing
that habits grew on him? eccentricities, weaknesses perhaps? It
was astonishing that a man of his intellect could stoop so low
as he did—but that was too harsh a phrase—could depend so
much as he did upon people's praise.

"Oh, but," said Lily, "think of his work!"

Whenever she "thought of his work" she always saw clearly
before her a large kitchen table. It was Andrew's doing. She
asked him what his father's books were about. "Subject and object and the nature of reality," Andrew had said. And when she
said Heavens, she had no notion what that meant. "Think of a
kitchen table then," he told her, "when you're not there."

So now she always saw, when she thought of Mr. Ramsay's work, a scrubbed kitchen table. It lodged now in the fork of a pear tree, for they had reached the orchard. And with a painful effort of concentration, she focused her mind, not upon the silver-bossed bark of the tree, or upon its fish-shaped leaves, but upon a phantom kitchen table, one of those scrubbed board tables, grained and knotted, whose virtue seems to have been laid bare by years of muscular integrity, which stuck there, its four legs in air. Naturally, if one's days were passed in this see-ing of angular essences, this reducing of lovely evenings, with all their flamingo clouds and blue and silver to a white deal four-legged table (and it was a mark of the finest minds so to do), naturally one could not be judged like an ordinary person.

Mr. Bankes liked her for bidding him "think of his work." He had thought of it, often and often. Times without number, he had said, "Ramsay is one of those men who do their best work before they are forty." He had made a definite contribu-tion to philosophy in one little book when he was only five and twenty; what came after was more or less amplification, repeti-tion. But the number of men who make a definite contribution to anything whatsoever is very small, he said, pausing by the pear tree, well brushed, scrupulously exact, exquisitely judicial. Suddenly, as if the movement of his hand had released it, the load of her accumulated impressions of him tilted up, and down poured in a ponderous avalanche all she felt about him. That was one sensation. Then up rose in a fume the essence of his being. That was another. She felt herself transfixed by the inten-sity of her perception; it was his severity; his goodness. I respect you (she addressed silently him in person) in every atom; you are not vain; you are entirely impersonal; you are finer than Mr. Ramsay; you are the finest human being that I know; you have neither wife nor child (without any sexual feeling, she longed to cherish that loneliness), you live for science (involuntarily, sections of potatoes rose before her eyes); praise would be an insult to you; generous, pure-hearted, heroic man! But simultaneously, she remembered how he had brought a valet all the way up here; objected to dogs on chairs; would prose for hours (until Mr. Ramsay slammed out of the room) about salt in vegetables and the iniquity of English cooks.

How then did it work out, all this? How did one judge people, think of them? How did one add up this and that and conclude that it was liking one felt, or disliking? And to those words, what meaning attached, after all? Standing now, apparently transfixed, by the pear tree, impressions poured in upon her of those two men, and to follow her thought was like following a voice which speaks too quickly to be taken down by one's pencil, and the voice was her own voice saying without prompting undeniable, everlasting, contradictory things, so that even the fissures and humps on the bark of the pear tree were irrevocably fixed there for eternity. You have greatness, she continued, but Mr. Ramsay has none of it. He is petty, selfish, vain, egotistical; he is spoilt; he is a tyrant; he wears Mrs. Ramsay to death; but he has what you (she addressed Mr. Bankes) have not; a fiery unworldliness; he knows nothing about trifles; he loves dogs and his children. He has eight. Mr. Bankes has none. Did he not come down in two coats the other night and let Mrs. Ramsay trim his hair into a pudding basin? All of this danced up and down, like a company of gnats, each separate, but all marvellously controlled in an invisible elastic net—danced up and down in Lily's mind, in and about the branches of the pear tree, where still hung in effigy the scrubbed kitchen table, symbol of her profound respect for Mr. Ramsay's mind, until her thought which had spun quicker and quicker exploded of its own intensity; she felt released; a shot went off close at hand, and there came, flying from its fragments, frightened, effusive, tumultuous, a flock of starlings.

"Jasper!" said Mr. Bankes. They turned the way the starlings flew, over the terrace. Following the scatter of swift-flying birds in the sky they stepped through the gap in the high hedge straight into Mr. Ramsay, who boomed tragically at them, "Some one had blundered!"

His eyes, glazed with emotion, defiant with tragic intensity, met theirs for a second, and trembled on the verge of recognition; but then, raising his hand, half-way to his face as if to avert, to brush off, in an agony of peevish shame, their normal gaze, as if he begged them to withhold for a moment what he knew to be inevitable, as if he impressed upon them his own child-like resentment of interruption, yet even in the moment of discovery was not to be routed utterly, but was determined to hold fast to something of this delicious emotion, this impure rhapsody of which he was ashamed, but in which he revelled—he turned abruptly, slammed his private door on them; and, Lily Briscoe and Mr. Bankes, looking uneasily up into the sky, observed that the flock of starlings which Jasper had routed with his gun had settled on the tops of the elm trees.

V

"AND EVEN if it isn't fine tomorrow," said Mrs. Ramsay, raising her eyes to glance at William Bankes and Lily Briscoe as they passed, "it will be another day. And now," she said, thinking that Lily's charm was her Chinese eyes, aslant in her white, puckered little face, but it would take a clever man to see it, "and now stand up, and let me measure your leg," for they might go to the Lighthouse after all, and she must see if the stocking did not need to be an inch or two longer in the leg.

Smiling, for it was an admirable idea, that had flashed upon her this very second—William and Lily should marry—she took the heather-mixture stocking, with its criss-cross of steel needles at the mouth of it, and measured it against James's leg.

"My dear, stand still," she said, for in his jealousy, not liking to serve as measuring block for the Lighthouse keeper's little boy, James fidgeted purposely; and if he did that, how could she see, was it too long, was it too short? she asked.

She looked up—what demon possessed him, her youngest, her cherished?—and saw the room, saw the chairs, thought them fearfully shabby. Their entrails, as Andrew said the other day, were all over the floor; but then what was the point, she asked, of buying good chairs to let them spoil up here all through the winter when the house, with only one old woman to see to it, positively dripped with wet? Never mind, the rent was precisely twopence halfpenny; the children loved it; it did her husband good to be three thousand, or if she must be accurate, three hundred miles from his libraries and his lectures and his disciples; and there was room for visitors. Mats, camp beds, crazy ghosts of chairs and tables whose London life of service was done—they did well enough here; and a photograph or two, and books. Books, she thought, grew of themselves. She never had time to read them. Alas! even the books that had been given her and inscribed by the hand of the poet himself: "For her whose wishes must be obeyed" ... "The happier Helen of our days" ... disgraceful to say, she had never read them. And Croom on the Mind and Bates on the Savage Customs of Polynesia ("My dear, stand still," she said)—neither of those could one send to the Lighthouse. At a certain moment, she supposed, the house would become so shabby that something must be done. If they could be taught to wipe their feet and not bring the beach in with them—that would be something. Crabs, she had to allow, if Andrew really wished to dissect them, or if Jasper believed that one could make soup from seaweed, one could not prevent it; or Rose's objects—shells, reeds, stones; for they were gifted, her children, but all in quite different ways. And the result of it was, she sighed, taking in the whole room from floor to ceiling, as she held the stocking against James's leg, that things got shabbier and got shabbier summer after summer. The mat was fading; the wall-paper was flapping. You couldn't tell any more that those were roses on it. Still, if every door in a house is left perpetually open, and no lockmaker in the whole of Scotland can mend a bolt, things must spoil. Every door was left open. She listened. The drawing-room door was open; the hall door was open; it sounded as if the bedroom doors were open; and certainly the window on the landing was open, for that she had opened herself. That windows should be open, and doors shut—simple as it was, could none of them remember it? She would go into the maids' bedrooms at night and find them sealed like ovens, except for Marie's, the Swiss girl, who would rather go without a bath than without fresh air, but then at home, she had said, "the mountains are so beautiful." She had said that last night looking out of the window with tears in her eyes. "The mountains are so beautiful." Her father was dying there, Mrs. Ramsay knew. He was leaving them fatherless. Scolding and demonstrating (how to make a bed, how to open a window, with hands that shut and spread like a French-woman's) all had folded itself quietly about her, when the girl spoke, as, after a flight through the sunshine the wings of a bird fold themselves quietly and the blue of its plumage changes from bright steel to soft purple. She had stood there silent for there was nothing to be said. He had cancer of the throat. At the recollection—how she had stood there, how the girl had said, "At home the mountains are so beautiful," and there was no hope, no hope whatever, she had a spasm of irritation, and speaking sharply, said to James:

"Stand still. Don't be tiresome," so that he knew instantly that her severity was real, and straightened his leg and she measured it.

The stocking was too short by half an inch at least, making allowance for the fact that Sorley's little boy would be less well grown than James.

"It's too short," she said, "ever so much too short."

Never did anybody look so sad. Bitter and black, half-way down, in the darkness, in the shaft which ran from the sunlight to the depths, perhaps a tear formed; a tear fell; the waters swayed this way and that, received it, and were at rest. Never did anybody look so sad.

But was it nothing but looks, people said? What was there behind it—her beauty and splendour? Had he blown his brains out, they asked, had he died the week before they were married—some other, earlier lover, of whom rumours reached one? Or was there nothing? nothing but an incomparable beauty which she lived behind, and could do nothing to disturb? For easily though she might have said at some moment of intimacy when stories of great passion, of love foiled, of ambition thwarted came her way how she too had known or felt or been through it herself, she never spoke. She was silent always. She knew then— she knew without having learnt. Her simplicity fathomed what clever people falsified. Her singleness of mind made her drop plumb like a stone, alight exact as a bird, gave her, naturally, this swoop and fall of the spirit upon truth which delighted, eased, sustained—falsely perhaps.

("Nature has but little clay," said Mr. Bankes once, much moved by her voice on the telephone, though she was only telling him a fact about a train, "like that of which she moulded you." He saw her at the end of the line very clearly Greek, straight, blue-eyed. How incongruous it seemed to be telephoning to a woman like that. The Graces assembling seemed to have joined hands in meadows of asphodel to compose that face. He would catch the 10:30 at Euston.

"Yet she's no more aware of her beauty than a child," said Mr. Bankes, replacing the receiver and crossing the room to see what progress the workmen were making with an hotel which they were building at the back of his house. And he thought of Mrs. Ramsay as he looked at that stir among the unfinished walls. For always, he thought, there was something incongruous to be worked into the harmony of her face. She clapped a deer-stalker's hat on her head; she ran across the lawn in goloshes to snatch a child from mischief. So that if it was her beauty merely that one thought of, one must remember the quivering thing, the living thing (they were carrying bricks up a little plank as he watched them), and work it into the picture; or if one thought of her simply as a woman, one must endow her with some freak of idiosyncrasy—she did not like admiration—or suppose some latent desire to doff her royalty of form as if her beauty bored her and all that men say of beauty, and she wanted only to be like other people, insignificant. He did not know. He did not know. He must go to his work.)

Knitting her reddish-brown hairy stocking, with her head outlined absurdly by the gilt frame, the green shawl which she had tossed over the edge of the frame, and the authenticated masterpiece by Michael Angelo, Mrs. Ramsay smoothed out what had been harsh in her manner a moment before, raised his head, and kissed her little boy on the forehead. "Let us find an-other picture to cut out," she said.

VI

BUT WHAT had happened?
Some one had blundered.

Starting from her musing she gave meaning to words which she had held meaningless in her mind for a long stretch of time. "Some one had blundered—" Fixing her short-sighted eyes upon her husband, who was now bearing down upon her, she gazed steadily until his closeness revealed to her (the jingle mated itself in her head) that something had happened, some one had blundered. But she could not for the life of her think what.

He shivered; he quivered. All his vanity, all his satisfaction in his own splendour, riding fell as a thunderbolt, fierce as a hawk at the head of his men through the valley of death, had been shattered, destroyed. Stormed at by shot and shell, boldly we rode and well, flashed through the valley of death, volleyed and thundered—straight into Lily Briscoe and William Bankes. He quivered; he shivered.

Not for the world would she have spoken to him, realising, from the familiar signs, his eyes averted, and some curious gathering together of his person, as if he wrapped himself about and needed privacy into which to regain his equilibrium, that he was outraged and anguished. She stroked James's head; she transferred to him what she felt for her husband, and, as she watched him chalk yellow the white dress shirt of a gentleman in the Army and Navy Stores catalogue, thought what a delight it would be to her should he turn out a great artist; and why should he not? He had a splendid forehead. Then, looking up, as her husband passed her once more, she was relieved to find that the ruin was veiled; domesticity triumphed; custom crooned its soothing rhythm, so that when stopping deliberately, as his turn came round again, at the window he bent quizzically and whimsically to tickle James's bare calf with a sprig of something, she twitted him for having dispatched "that poor young man," Charles Tansley. Tansley had had to go in and write his dissertation, he said.

"James will have to write *his* dissertation one of these days," he added ironically, flicking his sprig.

Hating his father, James brushed away the tickling spray with which in a manner peculiar to him, compound of severity and humour, he teased his youngest son's bare leg.

She was trying to get these tiresome stockings finished to send to Sorley's little boy tomorrow, said Mrs. Ramsay.

There wasn't the slightest possible chance that they could go to the Lighthouse tomorrow, Mr. Ramsay snapped out irascibly.

How did he know? she asked. The wind often changed.

The extraordinary irrationality of her remark, the folly of women's minds enraged him. He had ridden through the valley of death, been shattered and shivered; and now, she flew in the face of facts, made his children hope what was utterly out of the question, in effect, told lies. He stamped his foot on the stone step. "Damn you," he said. But what had she said? Simply that it might be fine tomorrow. So it might.

Not with the barometer falling and the wind due west.

To pursue truth with such astonishing lack of consideration for other people's feelings, to rend the thin veils of civilisation so wantonly, so brutally, was to her so horrible an outrage of human decency that, without replying, dazed and blinded, she bent her head as if to let the pelt of jagged hail, the drench of dirty water, bespatter her unrebuked. There was nothing to be said.

He stood by her in silence. Very humbly, at length, he said that he would step over and ask the Coastguards if she liked.

There was nobody whom she reverenced as she reverenced him.

She was quite ready to take his word for it, she said. Only then they need not cut sandwiches—that was all. They came to her, naturally, since she was a woman, all day long with this and that; one wanting this, another that; the children were growing up; she often felt she was nothing but a sponge sopped full of human emotions. Then he said, Damn you. He said, It must rain. He said, It won't rain; and instantly a Heaven of security opened before her. There was nobody she reverenced more. She was not good enough to tie his shoe strings, she felt.

Already ashamed of that petulance, of that gesticulation of the hands when charging at the head of his troops, Mr. Ramsay rather sheepishly prodded his son's bare legs once more, and then, as if he had her leave for it, with a movement which oddly reminded his wife of the great sea lion at the Zoo tumbling backwards after swallowing his fish and walloping off so that the water in the tank washes from side to side, he dived into the evening air which, already thinner, was taking the substance from leaves and hedges but, as if in return, restoring to roses and pinks a lustre which they had not had by day.

"Some one had blundered," he said again, striding off, up and down the terrace.

But how extraordinarily his note had changed! It was like the cuckoo; "in June he gets out of tune"; as if he were trying over, tentatively seeking, some phrase for a new mood, and having only this at hand, used it, cracked though it was. But it sounded ridiculous—"Some one had blundered"—said like that, almost as a question, without any conviction, melodiously. Mrs. Ramsay could not help smiling, and soon, sure enough, walking up and down, he hummed it, dropped it, fell silent.

He was safe, he was restored to his privacy. He stopped to light his pipe, looked once at his wife and son in the window, and as one raises one's eyes from a page in an express train and sees a farm, a tree, a cluster of cottages as an illustration, a confirmation of something on the printed page to which one returns, fortified, and satisfied, so without his distinguishing either his son or his wife, the sight of them fortified him and satisfied him and consecrated his effort to arrive at a perfectly clear understanding of the problem which now engaged the energies of his splendid mind.

It was a splendid mind. For if thought is like the keyboard of a piano, divided into so many notes, or like the alphabet is ranged in twenty-six letters all in order, then his splendid mind had no sort of difficulty in running over those letters one by one, firmly and accurately, until it had reached, say, the letter Q. He reached Q. Very few people in the whole of England ever reach Q. Here, stopping for one moment by the stone urn which held the geraniums, he saw, but now far, far away, like children picking up shells, divinely innocent and occupied with little trifles at their feet and somehow entirely defenceless against a doom which he perceived, his wife and son, together, in the window. They needed his protection; he gave it them. But after Q? What comes next? After Q there are a number of letters the last of which is scarcely visible to mortal eyes, but glimmers red in the distance. Z is only reached once by one man in a generation. Still, if he could reach R it would be something. Here at least was Q. He dug his heels in at Q. Q he was sure of. Q he could demonstrate. If Q then is Q—R— Here he knocked his pipe out, with two or three resonant taps on the handle of the urn, and proceeded. "Then R . . ." He braced himself. He clenched himself.

Qualities that would have saved a ship's company exposed on a broiling sea with six biscuits and a flask of water—endurance and justice, foresight, devotion, skill, came to his help. R is then—what is R?

A shutter, like the leathern eyelid of a lizard, flickered over the intensity of his gaze and obscured the letter R. In that flash of darkness he heard people saying—he was a failure—that R was beyond him. He would never reach R. On to R, once more. R—

Qualities that in a desolate expedition across the icy solitudes of the Polar region would have made him the leader, the guide, the counsellor, whose temper, neither sanguine nor despondent, surveys with equanimity what is to be and faces it, came to his help again. R——

The lizard's eye flickered once more. The veins on his forehead bulged. The geranium in the urn became startlingly visible and, displayed among its leaves, he could see, without wishing it, that old, that obvious distinction between the two classes of men; on the one hand the steady goers of superhuman strength who, plodding and persevering, repeat the whole alphabet in order, twenty-six letters in all, from start to finish; on the other the gifted, the inspired who, miraculously, lump all the letters together in one flash—the way of genius. He had not genius; he laid no claim to that: but he had, or might have had, the power to repeat every letter of the alphabet from A to Z accurately in order. Meanwhile, he stuck at Q. On, then, on to R.

Feelings that would not have disgraced a leader who, now that the snow has begun to fall and the mountain top is covered in mist, knows that he must lay himself down and die before morning comes, stole upon him, paling the colour of his eyes, giving him, even in the two minutes of his turn on the terrace, the bleached look of withered old age. Yet he would not die lying down; he would find some crag of rock, and there, his eyes fixed on the storm, trying to the end to pierce the darkness, he would die standing. He would never reach R.

He stood stock-still, by the urn, with the geranium flowing over it. How many men in a thousand million, he asked himself, reach Z after all? Surely the leader of a forlorn hope may ask himself that, and answer, without treachery to the expedition behind him, "One perhaps." One in a generation. Is he to be blamed then if he is not that one? provided he has toiled honestly, given to the best of his power, and till he has no more left

to give? And his fame lasts how long? It is permissible even for
a dying hero to think before he dies how men will speak of him
hereafter. His fame lasts perhaps two thousand years. And what
are two thousand years? (asked Mr. Ramsay ironically, staring at
the hedge). What, indeed, if you look from a mountain top
down the long wastes of the ages? The very stone one kicks
with one's boot will outlast Shakespeare. His own little light
would shine, not very brightly, for a year or two, and would then
be merged in some bigger light, and that in a bigger still. (He
looked into the hedge, into the intricacy of the twigs.) Who then
could blame the leader of that forlorn party which after all has
climbed high enough to see the waste of the years and the perishing of stars, if before death stiffens his limbs beyond the
power of movement he does a little consciously raise his numbed
fingers to his brow, and square his shoulders, so that when the
search party comes they will find him dead at his post, the fine
figure of a soldier? Mr. Ramsay squared his shoulders and stood
very upright by the urn.

Who shall blame him, if, so standing for a moment, he
dwells upon fame, upon search parties, upon cairns raised by
grateful followers over his bones? Finally, who shall blame the
leader of the doomed expedition, if, having adventured to the
uttermost, and used his strength wholly to the last ounce and
fallen asleep not much caring if he wakes or not, he now per-
ceives by some pricking in his toes that he lives, and does not
on the whole object to live, but requires sympathy, and whisky,
and some one to tell the story of his suffering to at once? Who
shall blame him? Who will not secretly rejoice when the hero
puts his armour off, and halts by the window and gazes at his
wife and son, who, very distant at first, gradually come closer
and closer, till lips and book and head are clearly before him,
though still lovely and unfamiliar from the intensity of his isolation and the waste of ages and the perishing of the stars, and

finally putting his pipe in his pocket and bending his magnificent head before her—who will blame him if he does homage to the beauty of the world?

VII

BUT HIS SON hated him. He hated him for coming up to them, for stopping and looking down on them; he hated him for interrupting them; he hated him for the exaltation and sublimity of his gestures; for the magnificence of his head; for his exactingness and egotism (for there he stood, commanding them to attend to him); but most of all he hated the twang and twitter of his father's emotion which, vibrating round them, disturbed the perfect simplicity and good sense of his relations with his mother. By looking fixedly at the page, he hoped to make him move on; by pointing his finger at a word, he hoped to recall his mother's attention, which, he knew angrily, wavered instantly his father stopped. But, no. Nothing would make Mr. Ramsay move on. There he stood, demanding sympathy.

Mrs. Ramsay, who had been sitting loosely, folding her son in her arm, braced herself, and, half turning, seemed to raise herself with an effort, and at once to pour erect into the air a rain of energy, a column of spray, looking at the same time animated and alive as if all her energies were being fused into force, burning and illuminating (quietly though she sat, taking up her stocking again), and into this delicious fecundity, this fountain and spray of life, the fatal sterility of the male plunged itself, like a beak of brass, barren and bare. He wanted sympathy. He was a failure, he said. Mrs. Ramsay flashed her needles. Mr. Ramsay repeated, never taking his eyes from her face, that he was a failure. She blew the words back at him. "Charles

Tansley . . ." she said. But he must have more than that. It was sympathy he wanted, to be assured of his genius, first of all, and then to be taken within the circle of life, warmed and soothed, to have his senses restored to him, his barrenness made fertile, and all the rooms of the house made full of life—the drawing-room; behind the drawing-room the kitchen; above the kitchen the bedrooms; and beyond them the nurseries; they must be furnished, they must be filled with life.

Charles Tansley thought him the greatest metaphysician of the time, she said. But he must have more than that. He must have sympathy. He must be assured that he too lived in the heart of life; was needed; not here only, but all over the world. Flashing her needles, confident, upright, she created drawing-room and kitchen, set them all aglow; bade him take his ease there, go in and out, enjoy himself. She laughed, she knitted. Standing between her knees, very stiff, James felt all her strength flaring up to be drunk and quenched by the beak of brass, the arid scimitar of the male, which smote mercilessly, again and again, demanding sympathy.

He was a failure, he repeated. Well, look then, feel then. Flashing her needles, glancing round about her, out of the window, into the room, at James himself, she assured him, beyond a shadow of a doubt, by her laugh, her poise, her competence (as a nurse carrying a light across a dark room assures a fractious child), that it was real; the house was full; the garden blowing. If he put implicit faith in her, nothing should hurt him; however deep he buried himself or climbed high, not for a second should he find himself without her. So boasting of her capacity to surround and protect, there was scarcely a shell of herself left for her to know herself by; all was so lavished and spent; and James, as he stood stiff between her knees, felt her rise in a rosy-flowered fruit tree laid with leaves and dancing boughs into

which the beak of brass, the arid scimitar of his father, the egotistical man, plunged and smote, demanding sympathy.

Filled with her words, like a child who drops off satisfied,
he said, at last, looking at her with humble gratitude, restored,
renewed, that he would take a turn; he would watch the children
playing cricket. He went.

Immediately, Mrs. Ramsay seemed to fold herself together,
one petal closed in another, and the whole fabric fell in exhaustion upon itself, so that she had only strength enough to move
her finger, in exquisite abandonment to exhaustion, across the
page of Grimm's fairy story, while there throbbed through her,
like a pulse in a spring which has expanded to its full width and
now gently ceases to beat, the rapture of successful creation.

Every throb of this pulse seemed, as he walked away, to en-
close her and her husband, and to give to each that solace which
two different notes, one high, one low, struck together, seem to
give each other as they combine. Yet, as the resonance died, and
she turned to the Fairy Tale again, Mrs. Ramsay felt not only exhausted in body (afterwards, not at the time, she always felt this)
but also there tinged her physical fatigue some faintly disagreeable sensation with another origin. Not that, as she read aloud
the story of the Fisherman's Wife, she knew precisely what it
came from; nor did she let herself put into words her dissatis-
faction when she realised, at the turn of the page when she
stopped and heard dully, ominously, a wave fall, how it came
from this: she did not like, even for a second, to feel finer than
her husband; and further, could not bear not being entirely sure,
when she spoke to him, of the truth of what she said. Universi-
ties and people wanting him, lectures and books and their being
of the highest importance—all that she did not doubt for a moment; but it was their relation, and his coming to her like that,
openly, so that any one could see, that discomposed her; for
then people said he depended on her, when they must know

that of the two he was infinitely the more important, and what
she gave the world, in comparison with what he gave, negligible.
But then again, it was the other thing too—not being able to
tell him the truth, being afraid, for instance, about the greenhouse roof and the expense it would be, fifty pounds perhaps,
to mend it; and then about his books, to be afraid that he might
guess, what she a little suspected, that his last book was not
quite his best book (she gathered that from William Bankes);
and then to hide small daily things, and the children seeing it,
and the burden it laid on them—all this diminished the entire
joy, the pure joy, of the two notes sounding together, and let the
sound die on her ear now with a dismal flatness.

A shadow was on the page; she looked up. It was Augustus
Carmichael shuffling past, precisely now, at the very moment
when it was painful to be reminded of the inadequacy of human
relationships, that the most perfect was flawed, and could not
bear the examination which, loving her husband, with her instinct for truth, she turned upon it; when it was painful to feel
herself convicted of unworthiness, and impeded in her proper
function by these lies, these exaggerations—it was at this moment when she was fretted thus ignobly in the wake of her exaltation, that Mr. Carmichael shuffled past, in his yellow
slippers, and some demon in her made it necessary for her to
call out, as he passed,

"Going indoors, Mr. Carmichael?"

VIII

HE SAID NOTHING. He took opium. The children said he had
stained his beard yellow with it. Perhaps. What was obvious to
her was that the poor man was unhappy, came to them every
year as an escape; and yet every year, she felt the same thing; he

did not trust her. She said, "I am going to the town. Shall I get you stamps, paper, tobacco?" and she felt him wince. He did not trust her. It was his wife's doing. She remembered that iniquity of his wife's towards him, which had made her turn to steel and adamant there, in the horrid little room in St. John's Wood, when with her own eyes she had seen that odious woman turn him out of the house. He was unkempt; he dropped things on his coat; he had the tiresomeness of an old man with nothing in the world to do; and she turned him out of the room. She said, in her odious way, "Now, Mrs. Ramsay and I want to have a little talk together," and Mrs. Ramsay could see, as if before her eyes, the innumerable miseries of his life. Had he money enough to buy tobacco? Did he have to ask her for it? half-a-crown? eighteenpence? Oh, she could not bear to think of the little indignities she made him suffer. And always now (why, she could not guess, except that it came probably from that woman somehow) he shrank from her. He never told her anything. But what more could she have done? There was a sunny room given up to him. The children were good to him. Never did she show a sign of not wanting him. She went out of her way indeed to be friendly. Do you want stamps, do you want tobacco? Here's a book you might like and so on. And after all—after all (here insensibly she drew herself together, physically, the sense of her own beauty becoming, as it did so seldom, present to her)—after all, she had not generally any difficulty in making people like her; for instance, George Manning; Mr. Wallace; famous as they were, they would come to her of an evening, quietly, and talk alone over her fire. She bore about with her, she could not help knowing it, the torch of her beauty; she carried it erect into any room that she entered; and after all, veil it as she might, and shrink from the monotony of bearing that it imposed on her, her beauty was apparent. She had been admired. She had been loved. She had entered rooms where mourners sat. Tears had flown in her presence. Men, and women too, letting go the multiplicity of things, had allowed themselves with her the relief of simplicity. It injured her that he should shrink. It hurt her. And yet not cleanly, not rightly. That was what she minded, coming as it did on top of her discontent with her husband; the sense she had now when Mr. Carmichael shuffled past, just nodding to her question, with a book beneath his arm, in his yellow slippers, that she was suspected; and that all this desire of hers to give, to help, was vanity. For her own self-satisfaction was it that she wished so instinctively to help, to give, that people might say of her, "O Mrs. Ramsay! dear Mrs. Ramsay . . . Mrs. Ramsay, of course!" and need her and send for her and admire her? Was it not secretly this that she wanted, and therefore when Mr. Carmichael shrank away from her, as he did at this moment, making off to some corner where he did acrostics endlessly, she did not feel merely snubbed back in her instinct, but made aware of the pettiness of some part of her, and of human relations, how flawed they are, how despicable, how self-seeking, at their best. Shabby and worn out, and not presumably (her cheeks were hollow, her hair was white) any longer a sight that filled the eyes with joy, she had better devote her mind to the story of the Fisherman and his Wife and so pacify that bundle of sensitiveness (none of her children was as sensitive as he was), her son James.

"The man's heart grew heavy," she read aloud, "and he would not go. He said to himself, 'It is not right,' and yet he went. And when he came to the sea the water was quite purple and dark blue, and grey and thick, and no longer so green and yellow, but it was still quiet. And he stood there and said——"

Mrs. Ramsay could have wished that her husband had not chosen that moment to stop. Why had he not gone as he said to watch the children playing cricket? But he did not speak; he looked; he nodded; he approved; he went on. He slipped, seeing before him that hedge which had over and over again rounded some pause, signified some conclusion, seeing his wife and child, seeing again the urns with the trailing of red geraniums which had so often decorated processes of thought, and bore, written up among their leaves, as if they were scraps of paper on which one scribbles notes in the rush of reading—he slipped, seeing all this, smoothly into speculation suggested by an article in *The Times* about the number of Americans who visit Shakespeare's house every year. If Shakespeare had never existed, he asked, would the world have differed much from what it is today? Does the progress of civilisation depend upon great men? Is the lot of the average human being better now than in the time of the Pharaohs? Is the lot of the average human being, however, he asked himself, the criterion by which we judge the measure of civilisation? Possibly not. Possibly the greatest good requires the existence of a slave class. The liftman in the Tube is an eternal necessity. The thought was distasteful to him. He tossed his head. To avoid it, he would find some way of snubbing the predominance of the arts. He would argue that the world exists for the average human being; that the arts are merely a decoration imposed on the top of human life; they do not express it. Nor is Shakespeare necessary to it. Not knowing precisely why it was that he wanted to disparage Shakespeare and come to the rescue of the man who stands eternally in the door of the lift, he picked a leaf sharply from the hedge. All this would have to be dished up for the young men at Cardiff next month, he thought; here, on his terrace, he was merely foraging and picknicking (he threw away the leaf that he had picked so peevishly) like a man who reaches from his horse to pick a bunch of roses, or stuffs his pockets with nuts as he ambles at his ease through the lanes and fields of a country known to him from boyhood. It was all familiar; this turning, that stile, that cut across the fields. Hours he would spend thus, with his pipe, of an evening, thinking up and down and in and out of the old familiar lanes and commons, which were all stuck about with the history of that campaign there, the life of this statesman here, with poems and with anecdotes, with figures too, this thinker, that soldier; all very brisk and clear; but at length the lane, the field, the common, the fruitful nut-tree and the flowering hedge led him on to that further turn of the road where he dismounted always, tied his horse to a tree, and proceeded on foot alone. He reached the edge of the lawn and looked out on the bay beneath.

It was his fate, his peculiarity, whether he wished it or not, to come out thus on a spit of land which the sea is slowly eating away, and there to stand, like a desolate sea-bird, alone. It was his power, his gift, suddenly to shed all superfluities, to shrink and diminish so that he looked barer and felt sparer, even physically, yet lost none of his intensity of mind, and so to stand on his little ledge facing the dark of human ignorance, how we know nothing and the sea eats away the ground we stand on— that was his fate, his gift. But having thrown away, when he dismounted, all gestures and fripperies, all trophies of nuts and roses, and shrunk so that not only fame but even his own name was forgotten by him, he kept even in that desolation a vigilance which spared no phantom and luxuriated in no vision, and it was in this guise that he inspired in William Bankes (intermittently) and in Charles Tansley (obsequiously) and in his wife now, when she looked up and saw him standing at the edge of the lawn, profoundly, reverence, and pity, and gratitude too, as a stake driven into the bed of a channel upon which the gulls perch and the waves beat inspires in merry boat-loads a feeling of gratitude for the duty it is taking upon itself of marking the channel out there in the floods alone.

"But the father of eight children has no choice." Muttering

half aloud, so he broke off, turned, sighed, raised his eyes, sought the figure of his wife reading stories to his little boy, filled his pipe. He turned from the sight of human ignorance and human fate and the sea eating the ground we stand on, which, had he been able to contemplate it fixedly might have led to something; and found consolation in trifles so slight compared with the august theme just now before him that he was disposed to slur that comfort over, to deprecate it, as if to be caught happy in a world of misery was for an honest man the most despicable of crimes. It was true; he was for the most part happy; he had his wife; he had his children; he had promised in six weeks' time to talk "some nonsense" to the young men of Cardiff about Locke, Hume, Berkeley, and the causes of the French Revolution. But this and his pleasure in it, his glory in the phrases he made, in the ardour of youth, in his wife's beauty, in the tributes that reached him from Swansea, Cardiff, Exeter, Southampton, Kidderminster, Oxford, Cambridge—all had to be deprecated and concealed under the phrase "talking nonsense," because, in effect, he had not done the thing he might have done. It was a disguise; it was the refuge of a man afraid to own his own feelings, who could not say, This is what I like—this is what I am; and rather pitiable and distasteful to William Bankes and Lily Briscoe, who wondered why such concealments should be necessary; why he needed always praise; why so brave a man in thought should be so timid in life; how strangely he was venerable and laughable at one and the same time.

Teaching and preaching is beyond human power, Lily suspected. (She was putting away her things.) If you are exalted you must somehow come a cropper. Mrs. Ramsay gave him what he asked too easily. Then the change must be so upsetting, Lily said. He comes in from his books and finds us all playing games and talking nonsense. Imagine what a change from the things he thinks about, she said.

He was bearing down upon them. Now he stopped dead and stood looking in silence at the sea. Now he had turned away again.

IX

YES, MR. BANKES said, watching him go. It was a thousand pities. (Lily had said something about his frightening her—he changed from one mood to another so suddenly.) Yes, said Mr. Bankes, it was a thousand pities that Ramsay could not behave a little more like other people. (For he liked Lily Briscoe; he could discuss Ramsay with her quite openly.) It was for that reason, he said, that the young don't read Carlyle. A crusty old grumbler who lost his temper if the porridge was cold, why should he preach to us? was what Mr. Bankes understood that young people said nowadays. It was a thousand pities if you thought, as he did, that Carlyle was one of the great teachers of mankind. Lily was ashamed to say that she had not read Carlyle since she was at school. But in her opinion one liked Mr. Ramsay all the better for thinking that if his little finger ached the whole world must come to an end. It was not *that* she minded. For who could be deceived by him? He asked you quite openly to flatter him, to admire him, his little dodges deceived nobody. What she disliked was his narrowness, his blindness, she said, looking after him.

"A bit of a hypocrite?" Mr. Bankes suggested, looking too at Mr. Ramsay's back, for was he not thinking of his friendship, and of Cam refusing to give him a flower, and of all those boys and girls, and his own house, full of comfort, but, since his wife's death, quiet rather? Of course, he had his work. . . . All the same, he rather wished Lily to agree that Ramsay was, as he said, "a bit of a hypocrite."

Lily Briscoe went on putting away her brushes, looking up, looking down. Looking up, there he was—Mr. Ramsay—advancing towards them, swinging, careless, oblivious, remote. A bit of a hypocrite? she repeated. Oh, no—the most sincere of men, the truest (here he was), the best; but, looking down, she thought, he is absorbed in himself, he is tyrannical, he is unjust; and kept looking down, purposely, for only so could she keep steady, staying with the Ramsays. Directly one looked up and saw them, what she called "being in love" flooded them. They became part of that unreal but penetrating and exciting universe which is the world seen through the eyes of love. The sky stuck to them; the birds sang through them. And, what was even more exciting, she felt, too, as she saw Mr. Ramsay bearing down and retreating, and Mrs. Ramsay sitting with James in the window and the cloud moving and the tree bending, how life, from being made up of little separate incidents which one lived one by one, became curled and whole like a wave which bore one up with it and threw one down with it, there, with a dash on the beach.

Mr. Bankes expected her to answer. And she was about to say something criticising Mrs. Ramsay, how she was alarming, too, in her way, high-handed, or words to that effect, when Mr. Bankes made it entirely unnecessary for her to speak by his rapture. For such it was considering his age, turned sixty, and his cleanliness and his impersonality, and the white scientific coat which seemed to clothe him. For him to gaze as Lily saw him gazing at Mrs. Ramsay was a rapture, equivalent, Lily felt, to the loves of dozens of young men (and perhaps Mrs. Ramsay had never excited the loves of dozens of young men). It was love, she thought, pretending to move her canvas, distilled and filtered; love that never attempted to clutch its object; but, like the love which mathematicians bear their symbols, or poets their phrases, was meant to be spread over the world and become part of the human gain. So it was indeed. The world by all means should have shared it, could Mr. Bankes have said why that woman pleased him so; why the sight of her reading a fairy tale to her boy had upon him precisely the same effect as the solution of a scientific problem, so that he rested in contemplation of it, and felt, as he felt when he had proved something absolute about the digestive system of plants, that barbarity was tamed, the reign of chaos subdued.

Such a rapture—for by what other name could one call it?—made Lily Briscoe forget entirely what she had been about to say. It was nothing of importance; something about Mrs. Ramsay. It paled beside this "rapture," this silent stare, for which she felt intense gratitude; for nothing so solaced her, eased her of the perplexity of life, and miraculously raised its burdens, as this sublime power, this heavenly gift, and one would no more disturb it, while it lasted, than break up the shaft of sunlight, lying level across the floor.

That people should love like this, that Mr. Bankes should feel this for Mrs. Ramsay (she glanced at him musing) was helpful, was exalting. She wiped one brush after another upon a piece of old rag, menially, on purpose. She took shelter from the reverence which covered all women; she felt herself praised. Let him gaze; she would steal a look at her picture.

She could have wept. It was bad, it was bad, it was infinitely bad! She could have done it differently of course; the colour could have been thinned and faded; the shapes etherealised; that was how Paunceforte would have seen it. But then she did not see it like that. She saw the colour burning on a framework of steel; the light of a butterfly's wing lying upon the arches of a cathedral. Of all that only a few random marks scrawled upon the canvas remained. And it would never be seen; never be hung even, and there was Mr. Tansley whispering in her ear, "Women can't paint, women can't write . . ."

She now remembered what she had been going to say about Mrs. Ramsay. She did not know how she would have put it; but it would have been something critical. She had been annoyed the other night by some highhandedness. Looking along the level of Mr. Bankes's glance at her, she thought that no woman could worship another woman in the way he worshipped; they could only seek shelter under the shade which Mr. Bankes extended over them both. Looking along his beam she added to it her different ray, thinking that she was unquestionably the loveliest of people (bowed over her book); the best perhaps; but also, different too from the perfect shape which one saw there. But why different, and how different? she asked herself, scraping her palette of all those mounds of blue and green which seemed to her like clods with no life in them now, yet she vowed, she would inspire them, force them to move, flow, do her bidding tomorrow. How did she differ? What was the spirit in her, the essential thing, by which, had you found a crumpled glove in the corner of a sofa, you would have known it, from its twisted finger, hers indisputably? She was like a bird for speed, an arrow for directness. She was wilful; she was commanding (of course, Lily reminded herself, I am thinking of her relations with women, and I am much younger, an insignificant person, living off the Brompton Road). She opened bedroom windows. She shut doors. (So she tried to start the tune of Mrs. Ramsay in her head.) Arriving late at night, with a light tap on one's bedroom door, wrapped in an old fur coat (for the setting of her beauty was always that—hasty, but apt), she would enact again whatever it might be—Charles Tansley losing his umbrella; Mr. Carmichael snuffling and sniffing; Mr. Bankes saying, "The vegetable salts are lost." All this she would adroitly shape; even maliciously twist; and, moving over to the window, in pretence that she must go,—it was dawn, she could see the sun rising,—half turn back, more intimately, but still always laughing, insist that she must, Minta must, they all must marry, since in the whole world whatever laurels might be tossed to her (but Mrs. Ramsay cared not a fig for her painting), or triumphs won by her (probably Mrs. Ramsay had had her share of those), and here she saddened, darkened, and came back to her chair, there could be no disputing this: an unmarried woman (she lightly took her hand for a moment), an unmarried woman has missed the best of life. The house seemed full of children sleeping and Mrs. Ramsay listening; shaded lights and regular breathing.

Oh, but, Lily would say, there was her father; her home; even, had she dared to say it, her painting. But all this seemed so little, so virginal, against the other. Yet, as the night wore on, and white lights parted the curtains, and even now and then some bird chirped in the garden, gathering a desperate courage she would urge her own exemption from the universal law; plead for it; she liked to be alone; she liked to be herself; she was not made for that; and so have to meet a serious stare from eyes of unparalleled depth, and confront Mrs. Ramsay's simple certainty (and she was childlike now) that her dear Lily, her little Brisk, was a fool. Then, she remembered, she had laid her head on Mrs. Ramsay's lap and laughed and laughed and laughed, laughed almost hysterically at the thought of Mrs. Ramsay presiding with immutable calm over destinies which she completely failed to understand. There she sat, simple, serious. She had recovered her sense of her now—this was the glove's twisted finger. But into what sanctuary had one penetrated? Lily Briscoe had looked up at last, and there was Mrs. Ramsay, unwitting entirely what had caused her laughter, still presiding, but now with every trace of wilfulness abolished, and in its stead, something clear as the space which the clouds at last uncover—the little space of sky which sleeps beside the moon.

Was it wisdom? Was it knowledge? Was it, once more, the deceptiveness of beauty, so that all one's perceptions, half-way

to truth, were tangled in a golden mesh? or did she lock up
within her some secret which certainly Lily Briscoe believed
people must have for the world to go on at all? Every one could
not be as helter skelter, hand to mouth as she was. But if they
knew, could they tell one what they knew? Sitting on the floor
with her arms round Mrs. Ramsay's knees, close as she could
get, smiling to think that Mrs. Ramsay would never know the
reason of that pressure, she imagined how in the chambers of
the mind and heart of the woman who was, physically, touching
her, were stood, like the treasures in the tombs of kings, tablets
bearing sacred inscriptions, which if one could spell them out,
would teach one everything, but they would never be offered
openly, never made public. What art was there, known to love
or cunning, by which one pressed through into those secret
chambers? What device for becoming, like waters poured into
one jar, inextricably the same, one with the object one adored?
Could the body achieve, or the mind, subtly mingling in the
intricate passages of the brain? or the heart? Could loving, as
people called it, make her and Mrs. Ramsay one? for it was not
knowledge but unity that she desired, not inscriptions on tablets,
nothing that could be written in any language known to men,
but intimacy itself, which is knowledge, she had thought, leaning her head on Mrs. Ramsay's knee.

Nothing happened. Nothing! Nothing! as she leant her head
against Mrs. Ramsay's knee. And yet, she knew knowledge and
wisdom were stored up in Mrs. Ramsay's heart. How then, she
had asked herself, did one know one thing or another thing
about people, sealed as they were? Only like a bee, drawn by
some sweetness or sharpness in the air intangible to touch or
taste, one haunted the dome-shaped hive, ranged the wastes of
the air over the countries of the world alone, and then haunted
the hives with their murmurs and their stirrings; the hives,

which were people. Mrs. Ramsay rose. Lily rose. Mrs. Ramsay went. For days there hung about her, as after a dream some subtle change is felt in the person one has dreamt of, more vividly than anything she said, the sound of murmuring and, as she sat in the wicker arm-chair in the drawing-room window she wore, to Lily's eyes, an august shape; the shape of a dome.

This ray passed level with Mr. Bankes's ray straight to Mrs. Ramsay sitting reading there with James at her knee. But now while she still looked, Mr. Bankes had done. He had put on his spectacles. He had stepped back. He had raised his hand. He had slightly narrowed his clear blue eyes, when Lily, rousing herself, saw what he was at, and winced like a dog who sees a hand raised to strike it. She would have snatched her picture off the easel, but she said to herself, One must. She braced herself to stand the awful trial of some one looking at her picture. One must, she said, one must. And if it must be seen, Mr. Bankes was less alarming than another. But that any other eyes should see the residue of her thirty-three years, the deposit of each day's living mixed with something more secret than she had ever spoken or shown in the course of all those days was an agony. At the same time it was immensely exciting.

Nothing could be cooler and quieter. Taking out a penknife, Mr. Bankes tapped the canvas with the bone handle. What did she wish to indicate by the triangular purple shape, "just there"? he asked.

It was Mrs. Ramsay reading to James, she said. She knew his objection—that no one could tell it for a human shape. But she had made no attempt at likeness, she said. For what reason had she introduced them then? he asked. Why indeed?—except that if there, in that corner, it was bright, here, in this, she felt the need of darkness. Simple, obvious, commonplace, as it was, Mr. Bankes was interested. Mother and child then—objects of universal veneration, and in this case the mother was famous for her beauty—might be reduced, he pondered, to a purple shadow without irreverence.

But the picture was not of them, she said. Or, not in his sense. There were other senses too in which one might reverence them. By a shadow here and a light there, for instance. Her tribute took that form if, as she vaguely supposed, a picture must be a tribute. A mother and child might be reduced to a shadow without irreverence. A light here required a shadow there. He considered. He was interested. He took it scientifically in complete good faith. The truth was that all his prejudices were on the other side, he explained. The largest picture in his drawing-room, which painters had praised, and valued at a higher price than he had given for it, was of the cherry trees in blossom on the banks of the Kennet. He had spent his honeymoon on the banks of the Kennet, he said. Lily must come and see that picture, he said. But now—he turned, with his glasses raised to the scientific examination of her canvas. The question being one of the relations of masses, of lights and shadows, which, to be honest, he had never considered before, he would like to have it explained—what then did she wish to make of it? And he indicated the scene before them. She looked. She could not show him what she wished to make of it, could not see it even herself, without a brush in her hand. She took up once more her old painting position with the dim eyes and the absent-minded manner, subduing all her impressions as a woman to something much more general; becoming once more under the power of that vision which she had seen clearly once and must now grope for among hedges and houses and mothers and children—her picture. It was a question, she remembered, how to connect this mass on the right hand with that on the left. She might do it by bringing the line of the branch across so; or break the vacancy in the foreground by an object (James perhaps) so. But the danger was that by doing that the unity of the whole might be broken. She stopped; she did not want to bore him; she took the canvas lightly off the easel.

But it had been seen; it had been taken from her. This man had shared with her something profoundly intimate. And, thanking Mr. Ramsay for it and Mrs. Ramsay for it and the hour and the place, crediting the world with a power which she had not suspected—that one could walk away down that long gallery not alone any more but arm in arm with somebody—the strangest feeling in the world, and the most exhilarating—she nicked the catch of her paint-box to, more firmly than was necessary, and the nick seemed to surround in a circle forever the paint-box, the lawn, Mr. Bankes, and that wild villain, Cam, dashing past.

X

FOR CAM GRAZED the easel by an inch; she would not stop for Mr. Bankes and Lily Briscoe; though Mr. Bankes, who would have liked a daughter of his own, held out his hand; she would not stop for her father, whom she grazed also by an inch; nor for her mother, who called "Cam! I want you a moment!" as she dashed past. She was off like a bird, bullet, or arrow, impelled by what desire, shot by whom, at what directed, who could say? What, what? Mrs. Ramsay pondered, watching her. It might be a vision—of a shell, of a wheelbarrow, of a fairy kingdom on the far side of the hedge; or it might be the glory of speed; no one knew. But when Mrs. Ramsay called "Cam!" a second time, the projectile dropped in mid career, and Cam came lagging back, pulling a leaf by the way, to her mother.

What was she dreaming about, Mrs. Ramsay wondered, seeing her engrossed, as she stood there, with some thought of her own, so that she had to repeat the message twice—ask Mildred if Andrew, Miss Doyle, and Mr. Rayley have come back?—The words seemed to be dropped into a well, where, if the waters were clear, they were also so extraordinarily distorting that, even as they descended, one saw them twisting about to make Heaven knows what pattern on the floor of the child's mind. What message would Cam give the cook? Mrs. Ramsay wondered. And indeed it was only by waiting patiently, and hearing that there was an old woman in the kitchen with very red cheeks, drinking soup out of a basin, that Mrs. Ramsay at last prompted that parrot-like instinct which had picked up Mildred's words quite accurately and could now produce them, if one waited, in a colourless singsong. Shifting from foot to foot, Cam repeated the words, "No, they haven't, and I've told Ellen to clear away tea."

Minta Doyle and Paul Rayley had not come back then. That could only mean, Mrs. Ramsay thought, one thing. She must accept him, or she must refuse him. This going off after luncheon for a walk, even though Andrew was with them—what could it mean? except that she had decided, rightly, Mrs. Ramsay thought (and she was very, very fond of Minta), to accept that good fellow, who might not be brilliant, but then, thought Mrs. Ramsay, realising that James was tugging at her, to make her go on reading aloud the Fisherman and his Wife, she did in her own heart infinitely prefer boobies to clever men who wrote dissertations; Charles Tansley, for instance. It must have happened, one way or the other, by now.

But she read, "Next morning the wife awoke first, and it was just daybreak, and from her bed she saw the beautiful country lying before her. Her husband was still stretching himself. . . ."

But how could Minta say now that she would not have him? Not if she agreed to spend whole afternoons trapesing about

the country alone—for Andrew would be off after his crabs—
but possibly Nancy was with them. She tried to recall the sight
of them standing at the hall door after lunch. There they stood,
looking at the sky, wondering about the weather, and she had
said, thinking partly to cover their shyness, partly to encourage
them to be off (for her sympathies were with Paul),

"There isn't a cloud anywhere within miles," at which she
could feel little Charles Tansley, who had followed them out,
snigger. But she did it on purpose. Whether Nancy was there or
not, she could not be certain, looking from one to the other in
her mind's eye.

She read on: "'Ah, wife,' said the man, 'why should we be
King? I do not want to be King.' 'Well,' said the wife, 'if you
won't be King, I will; go to the Flounder, for I will be King.'"

"Come in or go out, Cam," she said, knowing that Cam was
attracted only by the word "Flounder" and that in a moment
she would fidget and fight with James as usual. Cam shot off.
Mrs. Ramsay went on reading, relieved, for she and James
shared the same tastes and were comfortable together.

"And when he came to the sea, it was quite dark grey, and
the water heaved up from below, and smelt putrid. Then he
went and stood by it and said,

> 'Flounder, flounder, in the sea,
> Come, I pray thee, here to me;
> For my wife, good Ilsabil,
> Wills not as I'd have her will.'

'Well, what does she want then?' said the Flounder." And where
were they now? Mrs. Ramsay wondered, reading and thinking,
quite easily, both at the same time; for the story of the Fisherman and his Wife was like the bass gently accompanying a tune,
which now and then ran up unexpectedly into the melody. And

when should she be told? If nothing happened, she would have to speak seriously to Minta. For she could not go trapesing about all over the country, even if Nancy were with them (she tried again, unsuccessfully, to visualise their backs going down the path, and to count them). She was responsible to Minta's parents—the Owl and the Poker. Her nicknames for them shot into her mind as she read. The Owl and the Poker—yes, they would be annoyed if they heard—and they were certain to hear—that Minta, staying with the Ramsays, had been seen etcetera, etcetera, etcetera. "He wore a wig in the House of Commons and she ably assisted him at the head of the stairs," she repeated, fishing them up out of her mind by a phrase which, coming back from some party, she had made to amuse her husband. Dear, dear, Mrs. Ramsay said to herself, how did they produce this incongruous daughter? this tomboy Minta, with a hole in her stocking? How did she exist in that portentous atmosphere where the maid was always removing in a dustpan the sand that the parrot had scattered, and conversation was almost entirely reduced to the exploits—interesting perhaps, but limited after all—of that bird? Naturally, one had asked her to lunch, tea, dinner, finally to stay with them up at Finlay, which had resulted in some friction with the Owl, her mother, and more calling, and more conversation, and more sand, and really at the end of it, she had told enough lies about parrots to last her a lifetime (so she had said to her husband that night, coming back from the party). However, Minta came. . . . Yes, she came, Mrs. Ramsay thought, suspecting some thorn in the tangle of this thought; and disengaging it found it to be this: a woman had once accused her of "robbing her of her daughter's affections"; something Mrs. Doyle had said made her remember that charge again. Wishing to dominate, wishing to interfere, making people do what she wished—that was the charge against her, and she thought it most unjust. How could

she help being "like that" to look at? No one could accuse her
of taking pains to impress. She was often ashamed of her own
shabbiness. Nor was she domineering, nor was she tyrannical.
It was more true about hospitals and drains and the dairy.
About things like that she did feel passionately, and would, if she
had had the chance, have liked to take people by the scruff of
their necks and make them see. No hospital on the whole island.
It was a disgrace. Milk delivered at your door in London positively brown with dirt. It should be made illegal. A model dairy
and a hospital up here—those two things she would have liked
to do, herself. But how? With all these children? When they
were older, then perhaps she would have time; when they were
all at school.

Oh, but she never wanted James to grow a day older! or
Cam either. These two she would have liked to keep for ever just
as they were, demons of wickedness, angels of delight, never to
see them grow up into long-legged monsters. Nothing made up
for the loss. When she read just now to James, "and there were
numbers of soldiers with kettledrums and trumpets," and his
eyes darkened, she thought, why should they grow up and lose
all that? He was the most gifted, the most sensitive of her children. But all, she thought, were full of promise. Prue, a perfect
angel with the others, and sometimes now, at night especially,
she took one's breath away with her beauty. Andrew—even her
husband admitted that his gift for mathematics was extraordinary. And Nancy and Roger, they were both wild creatures now,
scampering about over the country all day long. As for Rose, her
mouth was too big, but she had a wonderful gift with her hands.
If they had charades, Rose made the dresses; made everything;
liked best arranging tables, flowers, anything. She did not like
it that Jasper should shoot birds; but it was only a stage; they
all went through stages. Why, she asked, pressing her chin on
James's head, should they grow up so fast? Why should they go

to school? She would have liked always to have had a baby. She was happiest carrying one in her arms. Then people might say she was tyrannical, domineering, masterful, if they chose; she did not mind. And, touching his hair with her lips, she thought, he will never be so happy again, but stopped herself, remembering how it angered her husband that she should say that. Still, it was true. They were happier now than they would ever be again. A tenpenny tea set made Cam happy for days. She heard them stamping and crowing on the floor above her head the moment they woke. They came bustling along the passage. Then the door sprang open and in they came, fresh as roses, staring, wide awake, as if this coming into the dining-room after breakfast, which they did every day of their lives, was a positive event to them, and so on, with one thing after another, all day long, until she went up to say good-night to them, and found them netted in their cots like birds among cherries and raspberries, still making up stories about some little bit of rubbish—something they had heard, something they had picked up in the garden. They had all their little treasures. . . . And so she went down and said to her husband, Why must they grow up and lose it all? Never will they be so happy again. And he was angry. Why take such a gloomy view of life? he said. It is not sensible. For it was odd; and she believed it to be true; that with all his gloom and desperation he was happier, more hopeful on the whole, than she was. Less exposed to human worries—perhaps that was it. He had always his work to fall back on. Not that she herself was "pessimistic," as he accused her of being. Only she thought life—and a little strip of time presented itself to her eyes—her fifty years. There it was before her—life. Life, she thought—but she did not finish her thought. She took a look at life, for she had a clear sense of it there, something real, something private, which she shared neither with her children nor with her husband. A sort of transaction went on between them, in which she was on one side, and life was on another, and she was always trying to get the better of it, as it was of her; and sometimes they parleyed (when she sat alone); there were, she remembered, great reconciliation scenes; but for the most part, oddly enough, she must admit that she felt this thing that she called life terrible, hostile, and quick to pounce on you if you gave it a chance. There were the eternal problems: suffering; death; the poor. There was always a woman dying of cancer even here. And yet she had said to all these children, You shall go through it all. To eight people she had said relentlessly that (and the bill for the greenhouse would be fifty pounds). For that reason, knowing what was before them—love and ambition and being wretched alone in dreary places—she had often the feeling, Why must they grow up and lose it all? And then she said to herself, brandishing her sword at life, Nonsense. They will be perfectly happy. And here she was, she reflected, feeling life rather sinister again, making Minta marry Paul Rayley; because whatever she might feel about her own transaction, she had had experiences which need not happen to every one (she did not name them to herself); she was driven on, too quickly she knew, almost as if it were an escape for her too, to say that people must marry; people must have children.

Was she wrong in this, she asked herself, reviewing her conduct for the past week or two, and wondering if she had indeed put any pressure upon Minta, who was only twenty-four, to make up her mind. She was uneasy. Had she not laughed about it? Was she not forgetting again how strongly she influenced people? Marriage needed—oh, all sorts of qualities (the bill for the greenhouse would be fifty pounds); one—she need not name it—that was essential; the thing she had with her husband. Had they that?

"Then he put on his trousers and ran away like a madman," she read. "But outside a great storm was raging and blowing so hard that he could scarcely keep his feet; houses and trees toppled over, the mountains trembled, rocks rolled into the sea, the sky was pitch black, and it thundered and lightened, and the sea came in with black waves as high as church towers and mountains, and all with white foam at the top."

She turned the page; there were only a few lines more, so that she would finish the story, though it was past bed-time. It was getting late. The light in the garden told her that; and the whitening of the flowers and something grey in the leaves conspired together, to rouse in her a feeling of anxiety. What it was about she could not think at first. Then she remembered; Paul and Minta and Andrew had not come back. She summoned before her again the little group on the terrace in front of the hall door, standing looking up into the sky. Andrew had his net and basket. That meant he was going to catch crabs and things. That meant he would climb out on to a rock; he would be cut off. Or coming back single file on one of those little paths above the cliff one of them might slip. He would roll and then crash. It was growing quite dark.

But she did not let her voice change in the least as she finished the story, and added, shutting the book, and speaking the last words as if she had made them up herself, looking into James's eyes: "And there they are living still at this very time."

"And that's the end," she said, and she saw in his eyes, as the interest of the story died away in them, something else take its place; something wondering, pale, like the reflection of a light, which at once made him gaze and marvel. Turning, she looked across the bay, and there, sure enough, coming regularly across the waves first two quick strokes and then one long steady stroke, was the light of the Lighthouse. It had been lit.

In a moment he would ask her, "Are we going to the Lighthouse?" And she would have to say, "No: not tomorrow; your father says not." Happily, Mildred came in to fetch them, and

the bustle distracted them. But he kept looking back over his
shoulder as Mildred carried him out, and she was certain that he
was thinking, we are not going to the Lighthouse tomorrow;
and she thought, he will remember that all his life.

XI

NO, SHE THOUGHT, putting together some of the pictures he
had cut out—a refrigerator, a mowing machine, a gentleman in
evening dress—children never forget. For this reason, it was so
important what one said, and what one did, and it was a relief
when they went to bed. For now she need not think about anybody. She could be herself, by herself. And that was what now
she often felt the need of—to think; well, not even to think. To
be silent; to be alone. All the being and the doing, expansive,
glittering, vocal, evaporated; and one shrunk, with a sense of
solemnity, to being oneself, a wedge-shaped core of darkness,
something invisible to others. Although she continued to knit,
and sat upright, it was thus that she felt herself; and this self having shed its attachments was free for the strangest adventures.
When life sank down for a moment, the range of experience
seemed limitless. And to everybody there was always this sense
of unlimited resources, she supposed; one after another, she,
Lily, Augustus Carmichael, must feel, our apparitions, the things
you know us by, are simply childish. Beneath it is all dark, it is
all spreading, it is unfathomably deep; but now and again we
rise to the surface and that is what you see us by. Her horizon
seemed to her limitless. There were all the places she had not
seen; the Indian plains; she felt herself pushing aside the thick
leather curtain of a church in Rome. This core of darkness could
go anywhere, for no one saw it. They could not stop it, she
thought, exulting. There was freedom, there was peace, there

was, most welcome of all, a summoning together, a resting on a platform of stability. Not as oneself did one find rest ever, in her experience (she accomplished here something dexterous with her needles) but as a wedge of darkness. Losing personality, one lost the fret, the hurry, the stir; and there rose to her lips always some exclamation of triumph over life when things came together in this peace, this rest, this eternity; and pausing there she looked out to meet that stroke of the Lighthouse, the long steady stroke, the last of the three, which was her stroke, for watching them in this mood always at this hour one could not help attaching oneself to one thing especially of the things one saw; and this thing, the long steady stroke, was her stroke. Often she found herself sitting and looking, sitting and looking, with her work in her hands until she became the thing she looked at—that light, for example. And it would lift up on it some little phrase or other which had been lying in her mind like that— "Children don't forget, children don't forget"—which she would repeat and begin adding to it, It will end, it will end, she said. It will come, it will come, when suddenly she added, We are in the hands of the Lord.

But instantly she was annoyed with herself for saying that. Who had said it? Not she; she had been trapped into saying something she did not mean. She looked up over her knitting and met the third stroke and it seemed to her like her own eyes meeting her own eyes, searching as she alone could search into her mind and her heart, purifying out of existence that lie, any lie. She praised herself in praising the light, without vanity, for she was stern, she was searching, she was beautiful like that light. It was odd, she thought, how if one was alone, one leant to inanimate things; trees, streams, flowers; felt they expressed one; felt they became one; felt they knew one, in a sense were one; felt an irrational tenderness thus (she looked at that long steady light) as for oneself. There rose, and she looked and looked with her needles suspended, there curled up off the floor of the mind, rose from the lake of one's being, a mist, a bride to meet her lover.

What brought her to say that: "We are in the hands of the Lord?" she wondered. The insincerity slipping in among the truths roused her, annoyed her. She returned to her knitting again. How could any Lord have made this world? she asked. With her mind she had always seized the fact that there is no reason, order, justice: but suffering, death, the poor. There was no treachery too base for the world to commit; she knew that. No happiness lasted; she knew that. She knitted with firm composure, slightly pursing her lips and, without being aware of it, so stiffened and composed the lines of her face in a habit of sternness that when her husband passed, though he was chuckling at the thought that Hume, the philosopher, grown enormously fat, had stuck in a bog, he could not help noting, as he passed, the sternness at the heart of her beauty. It saddened him, and her remoteness pained him, and he felt, as he passed, that he could not protect her, and, when he reached the hedge, he was sad. He could do nothing to help her. He must stand by and watch her. Indeed, the infernal truth was, he made things worse for her. He was irritable—he was touchy. He had lost his temper over the Lighthouse. He looked into the hedge, into its intricacy, its darkness.

Always, Mrs. Ramsay felt, one helped oneself out of solitude reluctantly by laying hold of some little odd or end, some sound, some sight. She listened, but it was all very still; cricket was over; the children were in their baths; there was only the sound of the sea. She stopped knitting; she held the long reddish-brown stocking dangling in her hands a moment. She saw the light again. With some irony in her interrogation, for when one woke at all, one's relations changed, she looked at the steady light, the pitiless, the remorseless, which was so much her, yet so little her, which had her at its beck and call (she woke in the night and saw it bent across their bed, stroking the floor), but for all that she thought, watching it with fascination, hypnotised, as if it were stroking with its silver fingers some sealed vessel in her brain whose bursting would flood her with delight, she had known happiness, exquisite happiness, intense happiness, and it silvered the rough waves a little more brightly, as daylight faded, and the blue went out of the sea and it rolled in waves of pure lemon which curved and swelled and broke upon the beach and the ecstasy burst in her eyes and waves of pure delight raced over the floor of her mind and she felt, It is enough! It is enough!

He turned and saw her. Ah! She was lovely, lovelier now than ever he thought. But he could not speak to her. He could not interrupt her. He wanted urgently to speak to her now that James was gone and she was alone at last. But he resolved, no; he would not interrupt her. She was aloof from him now in her beauty, in her sadness. He would let her be, and he passed her without a word, though it hurt him that she should look so distant, and he could not reach her, he could do nothing to help her. And again he would have passed her without a word had she not, at that very moment, given him of her own free will what she knew he would never ask, and called to him and taken the green shawl off the picture frame, and gone to him. For he wished, she knew, to protect her.

XII

SHE FOLDED the green shawl about her shoulders. She took his arm. His beauty was so great, she said, beginning to speak of Kennedy the gardener, at once he was so awfully handsome, that she couldn't dismiss him. There was a ladder against the greenhouse, and little lumps of putty stuck about, for they were beginning to mend the greenhouse. Yes, but as she strolled along with her husband, she felt that that particular source of worry had been placed. She had it on the tip of her tongue to say, as they strolled, "It'll cost fifty pounds," but instead, for her heart failed her about money, she talked about Jasper shooting birds, and he said, at once, soothing her instantly, that it was natural in a boy, and he trusted he would find better ways of amusing himself before long. Her husband was so sensible, so just. And so she said, "Yes; all children go through stages," and began considering the dahlias in the big bed, and wondering what about next year's flowers, and had he heard the children's nickname for Charles Tansley, she asked. The atheist, they called him, the little atheist. "He's not a polished specimen," said Mr. Ramsay. "Far from it," said Mrs. Ramsay.

She supposed it was all right leaving him to his own devices, Mrs. Ramsay said, wondering whether it was any use sending down bulbs; did they plant them? "Oh, he has his dissertation to write," said Mr. Ramsay. She knew all about *that,* said Mrs. Ramsay. He talked of nothing else. It was about the influence of somebody upon something. "Well, it's all he has to count on," said Mr. Ramsay. "Pray Heaven he won't fall in love with Prue," said Mrs. Ramsay. He'd disinherit her if she married him, said Mr. Ramsay. He did not look at the flowers, which his wife was considering, but at a spot about a foot or so above them. There was no harm in him, he added, and was just about to say that anyhow he was the only young man in England who admired his—— when he choked it back. He would not bother her again about his books. These flowers seemed creditable, Mr. Ramsay said, lowering his gaze and noticing something red, something brown. Yes, but then these she had put in with her own hands, said Mrs. Ramsay. The question was, what happened if she sent bulbs down; did Kennedy plant them? It was his incurable laziness; she added, moving on. If she stood over him all day long with a spade in her hand, he did sometimes do a stroke of work. So they strolled along, towards the red-hot pokers. "You're teaching your daughters to exaggerate," said Mr. Ramsay, reproving her. Her Aunt Camilla was far worse than she was, Mrs. Ramsay remarked. "Nobody ever held up your Aunt Camilla as a model of virtue that I'm aware of," said Mr. Ramsay. "She was the most beautiful woman I ever saw," said Mrs. Ramsay. "Somebody else was that," said Mr. Ramsay. Prue was going to be far more beautiful than she was, said Mrs. Ramsay. He saw no trace of it, said Mr. Ramsay. "Well, then, look tonight," said Mrs. Ramsay. They paused. He wished Andrew could be induced to work harder. He would lose every chance of a scholarship if he didn't. "Oh, scholarships!" she said. Mr. Ramsay thought her foolish for saying that about a serious thing like a scholarship. He should be very proud of Andrew if he got a scholarship, he said. She would be just as proud of him if he didn't, she answered. They disagreed always about this, but it did not matter. She liked him to believe in scholarships, and he liked her to be proud of Andrew whatever he did. Suddenly she remembered those little paths on the edge of the cliffs.

Wasn't it late? she asked. They hadn't come home yet. He flicked his watch carelessly open. But it was only just past seven. He held his watch open for a moment, deciding that he would tell her what he had felt on the terrace. To begin with, it was not reasonable to be so nervous. Andrew could look after himself. Then, he wanted to tell her that when he was walking on the terrace just now—here he became uncomfortable, as if he were breaking into that solitude, that aloofness, that remoteness of hers. . . . But she pressed him. What had he wanted to tell her, she asked, thinking it was about going to the Lighthouse; that he was sorry he had said "Damn you." But no. He did not like to see her look so sad, he said. Only wool gathering, she protested, flushing a little. They both felt uncomfortable, as if

they did not know whether to go on or go back. She had been
reading fairy tales to James, she said. No, they could not share
that; they could not say that.

They had reached the gap between the two clumps of red-
hot pokers, and there was the Lighthouse again, but she would
not let herself look at it. Had she known that he was looking at
her, she thought, she would not have let herself sit there, thinking. She disliked anything that reminded her that she had been
seen sitting thinking. So she looked over her shoulder, at the
town. The lights were rippling and running as if they were drops
of silver water held firm in a wind. And all the poverty, all the
suffering had turned to that, Mrs. Ramsay thought. The lights
of the town and of the harbour and of the boats seemed like a
phantom net floating there to mark something which had sunk.
Well, if he could not share her thoughts, Mr. Ramsay said to
himself, he would be off, then, on his own. He wanted to go on
thinking, telling himself the story how Hume was stuck in a bog;
he wanted to laugh. But first it was nonsense to be anxious
about Andrew. When he was Andrew's age he used to walk
about the country all day long, with nothing but a biscuit in his
pocket and nobody bothered about him, or thought that he had
fallen over a cliff. He said aloud he thought he would be off for
a day's walk if the weather held. He had had about enough of
Bankes and of Carmichael. He would like a little solitude. Yes,
she said. It annoyed him that she did not protest. She knew that
he would never do it. He was too old now to walk all day long
with a biscuit in his pocket. She worried about the boys, but not
about him. Years ago, before he had married, he thought, looking across the bay, as they stood between the clumps of red-hot
pokers, he had walked all day. He had made a meal off bread
and cheese in a public house. He had worked ten hours at a
stretch; an old woman just popped her head in now and again
and saw to the fire. That was the country he liked best, over

there; those sandhills dwindling away into darkness. One could walk all day without meeting a soul. There was not a house scarcely, not a single village for miles on end. One could worry things out alone. There were little sandy beaches where no one had been since the beginning of time. The seals sat up and looked at you. It sometimes seemed to him that in a little house out there, alone—he broke off, sighing. He had no right. The father of eight children—he reminded himself. And he would have been a beast and a cur to wish a single thing altered. Andrew would be a better man than he had been. Prue would be a beauty, her mother said. They would stem the flood a bit. That was a good bit of work on the whole—his eight children. They showed he did not damn the poor little universe entirely, for on an evening like this, he thought, looking at the land dwindling away, the little island seemed pathetically small, half swallowed up in the sea.

"Poor little place," he murmured with a sigh.

She heard him. He said the most melancholy things, but she noticed that directly he had said them he always seemed more cheerful than usual. All this phrase-making was a game, she thought, for if she had said half what he said, she would have blown her brains out by now.

It annoyed her, this phrase-making, and she said to him, in a matter-of-fact way, that it was a perfectly lovely evening. And what was he groaning about, she asked, half laughing, half complaining, for she guessed what he was thinking—he would have written better books if he had not married.

He was not complaining, he said. She knew that he did not complain. She knew that he had nothing whatever to complain of. And he seized her hand and raised it to his lips and kissed it with an intensity that brought the tears to her eyes, and quickly he dropped it.

They turned away from the view and began to walk up the

path where the silver-green spear-like plants grew, arm in arm. His arm was almost like a young man's arm, Mrs. Ramsay thought, thin and hard, and she thought with delight how strong he still was, though he was over sixty, and how untamed and optimistic, and how strange it was that being convinced, as he was, of all sorts of horrors, seemed not to depress him, but to cheer him. Was it not odd, she reflected? Indeed he seemed to her sometimes made differently from other people, born blind, deaf, and dumb, to the ordinary things, but to the extraordinary things, with an eye like an eagle's. His understanding often astonished her. But did he notice the flowers? No. Did he notice the view? No. Did he even notice his own daughter's beauty, or whether there was pudding on his plate or roast beef? He would sit at table with them like a person in a dream. And his habit of talking aloud, or saying poetry aloud, was growing on him, she was afraid; for sometimes it was awkward—

Best and brightest come away!

poor Miss Giddings, when he shouted that at her, almost jumped out of her skin. But then, Mrs. Ramsay, though instantly taking his side against all the silly Giddingses in the world, then, she thought, intimating by a little pressure on his arm that he walked up hill too fast for her, and she must stop for a moment to see whether those were fresh molehills on the bank, then, she thought, stooping down to look, a great mind like his must be different in every way from ours. All the great men she had ever known, she thought, deciding that a rabbit must have got in, were like that, and it was good for young men (though the atmosphere of lecture-rooms was stuffy and depressing to her beyond endurance almost) simply to hear him, simply to look at him. But without shooting rabbits, how was one to keep them down? she wondered. It might be a rabbit; it might be a mole.

Some creature anyhow was ruining her Evening Primroses. And looking up, she saw above the thin trees the first pulse of the full-throbbing star, and wanted to make her husband look at it; for the sight gave her such keen pleasure. But she stopped herself. He never looked at things. If he did, all he would say would be, Poor little world, with one of his sighs.

At that moment, he said, "Very fine," to please her, and pretended to admire the flowers. But she knew quite well that he did not admire them, or even realise that they were there. It was only to please her . . . Ah, but was that not Lily Briscoe strolling along with William Bankes? She focussed her short-sighted eyes upon the backs of a retreating couple. Yes, indeed it was. Did that not mean that they would marry? Yes, it must! What an admirable idea! They must marry!

XIII

HE HAD BEEN to Amsterdam, Mr. Bankes was saying as he strolled across the lawn with Lily Briscoe. He had seen the Rembrandts. He had been to Madrid. Unfortunately, it was Good Friday and the Prado was shut. He had been to Rome. Had Miss Briscoe never been to Rome? Oh, she should—— It would be a wonderful experience for her—the Sistine Chapel; Michael Angelo; and Padua, with its Giottos. His wife had been in bad health for many years, so that their sight-seeing had been on a modest scale.

She had been to Brussels; she had been to Paris, but only for a flying visit to see an aunt who was ill. She had been to Dresden; there were masses of pictures she had not seen; however, Lily Briscoe reflected, perhaps it was better not to see pictures: they only made one hopelessly discontented with one's own work. Mr. Bankes thought one could carry that point of view too far. We can't all be Titians and we can't all be Darwins, he said; at the same time he doubted whether you could have your Darwin and your Titian if it weren't for humble people like ourselves. Lily would have liked to pay him a compliment; you're not humble, Mr. Bankes, she would have liked to have said. But he did not want compliments (most men do, she thought), and she was a little ashamed of her impulse and said nothing while he remarked that perhaps what he was saying did not apply to pictures. Anyhow, said Lily, tossing off her little insincerity, she would always go on painting, because it interested her. Yes, said Mr. Bankes, he was sure she would, and, as they reached the end of the lawn he was asking her whether she had difficulty in finding subjects in London when they turned and saw the Ramsays. So that is marriage, Lily thought, a man and a woman looking at a girl throwing a ball. That is what Mrs. Ramsay tried to tell me the other night, she thought. For Mrs. Ramsay was wearing a green shawl, and they were standing close together watching Prue and Jasper throwing catches. And suddenly the meaning which, for no reason at all, as perhaps they are stepping out of the Tube or ringing a doorbell, descends on people, making them symbolical, making them representative, came upon them, and made them in the dusk standing, looking, the symbols of marriage, husband and wife. Then, after an instant, the symbolical outline which transcended the real figures sank down again, and they became, as they met them, Mr. and Mrs. Ramsay watching the children throwing catches. But still for a moment, though Mrs. Ramsay greeted them with her usual smile (oh, she's thinking we're going to get married, Lily thought) and said, "I have triumphed tonight," meaning that for once Mr. Bankes had agreed to dine with them and not run off to his own lodging where his man cooked vegetables properly; still, for one moment, there was a sense of things having been blown apart, of space, of irresponsibility as the ball soared high, and they followed it and lost it and saw the one star and the draped branches. In the failing light they all looked sharp-edged and ethereal and divided by great distances. Then, darting backwards over the vast space (for it seemed as if solidity had vanished altogether), Prue ran full tilt into them and caught the ball brilliantly high up in her left hand, and her mother said, "Haven't they come back yet?" whereupon the spell was broken. Mr. Ramsay felt free now to laugh out loud at the thought that Hume had stuck in a bog and an old woman rescued him on condition he said the Lord's Prayer, and chuckling to himself he strolled off to his study. Mrs. Ramsay, bringing Prue back into throwing catches again, from which she had escaped, asked,

"Did Nancy go with them?"

XIV

(CERTAINLY, NANCY had gone with them, since Minta Doyle had asked it with her dumb look, holding out her hand, as Nancy made off, after lunch, to her attic, to escape the horror of family life. She supposed she must go then. She did not want to go. She did not want to be drawn into it all. For as they walked along the road to the cliff Minta kept on taking her hand. Then she would let it go. Then she would take it again. What was it she wanted? Nancy asked herself. There was something, of course, that people wanted; for when Minta took her hand and held it, Nancy, reluctantly, saw the whole world spread out beneath her, as if it were Constantinople seen through a mist, and then, however heavy-eyed one might be, one must needs ask, "Is that Santa Sofia?" "Is that the Golden Horn?" So Nancy asked, when Minta took her hand. "What is it that she wants? Is it that?" And what was that? Here and there emerged from the mist (as Nancy looked down upon life spread beneath her) a pinnacle, a dome;

prominent things, without names. But when Minta dropped her hand, as she did when they ran down the hillside, all that, the dome, the pinnacle, whatever it was that had protruded through the mist, sank down into it and disappeared. Minta, Andrew observed, was rather a good walker. She wore more sensible clothes than most women. She wore very short skirts and black knickerbockers. She would jump straight into a stream and flounder across. He liked her rashness, but he saw that it would not do— she would kill herself in some idiotic way one of these days. She seemed to be afraid of nothing—except bulls. At the mere sight of a bull in a field she would throw up her arms and fly screaming, which was the very thing to enrage a bull of course. But she did not mind owning up to it in the least; one must admit that. She knew she was an awful coward about bulls, she said. She thought she must have been tossed in her perambulator when she was a baby. She didn't seem to mind what she said or did. Suddenly now she pitched down on the edge of the cliff and began to sing some song about

Damn your eyes, damn your eyes.

They all had to join in and sing the chorus, and shout out together:

Damn your eyes, damn your eyes,

but it would be fatal to let the tide come in and cover up all the good hunting-grounds before they got on to the beach.

"Fatal," Paul agreed, springing up, and as they went slithering down, he kept quoting the guidebook about "these islands being justly celebrated for their park-like prospects and the extent and variety of their marine curiosities." But it would not do altogether, this shouting and damning your eyes, Andrew felt, picking his way down the cliff, this clapping him on the back, and calling him "old fellow" and all that; it would not altogether do. It was the worst of taking women on walks. Once on the beach they separated, he going out on to the Pope's Nose, taking his shoes off, and rolling his socks in them and letting that couple look after themselves; Nancy waded out to her own rocks and searched her own pools and let that couple look after themselves. She crouched low down and touched the smooth rubber-like sea anemones, who were stuck like lumps of jelly to the side of the rock. Brooding, she changed the pool into the sea, and made the minnows into sharks and whales, and cast vast clouds over this tiny world by holding her hand against the sun, and so brought darkness and desolation, like God himself, to millions of ignorant and innocent creatures, and then took her hand away suddenly and let the sun stream down. Out on the pale criss-crossed sand, high-stepping, fringed, gauntleted, stalked some fantastic leviathan (she was still enlarging the pool), and slipped into the vast fissures of the mountain side. And then, letting her eyes slide imperceptibly above the pool and rest on that wavering line of sea and sky, on the tree trunks which the smoke of steamers made waver upon the horizon, she became with all that power sweeping savagely in and inevitably withdrawing, hypnotised, and the two senses of that vastness and this tininess (the pool had diminished again) flowering within it made her feel that she was bound hand and foot and unable to move by the intensity of feelings which reduced her own body, her own life, and the lives of all the people in the world, for ever, to nothingness. So listening to the waves, crouching over the pool, she brooded.

And Andrew shouted that the sea was coming in, so she leapt splashing through the shallow waves on to the shore and ran up the beach and was carried by her own impetuosity and her desire for rapid movement right behind a rock and there—

oh, heavens! in each other's arms, were Paul and Minta kissing probably. She was outraged, indignant. She and Andrew put on their shoes and stockings in dead silence without saying a thing about it. Indeed they were rather sharp with each other. She might have called him when she saw the crayfish or whatever it was, Andrew grumbled. However, they both felt, it's not our fault. They had not wanted this horrid nuisance to happen. All the same it irritated Andrew that Nancy should be a woman, and Nancy that Andrew should be a man, and they tied their shoes very neatly and drew the bows rather tight.

It was not until they had climbed right up on to the top of the cliff again that Minta cried out that she had lost her grandmother's brooch—her grandmother's brooch, the sole ornament she possessed—a weeping willow, it was (they must remember it) set in pearls. They must have seen it, she said, with the tears running down her cheeks, the brooch which her grandmother had fastened her cap with till the last day of her life. Now she had lost it. She would rather have lost anything than that! She would go back and look for it. They all went back. They poked and peered and looked. They kept their heads very low, and said things shortly and gruffly. Paul Rayley searched like a madman all about the rock where they had been sitting. All this pother about a brooch really didn't do at all, Andrew thought, as Paul told him to make a "thorough search between this point and that." The tide was coming in fast. The sea would cover the place where they had sat in a minute. There was not a ghost of a chance of their finding it now. "We shall be cut off!" Minta shrieked, suddenly terrified. As if there were any danger of that! It was the same as the bulls all over again—she had no control over her emotions, Andrew thought. Women hadn't. The wretched Paul had to pacify her. The men (Andrew and Paul at once became manly, and different from usual) took counsel briefly and decided that they would plant Rayley's stick

where they had sat and come back at low tide again. There was
nothing more that could be done now. If the brooch was there,
it would still be there in the morning, they assured her, but
Minta still sobbed, all the way up to the top of the cliff. It was
her grandmother's brooch; she would rather have lost anything
but that, and yet Nancy felt, it might be true that she minded
losing her brooch, but she wasn't crying only for that. She was
crying for something else. We might all sit down and cry, she
felt. But she did not know what for.

They drew ahead together, Paul and Minta, and he comforted her, and said how famous he was for finding things.
Once when he was a little boy he had found a gold watch. He
would get up at daybreak and he was positive he would find it.
It seemed to him that it would be almost dark, and he would be
alone on the beach, and somehow it would be rather dangerous.
He began telling her, however, that he would certainly find it,
and she said that she would not hear of his getting up at dawn:
it was lost: she knew that: she had had a presentiment when she
put it on that afternoon. And secretly he resolved that he would
not tell her, but he would slip out of the house at dawn when
they were all asleep and if he could not find it he would go to
Edinburgh and buy her another, just like it but more beautiful.
He would prove what he could do. And as they came out on the
hill and saw the lights of the town beneath them, the lights coming out suddenly one by one seemed like things that were going
to happen to him—his marriage, his children, his house; and
again he thought, as they came out on to the high road, which
was shaded with high bushes, how they would retreat into solitude together, and walk on and on, he always leading her, and
she pressing close to his side (as she did now). As they turned
by the cross roads he thought what an appalling experience he
had been through, and he must tell someone—Mrs. Ramsay of
course, for it took his breath away to think what he had been

and done. It had been far and away the worst moment of his life when he asked Minta to marry him. He would go straight to Mrs. Ramsay, because he felt somehow that she was the person who had made him do it. She had made him think he could do anything. Nobody else took him seriously. But she made him believe that he could do whatever he wanted. He had felt her eyes on him all day today, following him about (though she never said a word) as if she were saying, "Yes, you can do it. I believe in you. I expect it of you." She had made him feel all that, and directly they got back (he looked for the lights of the house above the bay) he would go to her and say, "I've done it, Mrs. Ramsay; thanks to you." And so turning into the lane that led to the house he could see lights moving about in the upper windows. They must be awfully late then. People were getting ready for dinner. The house was all lit up, and the lights after the darkness made his eyes feel full, and he said to himself, childishly, as he walked up the drive, Lights, lights, lights, and repeated in a dazed way, Lights, lights, lights, as they came into the house staring about him with his face quite stiff. But, good heavens, he said to himself, putting his hand to his tie, I must not make a fool of myself.)

XV

"YES," SAID PRUE, in her considering way, answering her mother's question, "I think Nancy did go with them."

XVI

WELL THEN, Nancy had gone with them, Mrs. Ramsay supposed, wondering, as she put down a brush, took up a comb, and said "Come in" to a tap at the door (Jasper and Rose came in), whether the fact that Nancy was with them made it less likely or more likely that anything would happen; it made it less likely, somehow, Mrs. Ramsay felt, very irrationally, except that after all holocaust on such a scale was not probable. They could not all be drowned. And again she felt alone in the presence of her old antagonist, life.

Jasper and Rose said that Mildred wanted to know whether she should wait dinner.

"Not for the Queen of England," said Mrs. Ramsay emphatically.

"Not for the Empress of Mexico," she added, laughing at Jasper; for he shared his mother's vice: he, too, exaggerated.

And if Rose liked, she said, while Jasper took the message, she might choose which jewels she was to wear. When there are fifteen people sitting down to dinner, one cannot keep things waiting for ever. She was now beginning to feel annoyed with them for being so late; it was inconsiderate of them, and it annoyed her on top of her anxiety about them, that they should choose this very night to be out late, when, in fact, she wished the dinner to be particularly nice, since William Bankes had at last consented to dine with them; and they were having Mildred's masterpiece—Bœuf en Daube. Everything depended upon things being served up to the precise moment they were ready. The beef, the bay leaf, and the wine—all must be done to a turn. To keep it waiting was out of the question. Yet of course tonight, of all nights, out they went, and they came in late, and things had to be sent out, things had to be kept hot; the Bœuf en Daube would be entirely spoilt.

Jasper offered her an opal necklace; Rose a gold necklace. Which looked best against her black dress? Which did indeed, said Mrs. Ramsay absentmindedly, looking at her neck and shoulders (but avoiding her face) in the glass. And then, while the children rummaged among her things, she looked out of the window at a sight which always amused her—the rooks trying to decide which tree to settle on. Every time, they seemed to change their minds and rose up into the air again, because, she thought, the old rook, the father rook, old Joseph was her name for him, was a bird of a very trying and difficult disposition. He was a disreputable old bird, with half his wing feathers missing. He was like some seedy old gentleman in a top hat she had seen playing the horn in front of a public house.

"Look!" she said, laughing. They were actually fighting. Joseph and Mary were fighting. Anyhow they all went up again, and the air was shoved aside by their black wings and cut into exquisite scimitar shapes. The movement of the wings beating out, out, out—she could never describe it accurately enough to please herself—was one of the loveliest of all to her. Look at that, she said to Rose, hoping that Rose would see it more clearly than she could. For one's children so often gave one's own perceptions a little thrust forwards.

But which was it to be? They had all the trays of her jewel-case open. The gold necklace, which was Italian, or the opal necklace, which Uncle James had brought her from India; or should she wear her amethysts?

"Choose, dearests, choose," she said, hoping that they would make haste.

But she let them take their time to choose: she let Rose, particularly, take up this and then that, and hold her jewels against the black dress, for this little ceremony of choosing jewels, which was gone through every night, was what Rose liked best, she knew. She had some hidden reason of her own for attaching great importance to this choosing what her mother was to wear. What was the reason, Mrs. Ramsay wondered, standing still to let her clasp the necklace she had chosen, divining, through her own past, some deep, some buried, some quite speechless feeling that one had for one's mother at Rose's age. Like all feelings felt for oneself, Mrs. Ramsay thought, it made one sad. It was so inadequate, what one could give in return; and what Rose felt was quite out of proportion to anything she actually was. And Rose would grow up; and Rose would suffer, she supposed, with these deep feelings, and she said she was ready now, and they would go down, and Jasper, because he was the gentleman, should give her his arm, and Rose, as she was the lady, should carry her handkerchief (she gave her the handkerchief), and what else? oh, yes, it might be cold: a shawl. Choose me a shawl, she said, for that would please Rose, who was bound to suffer so. "There," she said, stopping by the window on the landing, "there they are again." Joseph had settled on another tree-top. "Don't you think they mind," she said to Jasper, "having their wings broken?" Why did he want to shoot poor old Joseph and Mary? He shuffled a little on the stairs, and felt rebuked, but not seriously, for she did not understand the fun of shooting birds; and they did not feel; and being his mother she lived away in another division of the world, but he rather liked her stories about Mary and Joseph. She made him laugh. But how did she know that those were Mary and Joseph? Did she think the same birds came to the same trees every night? he asked. But here, suddenly, like all grown-up people, she ceased to pay him the least attention. She was listening to a clatter in the hall.

"They've come back!" she exclaimed, and at once she felt much more annoyed with them than relieved. Then she wondered, had it happened? She would go down and they would tell her—but no. They could not tell her anything, with all these people about. So she must go down and begin dinner and wait. And, like some queen who, finding her people gathered in the hall, looks down upon them, and descends among them, and acknowledges their tributes silently, and accepts their devotion and their prostration before her (Paul did not move a muscle but looked straight before him as she passed) she went down, and crossed the hall and bowed her head very slightly, as if she accepted what they could not say: their tribute to her beauty.

But she stopped. There was a smell of burning. Could they have let the Bœuf en Daube overboil? she wondered, pray heaven not! when the great clangour of the gong announced solemnly, authoritatively, that all those scattered about, in attics, in bedrooms, on little perches of their own, reading, writing, putting the last smooth to their hair, or fastening dresses, must leave all that, and the little odds and ends on their washing-tables and dressing-tables, and the novels on the bed-tables, and the diaries which were so private, and assemble in the dining-room for dinner.

XVII

BUT WHAT have I done with my life? thought Mrs. Ramsay, taking her place at the head of the table, and looking at all the plates making white circles on it. "William, sit by me," she said. "Lily," she said, wearily, "over there." They had that—Paul Rayley and Minta Doyle—she, only this—an infinitely long table and plates and knives. At the far end, was her husband, sitting down, all in a heap, frowning. What at? She did not know. She did not mind. She could not understand how she had ever felt any emotion or affection for him. She had a sense of being past everything, through everything, out of every-thing, as she helped the soup, as if there was an eddy—there—and one could be in it, or one could be out of it, and she was out of it. It's all come to an end, she thought, while they came in one after another, Charles Tansley—"Sit there, please," she said—Augustus Carmichael—and sat down. And meanwhile she waited, passively, for some one to answer her, for something to happen. But this is not a thing, she thought, ladling out soup, that one says.

Raising her eyebrows at the discrepancy—that was what she was thinking, this was what she was doing—ladling out soup—she felt, more and more strongly, outside that eddy; or as if a shade had fallen, and, robbed of colour, she saw things truly. The room (she looked round it) was very shabby. There was no beauty anywhere. She forebore to look at Mr. Tansley. Nothing seemed to have merged. They all sat separate. And the whole of the effort of merging and flowing and creating rested on her. Again she felt, as a fact without hostility, the sterility of men, for if she did not do it nobody would do it, and so, giving herself the little shake that one gives a watch that has stopped, the old familiar pulse began beating, as the watch begins ticking—one, two, three, one, two, three. And so on and so on, she repeated, listening to it, sheltering and fostering the still feeble pulse as one might guard a weak flame with a newspaper. And so then, she concluded, addressing herself by bending silently in his direction to William Bankes—poor man! who had no wife, and no children and dined alone in lodgings except for tonight; and in pity for him, life being now strong enough to bear her on again, she began all this business, as a sailor not without weariness sees the wind fill his sail and yet hardly wants to be off again and thinks how, had the ship sunk, he would have whirled round and round and found rest on the floor of the sea.

"Did you find your letters? I told them to put them in the hall for you," she said to William Bankes.

Lily Briscoe watched her drifting into that strange no-man's land where to follow people is impossible and yet their going inflicts such a chill on those who watch them that they always try at least to follow them with their eyes as one follows a fading ship until the sails have sunk beneath the horizon.

How old she looks, how worn she looks, Lily thought, and how remote. Then when she turned to William Bankes, smiling, it was as if the ship had turned and the sun had struck its sails again, and Lily thought with some amusement because she was relieved, Why does she pity him? For that was the impression she gave, when she told him that his letters were in the hall. Poor William Bankes, she seemed to be saying, as if her own weariness had been partly pitying people, and the life in her, her resolve to live again, had been stirred by pity. And it was not true, Lily thought; it was one of those misjudgments of hers that seemed to be instinctive and to arise from some need of her own rather than of other people's. He is not in the least pitiable. He has his work, Lily said to herself. She remembered, all of a sudden as if she had found a treasure, that she had her work. In a flash she saw her picture, and thought, Yes, I shall put the tree further in the middle; then I shall avoid that awkward space. That's what I shall do. That's what has been puzzling me. She took up the salt cellar and put it down again on a flower in pattern in the table-cloth, so as to remind herself to move the tree.

"It's odd that one scarcely gets anything worth having by post, yet one always wants one's letters," said Mr. Bankes.

What damned rot they talk, thought Charles Tansley, laying down his spoon precisely in the middle of his plate, which he had swept clean, as if, Lily thought (he sat opposite to her with his back to the window precisely in the middle of view), he were determined to make sure of his meals. Everything about him had that meagre fixity, that bare unloveliness. But nevertheless, the fact remained, it was impossible to dislike any one if one looked at them. She liked his eyes; they were blue, deep set, frightening.

"Do you write many letters, Mr. Tansley?" asked Mrs. Ramsay, pitying him too, Lily supposed; for that was true of Mrs. Ramsay—she pitied men always as if they lacked something—women never, as if they had something. He wrote to his mother;

otherwise he did not suppose he wrote one letter a month, said Mr. Tansley, shortly.

For he was not going to talk the sort of rot these people wanted him to talk. He was not going to be condescended to by these silly women. He had been reading in his room, and now he came down and it all seemed to him silly, superficial, flimsy. Why did they dress? He had come down in his ordinary clothes. He had not got any dress clothes. "One never gets anything worth having by post"—that was the sort of thing they were always saying. They made men say that sort of thing. Yes, it was pretty well true, he thought. They never got anything worth having from one year's end to another. They did nothing but talk, talk, talk, eat, eat, eat. It was the women's fault. Women made civilisation impossible with all their "charm," all their silliness.

"No going to the Lighthouse tomorrow, Mrs. Ramsay," he said, asserting himself. He liked her; he admired her; he still thought of the man in the drain-pipe looking up at her; but he felt it necessary to assert himself.

He was really, Lily Briscoe thought, in spite of his eyes, but then look at his nose, look at his hands, the most uncharming human being she had ever met. Then why did she mind what he said? Women can't write, women can't paint—what did that matter coming from him, since clearly it was not true to him but for some reason helpful to him, and that was why he said it? Why did her whole being bow, like corn under a wind, and erect itself again from this abasement only with a great and rather painful effort? She must make it once more. There's the sprig on the table-cloth; there's my painting; I must move the tree to the middle; that matters—nothing else. Could she not hold fast to that, she asked herself, and not lose her temper, and not argue; and if she wanted revenge take it by laughing at him?

"Oh, Mr. Tansley," she said, "do take me to the Lighthouse with you. I should so love it."

She was telling lies he could see. She was saying what she did not mean to annoy him, for some reason. She was laughing at him. He was in his old flannel trousers. He had no others. He felt very rough and isolated and lonely. He knew that she was trying to tease him for some reason; she didn't want to go to the Lighthouse with him; she despised him: so did Prue Ramsay; so did they all. But he was not going to be made a fool of by women, so he turned deliberately in his chair and looked out of the window and said, all in a jerk, very rudely, it would be too rough for her tomorrow. She would be sick.

It annoyed him that she should have made him speak like that, with Mrs. Ramsay listening. If only he could be alone in his room working, he thought, among his books. That was where he felt at his ease. And he had never run a penny into debt; he had never cost his father a penny since he was fifteen; he had helped them at home out of his savings; he was educating his sister. Still, he wished he had known how to answer Miss Briscoe properly; he wished it had not come out all in a jerk like that. "You'd be sick." He wished he could think of something to say to Mrs. Ramsay, something which would show her that he was not just a dry prig. That was what they all thought him. He turned to her. But Mrs. Ramsay was talking about people he had never heard of to William Bankes.

"Yes, take it away," she said briefly, interrupting what she was saying to Mr. Bankes to speak to the maid. "It must have been fifteen—no, twenty years ago—that I last saw her," she was saying, turning back to him again as if she could not lose a moment of their talk, for she was absorbed by what they were saying. So he had actually heard from her this evening! And was Carrie still living at Marlow, and was everything still the same? Oh, she could remember as if it were yesterday—going on the river, feeling very cold. But if the Mannings made a plan they stuck to it. Never should she forget Herbert killing a wasp with a teaspoon on the bank! And it was still going on, Mrs. Ramsay mused, gliding like a ghost among the chairs and tables of that drawing-room on the banks of the Thames where she had been so very, very cold twenty years ago; but now she went among them like a ghost; and it fascinated her, as if, while she had changed, that particular day, now become very still and beautiful, had remained there, all these years. Had Carrie written to him herself? she asked.

"Yes. She says they're building a new billiard room," he said. No! No! That was out of the question! Building a new billiard room! It seemed to her impossible.

Mr. Bankes could not see that there was anything very odd about it. They were very well off now. Should he give her love to Carrie?

"Oh," said Mrs. Ramsay with a little start, "No," she added, reflecting that she did not know this Carrie who built a new billiard room. But how strange, she repeated, to Mr. Bankes's amusement, that they should be going on there still. For it was extraordinary to think that they had been capable of going on living all these years when she had not thought of them more than once all that time. How eventful her own life had been, during those same years. Yet perhaps Carrie Manning had not thought about her either. The thought was strange and distasteful.

"People soon drift apart," said Mr. Bankes, feeling, however, some satisfaction when he thought that after all he knew both the Mannings and the Ramsays. He had not drifted apart he thought, laying down his spoon and wiping his clean-shaven lips punctiliously. But perhaps he was rather unusual, he thought, in this; he never let himself get into a groove. He had friends in all circles. . . . Mrs. Ramsay had to break off here to tell the maid something about keeping food hot. That was why he preferred dining alone. All those interruptions annoyed him.

Well, thought William Bankes, preserving a demeanour of exquisite courtesy and merely spreading the fingers of his left hand on the table-cloth as a mechanic examines a tool beautifully polished and ready for use in an interval of leisure, such are the sacrifices one's friends ask of one. It would have hurt her if he had refused to come. But it was not worth it for him. Looking at his hand he thought that if he had been alone dinner would have been almost over now; he would have been free to work. Yes, he thought, it is a terrible waste of time. The children were dropping in still. "I wish one of you would run up to Roger's room," Mrs. Ramsay was saying. How trifling it all is, how boring it all is, he thought, compared with the other thing—work. Here he sat drumming his fingers on the table-cloth when he might have been—he took a flashing bird's-eye view of his work. What a waste of time it all was to be sure! Yet, he thought, she is one of my oldest friends. I am by way of being devoted to her. Yet now, at this moment her presence meant absolutely nothing to him: her beauty meant nothing to him; her sitting with her little boy at the window—nothing, nothing. He wished only to be alone and to take up that book. He felt uncomfortable; he felt treacherous, that he could sit by her side and feel nothing for her. The truth was that he did not enjoy family life. It was in this sort of state that one asked oneself, What does one live for? Why, one asked oneself, does one take all these pains for the human race to go on? Is it so very desirable? Are we attractive as a species? Not so very, he thought, looking at those rather untidy boys. His favourite, Cam, was in bed, he supposed. Foolish questions, vain questions, questions one never asked if one was occupied. Is human life this? Is human life that? One never had time to think about it. But here he was asking himself that sort of question, because Mrs. Ramsay was giving orders to servants, and also because it had struck him, thinking how surprised Mrs. Ramsay was that Carrie Manning should still exist, that friendships, even the best of them, are frail things. One drifts apart. He reproached himself again. He was sitting beside Mrs. Ramsay and he had nothing in the world to say to her.

"I'm so sorry," said Mrs. Ramsay, turning to him at last. He felt rigid and barren, like a pair of boots that have been soaked and gone dry so that you can hardly force your feet into them. Yet he must force his feet into them. He must make himself talk. Unless he were very careful, she would find out this treachery of his; that he did not care a straw for her, and that would not be at all pleasant, he thought. So he bent his head courteously in her direction.

"How you must detest dining in this bear garden," she said, making use, as she did when she was distracted, of her social manner. So, when there is a strife of tongues, at some meeting, the chairman, to obtain unity, suggests that every one shall speak in French. Perhaps it is bad French; French may not contain the words that express the speaker's thoughts; nevertheless speaking French imposes some order, some uniformity. Replying to her in the same language, Mr. Bankes said, "No, not at all," and Mr. Tansley, who had no knowledge of this language, even spoke thus in words of one syllable, at once suspected its insincerity. They did talk nonsense, he thought, the Ramsays; and he pounced on this fresh instance with joy, making a note which, one of these days, he would read aloud, to one or two friends. There, in a society where one could say what one liked he would sarcastically describe "staying with the Ramsays" and what nonsense they talked. It was worth while doing it once, he would say; but not again. The women bored one so, he would say. Of course Ramsay had dished himself by marrying a beautiful woman and having eight children. It would shape itself something like that, but now, at this moment, sitting stuck there with an empty seat beside him, nothing had shaped itself at all.

It was all in scraps and fragments. He felt extremely, even physically, uncomfortable. He wanted somebody to give him a chance of asserting himself. He wanted it so urgently that he fidgeted in his chair, looked at this person, then at that person, tried to break into their talk, opened his mouth and shut it again. They were talking about the fishing industry. Why did no one ask him his opinion? What did they know about the fishing industry?

Lily Briscoe knew all that. Sitting opposite him, could she not see, as in an X-ray photograph, the ribs and thigh bones of the young man's desire to impress himself, lying dark in the mist of his flesh—that thin mist which convention had laid over his burning desire to break into the conversation? But, she thought, screwing up her Chinese eyes, and remembering how he sneered at women, "can't paint, can't write," why should I help him to relieve himself?

There is a code of behaviour, she knew, whose seventh article (it may be) says that on occasions of this sort it behooves the woman, whatever her own occupation may be, to go to the help of the young man opposite so that he may expose and relieve the thigh bones, the ribs, of his vanity, of his urgent desire to assert himself; as indeed it is their duty, she reflected, in her old maidenly fairness, to help us, suppose the Tube were to burst into flames. Then, she thought, I should certainly expect Mr. Tansley to get me out. But how would it be, she thought, if neither of us did either of these things? So she sat there smiling.

"You're not planning to go to the Lighthouse, are you, Lily," said Mrs. Ramsay. "Remember poor Mr. Langley; he had been round the world dozens of times, but he told me he never suffered as he did when my husband took him there. Are you a good sailor, Mr. Tansley?" she asked.

Mr. Tansley raised a hammer: swung it high in air; but realising, as it descended, that he could not smite that butterfly with

such an instrument as this, said only that he had never been sick
in his life. But in that one sentence lay compact, like gunpowder, that his grandfather was a fisherman; his father a chemist;
that he had worked his way up entirely himself; that he was
proud of it; that he was Charles Tansley—a fact that nobody
there seemed to realise; but one of these days every single person would know it. He scowled ahead of him. He could almost
pity these mild cultivated people, who would be blown sky high,
like bales of wool and barrels of apples, one of these days by the
gunpowder that was in him.

"Will you take me, Mr. Tansley?" said Lily, quickly, kindly,
for, of course, if Mrs. Ramsay said to her, as in effect she did, "I
am drowning, my dear, in seas of fire. Unless you apply some
balm to the anguish of this hour and say something nice to that
young man there, life will run upon the rocks—indeed I hear
the grating and the growling at this minute. My nerves are taut
as fiddle strings. Another touch and they will snap"—when
Mrs. Ramsay said all this, as the glance in her eyes said it, of
course for the hundred and fiftieth time Lily Briscoe had to re-
nounce the experiment—what happens if one is not nice to
that young man there—and be nice.

Judging the turn in her mood correctly—that she was
friendly to him now—he was relieved of his egotism, and told
her how he had been thrown out of a boat when he was a baby;
how his father used to fish him out with a boat-hook; that was
how he had learnt to swim. One of his uncles kept the light on
some rock or other off the Scottish coast, he said. He had been
there with him in a storm. This was said loudly in a pause. They
had to listen to him when he said that he had been with his
uncle in a lighthouse in a storm. Ah, thought Lily Briscoe, as the
conversation took this auspicious turn, and she felt Mrs. Ramsay's gratitude (for Mrs. Ramsay was free now to talk for a mo-

ment herself), ah, she thought, but what haven't I paid to get it
for you? She had not been sincere.

She had done the usual trick—been nice. She would never
know him. He would never know her. Human relations were all
like that, she thought, and the worst (if it had not been for Mr.
Bankes) were between men and women. Inevitably these were
extremely insincere she thought. Then her eye caught the salt
cellar, which she had placed there to remind her, and she remembered that next morning she would move the tree further
towards the middle, and her spirits rose so high at the thought
of painting tomorrow that she laughed out loud at what Mr.
Tansley was saying. Let him talk all night if he liked it.

"But how long do they leave men on a Lighthouse?" she
asked. He told her. He was amazingly well informed. And as he
was grateful, and as he liked her, and as he was beginning to
enjoy himself, so now, Mrs. Ramsay thought, she could return
to that dream land, that unreal but fascinating place, the Mannings' drawing-room at Marlow twenty years ago; where one
moved about without haste or anxiety, for there was no future
to worry about. She knew what had happened to them, what to
her. It was like reading a good book again, for she knew the end
of that story, since it had happened twenty years ago, and life,
which shot down even from this dining-room table in cascades,
heaven knows where, was sealed up there, and lay, like a lake,
placidly between its banks. He said they had built a billiard
room—was it possible? Would William go on talking about the
Mannings? She wanted him to. But, no—for some reason he
was no longer in the mood. She tried. He did not respond. She
could not force him. She was disappointed.

"The children are disgraceful," she said, sighing. He said
something about punctuality being one of the minor virtues
which we do not acquire until later in life.

"If at all," said Mrs. Ramsay merely to fill up space, thinking what an old maid William was becoming. Conscious of his treachery, conscious of her wish to talk about something more intimate, yet out of mood for it at present, he felt come over him the disagreeableness of life, sitting there, waiting. Perhaps the others were saying something interesting? What were they saying?

That the fishing season was bad; that the men were emigrating. They were talking about wages and unemployment. The young man was abusing the government. William Bankes, thinking what a relief it was to catch on to something of this sort when private life was disagreeable, heard him say something about "one of the most scandalous acts of the present government." Lily was listening; Mrs. Ramsay was listening; they were all listening. But already bored, Lily felt that something was lacking; Mr. Bankes felt that something was lacking. Pulling her shawl round her Mrs. Ramsay felt that something was lacking. All of them bending themselves to listen thought, "Pray heaven that the inside of my mind may not be exposed," for each thought, "The others are feeling this. They are outraged and indignant with the government about the fishermen. Whereas, I feel nothing at all." But perhaps, thought Mr. Bankes, as he looked at Mr. Tansley, here is the man. One was always waiting for the man. There was always a chance. At any moment the leader might arise; the man of genius, in politics as in anything else. Probably he will be extremely disagreeable to us old fogies, thought Mr. Bankes, doing his best to make allowances, for he knew by some curious physical sensation, as of nerves erect in his spine, that he was jealous, for himself partly, partly more probably for his work, for his point of view, for his science; and therefore he was not entirely open-minded or altogether fair, for Mr. Tansley seemed to be saying, You have wasted your lives. You are all of you wrong. Poor old fogies, you're hopelessly behind the times. He seemed to be rather cocksure, this young man; and his manners were bad. But Mr. Bankes bade himself observe, he had courage; he had ability; he was extremely well up in the facts. Probably, Mr. Bankes thought, as Tansley abused the government, there is a good deal in what he says.

"Tell me now..." he said. So they argued about politics, and Lily looked at the leaf on the table-cloth; and Mrs. Ramsay, leaving the argument entirely in the hands of the two men, wondered why she was so bored by this talk, and wished, looking at her husband at the other end of the table, that he would say something. One word, she said to herself. For if he said a thing, it would make all the difference. He went to the heart of things. He cared about fishermen and their wages. He could not sleep for thinking of them. It was altogether different when he spoke; one did not feel then, pray heaven you don't see how little I care, because one did care. Then, realising that it was because she admired him so much that she was waiting for him to speak, she felt as if somebody had been praising her husband to her and their marriage, and she glowed all over without realising that it was she herself who had praised him. She looked at him thinking to find this in his face; he would be looking magnificent. . . . But not in the least! He was screwing his face up, he was scowling and frowning, and flushing with anger. What on earth was it about? she wondered. What could be the matter? Only that poor old Augustus had asked for another plate of soup—that was all. It was unthinkable, it was detestable (so he signalled to her across the table) that Augustus should be beginning his soup over again. He loathed people eating when he had finished. She saw his anger fly like a pack of hounds into his eyes, his brow, and she knew that in a moment something violent would explode, and then—thank goodness! she saw him clutch himself and clap a brake on the wheel, and the whole of his body seemed to emit sparks but not words. He sat there scowling. He had said nothing, he would have her observe. Let her give him the credit for that! But why after all should poor Augustus not ask for another plate of soup? He had merely touched Ellen's arm and said:

"Ellen, please, another plate of soup," and then Mr. Ramsay scowled like that.

And why not? Mrs. Ramsay demanded. Surely they could let Augustus have his soup if he wanted it. He hated people wallowing in food, Mr. Ramsay frowned at her. He hated everything dragging on for hours like this. But he had controlled himself, Mr. Ramsay would have her observe, disgusting though the sight was. But why show it so plainly, Mrs. Ramsay demanded (they looked at each other down the long table sending these questions and answers across, each knowing exactly what the other felt). Everybody could see, Mrs. Ramsay thought. There was Rose gazing at her father, there was Roger gazing at his father; both would be off in spasms of laughter in another second, she knew, and so she said promptly (indeed it was time):

"Light the candles," and they jumped up instantly and went and fumbled at the sideboard.

Why could he never conceal his feelings? Mrs. Ramsay wondered, and she wondered if Augustus Carmichael had noticed. Perhaps he had; perhaps he had not. She could not help respecting the composure with which he sat there, drinking his soup. If he wanted soup, he asked for soup. Whether people laughed at him or were angry with him he was the same. He did not like her, she knew that; but partly for that very reason she respected him, and looking at him, drinking soup, very large and calm in the failing light, and monumental, and contemplative, she wondered what he did feel then, and why he was always content and dignified; and she thought how devoted he was to Andrew, and would call him into his room, and Andrew said, "show him things." And there he would lie all day long on the lawn brooding presumably over his poetry, till he reminded one of a cat watching birds, and then he clapped his paws together when he had found the word, and her husband said, "Poor old Augustus—he's a true poet," which was high praise from her husband.

Now eight candles were stood down the table, and after the first stoop the flames stood upright and drew with them into visibility the long table entire, and in the middle a yellow and purple dish of fruit. What had she done with it, Mrs. Ramsay wondered, for Rose's arrangement of the grapes and pears, of the horny pink-lined shell, of the bananas, made her think of a trophy fetched from the bottom of the sea, of Neptune's banquet, of the bunch that hangs with vine leaves over the shoulder of Bacchus (in some picture), among the leopard skins and the torches lolloping red and gold. . . . Thus brought up suddenly into the light it seemed possessed of great size and depth, was like a world in which one could take one's staff and climb hills, she thought, and go down into valleys, and to her pleasure (for it brought them into sympathy momentarily) she saw that Augustus too feasted his eyes on the same plate of fruit, plunged in, broke off a bloom there, a tassel here, and returned, after feasting, to his hive. That was his way of looking, different from hers. But looking together united them.

Now all the candles were lit up, and the faces on both sides of the table were brought nearer by the candlelight, and composed, as they had not been in the twilight, into a party round a table, for the night was now shut off by panes of glass, which, far from giving any accurate view of the outside world, rippled it so strangely that here, inside the room, seemed to be order and dry land; there, outside, a reflection in which things waved and vanished, waterily.

Some change at once went through them all, as if this had really happened, and they were all conscious of making a party together in a hollow, on an island; had their common cause

against that fluidity out there. Mrs. Ramsay, who had been uneasy, waiting for Paul and Minta to come in, and unable, she felt,
to settle to things, now felt her uneasiness changed to expectation. For now they must come, and Lily Briscoe, trying to
analyse the cause of the sudden exhilaration, compared it with
that moment on the tennis lawn, when solidity suddenly vanished, and such vast spaces lay between them; and now the same
effect was got by the many candles in the sparely furnished
room, and the uncurtained windows, and the bright mask-like
look of faces seen by candlelight. Some weight was taken off
them; anything might happen, she felt. They must come now,
Mrs. Ramsay thought, looking at the door, and at that instant,
Minta Doyle, Paul Rayley, and a maid carrying a great dish in her
hands came in together. They were awfully late; they were horribly late, Minta said, as they found their way to different ends
of the table.

"I lost my brooch—my grandmother's brooch," said Minta
with a sound of lamentation in her voice, and a suffusion in her
large brown eyes, looking down, looking up, as she sat by Mr.
Ramsay, which roused his chivalry so that he bantered her.

How could she be such a goose, he asked, as to scramble
about the rocks in jewels?

She was by way of being terrified of him—he was so fearfully clever, and the first night when she had sat by him, and he
talked about George Eliot, she had been really frightened, for
she had left the third volume of *Middlemarch* in the train and she
never knew what happened in the end; but afterwards she got
on perfectly, and made herself out even more ignorant than she
was, because he liked telling her she was a fool. And so tonight,
directly he laughed at her, she was not frightened. Besides, she
knew, directly she came into the room that the miracle had happened; she wore her golden haze. Sometimes she had it; sometimes not. She never knew why it came or why it went, or if she

had it until she came into the room and then she knew instantly by the way some man looked at her. Yes, tonight she had it, tremendously; she knew that by the way Mr. Ramsay told her not to be a fool. She sat beside him, smiling.

It must have happened then, thought Mrs. Ramsay; they are engaged. And for a moment she felt what she had never expected to feel again—jealousy. For he, her husband, felt it too—Minta's glow; he liked these girls, these golden-reddish girls, with something flying, something a little wild and harum-scarum about them, who didn't "scrape their hair off," weren't, as he said about poor Lily Briscoe, ". . . skimpy." There was some quality which she herself had not, some lustre, some rich-ness, which attracted him, amused him, led him to make favourites of girls like Minta. They might cut his hair from him, plait him watch-chains, or interrupt him at his work, hailing him (she heard them), "Come along, Mr. Ramsay; it's our turn to beat them now," and out he came to play tennis.

But indeed she was not jealous, only, now and then, when she made herself look in her glass a little resentful that she had grown old, perhaps, by her own fault. (The bill for the green-house and all the rest of it.) She was grateful to them for laugh-ing at him. ("How many pipes have you smoked today, Mr. Ramsay?" and so on), till he seemed a young man; a man very attractive to women, not burdened, not weighed down with the greatness of his labours and the sorrows of the world and his fame or his failure, but again as she had first known him, gaunt but gallant; helping her out of a boat, she remembered; with de-lightful ways, like that (she looked at him, and he looked aston-ishingly young, teasing Minta). For herself—"Put it down there," she said, helping the Swiss girl to place gently before her the huge brown pot in which was the Bœuf en Daube—for her own part, she liked her boobies. Paul must sit by her. She had kept a place for him. Really, she sometimes thought she liked

the boobies best. They did not bother one with their dissertations. How much they missed, after all, these very clever men!
How dried up they did become, to be sure. There was something, she thought as he sat down, very charming about Paul.
His manners were delightful to her, and his sharp-cut nose and
his bright blue eyes. He was so considerate. Would he tell her—
now that they were all talking again—what had happened?

"We went back to look for Minta's brooch," he said, sitting
down by her. "We"—that was enough. She knew from the effort, the rise in his voice to surmount a difficult word that it was
the first time he had said "we." "We did this, we did that."
They'll say that all their lives, she thought, and an exquisite scent
of olives and oil and juice rose from the great brown dish as
Marthe, with a little flourish, took the cover off. The cook had
spent three days over that dish. And she must take great care,
Mrs. Ramsay thought, diving into the soft mass, to choose a specially tender piece for William Bankes. And she peered into the
dish, with its shiny walls and its confusion of savoury brown
and yellow meats and its bay leaves and its wine, and thought,
This will celebrate the occasion—a curious sense rising in her,
at once freakish and tender, of celebrating a festival, as if two
emotions were called up in her, one profound—for what could
be more serious than the love of man for woman, what more
commanding, more impressive, bearing in its bosom the seeds
of death; at the same time these lovers, these people entering
into illusion glittering eyed, must be danced round with mock-
ery, decorated with garlands.

"It is a triumph," said Mr. Bankes, laying his knife down for
a moment. He had eaten attentively. It was rich; it was tender.
It was perfectly cooked. How did she manage these things in the
depths of the country? he asked her. She was a wonderful
woman. All his love, all his reverence, had returned; and she
knew it.

"It is a French recipe of my grandmother's," said Mrs. Ramsay, speaking with a ring of great pleasure in her voice. Of course it was French. What passes for cookery in England is an abomination (they agreed). It is putting cabbages in water. It is roasting meat till it is like leather. It is cutting off the delicious skins of vegetables. "In which," said Mr. Bankes, "all the virtue of the vegetable is contained." And the waste, said Mrs. Ramsay. A whole French family could live on what an English cook throws away. Spurred on by her sense that William's affection had come back to her, and that everything was all right again, and that her suspense was over, and that now she was free both to triumph and to mock, she laughed, she gesticulated, till Lily thought, How childlike, how absurd she was, sitting up there with all her beauty opened again in her, talking about the skins of vegetables. There was something frightening about her. She was irresistible. Always she got her own way in the end, Lily thought. Now she had brought this off—Paul and Minta, one might suppose, were engaged. Mr. Bankes was dining here. She put a spell on them all, by wishing, so simply, so directly, and Lily contrasted that abundance with her own poverty of spirit, and supposed that it was partly that belief (for her face was all lit up—without looking young, she looked radiant) in this strange, this terrifying thing, which made Paul Rayley, sitting at her side, all of a tremor, yet abstract, absorbed, silent. Mrs. Ramsay, Lily felt, as she talked about the skins of vegetables, exalted that, worshipped that; held her hands over it to warm them, to protect it, and yet, having brought it all about, somehow laughed, led her victims, Lily felt, to the altar. It came over her too now—the emotion, the vibration, of love. How inconspicuous she felt herself by Paul's side! He, glowing, burning; she, aloof, satirical; he, bound for adventure; she, moored to the shore; he, launched, incautious; she, solitary, left out—and, ready to implore a share, if it were a disaster, in his disaster, she said shyly:

"When did Minta lose her brooch?"

He smiled the most exquisite smile, veiled by memory, tinged by dreams. He shook his head. "On the beach," he said.

"I'm going to find it," he said, "I'm getting up early." This being kept secret from Minta, he lowered his voice, and turned his eyes to where she sat, laughing, beside Mr. Ramsay.

Lily wanted to protest violently and outrageously her desire to help him, envisaging how in the dawn on the beach she would be the one to pounce on the brooch half-hidden by some stone, and thus herself be included among the sailors and adventurers. But what did he reply to her offer? She actually said with an emotion that she seldom let appear, "Let me come with you," and he laughed. He meant yes or no—either perhaps. But it was not his meaning—it was the odd chuckle he gave, as if he had said, Throw yourself over the cliff if you like, I don't care. He turned on her cheek the heat of love, its horror, its cruelty, its unscrupulosity. It scorched her, and Lily, looking at Minta, being charming to Mr. Ramsay at the other end of the table, flinched for her exposed to these fangs, and was thankful. For at any rate, she said to herself, catching sight of the salt cellar on the pattern, she need not marry, thank Heaven: she need not undergo that degradation. She was saved from that dilution. She would move the tree rather more to the middle.

Such was the complexity of things. For what happened to her, especially staying with the Ramsays, was to be made to feel violently two opposite things at the same time; that's what you feel, was one; that's what I feel, was the other, and then they fought together in her mind, as now. It is so beautiful, so exciting, this love, that I tremble on the verge of it, and offer, quite out of my own habit, to look for a brooch on a beach; also it is the stupidest, the most barbaric of human passions, and turns a nice young man with a profile like a gem's (Paul's was exquisite) into a bully with a crowbar (he was swaggering, he was insolent) in the Mile End Road. Yet, she said to herself, from the dawn of time odes have been sung to love; wreaths heaped and roses; and if you asked nine people out of ten they would say they wanted nothing but this—love; while the women, judging from her own experience, would all the time be feeling, This is not what we want; there is nothing more tedious, puerile, and inhumane than this; yet it is also beautiful and necessary. Well then, well then? she asked, somehow expecting the others to go on with the argument, as if in an argument like this one threw one's own little bolt which fell short obviously and left the others to carry it on. So she listened again to what they were saying in case they should throw any light upon the question of love.

"Then," said Mr. Bankes, "there is that liquid the English call coffee."

"Oh, coffee!" said Mrs. Ramsay. But it was much rather a question (she was thoroughly roused, Lily could see, and talked very emphatically) of real butter and clean milk. Speaking with warmth and eloquence, she described the iniquity of the English dairy system, and in what state milk was delivered at the door, and was about to prove her charges, for she had gone into the matter, when all round the table, beginning with Andrew in the middle, like a fire leaping from tuft to tuft of furze, her children laughed; her husband laughed; she was laughed at, fire-encircled, and forced to vail her crest, dismount her batteries, and only retaliate by displaying the raillery and ridicule of the table to Mr. Bankes as an example of what one suffered if one attacked the prejudices of the British Public.

Purposely, however, for she had it on her mind that Lily, who had helped her with Mr. Tansley, was out of things, she exempted her from the rest; said "Lily anyhow agrees with me," and so drew her in, a little fluttered, a little startled. (For she was thinking about love.) They were both out of things, Mrs. Ramsay had been thinking, both Lily and Charles Tansley. Both suffered from the glow of the other two. He, it was clear, felt himself utterly in the cold; no woman would look at him with Paul Rayley in the room. Poor fellow! Still, he had his dissertation, the influence of somebody upon something: he could take care of himself. With Lily it was different. She faded, under Minta's glow; became more inconspicuous than ever, in her little grey dress with her little puckered face and her little Chinese eyes. Everything about her was so small. Yet, thought Mrs. Ramsay, comparing her with Minta, as she claimed her help (for Lily should bear her out, she talked no more about her dairies than her husband did about his boots—he would talk by the hour about his boots) of the two, Lily at forty will be the better. There was in Lily a thread of something; a flare of something; something of her own which Mrs. Ramsay liked very much indeed, but no man would, she feared. Obviously, not, unless it were a much older man, like William Bankes. But then ne cared, well, Mrs. Ramsay sometimes thought that he cared, since his wife's death, perhaps for her. He was not "in love" of course; it was one of those unclassified affections of which there are so many. Oh, but nonsense, she thought; William must marry Lily. They have so many things in common. Lily is so fond of flowers. They are both cold and aloof and rather self-sufficing. She must arrange for them to take a long walk together.

Foolishly, she had set them opposite each other. That could be remedied tomorrow. If it were fine, they should go for a picnic. Everything seemed possible. Everything seemed right. Just now (but this cannot last, she thought, dissociating herself from the moment while they were all talking about boots) just now she had reached security; she hovered like a hawk suspended; like a flag floated in an element of joy which filled every nerve of her body fully and sweetly, not noisily, solemnly rather, for it arose, she thought, looking at them all eating there, from hus-

band and children and friends; all of which rising in this profound stillness (she was helping William Bankes to one very
small piece more, and peered into the depths of the earthenware
pot) seemed now for no special reason to stay there like a
smoke, like a fume rising upwards, holding them safe together.
Nothing need be said; nothing could be said. There it was, all
round them. It partook, she felt, carefully helping Mr. Bankes to
a specially tender piece, of eternity; as she had already felt about
something different once before that afternoon; there is a co-
herence in things, a stability; something, she meant, is immune
from change, and shines out (she glanced at the window with
its ripple of reflected lights) in the face of the flowing, the fleet-
ing, the spectral, like a ruby; so that again tonight she had the
feeling she had had once today, already, of peace, of rest. Of
such moments, she thought, the thing is made that endures.

"Yes," she assured William Bankes, "there is plenty for
everybody."

"Andrew," she said, "hold your plate lower, or I shall spill
it." (The Bœuf en Daube was a perfect triumph.) Here, she felt,
putting the spoon down, was the still space that lies about the
heart of things, where one could move or rest; could wait now
(they were all helped) listening; could then, like a hawk which
lapses suddenly from its high station, flaunt and sink on laughter easily, resting her whole weight upon what at the other end
of the table her husband was saying about the square root of
one thousand two hundred and fifty-three. That was the number, it seemed, on his watch.

What did it all mean? To this day she had no notion. A
square root? What was that? Her sons knew. She leant on them;
on cubes and square roots; that was what they were talking about
now; on Voltaire and Madame de Staël; on the character of
Napoleon; on the French system of land tenure; on Lord Rosebery; on Creevey's Memoirs: she let it uphold her and sustain her,

this admirable fabric of the masculine intelligence, which ran up and down, crossed this way and that, like iron girders spanning the swaying fabric, upholding the world, so that she could trust herself to it utterly, even shut her eyes, or flicker them for a moment, as a child staring up from its pillow winks at the myriad layers of the leaves of a tree. Then she woke up. It was still being fabricated. William Bankes was praising the Waverley novels.

He read one of them every six months, he said. And why should that make Charles Tansley angry? He rushed in (all, thought Mrs. Ramsay, because Prue will not be nice to him) and denounced the Waverley novels when he knew nothing about it, nothing about it whatsoever, Mrs. Ramsay thought, observing him rather than listening to what he said. She could see how it was from his manner—he wanted to assert himself, and so it would always be with him till he got his Professorship or married his wife, and so need not be always saying, "I—I—I." For that was what his criticism of poor Sir Walter, or perhaps it was Jane Austen, amounted to. "I—I—I." He was thinking of himself and the impression he was making, as she could tell by the sound of his voice, and his emphasis and his uneasiness. Success would be good for him. At any rate they were off again. Now she need not listen. It could not last, she knew, but at the moment her eyes were so clear that they seemed to go round the table unveiling each of these people, and their thoughts and their feelings, without effort like a light stealing under water so that its ripples and the reeds in it and the minnows balancing themselves, and the sudden silent trout are all lit up hanging, trembling. So she saw them; she heard them; but whatever they said had also this quality, as if what they said was like the movement of a trout when, at the same time, one can see the ripple and the gravel, something to the right, something to the left; and the whole is held together; for whereas in active life she would be netting and separating one thing from another; she would be saying she liked the Waverley novels or had not read them; she would be urging herself forward; now she said nothing. For the moment, she hung suspended.

"Ah, but how long do you think it'll last?" said somebody. It was as if she had antennæ trembling out from her, which, intercepting certain sentences, forced them upon her attention. This was one of them. She scented danger for her husband. A question like that would lead, almost certainly, to something being said which reminded him of his own failure. How long would he be read—he would think at once. William Bankes (who was entirely free from all such vanity) laughed, and said he attached no importance to changes in fashion. Who could tell what was going to last—in literature or indeed in anything else?

"Let us enjoy what we do enjoy," he said. His integrity seemed to Mrs. Ramsay quite admirable. He never seemed for a moment to think, But how does this affect me? But then if you had the other temperament, which must have praise, which must have encouragement, naturally you began (and she knew that Mr. Ramsay was beginning) to be uneasy; to want somebody to say, Oh, but your work will last, Mr. Ramsay, or something like that. He showed his uneasiness quite clearly now by saying, with some irritation, that, anyhow, Scott (or was it Shakespeare?) would last him his lifetime. He said it irritably. Everybody, she thought, felt a little uncomfortable, without knowing why. Then Minta Doyle, whose instinct was fine, said bluffly, absurdly, that she did not believe that any one really enjoyed reading Shakespeare. Mr. Ramsay said grimly (but his mind was turned away again) that very few people liked it as much as they said they did. But, he added, there is considerable merit in some of the plays nevertheless, and Mrs. Ramsay saw that it would be all right for the moment anyhow; he would laugh at Minta, and she, Mrs. Ramsay saw, realising his extreme anxiety about himself, would, in her own way, see that he was

taken care of, and praise him, somehow or other. But she
wished it was not necessary: perhaps it was her fault that it was
necessary. Anyhow, she was free now to listen to what Paul Rayley was trying to say about books one had read as a boy. They
lasted, he said. He had read some of Tolstoi at school. There
was one he always remembered, but he had forgotten the name.
Russian names were impossible, said Mrs. Ramsay. "Vronsky,"
said Paul. He remembered that because he always thought it
such a good name for a villain. "Vronsky," said Mrs. Ramsay;
"Oh, *Anna Karenina,*" but that did not take them very far; books
were not in their line. No, Charles Tansley would put them both
right in a second about books, but it was all so mixed up with,
Am I saying the right thing? Am I making a good impression?
that, after all, one knew more about him than about Tolstoi,
whereas, what Paul said was about the thing, simply, not himself, nothing else. Like all stupid people, he had a kind of mod-
esty too, a consideration for what you were feeling, which, once
in a way at least, she found attractive. Now he was thinking, not
about himself or about Tolstoi, but whether she was cold,
whether she felt a draught, whether she would like a pear.

No, she said, she did not want a pear. Indeed she had been
keeping guard over the dish of fruit (without realising it) jeal-
ously, hoping that nobody would touch it. Her eyes had been
going in and out among the curves and shadows of the fruit,
among the rich purples of the lowland grapes, then over the
horny ridge of the shell, putting a yellow against a purple, a
curved shape against a round shape, without knowing why she
did it, or why, every time she did it, she felt more and more
serene; until, oh, what a pity that they should do it—a hand
reached out, took a pear, and spoilt the whole thing. In sympathy she looked at Rose. She looked at Rose sitting between
Jasper and Prue. How odd that one's child should do that!

How odd to see them sitting there, in a row, her children, Jasper, Rose, Prue, Andrew, almost silent, but with some joke of their own going on, she guessed, from the twitching at their lips. It was something quite apart from everything else, something they were hoarding up to laugh over in their own room. It was not about their father, she hoped. No, she thought not. What was it, she wondered, sadly rather, for it seemed to her that they would laugh when she was not there. There was all that hoarded behind those rather set, still, mask-like faces, for they did not join in easily; they were like watchers, surveyors, a little raised or set apart from the grown-up people. But when she looked at Prue tonight, she saw that this was not now quite true of her. She was just beginning, just moving, just descending. The faintest light was on her face, as if the glow of Minta opposite, some excitement, some anticipation of happiness was reflected in her, as if the sun of the love of men and women rose over the rim of the table-cloth, and without knowing what it was she bent towards it and greeted it. She kept looking at Minta, shyly, yet curiously, so that Mrs. Ramsay looked from one to the other and said, speaking to Prue in her own mind, You will be as happy as she is one of these days. You will be much happier, she added, because you are my daughter, she meant; her own daughter must be happier than other people's daughters. But dinner was over. It was time to go. They were only playing with things on their plates. She would wait until they had done laughing at some story her husband was telling. He was having a joke with Minta about a bet. Then she would get up.

She liked Charles Tansley, she thought, suddenly; she liked his laugh. She liked him for being so angry with Paul and Minta. She liked his awkwardness. There was a lot in that young man after all. And Lily, she thought, putting her napkin beside her plate, she always has some joke of her own. One need never bother about Lily. She waited. She tucked her napkin under the edge of her plate. Well, were they done now? No. That story had led to another story. Her husband was in great spirits tonight, and wishing, she supposed, to make it all right with old Augustus after that scene about the soup, had drawn him in—they were telling stories about some one they had both known at college. She looked at the window in which the candle flames burnt brighter now that the panes were black, and looking at that outside the voices came to her very strangely, as if they were voices at a service in a cathedral, for she did not listen to the words. The sudden bursts of laughter and then one voice (Minta's) speaking alone, reminded her of men and boys crying out the Latin words of a service in some Roman Catholic cathedral. She waited. Her husband spoke. He was repeating something, and she knew it was poetry from the rhythm and the ring of exultation, and melancholy in his voice:

> Come out and climb the garden path,
>   Luriana Lurilee.
> The China rose is all abloom and buzzing with the
>   yellow bee.

The words (she was looking at the window) sounded as if they were floating like flowers on water out there, cut off from them all, as if no one had said them, but they had come into existence of themselves.

"And all the lives we ever lived and all the lives to be are full of trees and changing leaves." She did not know what they meant, but, like music, the words seemed to be spoken by her own voice, outside her self, saying quite easily and naturally what had been in her mind the whole evening while she said different things. She knew, without looking round, that every one at the table was listening to the voice saying:

> I wonder if it seems to you,
>   Luriana, Lurilee

with the same sort of relief and pleasure that she had, as if this were, at last, the natural thing to say, this were their own voice speaking.

But the voice stopped. She looked round. She made herself get up. Augustus Carmichael had risen and, holding his table napkin so that it looked like a long white robe he stood chanting:

> To see the Kings go riding by
> Over lawn and daisy lea
> With their palm leaves and cedar sheaves,
>   Luriana, Lurilee,

and as she passed him, he turned slightly towards her repeating the last words:

> Luriana, Lurilee

and bowed to her as if he did her homage. Without knowing why, she felt that he liked her better than he had ever done before; and with a feeling of relief and gratitude she returned his bow and passed through the door which he held open for her.

It was necessary now to carry everything a step further. With her foot on the threshold she waited a moment longer in a scene which was vanishing even as she looked, and then, as she moved and took Minta's arm and left the room, it changed, it shaped itself differently; it had become, she knew, giving one last look at it over her shoulder, already the past.

XVIII

As USUAL, Lily thought. There was always something that had to be done at that precise moment, something that Mrs. Ramsay had decided for reasons of her own to do instantly, it might be with every one standing about making jokes, as now, not being able to decide whether they were going into the smoking-room, into the drawing-room, up to the attics. Then one saw Mrs. Ramsay in the midst of this hubbub standing there with Minta's arm in hers, bethink her, "Yes, it is time for that now," and so make off at once with an air of secrecy to do something alone. And directly she went a sort of disintegration set in; they wavered about, went different ways, Mr. Bankes took Charles Tansley by the arm and went off to finish on the terrace the discussion they had begun at dinner about politics, thus giving a turn to the whole poise of the evening, making the weight fall in a different direction, as if, Lily thought, seeing them go, and hearing a word or two about the policy of the Labour Party, they had gone up on to the bridge of the ship and were taking their bearings; the change from poetry to politics struck her like that; so Mr. Bankes and Charles Tansley went off, while the others stood looking at Mrs. Ramsay going upstairs in the lamplight alone. Where, Lily wondered, was she going so quickly?

Not that she did in fact run or hurry; she went indeed rather slowly. She felt rather inclined just for a moment to stand still after all that chatter, and pick out one particular thing; the thing that mattered; to detach it; separate it off; clean it of all the emotions and odds and ends of things, and so hold it before her, and

bring it to the tribunal where, ranged about in conclave, sat the
judges she had set up to decide these things. Is it good, is it bad,
is it right or wrong? Where are we all going to? and so on. So
she righted herself after the shock of the event, and quite un-
consciously and incongruously, used the branches of the elm
trees outside to help her to stabilise her position. Her world was
changing: they were still. The event had given her a sense of
movement. All must be in order. She must get that right and
that right, she thought, insensibly approving of the dignity of
the trees' stillness, and now again of the superb upward rise (like
the beak of a ship up a wave) of the elm branches as the wind
raised them. For it was windy (she stood a moment to look out).
It was windy, so that the leaves now and then brushed open a
star, and the stars themselves seemed to be shaking and darting
light and trying to flash out between the edges of the leaves. Yes,
that was done then, accomplished; and as with all things done,
became solemn. Now one thought of it, cleared of chatter and
emotion, it seemed always to have been, only was shown now
and so being shown, struck everything into stability. They
would, she thought, going on again, however long they lived,
come back to this night; this moon; this wind; this house: and
to her too. It flattered her, where she was most susceptible of
flattery, to think how, wound about in their hearts, however long
they lived she would be woven; and this, and this, and this, she
thought, going upstairs, laughing, but affectionately, at the sofa
on the landing (her mother's); at the rocking-chair (her father's);
at the map of the Hebrides. All that would be revived again in
the lives of Paul and Minta; "the Rayleys"—she tried the new
name over; and she felt, with her hand on the nursery door, that
community of feeling with other people which emotion gives as
if the walls of partition had become so thin that practically (the
feeling was one of relief and happiness) it was all one stream,

and chairs, tables, maps, were hers, were theirs, it did not matter whose, and Paul and Minta would carry it on when she was dead.

She turned the handle, firmly, lest it should squeak, and went in, pursing her lips slightly, as if to remind herself that she must not speak aloud. But directly she came in she saw, with annoyance, that the precaution was not needed. The children were not asleep. It was most annoying. Mildred should be more careful. There was James wide awake and Cam sitting bolt upright, and Mildred out of bed in her bare feet, and it was almost eleven and they were all talking. What was the matter? It was that horrid skull again. She had told Mildred to move it, but Mildred, of course, had forgotten, and now there was Cam wide awake, and James wide awake quarrelling when they ought to have been asleep hours ago. What had possessed Edward to send them this horrid skull? She had been so foolish as to let them nail it up there. It was nailed fast, Mildred said, and Cam couldn't go to sleep with it in the room, and James screamed if she touched it.

Then Cam must go to sleep (it had great horns said Cam)— must go to sleep and dream of lovely palaces, said Mrs. Ramsay, sitting down on the bed by her side. She could see the horns, Cam said, all over the room. It was true. Wherever they put the light (and James could not sleep without a light) there was always a shadow somewhere.

"But think, Cam, it's only an old pig," said Mrs. Ramsay, "a nice black pig like the pigs at the farm." But Cam thought it was a horrid thing, branching at her all over the room.

"Well then," said Mrs. Ramsay, "we will cover it up," and they all watched her go to the chest of drawers, and open the little drawers quickly one after another, and not seeing anything that would do, she quickly took her own shawl off and wound it round the skull, round and round and round, and then she came back to Cam and laid her head almost flat on the pillow beside Cam's and said how lovely it looked now; how the fairies would love it; it was like a bird's nest; it was like a beautiful mountain such as she had seen abroad, with valleys and flowers and bells ringing and birds singing and little goats and antelopes and . . . She could see the words echoing as she spoke them rhythmically in Cam's mind, and Cam was repeating after her how it was like a mountain, a bird's nest, a garden, and there were little antelopes, and her eyes were opening and shutting, and Mrs. Ramsay went on speaking still more monotonously, and more rhythmically and more nonsensically, how she must shut her eyes and go to sleep and dream of mountains and valleys and stars falling and parrots and antelopes and gardens, and everything lovely, she said, raising her head very slowly and speaking more and more mechanically, until she sat upright and saw that Cam was asleep.

Now, she whispered, crossing over to his bed, James must go to sleep too, for see, she said, the boar's skull was still there; they had not touched it; they had done just what he wanted; it was there quite unhurt. He made sure that the skull was still there under the shawl. But he wanted to ask her something more. Would they go to the Lighthouse tomorrow?

No, not tomorrow, she said, but soon, she promised him; the next fine day. He was very good. He lay down. She covered him up. But he would never forget, she knew, and she felt angry with Charles Tansley, with her husband, and with herself, for she had raised his hopes. Then feeling for her shawl and remembering that she had wrapped it round the boar's skull, she got up, and pulled the window down another inch or two, and heard the wind, and got a breath of the perfectly indifferent chill night air and murmured good-night to Mildred and left the room and let the tongue of the door slowly lengthen in the lock and went out.

She hoped he would not bang his books on the floor above their heads, she thought, still thinking how annoying Charles

Tansley was. For neither of them slept well; they were excitable children, and since he said things like that about the Lighthouse, it seemed to her likely that he would knock a pile of books over, just as they were going to sleep, clumsily sweeping them off the table with his elbow. For she supposed that he had gone upstairs to work. Yet he looked so desolate; yet she would feel relieved when he went; yet she would see that he was better treated tomorrow; yet he was admirable with her husband; yet his manners certainly wanted improving; yet she liked his laugh—thinking this, as she came downstairs, she noticed that she could now see the moon itself through the staircase window—the yellow harvest moon—and turned, and they saw her, standing above them on the stairs.

"That's my mother," thought Prue. Yes; Minta should look at her; Paul Rayley should look at her. That is the thing itself, she felt, as if there were only one person like that in the world; her mother. And, from having been quite grown up, a moment before, talking with the others, she became a child again, and what they had been doing was a game, and would her mother sanction their game, or condemn it, she wondered. And thinking what a chance it was for Minta and Paul and Lily to see her, and feeling what an extraordinary stroke of fortune it was for her, to have her, and how she would never grow up and never leave home, she said, like a child, "We thought of going down to the beach to watch the waves."

Instantly, for no reason at all, Mrs. Ramsay became like a girl of twenty, full of gaiety. A mood of revelry suddenly took possession of her. Of course they must go; of course they must go, she cried, laughing; and running down the last three or four steps quickly, she began turning from one to the other and laughing and drawing Minta's wrap round her and saying she only wished she could come too, and would they be very late, and had any of them got a watch?

"Yes, Paul has," said Minta. Paul slipped a beautiful gold watch out of a little wash-leather case to show her. And as he held it in the palm of his hand before her, he felt, "She knows all about it. I need not say anything." He was saying to her as he showed her the watch, "I've done it, Mrs. Ramsay. I owe it all to you." And seeing the gold watch lying in his hand, Mrs. Ramsay felt, How extraordinarily lucky Minta is! She is marrying a man who has a gold watch in a wash-leather bag!

"How I wish I could come with you!" she cried. But she was withheld by something so strong that she never even thought of asking herself what it was. Of course it was impossible for her to go with them. But she would have liked to go, had it not been for the other thing, and tickled by the absurdity of her thought (how lucky to marry a man with a wash-leather bag for his watch) she went with a smile on her lips into the other room, where her husband sat reading.

XIX

OF COURSE, she said to herself, coming into the room, she had to come here to get something she wanted. First she wanted to sit down in a particular chair under a particular lamp. But she wanted something more, though she did not know, could not think what it was that she wanted. She looked at her husband (taking up her stocking and beginning to knit), and saw that he did not want to be interrupted—that was clear. He was reading something that moved him very much. He was half smiling and then she knew he was controlling his emotion. He was tossing the pages over. He was acting it—perhaps he was thinking himself the person in the book. She wondered what book it was. Oh, it was one of old Sir Walter's she saw, adjusting the shade of her lamp so that the light fell on her knitting. For Charles

Tansley had been saying (she looked up as if she expected to hear the crash of books on the floor above), had been saying that people don't read Scott any more. Then her husband thought, "That's what they'll say of me"; so he went and got one of those books. And if he came to the conclusion "That's true" what Charles Tansley said, he would accept it about Scott. (She could see that he was weighing, considering, putting this with that as he read.) But not about himself. He was always uneasy about himself. That troubled her. He would always be worrying about his own books—will they be read, are they good, why aren't they better, what do people think of me? Not liking to think of him so, and wondering if they had guessed at dinner why he suddenly became irritable when they talked about fame and books lasting, wondering if the children were laughing at that, she twitched the stocking out, and all the fine gravings came drawn with steel instruments about her lips and forehead, and she grew still like a tree which has been tossing and quivering and now, when the breeze falls, settles, leaf by leaf, into quiet.

It didn't matter, any of it, she thought. A great man, a great book, fame—who could tell? She knew nothing about it. But it was his way with him, his truthfulness—for instance at dinner she had been thinking quite instinctively, If only he would speak! She had complete trust in him. And dismissing all this, as one passes in diving now a weed, now a straw, now a bubble, she felt again, sinking deeper, as she had felt in the hall when the others were talking, There is something I want—something I have come to get, and she fell deeper and deeper without knowing quite what it was, with her eyes closed. And she waited a little, knitting, wondering, and slowly those words they had said at dinner, "the China rose is all abloom and buzzing with the honey bee," began washing from side to side of her mind rhythmically, and as they washed, words, like little shaded lights, one red, one blue, one yellow, lit up in the dark of her mind, and seemed leaving their perches up there to fly across and across, or to cry out and to be echoed; so she turned and felt on the table beside her for a book.

> And all the lives we ever lived
> And all the lives to be,
> Are full of trees and changing leaves,

she murmured, sticking her needles into the stocking. And she opened the book and began reading here and there at random, and as she did so she felt that she was climbing backwards, upwards, shoving her way up under petals that curved over her, so that she only knew this is white, or this is red. She did not know at first what the words meant at all.

> Steer, hither steer your winged pines, all beaten Mariners

she read and turned the page, swinging herself, zigzagging this way and that, from one line to another as from one branch to another, from one red and white flower to another, until a little sound roused her—her husband slapping his thighs. Their eyes met for a second; but they did not want to speak to each other. They had nothing to say, but something seemed, nevertheless, to go from him to her. It was the life, it was the power of it, it was the tremendous humour, she knew, that made him slap his thighs. Don't interrupt me, he seemed to be saying, don't say anything; just sit there. And he went on reading. His lips twitched. It filled him. It fortified him. He clean forgot all the little rubs and digs of the evening, and how it bored him unutterably to sit still while people ate and drank interminably, and his being so irritable with his wife and so touchy and minding when they passed his books over as if they didn't exist at all. But now, he felt, it didn't matter a damn who reached Z (if thought ran like an alphabet from A to Z). Somebody would reach it—if not he, then another. This man's strength and sanity, his feeling for straightforward simple things, these fishermen, the poor old crazed creature in Mucklebackit's cottage made him feel so vigorous, so relieved of something that he felt roused and triumphant and could not choke back his tears. Raising the book a little to hide his face, he let them fall and shook his head from side to side and forgot himself completely (but not one or two reflections about morality and French novels and English novels and Scott's hands being tied but his view perhaps being as true as the other view), forgot his own bothers and failures completely in poor Steenie's drowning and Mucklebackit's sorrow (that was Scott at his best) and the astonishing delight and feeling of vigour that it gave him.

Well, let them improve upon that, he thought as he finished the chapter. He felt that he had been arguing with somebody, and had got the better of him. They could not improve upon that, whatever they might say; and his own position became more secure. The lovers were fiddlesticks, he thought, collecting it all in his mind again. That's fiddlesticks, that's first-rate, he thought, putting one thing beside another. But he must read it again. He could not remember the whole shape of the thing. He had to keep his judgement in suspense. So he returned to the other thought—if young men did not care for this, naturally they did not care for him either. One ought not to complain, thought Mr. Ramsay, trying to stifle his desire to complain to his wife that young men did not admire him. But he was determined; he would not bother her again. Here he looked at her reading. She looked very peaceful, reading. He liked to think that every one had taken themselves off and that he and she were alone. The whole of life did not consist in going to bed with a woman, he thought, returning to Scott and Balzac, to the English novel and the French novel.

Mrs. Ramsay raised her head and like a person in a light sleep seemed to say that if he wanted her to wake she would, she really would, but otherwise, might she go on sleeping, just a little longer, just a little longer? She was climbing up those branches, this way and that, laying hands on one flower and then another.

"Nor praise the deep vermilion in the rose," she read, and so reading she was ascending, she felt, on to the top, on to the summit. How satisfying! How restful! All the odds and ends of the day stuck to this magnet; her mind felt swept, felt clean. And then there it was, suddenly entire; she held it in her hands, beautiful and reasonable, clear and complete, the essence sucked out of life and held rounded here—the sonnet.

But she was becoming conscious of her husband looking at her. He was smiling at her, quizzically, as if he were ridiculing her gently for being asleep in broad daylight, but at the same time he was thinking, Go on reading. You don't look sad now, he thought. And he wondered what she was reading, and exaggerated her ignorance, her simplicity, for he liked to think that she was not clever, not book-learned at all. He wondered if she understood what she was reading. Probably not, he thought. She was astonishingly beautiful. Her beauty seemed to him, if that were possible, to increase

> Yet seem'd it winter still, and, you away,
> As with your shadow I with these did play,

she finished.

"Well?" she said, echoing his smile dreamily, looking up from her book.

As with your shadow I with these did play,

she murmured, putting the book on the table.

What had happened, she wondered, as she took up her knitting, since she had seen him alone? She remembered dressing, and seeing the moon; Andrew holding his plate too high at dinner; being depressed by something William had said; the birds in the trees; the sofa on the landing; the children being awake; Charles Tansley waking them with his books falling—oh, no, that she had invented; and Paul having a wash-leather case for his watch. Which should she tell him about?

"They're engaged," she said, beginning to knit, "Paul and Minta."

"So I guessed," he said. There was nothing very much to be said about it. Her mind was still going up and down, up and down with the poetry; he was still feeling very vigorous, very forthright, after reading about Steenie's funeral. So they sat silent. Then she became aware that she wanted him to say something.

Anything, anything, she thought, going on with her knitting. Anything will do.

"How nice it would be to marry a man with a wash-leather bag for his watch," she said, for that was the sort of joke they had together.

He snorted. He felt about this engagement as he always felt about any engagement; the girl is much too good for that young man. Slowly it came into her head, why is it then that one wants people to marry? What was the value, the meaning of things? (Every word they said now would be true.) Do say something, she thought, wishing only to hear his voice. For the shadow, the thing folding them in was beginning, she felt, to close round her again. Say anything, she begged, looking at him, as if for help.

He was silent, swinging the compass on his watch-chain to and fro, and thinking of Scott's novels and Balzac's novels. But through the crepuscular walls of their intimacy, for they were drawing together, involuntarily, coming side by side, quite close, she could feel his mind like a raised hand shadowing her mind; and he was beginning, now that her thoughts took a turn he disliked—towards this "pessimism" as he called it—to fidget, though he said nothing, raising his hand to his forehead, twisting a lock of hair, letting it fall again.

"You won't finish that stocking tonight," he said, pointing to her stocking. That was what she wanted—the asperity in his voice reproving her. If he says it's wrong to be pessimistic probably it is wrong, she thought; the marriage will turn out all right.

"No," she said, flattening the stocking out upon her knee, "I shan't finish it."

And what then? For she felt that he was still looking at her, but that his look had changed. He wanted something—wanted the thing she always found it so difficult to give him; wanted her to tell him that she loved him. And that, no, she could not do. He found talking so much easier than she did. He could say things—she never could. So naturally it was always he that said the things, and then for some reason he would mind this suddenly, and would reproach her. A heartless woman he called her; she never told him that she loved him. But it was not so—it was not so. It was only that she never could say what she felt. Was there no crumb on his coat? Nothing she could do for him? Getting up, she stood at the window with the reddish-brown stocking in her hands, partly to turn away from him, partly because she remembered how beautiful it often is—the sea at night. But she knew that he had turned his head as she turned; he was watching her. She knew that he was thinking, You are more beautiful than ever. And she felt herself very beautiful.

Will you not tell me just for once that you love me? He was thinking that, for he was roused, what with Minta and his book, and its being the end of the day and their having quarrelled about going to the Lighthouse. But she could not do it; she could not say it. Then, knowing that he was watching her, instead of saying anything she turned, holding her stocking, and looked at him. And as she looked at him she began to smile, for though she had not said a word, he knew, of course he knew, that she loved him. He could not deny it. And smiling she looked out of the window and said (thinking to herself, Nothing on earth can equal this happiness)—

"Yes, you were right. It's going to be wet tomorrow. You won't be able to go." And she looked at him smiling. For she had triumphed again. She had not said it: yet he knew.

Time Passes

I

"Well, we must wait for the future to show," said Mr. Bankes, coming in from the terrace.

"It's almost too dark to see," said Andrew, coming up from the beach.

"One can hardly tell which is the sea and which is the land," said Prue.

"Do we leave that light burning?" said Lily as they took their coats off indoors.

"No," said Prue, "not if every one's in."

"Andrew," she called back, "just put out the light in the hall."

One by one the lamps were all extinguished, except that Mr. Carmichael, who liked to lie awake a little reading Virgil, kept his candle burning rather longer than the rest.

II

So with the lamps all put out, the moon sunk, and a thin rain drumming on the roof a downpouring of immense darkness began. Nothing, it seemed, could survive the flood, the profusion of darkness which, creeping in at keyholes and crevices, stole round window blinds, came into bedrooms, swallowed up here a jug and basin, there a bowl of red and yellow dahlias, there the sharp edges and firm bulk of a chest of drawers. Not only was furniture confounded; there was scarcely anything left of body or mind by which one could say, "This is he" or "This is she." Sometimes a hand was raised as if to clutch something or ward off something, or somebody groaned, or somebody laughed aloud as if sharing a joke with nothingness.

Nothing stirred in the drawing-room or in the dining-room or on the staircase. Only through the rusty hinges and swollen sea-moistened woodwork certain airs, detached from the body of the wind (the house was ramshackle after all) crept round corners and ventured indoors. Almost one might imagine them, as they entered the drawing-room questioning and wondering, toying with the flap of hanging wall-paper, asking, would it hang much longer, when would it fall? Then smoothly brushing the walls, they passed on musingly as if asking the red and yellow roses on the wall-paper whether they would fade, and questioning (gently, for there was time at their disposal) the torn letters in the waste-paper basket, the flowers, the books, all of which were now open to them and asking, Were they allies? Were they enemies? How long would they endure?

So some random light directing them with its pale footfall upon stair and mat, from some uncovered star, or wandering ship, or the Lighthouse even, the little airs mounted the staircase and nosed round bedroom doors. But here surely, they must cease. Whatever else may perish and disappear, what lies here is steadfast. Here one might say to those sliding lights, those fumbling airs that breathe and bend over the bed itself, here you can neither touch nor destroy. Upon which, wearily, ghostlily, as if they had feather-light fingers and the light persistency of feathers, they would look, once, on the shut eyes, and the loosely clasping fingers, and fold their garments wearily and disappear. And so, nosing, rubbing, they went to the window on

the staircase, to the servants' bedrooms, to the boxes in the attics; descending, blanched the apples on the dining-room table,
fumbled the petals of roses, tried the picture on the easel,
brushed the mat and blew a little sand along the floor. At length,
desisting, all ceased together, gathered together, all sighed together; all together gave off an aimless gust of lamentation to
which some door in the kitchen replied; swung wide; admitted
nothing; and slammed to.

[Here Mr. Carmichael, who was reading Virgil, blew out his
candle. It was midnight.]

III

BUT WHAT after all is one night? A short space, especially when
the darkness dims so soon, and so soon a bird sings, a cock
crows, or a faint green quickens, like a turning leaf, in the hollow of the wave. Night, however, succeeds to night. The winter
holds a pack of them in store and deals them equally, evenly,
with indefatigable fingers. They lengthen; they darken. Some of
them hold aloft clear planets, plates of brightness. The autumn
trees, ravaged as they are, take on the flash of tattered flags
kindling in the gloom of cool cathedral caves where gold letters
on marble pages describe death in battle and how bones bleach
and burn far away in Indian sands. The autumn trees gleam in
the yellow moonlight, in the light of harvest moons, the light
which mellows the energy of labour, and smooths the stubble,
and brings the wave lapping blue to the shore.

It seemed now as if, touched by human penitence and all its
toil, divine goodness had parted the curtain and displayed behind it, single, distinct, the hare erect; the wave falling; the boat
rocking; which, did we deserve them, should be ours always. But
alas, divine goodness, twitching the cord, draws the curtain; it

does not please him; he covers his treasures in a drench of hail, and so breaks them, so confuses them that it seems impossible that their calm should ever return or that we should ever compose from their fragments a perfect whole or read in the littered pieces the clear words of truth. For our penitence deserves a glimpse only; our toil respite only.

The nights now are full of wind and destruction; the trees plunge and bend and their leaves fly helter skelter until the lawn is plastered with them and they lie packed in gutters and choke rain-pipes and scatter damp paths. Also the sea tosses itself and breaks itself, and should any sleeper fancying that he might find on the beach an answer to his doubts, a sharer of his solitude, throw off his bedclothes and go down by himself to walk on the sand, no image with semblance of serving and divine promptitude comes readily to hand bringing the night to order and making the world reflect the compass of the soul. The hand dwindles in his hand; the voice bellows in his ear. Almost it would appear that it is useless in such confusion to ask the night those questions as to what, and why, and wherefore, which tempt the sleeper from his bed to seek an answer.

[Mr. Ramsay, stumbling along a passage one dark morning, stretched his arms out, but Mrs. Ramsay having died rather suddenly the night before, his arms, though stretched out, remained empty.]

IV

SO WITH the house empty and the doors locked and the mattresses rolled round, those stray airs, advance guards of great armies, blustered in, brushed bare boards, nibbled and fanned, met nothing in bedroom or drawing-room that wholly resisted them but only hangings that flapped, wood that creaked, the bare legs of tables, saucepans and china already furred, tarnished, cracked. What people had shed and left—a pair of shoes, a shooting cap, some faded skirts and coats in wardrobes—those alone kept the human shape and in the emptiness indicated how once they were filled and animated; how once hands were busy with hooks and buttons; how once the looking-glass had held a face; had held a world hollowed out in which a figure turned, a hand flashed, the door opened, in came children rushing and tumbling; and went out again. Now, day after day, light turned, like a flower reflected in water, its sharp image on the wall opposite. Only the shadows of the trees, flourishing in the wind, made obeisance on the wall, and for a moment darkened the pool in which light reflected itself; or birds, flying, made a soft spot flutter slowly across the bedroom floor.

So loveliness reigned and stillness, and together made the shape of loveliness itself, a form from which life had parted; solitary like a pool at evening, far distant, seen from a train window, vanishing so quickly that the pool, pale in the evening, is scarcely robbed of its solitude, though once seen. Loveliness and stillness clasped hands in the bedroom, and among the shrouded jugs and sheeted chairs even the prying of the wind, and the soft nose of the clammy sea airs, rubbing, snuffling, iterating, and reiterating their questions—"Will you fade? Will you perish?"—scarcely disturbed the peace, the indifference, the air of pure integrity, as if the question they asked scarcely needed that they should answer: we remain.

Nothing it seemed could break that image, corrupt that innocence, or disturb the swaying mantle of silence which, week after week, in the empty room, wove into itself the falling cries of birds, ships hooting, the drone and hum of the fields, a dog's bark, a man's shout, and folded them round the house in silence. Once only a board sprang on the landing; once in the middle of the night with a roar, with a rupture, as after centuries of quiescence, a rock rends itself from the mountain and hurtles crashing into the valley, one fold of the shawl loosened and swung to and fro. Then again peace descended; and the shadow wavered; light bent to its own image in adoration on the bedroom wall; and Mrs. McNab, tearing the veil of silence with hands that had stood in the wash-tub, grinding it with boots that had crunched the shingle, came as directed to open all windows, and dust the bedrooms.

V

AS SHE LURCHED (for she rolled like a ship at sea) and leered (for her eyes fell on nothing directly, but with a sidelong glance that deprecated the scorn and anger of the world—she was witless, she knew it), as she clutched the banisters and hauled herself upstairs and rolled from room to room, she sang. Rubbing the glass of the long looking-glass and leering sideways at her swinging figure a sound issued from her lips—something that had been gay twenty years before on the stage perhaps, had been hummed and danced to, but now, coming from the toothless, bonneted, care-taking woman, was robbed of meaning, was like the voice of witlessness, humour, persistency itself, trodden down but springing up again, so that as she lurched, dusting, wiping, she seemed to say how it was one long sorrow and trouble, how it was getting up and going to bed again, and bringing things out and putting them away again. It was not easy or snug this world she had known for close on seventy years. Bowed down she was with weariness. How long, she asked, creaking and groaning on her knees under the bed, dusting the boards, how long shall it endure? but hobbled to her feet again, pulled herself up, and again with her sidelong leer which slipped and turned aside even from her own face, and her own sorrows, stood and gaped in the glass, aimlessly smiling, and began again the old amble and hobble, taking up mats, putting down china, looking sideways in the glass, as if, after all, she had her consolations, as if indeed there twined about her dirge some incorrigible hope. Visions of joy there must have been at the wash-tub, say with her children (yet two had been base-born and one had deserted her), at the public-house, drinking; turning over scraps in her drawers. Some cleavage of the dark there must have been, some channel in the depths of obscurity through which light enough issued to twist her face grinning in the glass and make her, turning to her job again, mumble out the old music hall song. The mystic, the visionary, walking the beach on a fine night, stirring a puddle, looking at a stone, asking themselves "What am I," "What is this?" had suddenly an answer vouchsafed them: (they could not say what it was) so that they were warm in the frost and had comfort in the desert. But Mrs. McNab continued to drink and gossip as before.

VI

THE SPRING without a leaf to toss, bare and bright like a virgin fierce in her chastity, scornful in her purity, was laid out on fields wide-eyed and watchful and entirely careless of what was done or thought by the beholders. [Prue Ramsay, leaning on her father's arm, was given in marriage. What, people said, could have been more fitting? And, they added, how beautiful she looked!]

As summer neared, as the evenings lengthened, there came to the wakeful, the hopeful, walking the beach, stirring the pool, imaginations of the strangest kind—of flesh turned to atoms which drove before the wind, of stars flashing in their hearts, of cliff, sea, cloud, and sky brought purposely together to assemble outwardly the scattered parts of the vision within. In those mirrors, the minds of men, in those pools of uneasy water, in which clouds for ever turn and shadows form, dreams persisted, and it was impossible to resist the strange intimation which every gull, flower, tree, man and woman, and the white earth itself seemed to declare (but if questioned at once to withdraw) that good triumphs, happiness prevails, order rules; or to resist the extraordinary stimulus to range hither and thither in search of some absolute good, some crystal of intensity, remote from the known pleasures and familiar virtues, something alien to the processes of domestic life, single, hard, bright, like a diamond in the sand, which would render the possessor secure. Moreover, softened and acquiescent, the spring with her bees humming and gnats dancing threw her cloak about her, veiled her eyes, averted her head, and among passing shadows and flights of small rain seemed to have taken upon her a knowledge of the sorrows of mankind.

[Prue Ramsay died that summer in some illness connected with childbirth, which was indeed a tragedy, people said, everything, they said, had promised so well.]

And now in the heat of summer the wind sent its spies about the house again. Flies wove a web in the sunny rooms; weeds that had grown close to the glass in the night tapped methodically at the window-pane. When darkness fell, the stroke of the Lighthouse, which had laid itself with such authority upon the carpet in the darkness, tracing its pattern, came now in the softer light of spring mixed with moonlight gliding gently as if it laid its caress and lingered steathily and looked and came lovingly again. But in the very lull of this loving caress, as the long stroke leant upon the bed, the rock was rent asunder; another fold of the shawl loosened; there it hung, and swayed. Through the short summer nights and the long summer days, when the empty rooms seemed to murmur with the echoes of the fields and the hum of flies, the long streamer waved gently, swayed aimlessly; while the sun so striped and barred the rooms and filled them with yellow haze that Mrs. McNab, when she broke in and lurched about, dusting, sweeping, looked like a tropical fish oaring its way through sun-lanced waters.

But slumber and sleep though it might there came later in the summer ominous sounds like the measured blows of hammers dulled on felt, which, with their repeated shocks still further loosened the shawl and cracked the tea-cups. Now and again some glass tinkled in the cupboard as if a giant voice had shrieked so loud in its agony that tumblers stood inside a cupboard vibrated too. Then again silence fell; and then, night after night, and sometimes in plain mid-day when the roses were bright and light turned on the wall its shape clearly there seemed to drop into this silence, this indifference, this integrity, the thud of something falling.

[A shell exploded. Twenty or thirty young men were blown up in France, among them Andrew Ramsay, whose death, mercifully, was instantaneous.]

At that season those who had gone down to pace the beach and ask of the sea and sky what message they reported or what vision they affirmed had to consider among the usual tokens of divine bounty—the sunset on the sea, the pallor of dawn, the moon rising, fishing-boats against the moon, and children making mud pies or pelting each other with handfuls of grass, something out of harmony with this jocundity and this serenity. There was the silent apparition of an ashen-coloured ship for instance, come, gone; there was a purplish stain upon the bland surface of the sea as if something had boiled and bled, invisibly, beneath. This intrusion into a scene calculated to stir the most sublime reflections and lead to the most comfortable conclusions stayed their pacing. It was difficult blandly to overlook them; to abolish their significance in the landscape; to continue, as one walked by the sea, to marvel how beauty outside mirrored beauty within.

Did Nature supplement what man advanced? Did she complete what he began? With equal complacence she saw his misery, his meanness, and his torture. That dream, of sharing, completing, of finding in solitude on the beach an answer, was then but a reflection in a mirror, and the mirror itself was but the surface glassiness which forms in quiescence when the nobler powers sleep beneath? Impatient, despairing yet loth to go (for beauty offers her lures, has her consolations), to pace the beach was impossible; contemplation was unendurable; the mirror was broken.

[Mr. Carmichael brought out a volume of poems that spring, which had an unexpected success. The war, people said, had revived their interest in poetry.]

VII

NIGHT AFTER NIGHT, summer and winter, the torment of storms, the arrow-like stillness of fine weather, held their court without interference. Listening (had there been any one to listen) from the upper rooms of the empty house only gigantic chaos streaked with lightning could have been heard tumbling and tossing, as the winds and waves disported themselves like the amorphous bulks of leviathans whose brows are pierced by no light of reason, and mounted one on top of another, and lunged and plunged in the darkness or the daylight (for night and day, month and year ran shapelessly together) in idiot games, until it seemed as if the universe were battling and tumbling, in brute confusion and wanton lust aimlessly by itself.

In spring the garden urns, casually filled with wind-blown plants, were gay as ever. Violets came and daffodils. But the stillness and the brightness of the day were as strange as the chaos and tumult of night, with the trees standing there, and the flowers standing there, looking before them, looking up, yet beholding nothing, eyeless, and so terrible.

VIII

THINKING NO HARM, for the family would not come, never again, some said, and the house would be sold at Michaelmas perhaps, Mrs. McNab stooped and picked a bunch of flowers to take home with her. She laid them on the table while she dusted. She was fond of flowers. It was a pity to let them waste. Suppose the house were sold (she stood arms akimbo in front of the looking-glass) it would want seeing to—it would. There it had stood all these years without a soul in it. The books and things were mouldy, for, what with the war and help being hard to get, the house had not been cleaned as she could have wished. It was beyond one person's strength to get it straight now. She was too old. Her legs pained her. All those books needed to be laid out on the grass in the sun; there was plaster fallen in the hall; the rain-pipe had blocked over the study window and let the water in; the carpet was ruined quite. But people should come themselves; they should have sent somebody down to see. For there were clothes in the cupboards; they had left clothes in all the bedrooms. What was she to do with them? They had the moth in them—Mrs. Ramsay's things. Poor lady! She would never want *them* again. She was dead, they said; years ago, in London. There was the old grey cloak she wore gardening (Mrs. McNab fingered it). She could see her, as she came up the drive with the washing, stooping over her flowers (the garden was a pitiful sight now, all run to riot, and rabbits scuttling at you out of the beds)—she could see her with one of the children by her in that grey cloak. There were boots and shoes; and a brush and comb left on the dressing-table, for all the world as if she expected to come back tomorrow. (She had died very sudden at the end, they said.) And once they had been coming, but had put off coming, what with the war, and travel being so difficult these days; they had never come all these years; just sent her money; but never wrote, never came, and expected to find things as they had left them, ah, dear! Why the dressing-table drawers were full of things (she pulled them open), handkerchiefs, bits of ribbon. Yes, she could see Mrs. Ramsay as she came up the drive with the washing.

"Good-evening, Mrs. McNab," she would say.

She had a pleasant way with her. The girls all liked her. But, dear, many things had changed since then (she shut the drawer); many families had lost their dearest. So she was dead; and Mr. Andrew killed; and Miss Prue dead too, they said, with her first baby; but every one had lost some one these years. Prices had gone up shamefully, and didn't come down again neither. She could well remember her in her grey cloak.

"Good-evening, Mrs. McNab," she said, and told cook to keep a plate of milk soup for her—quite thought she wanted it, carrying that heavy basket all the way up from town. She could see her now, stooping over her flowers; and faint and flickering, like a yellow beam or the circle at the end of a telescope, a lady in a grey cloak, stooping over her flowers, went wandering over the bedroom wall, up the dressing-table, across the wash-stand, as Mrs. McNab hobbled and ambled, dusting, straightening. And cook's name now? Mildred? Marian?—some name like that. Ah, she had forgotten—she did forget things. Fiery, like all red-haired women. Many a laugh they had had. She was always welcome in the kitchen. She made them laugh, she did. Things were better then than now.

She sighed; there was too much work for one woman. She wagged her head this side and that. This had been the nursery. Why, it was all damp in here; the plaster was falling. Whatever did they want to hang a beast's skull there? gone mouldy too. And rats in all the attics. The rain came in. But they never sent; never came. Some of the locks had gone, so the doors banged. She didn't like to be up here at dusk alone neither. It was too much for one woman, too much, too much. She creaked, she moaned. She banged the door. She turned the key in the lock, and left the house alone, shut up, locked.

IX

THE HOUSE was left; the house was deserted. It was left like a shell on a sandhill to fill with dry salt grains now that life had left it. The long night seemed to have set in; the trifling airs, nibbling, the clammy breaths, fumbling, seemed to have triumphed. The saucepan had rusted and the mat decayed. Toads had nosed their way in. Idly, aimlessly, the swaying shawl swung to and fro. A thistle thrust itself between the tiles in the larder. The swallows nested in the drawing-room; the floor was strewn with straw; the plaster fell in shovelfuls; rafters were laid bare; rats carried off this and that to gnaw behind the wainscots. Tortoise-shell butterflies burst from the chrysalis and pattered their life out on the window-pane. Poppies sowed themselves among the dahlias; the lawn waved with long grass; giant artichokes towered among roses; a fringed carnation flowered among the cabbages; while the gentle tapping of a weed at the window had become, on winters' nights, a drumming from sturdy trees and thorned briars which made the whole room green in summer.

What power could now prevent the fertility, the insensibility of nature? Mrs. McNab's dream of a lady, of a child, of a plate of milk soup? It had wavered over the walls like a spot of sunlight and vanished. She had locked the door; she had gone. It was beyond the strength of one woman, she said. They never sent. They never wrote. There were things up there rotting in the drawers—it was a shame to leave them so, she said. The place was gone to rack and ruin. Only the Lighthouse beam entered the rooms for a moment, sent its sudden stare over bed and wall in the darkness of winter, looked with equanimity at the thistle and the swallow, the rat and the straw. Nothing now withstood them; nothing said no to them. Let the wind blow; let the poppy seed itself and the carnation mate with the cabbage. Let the swallow build in the drawing-room, and the thistle thrust aside the tiles, and the butterfly sun itself on the faded chintz of the arm-chairs. Let the broken glass and the china lie out on the lawn and be tangled over with grass and wild berries.

For now had come that moment, that hesitation when dawn trembles and night pauses, when if a feather alight in the scale it will be weighed down. One feather, and the house, sinking, falling, would have turned and pitched downwards to the depths of darkness. In the ruined room, picnickers would have lit their kettles; lovers sought shelter there, lying on the bare boards; and the shepherd stored his dinner on the bricks, and the tramp slept with his coat round him to ward off the cold. Then the roof would have fallen; briars and hemlocks would have blotted out path, step, and window; would have grown, unequally but lustily over the mound, until some trespasser, losing his way, could have told only by a red-hot poker among the nettles, or a scrap of china in the hemlock that here once some one had lived; there had been a house.

If the feather had fallen, if it had tipped the scale downwards, the whole house would have plunged to the depths to lie upon the sands of oblivion. But there was a force working; something not highly conscious; something that leered, something that lurched; something not inspired to go about its work with dignified ritual or solemn chanting. Mrs. McNab groaned; Mrs. Bast creaked. They were old; they were stiff; their legs ached. They came with their brooms and pails at last; they got to work. All of a sudden, would Mrs. McNab see that the house was ready, one of the young ladies wrote: would she get this done; would she get that done; all in a hurry. They might be coming for the summer; had left everything to the last; expected to find things as they had left them. Slowly and painfully, with broom and pail, mopping, scouring, Mrs. McNab, Mrs. Bast, stayed the corruption and the rot; rescued from the pool of Time that was fast closing over them now a basin, now a cupboard; fetched up from oblivion all the Waverley novels and a tea-set one morning; in the afternoon restored to sun and air a brass fender and a set of steel fire-irons. George, Mrs. Bast's son, caught the rats, and cut the grass. They had the builders. Attended with the creaking of hinges and the screeching of bolts, the slamming and banging of damp-swollen woodwork some rusty laborious birth seemed to be taking place, as the women, stooping, rising, groaning, singing, slapped and slammed, upstairs now, now down in the cellars. Oh, they said, the work!

They drank their tea in the bedroom sometimes, or in the study; breaking off work at mid-day with the smudge on their faces, and their old hands clasped and cramped with the broom handles. Flopped on chairs, they contemplated now the magnificent conquest over taps and bath; now the more arduous, more partial triumph over long rows of books, black as ravens once, now white-stained, breeding pale mushrooms and secreting furtive spiders. Once more, as she felt the tea warm in her, the telescope fitted itself to Mrs. McNab's eyes, and in a ring of light she saw the old gentleman, lean as a rake, wagging his head, as she came up with the washing, talking to himself, she supposed, on the lawn. He never noticed her. Some said he was dead; some said she was dead. Which was it? Mrs. Bast didn't know for certain either. The young gentleman was dead. That she was sure. She had read his name in the papers.

There was the cook now, Mildred, Marian, some such name as that—a red-headed woman, quick-tempered like all her sort, but kind, too, if you knew the way with her. Many a laugh they had had together. She saved a plate of soup for Maggie; a bite of ham, sometimes; whatever was over. They lived well in those days. They had everything they wanted (glibly, jovially, with the tea hot in her, she unwound her ball of memories, sitting in the wicker arm-chair by the nursery fender). There was always plenty doing, people in the house, twenty staying sometimes, and washing up till long past midnight.

Mrs. Bast (she had never known them; had lived in Glasgow at that time) wondered, putting her cup down, whatever they hung that beast's skull there for? Shot in foreign parts no doubt.

It might well be, said Mrs. McNab, wantoning on with her memories; they had friends in eastern countries; gentlemen staying there, ladies in evening dress; she had seen them once through the dining-room door all sitting at dinner. Twenty she dared say all in their jewellery, and she asked to stay help wash up, might be till after midnight.

Ah, said Mrs. Bast, they'd find it changed. She leant out of the window. She watched her son George scything the grass. They might well ask, what had been done to it? seeing how old Kennedy was supposed to have charge of it, and then his leg got so bad after he fell from the cart; and perhaps then no one for a year, or the better part of one; and then Davie Macdonald, and seeds might be sent, but who should say if they were ever planted? They'd find it changed.

She watched her son scything. He was a great one for work—one of those quiet ones. Well they must be getting along with the cupboards, she supposed. They hauled themselves up.

At last, after days of labour within, of cutting and digging without, dusters were flicked from the windows, the windows were shut to, keys were turned all over the house; the front door was banged; it was finished.

And now as if the cleaning and the scrubbing and the scything and the mowing had drowned it there rose that half-heard melody, that intermittent music which the ear half catches but lets fall; a bark, a bleat; irregular, intermittent, yet somehow related; the hum of an insect, the tremor of cut grass, dissevered yet somehow belonging; the jar of a dorbeetle, the squeak of a wheel, loud, low, but mysteriously related; which the ear strains to bring together and is always on the verge of harmonising, but they are never quite heard, never fully harmonised, and at last, in the evening, one after another the sounds die out, and the harmony falters, and silence falls. With the sunset sharpness was lost, and like mist rising, quiet rose, quiet spread, the wind settled; loosely the world shook itself down to sleep, darkly here without a light to it, save what came green suffused through leaves, or pale on the white flowers in the bed by the window.

(Lily Briscoe had her bag carried up to the house late one evening in September.)

X

THEN INDEED peace had come. Messages of peace breathed from the sea to the shore. Never to break its sleep any more, to lull it rather more deeply to rest, and whatever the dreamers dreamt holily, dreamt wisely, to confirm—what else was it murmuring—as Lily Briscoe laid her head on the pillow in the clean still room and heard the sea. Through the open window the voice of the beauty of the world came murmuring, too softly to hear exactly what it said—but what mattered if the meaning were plain? entreating the sleepers (the house was full again; Mrs. Beckwith was staying there, also Mr. Carmichael), if they would not actually come down to the beach itself at least to lift the blind and look out. They would see then night flowing down in purple; his head crowned; his sceptre jewelled; and how in his eyes a child might look. And if they still faltered (Lily was tired out with travelling and slept almost at once; but Mr. Carmichael read a book by candlelight), if they still said no, that it was vapour, this splendour of his, and the dew had more power than he, and they preferred sleeping; gently then without complaint, or argument, the voice would sing its song. Gently the waves would break (Lily heard them in her sleep); tenderly the light fell (it seemed to come through her eyelids). And it all looked, Mr. Carmichael thought, shutting his book, falling asleep, much as it used to look.

Indeed the voice might resume, as the curtains of dark wrapped themselves over the house, over Mrs. Beckwith, Mr. Carmichael, and Lily Briscoe so that they lay with several folds of blackness on their eyes, why not accept this, be content with this, acquiesce and resign? The sigh of all the seas breaking in measure round the isles soothed them; the night wrapped them; nothing broke their sleep, until, the birds beginning and the dawn weaving their thin voices in to its whiteness, a cart grinding, a dog somewhere barking, the sun lifted the curtains, broke the veil on their eyes, and Lily Briscoe stirring in her sleep. She clutched at her blankets as a faller clutches at the turf on the edge of a cliff. Her eyes opened wide. Here she was again, she thought, sitting bolt upright in bed. Awake.

THE LIGHTHOUSE

I

WHAT DOES it mean then, what can it all mean? Lily Briscoe asked herself, wondering whether, since she had been left alone, it behooved her to go to the kitchen to fetch another cup of coffee or wait here. What does it mean?—a catchword that was, caught up from some book, fitting her thought loosely, for she could not, this first morning with the Ramsays, contract her feelings, could only make a phrase resound to cover the blankness of her mind until these vapours had shrunk. For really, what did she feel, come back after all these years and Mrs. Ramsay dead? Nothing, nothing—nothing that she could express at all.

She had come late last night when it was all mysterious, dark. Now she was awake, at her old place at the breakfast table, but alone. It was very early too, not yet eight. There was this expedition—they were going to the Lighthouse, Mr. Ramsay, Cam, and James. They should have gone already—they had to catch the tide or something. And Cam was not ready and James was not ready and Nancy had forgotten to order the sandwiches and Mr. Ramsay had lost his temper and banged out of the room.

"What's the use of going now?" he had stormed.

Nancy had vanished. There he was, marching up and down the terrace in a rage. One seemed to hear doors slamming and voices calling all over the house. Now Nancy burst in, and asked, looking round the room, in a queer half dazed, half desperate way, "What does one send to the Lighthouse?" as if she were forcing herself to do what she despaired of ever being able to do.

What does one send to the Lighthouse indeed! At any other time Lily could have suggested reasonably tea, tobacco, newspapers. But this morning everything seemed so extraordinarily queer that a question like Nancy's—What does one send to the Lighthouse?—opened doors in one's mind that went banging and swinging to and fro and made one keep asking, in a stupefied gape, What does one send? What does one do? Why is one sitting here, after all?

Sitting alone (for Nancy went out again) among the clean cups at the long table, she felt cut off from other people, and able only to go on watching, asking, wondering. The house, the place, the morning, all seemed strangers to her. She had no attachment here, she felt, no relations with it, anything might happen, and whatever did happen, a step outside, a voice calling ("It's not in the cupboard; it's on the landing," some one cried), was a question, as if the link that usually bound things together had been cut, and they floated up here, down there, off, anyhow. How aimless it was, how chaotic, how unreal it was, she thought, looking at her empty coffee cup. Mrs. Ramsay dead; Andrew killed; Prue dead too—repeat it as she might, it roused no feeling in her. And we all get together in a house like this on a morning like this, she said, looking out of the window. It was a beautiful still day.

Suddenly Mr. Ramsay raised his head as he passed and looked straight at her, with his distraught wild gaze which was yet so penetrating, as if he saw you, for one second, for the first time, for ever; and she pretended to drink out of her empty coffee cup so as to escape him—to escape his demand on her, to put aside a moment longer that imperious need. And he shook his head at her, and strode on ("Alone" she heard him say, "Perished" she heard him say) and like everything else this strange morning the words became symbols, wrote themselves all over the grey-green walls. If only she could put them together, she felt, write them out in some sentence, then she would have got at the truth of things. Old Mr. Carmichael came padding softly in, fetched his coffee, took his cup and made off to sit in the sun. The extraordinary unreality was frightening; but it was also exciting. Going to the Lighthouse. But what does one send to the Lighthouse? Perished. Alone. The grey-green light on the wall opposite. The empty places. Such were some of the parts, but how bring them together? she asked. As if any interruption would break the frail shape she was building on the table she turned her back to the window lest Mr. Ramsay should see her. She must escape somewhere, be alone somewhere. Suddenly she remembered. When she had sat there last ten years ago there had been a little sprig or leaf pattern on the table-cloth, which she had looked at in a moment of revelation. There had been a problem about a foreground of a picture. Move the tree to the middle, she had said. She had never finished that picture. She would paint that picture now. It had been knocking about in her mind all these years. Where were her paints, she wondered? Her paints, yes. She had left them in the hall last night. She would start at once. She got up quickly, before Mr. Ramsay turned.

She fetched herself a chair. She pitched her easel with her precise old-maidish movements on the edge of the lawn, not too close to Mr. Carmichael, but close enough for his protection. Yes, it must have been precisely here that she had stood ten years ago. There was the wall; the hedge; the tree. The question was of some relation between those masses. She had borne it in her mind all these years. It seemed as if the solution had come to her: she knew now what she wanted to do.

But with Mr. Ramsay bearing down on her, she could do nothing. Every time he approached—he was walking up and down the terrace—ruin approached, chaos approached. She could not paint. She stooped, she turned; she took up this rag; she squeezed that tube. But all she did was to ward him off a moment. He made it impossible for her to do anything. For if she gave him the least chance, if he saw her disengaged a moment, looking his way a moment, he would be on her, saying, as he had said last night, "You find us much changed." Last night he had got up and stopped before her, and said that. Dumb and staring though they had all sat, the six children whom they used to call after the Kings and Queens of England—the Red, the Fair, the Wicked, the Ruthless—she felt how they raged under it. Kind old Mrs. Beckwith said something sensible. But it was a house full of unrelated passions—she had felt that all the evening. And on top of this chaos Mr. Ramsay got up, pressed her hand, and said: "You will find us much changed" and none of them had moved or had spoken; but had sat there as if they were forced to let him say it. Only James (certainly the Sullen) scowled at the lamp; and Cam screwed her handkerchief round her finger. Then he reminded them that they were going to the Lighthouse tomorrow. They must be ready, in the hall, on the stroke of half-past seven. Then, with his hand on the door, he stopped; he turned upon them. Did they not want to go? he demanded. Had they dared say No (he had some reason for wanting it) he would have flung himself tragically backwards into the bitter waters of despair. Such a gift he had for gesture. He looked like a king in exile. Doggedly James said yes. Cam stumbled more wretchedly. Yes, oh, yes, they'd both be ready, they said. And it struck her, this was tragedy—not palls, dust, and the shroud; but children coerced, their spirits subdued. James was sixteen, Cam, seventeen, perhaps. She had looked round for some one who was not there, for Mrs. Ramsay, presumably. But there was only kind Mrs. Beckwith turning over her sketches under the lamp. Then, being tired, her mind still rising and falling with the sea, the taste and smell that places have after long absence possessing her, the candles wavering in her eyes, she had lost herself and gone under. It was a wonderful night, starlit; the waves sounded as they went upstairs; the moon surprised them, enormous, pale, as they passed the staircase window. She had slept at once.

She set her clean canvas firmly upon the easel, as a barrier, frail, but she hoped sufficiently substantial to ward off Mr. Ramsay and his exactingness. She did her best to look, when his back was turned, at her picture; that line there, that mass there. But it was out of the question. Let him be fifty feet away, let him not even speak to you, let him not even see you, he permeated, he prevailed, he imposed himself. He changed everything. She could not see the colour; she could not see the lines; even with his back turned to her, she could only think, But he'll be down on me in a moment, demanding—something she felt she could not give him. She rejected one brush; she chose another. When would those children come? When would they all be off? she fidgeted. That man, she thought, her anger rising in her, never gave; that man took. She, on the other hand, would be forced to give. Mrs. Ramsay had given. Giving, giving, giving, she had died—and had left all this. Really, she was angry with Mrs. Ramsay. With the brush slightly trembling in her fingers she looked at the hedge, the step, the wall. It was all Mrs. Ramsay's doing. She was dead. Here was Lily, at forty-four, wasting her time, unable to do a thing, standing there, playing at painting, playing at the one thing one did not play at, and it was all Mrs. Ramsay's fault. She was dead. The step where she used to sit was empty. She was dead.

But why repeat this over and over again? Why be always trying to bring up some feeling she had not got? There was a kind

of blasphemy in it. It was all dry: all withered: all spent. They
ought not to have asked her; she ought not to have come. One
can't waste one's time at forty-four, she thought. She hated playing at painting. A brush, the one dependable thing in a world of
strife, ruin, chaos—that one should not play with, knowingly
even: she detested it. But he made her. You shan't touch your
canvas, he seemed to say, bearing down on her, till you've given
me what I want of you. Here he was, close upon her again,
greedy, distraught. Well, thought Lily in despair, letting her right
hand fall at her side, it would be simpler then to have it over.
Surely, she could imitate from recollection the glow, the rhapsody, the self-surrender, she had seen on so many women's faces
(on Mrs. Ramsay's, for instance) when on some occasion like
this they blazed up—she could remember the look on Mrs.
Ramsay's face—into a rapture of sympathy, of delight in the
reward they had, which, though the reason of it escaped her,
evidently conferred on them the most supreme bliss of which
human nature was capable. Here he was, stopped by her side.
She would give him what she could.

II

SHE SEEMED to have shrivelled slightly, he thought. She looked
a little skimpy, wispy; but not unattractive. He liked her. There
had been some talk of her marrying William Bankes once, but
nothing had come of it. His wife had been fond of her. He had
been a little out of temper too at breakfast. And then, and
then—this was one of those moments when an enormous need
urged him, without being conscious what it was, to approach
any woman, to force them, he did not care how, his need was
so great, to give him what he wanted: sympathy.

Was anybody looking after her? he said. Had she everything she wanted?

"Oh, thanks, everything," said Lily Briscoe nervously. No; she could not do it. She ought to have floated off instantly upon some wave of sympathetic expansion: the pressure on her was tremendous. But she remained stuck. There was an awful pause. They both looked at the sea. Why, thought Mr. Ramsay, should she look at the sea when I am here? She hoped it would be calm enough for them to land at the Lighthouse, she said. The Lighthouse! The Lighthouse! What's that got to do with it? he thought impatiently. Instantly, with the force of some primeval gust (for really he could not restrain himself any longer), there issued from him such a groan that any other woman in the whole world would have done something, said something—all except myself, thought Lily, girding at herself bitterly, who am not a woman, but a peevish, ill-tempered, dried-up old maid, presumably.

Mr. Ramsay sighed to the full. He waited. Was she not going to say anything? Did she not see what he wanted from her? Then he said he had a particular reason for wanting to go to the Lighthouse. His wife used to send the men things. There was a poor boy with a tuberculous hip, the lightkeeper's son. He sighed profoundly. He sighed significantly. All Lily wished was that this enormous flood of grief, this insatiable hunger for sympathy, this demand that she should surrender herself up to him entirely, and even so he had sorrows enough to keep her supplied for ever, should leave her, should be diverted (she kept looking at the house, hoping for an interruption) before it swept her down in its flow.

"Such expeditions," said Mr. Ramsay, scraping the ground with his toe, "are very painful." Still Lily said nothing. (She is a stock, she is a stone, he said to himself.) "They are very exhausting," he said, looking, with a sickly look that nauseated her (he

was acting, she felt, this great man was dramatising himself), at
his beautiful hands. It was horrible, it was indecent. Would they
never come, she asked, for she could not sustain this enormous
weight of sorrow, support these heavy draperies of grief (he had
assumed a pose of extreme decrepitude; he even tottered a little
as he stood there) a moment longer.

Still she could say nothing; the whole horizon seemed swept
bare of objects to talk about; could only feel, amazedly, as Mr.
Ramsay stood there, how his gaze seemed to fall dolefully over
the sunny grass and discolour it, and cast over the rubicund,
drowsy, entirely contented figure of Mr. Carmichael, reading a
French novel on a deck-chair, a veil of crape, as if such an existence, flaunting its prosperity in a world of woe, were enough
to provoke the most dismal thoughts of all. Look at him, he
seemed to be saying, look at me; and indeed, all the time he was
feeling, Think of me, think of me. Ah, could that bulk only be
wafted alongside of them, Lily wished; had she only pitched
her easel a yard or two closer to him; a man, any man, would
staunch this effusion, would stop these lamentations. A woman,
she had provoked this horror; a woman, she should have known
how to deal with it. It was immensely to her discredit, sexually,
to stand there dumb. One said—what did one say?—Oh, Mr.
Ramsay! Dear Mr. Ramsay! That was what that kind old lady
who sketched, Mrs. Beckwith, would have said instantly, and
rightly. But, no. They stood there, isolated from the rest of the
world. His immense self-pity, his demand for sympathy poured
and spread itself in pools at her feet, and all she did, miserable
sinner that she was, was to draw her skirts a little closer round
her ankles, lest she should get wet. In complete silence she
stood there, grasping her paint brush.

Heaven could never be sufficiently praised! She heard
sounds in the house. James and Cam must be coming. But Mr.
Ramsay, as if he knew that his time ran short, exerted upon her

solitary figure the immense pressure of his concentrated woe; his age; his frailty; his desolation; when suddenly, tossing his head impatiently, in his annoyance—for after all, what woman could resist him?—he noticed that his boot-laces were untied. Remarkable boots they were too, Lily thought, looking down at them: sculptured; colossal; like everything that Mr. Ramsay wore, from his frayed tie to his half-buttoned waistcoat, his own indisputably. She could see them walking to his room of their own accord, expressive in his absence of pathos, surliness, ill-temper, charm.

"What beautiful boots!" she exclaimed. She was ashamed of herself. To praise his boots when he asked her to solace his soul; when he had shown her his bleeding hands, his lacerated heart, and asked her to pity them, then to say, cheerfully, "Ah, but what beautiful boots you wear!" deserved, she knew, and she looked up expecting to get it, in one of his sudden roars of ill-temper, complete annihilation.

Instead, Mr. Ramsay smiled. His pall, his draperies, his infirmities fell from him. Ah, yes, he said, holding his foot up for her to look at, they were first-rate boots. There was only one man in England who could make boots like that. Boots are among the chief curses of mankind, he said. "Bootmakers make it their business," he exclaimed, "to cripple and torture the human foot." They are also the most obstinate and perverse of mankind. It had taken him the best part of his youth to get boots made as they should be made. He would have her observe (he lifted his right foot and then his left) that she had never seen boots made quite that shape before. They were made of the finest leather in the world, also. Most leather was mere brown paper and cardboard. He looked complacently at his foot, still held in the air. They had reached, she felt, a sunny island where peace dwelt, sanity reigned and the sun for ever shone, the blessed island of good boots. Her heart warmed to him. "Now

let me see if you can tie a knot," he said. He poohpoohed her
feeble system. He showed her his own invention. Once you tied
it, it never came undone. Three times he knotted her shoe; three
times he unknotted it.

Why, at this completely inappropriate moment, when he
was stooping over her shoe, should she be so tormented with
sympathy for him that, as she stooped too, the blood rushed to
her face, and, thinking of her callousness (she had called him
a play-actor) she felt her eyes swell and tingle with tears? Thus
occupied he seemed to her a figure of infinite pathos. He tied
knots. He bought boots. There was no helping Mr. Ramsay
on the journey he was going. But now just as she wished to
say something, could have said something, perhaps, here they
were—Cam and James. They appeared on the terrace. They
came, lagging, side by side, a serious, melancholy couple.

But why was it like *that* that they came? She could not help
feeling annoyed with them; they might have come more cheerfully; they might have given him what, now that they were off,
she would not have the chance of giving him. For she felt a sudden emptiness; a frustration. Her feeling had come too late;
there it was ready; but he no longer needed it. He had become
a very distinguished, elderly man, who had no need of her whatsoever. She felt snubbed. He slung a knapsack round his shoulders. He shared out the parcels—there were a number of them,
ill tied in brown paper. He sent Cam for a cloak. He had all the
appearance of a leader making ready for an expedition. Then,
wheeling about, he led the way with his firm military tread, in
those wonderful boots, carrying brown paper parcels, down the
path, his children following him. They looked, she thought, as
if fate had devoted them to some stern enterprise, and they
went to it, still young enough to be drawn acquiescent in their
father's wake, obediently, but with a pallor in their eyes which
made her feel that they suffered something beyond their years

in silence. So they passed the edge of the lawn, and it seemed to Lily that she watched a procession go, drawn on by some stress of common feeling which made it, faltering and flagging as it was, a little company bound together and strangely impressive to her. Politely, but very distantly, Mr. Ramsay raised his hand and saluted her as they passed.

But what a face, she thought, immediately finding the sympathy which she had not been asked to give troubling her for expression. What had made it like that? Thinking, night after night, she supposed—about the reality of kitchen tables, she added, remembering the symbol which in her vagueness as to what Mr. Ramsay did think about Andrew had given her. (He had been killed by the splinter of a shell instantly, she bethought her.) The kitchen table was something visionary, austere; something bare, hard, not ornamental. There was no colour to it; it was all edges and angles; it was uncompromisingly plain. But Mr. Ramsay kept always his eyes fixed upon it, never allowed himself to be distracted or deluded, until his face became worn too and ascetic and partook of this unornamented beauty which so deeply impressed her. Then, she recalled (standing where he had left her, holding her brush), worries had fretted it—not so nobly. He must have had his doubts about that table, she supposed; whether the table was a real table; whether it was worth the time he gave to it; whether he was able after all to find it. He had had doubts, she felt, or he would have asked less of people. That was what they talked about late at night sometimes, she suspected; and then next day Mrs. Ramsay looked tired, and Lily flew into a rage with him over some absurd little thing. But now he had nobody to talk to about that table, or his boots, or his knots; and he was like a lion seeking whom he could devour, and his face had that touch of desperation, of exaggeration in it which alarmed her, and made her pull her skirts about her. And then, she recalled, there was that sudden revivification, that sudden flare (when she praised his boots), that sudden recovery of vitality and interest in ordinary human things, which too passed and changed (for he was always changing, and hid nothing) into that other final phase which was new to her and had, she owned, made herself ashamed of her own irritability, when it seemed as if he had shed worries and ambitions, and the hope of sympathy and the desire for praise, had entered some other region, was drawn on, as if by curiosity, in dumb colloquy, whether with himself or another, at the head of that little procession out of one's range. An extraordinary face! The gate banged.

III

SO THEY'RE GONE, she thought, sighing with relief and disappointment. Her sympathy seemed to be cast back on her, like a bramble sprung across her face. She felt curiously divided, as if one part of her were drawn out there—it was a still day, hazy; the Lighthouse looked this morning at an immense distance; the other had fixed itself doggedly, solidly, here on the lawn. She saw her canvas as if it had floated up and placed itself white and uncompromising directly before her. It seemed to rebuke her with its cold stare for all this hurry and agitation; this folly and waste of emotion; it drastically recalled her and spread through her mind first a peace, as her disorderly sensations (he had gone and she had been so sorry for him and she had said nothing) trooped off the field; and then, emptiness. She looked blankly at the canvas, with its uncompromising white stare; from the canvas to the garden. There was something (she stood screwing up her little Chinese eyes in her small puckered face), something she remembered in the relations of those lines cutting across, slicing down, and in the mass of the hedge with its green cave of blues and browns, which had stayed in her mind; which had tied a knot in her mind so that at odds and ends of time, involuntarily, as she walked along the Brompton Road, as she brushed her hair, she found herself painting that picture, passing her eye over it, and untying the knot in imagination. But there was all the difference in the world between this planning airily away from the canvas, and actually taking her brush and making the first mark.

She had taken the wrong brush in her agitation at Mr. Ramsay's presence, and her easel, rammed into the earth so nervously, was at the wrong angle. And now that she had put that right, and in so doing had subdued the impertinences and irrelevances that plucked her attention and made her remember how she was such and such a person, had such and such relations to people, she took her hand and raised her brush. For a moment it stayed trembling in a painful but exciting ecstasy in the air. Where to begin?—that was the question at what point to make the first mark? One line placed on the canvas committed her to innumerable risks, to frequent and irrevocable decisions. All that in idea seemed simple became in practice immediately complex; as the waves shape themselves symmetrically from the cliff top, but to the swimmer among them are divided by steep gulfs, and foaming crests. Still the risk must be run; the mark made.

With a curious physical sensation, as if she were urged forward and at the same time must hold herself back, she made her first quick decisive stroke. The brush descended. It flickered brown over the white canvas; it left a running mark. A second time she did it—a third time. And so pausing and so flickering, she attained a dancing rhythmical movement, as if the pauses were one part of the rhythm and the strokes another, and all were related; and so, lightly and swiftly pausing, striking, she scored her canvas with brown running nervous lines which had no sooner settled there than they enclosed (she felt it looming out at her) a space. Down in the hollow of one wave she saw the next wave towering higher and higher above her. For what could be more formidable than that space? Here she was again, she thought, stepping back to look at it, drawn out of gossip, out of living, out of community with people into the presence of this formidable ancient enemy of hers—this other thing, this truth, this reality, which suddenly laid hands on her, emerged stark at the back of appearances and commanded her attention. She was half unwilling, half reluctant. Why always be drawn out and haled away? Why not left in peace, to talk to Mr. Carmichael on the lawn? It was an exacting form of intercourse anyhow. Other worshipful objects were content with worship; men, women, God, all let one kneel prostrate; but this form, were it only the shape of a white lamp-shade looming on a wicker table, roused one to perpetual combat, challenged one to a fight in which one was bound to be worsted. Always (it was in her nature, or in her sex, she did not know which) before she exchanged the fluidity of life for the concentration of painting she had a few moments of nakedness when she seemed like an unborn soul, a soul reft of body, hesitating on some windy pinnacle and exposed without protection to all the blasts of doubt. Why then did she do it? She looked at the canvas, lightly scored with running lines. It would be hung in the servants' bedrooms. It would be rolled up and stuffed under a sofa. What was the good of doing it then, and she heard some voice saying she couldn't paint, saying she couldn't create, as if she were caught up in one of those habitual currents in which after a certain time experience forms in the mind, so that one repeats words without being aware any longer who originally spoke them.

Can't paint, can't write, she murmured monotonously, anxiously considering what her plan of attack should be. For the mass loomed before her; it protruded; she felt it pressing on her eyeballs. Then, as if some juice necessary for the lubrication of her faculties were spontaneously squirted, she began precariously dipping among the blues and umbers, moving her brush hither and thither, but it was now heavier and went slower, as if it had fallen in with some rhythm which was dictated to her (she kept looking at the hedge, at the canvas) by what she saw, so that while her hand quivered with life, this rhythm was strong enough to bear her along with it on its current. Certainly she was losing consciousness of outer things. And as she lost consciousness of outer things, and her name and her personality and her appearance, and whether Mr. Carmichael was there or not, her mind kept throwing up from its depths, scenes, and names, and sayings, and memories and ideas, like a fountain spurting over that glaring, hideously difficult white space, while she modelled it with greens and blues.

Charles Tansley used to say that, she remembered, women can't paint, can't write. Coming up behind her, he had stood close beside her, a thing she hated, as she painted here on this very spot. "Shag tobacco," he said, "fivepence an ounce," parading his poverty, his principles. (But the war had drawn the sting of her femininity. Poor devils, one thought, poor devils, of both sexes.) He was always carrying a book about under his arm—a purple book. He "worked." He sat, she remembered, working in a blaze of sun. At dinner he would sit right in the middle of the view. But after all, she reflected, there was the scene on the beach. One must remember that. It was a windy morning. They had all gone down to the beach. Mrs. Ramsay sat down and wrote letters by a rock. She wrote and wrote. "Oh," she said, looking up at something floating in the sea, "is it a lobster pot? Is it an upturned boat?" She was so short-sighted that she could not see, and then Charles Tansley became as nice as he could possibly be. He began playing ducks and drakes. They chose little flat black stones and sent them skipping over the waves.

Every now and then Mrs. Ramsay looked up over her spectacles and laughed at them. What they said she could not remember, but only she and Charles throwing stones and getting on very well all of a sudden and Mrs. Ramsay watching them. She was highly conscious of that. Mrs. Ramsay, she thought, stepping back and screwing up her eyes. (It must have altered the design a good deal when she was sitting on the step with James. There must have been a shadow.) When she thought of herself and Charles throwing ducks and drakes and of the whole scene on the beach, it seemed to depend somehow upon Mrs. Ramsay sitting under the rock, with a pad on her knee, writing letters. (She wrote innumerable letters, and sometimes the wind took them and she and Charles just saved a page from the sea.) But what a power was in the human soul! she thought. That woman sitting there writing under the rock resolved everything into simplicity; made these angers, irritations fall off like old rags; she brought together this and that and then this, and so made out of that miserable silliness and spite (she and Charles squabbling, sparring, had been silly and spiteful) something—this scene on the beach for example, this moment of friendship and liking—which survived, after all these years complete, so that she dipped into it to re-fashion her memory of him, and there it stayed in the mind affecting one almost like a work of art.

"Like a work of art," she repeated, looking from her canvas to the drawing-room steps and back again. She must rest for a moment. And, resting, looking from one to the other vaguely, the old question which traversed the sky of the soul perpetually, the vast, the general question which was apt to particularise itself at such moments as these, when she released faculties that had been on the strain, stood over her, paused over her, darkened over her. What is the meaning of life? That was all—a simple question; one that tended to close in on one with years. The great revelation had never come. The great revelation per-

haps never did come. Instead there were little daily miracles, il-
luminations, matches struck unexpectedly in the dark; here was
one. This, that, and the other; herself and Charles Tansley and
the breaking wave; Mrs. Ramsay bringing them together; Mrs.
Ramsay saying, "Life stand still here"; Mrs. Ramsay making of
the moment something permanent (as in another sphere Lily
herself tried to make of the moment something permanent)—
this was of the nature of a revelation. In the midst of chaos
there was shape; this eternal passing and flowing (she looked at
the clouds going and the leaves shaking) was struck into stability. Life stand still here, Mrs. Ramsay said. "Mrs. Ramsay! Mrs.
Ramsay!" she repeated. She owed it all to her.

All was silence. Nobody seemed yet to be stirring in the
house. She looked at it there sleeping in the early sunlight with
its windows green and blue with the reflected leaves. The faint
thought she was thinking of Mrs. Ramsay seemed in conso-
nance with this quiet house; this smoke; this fine early morning
air. Faint and unreal, it was amazingly pure and exciting. She
hoped nobody would open the window or come out of the
house, but that she might be left alone to go on thinking, to go
on painting. She turned to her canvas. But impelled by some curiosity, driven by the discomfort of the sympathy which she held
undischarged, she walked a pace or so to the end of the lawn to
see whether, down there on the beach, she could see that little
company setting sail. Down there among the little boats which
floated, some with their sails furled, some slowly, for it was very
calm moving away, there was one rather apart from the others.
The sail was even now being hoisted. She decided that there in
that very distant and entirely silent little boat Mr. Ramsay was
sitting with Cam and James. Now they had got the sail up; now
after a little flagging and hesitation the sails filled and, shrouded
in profound silence, she watched the boat take its way with de-
liberation past the other boats out to sea.

IV

THE SAILS flapped over their heads. The water chuckled and slapped the sides of the boat, which drowsed motionless in the sun. Now and then the sails rippled with a little breeze in them, but the ripple ran over them and ceased. The boat made no motion at all. Mr. Ramsay sat in the middle of the boat. He would be impatient in a moment, James thought, and Cam thought, looking at her father, who sat in the middle of the boat between them (James steered; Cam sat alone in the bow) with his legs tightly curled. He hated hanging about. Sure enough, after fidgeting a second or two, he said something sharp to Macalister's boy, who got out his oars and began to row. But their father, they knew, would never be content until they were flying along. He would keep looking for a breeze, fidgeting, saying things under his breath, which Macalister and Macalister's boy would overhear, and they would both be made horribly uncomfortable. He had made them come. He had forced them to come. In their anger they hoped that the breeze would never rise, that he might be thwarted in every possible way, since he had forced them to come against their wills.

All the way down to the beach they had lagged behind together, though he bade them "Walk up, walk up," without speaking. Their heads were bent down, their heads were pressed down by some remorseless gale. Speak to him they could not. They must come; they must follow. They must walk behind him carrying brown paper parcels. But they vowed, in silence, as they walked, to stand by each other and carry out the great compact—to resist tyranny to the death. So there they would sit, one at one end of the boat, one at the other, in silence. They would say nothing, only look at him now and then where he sat with his legs twisted, frowning and fidgeting, and pishing and pshawing and muttering things to himself, and waiting impatiently for a breeze. And they hoped it would be calm. They hoped he would be thwarted. They hoped the whole expedition would fail, and they would have to put back, with their parcels, to the beach.

But now, when Macalister's boy had rowed a little way out, the sails slowly swung round, the boat quickened itself, flattened itself, and shot off. Instantly, as if some great strain had been relieved, Mr. Ramsay uncurled his legs, took out his tobacco pouch, handed it with a little grunt to Macalister, and felt, they knew, for all they suffered, perfectly content. Now they would sail on for hours like this, and Mr. Ramsay would ask old Macalister a question—about the great storm last winter probably—and old Macalister would answer it, and they would puff their pipes together, and Macalister would take a tarry rope in his fingers, tying or untying some knot, and the boy would fish, and never say a word to any one. James would be forced to keep his eye all the time on the sail. For if he forgot, then the sail puckered and shivered, and the boat slackened, and Mr. Ramsay would say sharply, "Look out! Look out!" and old Macalister would turn slowly on his seat. So they heard Mr. Ramsay asking some question about the great storm at Christmas. "She comes driving round the point," old Macalister said, describing the great storm last Christmas, when ten ships had been driven into the bay for shelter, and he had seen "one there, one there, one there" (he pointed slowly round the bay. Mr. Ramsay followed him, turning his head). He had seen four men clinging to the mast. Then she was gone. "And at last we shoved her off," he went on (but in their anger and their silence they only caught a word here and there, sitting at opposite ends of the boat, united by their compact to fight tyranny to the death). At last they had shoved her off, they had launched the lifeboat, and they had got her out past the point—Macalister told the story; and though they only caught a word here and there, they were conscious all the time of their father—how he leant forward, how he brought his voice into tune with Macalister's voice; how, puffing at his pipe, and looking there and there where Macalister pointed, he relished the thought of the storm and the dark night and the fishermen striving there. He liked that men should labour and sweat on the windy beach at night; pitting muscle and brain against the waves and the wind; he liked men to work like that, and women to keep house, and sit beside sleeping children indoors, while men were drowned, out there in a storm. So James could tell, so Cam could tell (they looked at him, they looked at each other), from his toss and his vigilance and the ring in his voice, and the little tinge of Scottish accent which came into his voice, making him seem like a peasant himself, as he questioned Macalister about the eleven ships that had been driven into the bay in a storm. Three had sunk.

He looked proudly where Macalister pointed; and Cam thought, feeling proud of him without knowing quite why, had he been there he would have launched the lifeboat, he would have reached the wreck, Cam thought. He was so brave, he was so adventurous, Cam thought. But she remembered. There was the compact; to resist tyranny to the death. Their grievance weighed them down. They had been forced; they had been bidden. He had borne them down once more with his gloom and his authority, making them do his bidding, on this fine morning, come, because he wished it, carrying these parcels, to the Lighthouse; take part in these rites he went through for his own pleasure in memory of dead people, which they hated, so that they lagged after him, and all the pleasure of the day was spoilt.

Yes, the breeze was freshening. The boat was leaning, the water was sliced sharply and fell away in green cascades, in bubbles, in cataracts. Cam looked down into the foam, into the sea with all its treasure in it, and its speed hypnotised her, and the tie between her and James sagged a little. It slackened a little. She began to think, How fast it goes. Where are we going? and the movement hypnotised her, while James, with his eye fixed on the sail and on the horizon, steered grimly. But he began to think as he steered that he might escape; he might be quit of it all. They might land somewhere; and be free then. Both of them, looking at each other for a moment, had a sense of escape and exaltation, what with the speed and the change. But the breeze bred in Mr. Ramsay too the same excitement, and, as old Macalister turned to fling his line overboard, he cried out aloud.

"We perished," and then again, "each alone." And then with his usual spasm of repentance or shyness, pulled himself up, and waved his hand towards the shore.

"See the little house," he said pointing, wishing Cam to look. She raised herself reluctantly and looked. But which was it? She could no longer make out, there on the hillside, which was their house. All looked distant and peaceful and strange. The shore seemed refined, far away, unreal. Already the little distance they had sailed had put them far from it and given it the changed look, the composed look, of something receding in which one has no longer any part. Which was their house? She could not see it.

"But I beneath a rougher sea," Mr. Ramsay murmured. He had found the house and so seeing it, he had also seen himself there; he had seen himself walking on the terrace, alone. He was walking up and down between the urns; and he seemed to himself very old and bowed. Sitting in the boat, he bowed, he crouched himself, acting instantly his part—the part of a desolate man, widowed, bereft; and so called up before him in hosts people sympathising with him; staged for himself as he sat in the boat, a little drama; which required of him decrepitude and exhaustion and sorrow (he raised his hands and looked at the thinness of them, to confirm his dream) and then there was given him in abundance women's sympathy, and he imagined how they would soothe him and sympathise with him, and so getting in his dream some reflection of the exquisite pleasure women's sympathy was to him, he sighed and said gently and mournfully,

> But I beneath a rougher sea
> Was whelmed in deeper gulfs than he,

so that the mournful words were heard quite clearly by them all. Cam half started on her seat. It shocked her—it outraged her. The movement roused her father; and he shuddered, and broke off, exclaiming: "Look! Look!" so urgently that James also turned his head to look over his shoulder at the island. They all looked. They looked at the island.

But Cam could see nothing. She was thinking how all those paths and the lawn, thick and knotted with the lives they had lived there, were gone: were rubbed out; were past; were unreal, and now this was real; the boat and the sail with its patch; Macalister with his earrings; the noise of the waves—all this was real. Thinking this, she was murmuring to herself, "We perished, each alone," for her father's words broke and broke again in her mind, when her father, seeing her gazing so vaguely, began to tease her. Didn't she know the points of the compass? he asked. Didn't she know the North from the South? Did she really think they lived right out there? And he pointed again, and showed her where their house was, there, by those trees. He wished she would try to be more accurate, he said: "Tell me— which is East, which is West?" he said, half laughing at her, half scolding her, for he could not understand the state of mind of any one, not absolutely imbecile, who did not know the points of the compass. Yet she did not know. And seeing her gazing, with her vague, now rather frightened, eyes fixed where no house was Mr. Ramsay forgot his dream; how he walked up and down between the urns on the terrace; how the arms were stretched out to him. He thought, women are always like that; the vagueness of their minds is hopeless; it was a thing he had never been able to understand; but so it was. It had been so with her—his wife. They could not keep anything clearly fixed in their minds. But he had been wrong to be angry with her; moreover, did he not rather like this vagueness in women? It was part of their extraordinary charm. I will make her smile at me, he thought. She looks frightened. She was so silent. He clutched his fingers, and determined that his voice and his face and all the quick expressive gestures which had been at his command making people pity him and praise him all these years should subdue themselves. He would make her smile at him. He would find some simple easy thing to say to her. But what? For, wrapped up in his work as he was, he forgot the sort of thing one said. There was a puppy. They had a puppy. Who was looking after the puppy today? he asked. Yes, thought James pitilessly, seeing his sister's head against the sail, now she will give way. I shall be left to fight the tyrant alone. The compact would be left to him to carry out. Cam would never resist tyranny to the death, he thought grimly, watching her face, sad, sulky, yielding. And as sometimes happens when a cloud falls on a green hillside and gravity descends and there among all the surrounding hills is gloom and sorrow, and it seems as if the hills themselves must ponder the fate of the clouded, the darkened, either in pity, or maliciously rejoicing in her dismay: so Cam now felt herself overcast, as she sat there among calm, resolute people and wondered how to answer her father about the puppy; how to resist his entreaty—forgive me, care for me; while James the lawgiver, with the tablets of eternal wisdom laid open on his knee (his hand on the tiller had become symbolical to her), said, Resist him. Fight him. He said so rightly; justly. For they must fight tyranny to the death, she thought. Of all human qualities she reverenced justice most. Her brother was most god-like, her father most suppliant. And to which did she yield, she thought, sitting between them, gazing at the shore whose points were all unknown to her, and thinking how the lawn and the terrace and the house were smoothed away now and peace dwelt there.

"Jasper," she said sullenly. He'd look after the puppy.

And what was she going to call him? her father persisted. He had had a dog when he was a little boy, called Frisk. She'll give way, James thought, as he watched a look come upon her face, a look he remembered. They look down, he thought, at their knitting or something. Then suddenly they look up. There was a flash of blue, he remembered, and then somebody sitting with him laughed, surrendered, and he was very angry. It must have been his mother, he thought, sitting on a low chair, with his father standing over her. He began to search among the infinite series of impressions which time had laid down, leaf upon leaf, fold upon fold softly, incessantly upon his brain; among scents, sounds; voices, harsh, hollow, sweet; and lights passing, and brooms tapping; and the wash and hush of the sea, how a man had marched up and down and stopped dead, upright, over them. Meanwhile, he noticed, Cam dabbled her fingers in the water, and stared at the shore and said nothing. No, she won't give way, he thought; she's different, he thought. Well, if Cam would not answer him, he would not bother her, Mr. Ramsay decided, feeling in his pocket for a book. But she would answer him; she wished, passionately, to move some obstacle that lay upon her tongue and to say, Oh, yes, Frisk. I'll call him Frisk. She wanted even to say, Was that the dog that found its way over the moor alone? But try as she might, she could think of nothing to say like that, fierce and loyal to the compact, yet passing on to her father, unsuspected by James, a private token of the love she felt for him. For she thought, dabbling her hand (and now Macalister's boy had caught a mackerel, and it lay kicking on the floor, with blood on its gills) for she thought, looking at James who kept his eyes dispassionately on the sail, or glanced now and then for a second at the horizon, you're not exposed to it, to this pressure and division of feeling, this extraordinary temptation. Her father was feeling in his pockets; in another second, he would have found his book. For no one attracted her more; his hands were beautiful, and his feet, and his voice, and his words, and his haste, and his temper, and his oddity, and his passion, and his saying straight out before every one, we perish, each alone, and his remoteness. (He had opened his book.) But what remained intolerable, she thought, sitting upright, and watching Macalister's boy tug the hook out of the gills of another fish, was that crass blindness and tyranny of his which had poisoned her childhood and raised bitter storms, so that even now she woke in the night trembling with rage and remembered some command of his; some insolence: "Do this," "Do that," his dominance: his "Submit to me."

So she said nothing, but looked doggedly and sadly at the shore, wrapped in its mantle of peace; as if the people there had fallen asleep, she thought; were free like smoke, were free to come and go like ghosts. They have no suffering there, she thought.

V

YES, THAT is their boat, Lily Briscoe decided, standing on the edge of the lawn. It was the boat with greyish-brown sails, which she saw now flatten itself upon the water and shoot off across the bay. There he sits, she thought, and the children are quite silent still. And she could not reach him either. The sympathy she had not given him weighed her down. It made it difficult for her to paint.

She had always found him difficult. She never had been able to praise him to his face, she remembered. And that reduced their relationship to something neutral, without that element of sex in it which made his manner to Minta so gallant, almost gay. He would pick a flower for her, lend her his books. But could he believe that Minta read them? She dragged them about the garden, sticking in leaves to mark the place.

"D'you remember, Mr. Carmichael?" she was inclined to ask, looking at the old man. But he had pulled his hat half over his forehead; he was asleep, or he was dreaming, or he was lying there catching words, she supposed.

"D'you remember?" she felt inclined to ask him as she passed him, thinking again of Mrs. Ramsay on the beach; the cask bobbing up and down; and the pages flying. Why, after all these years had that survived, ringed round, lit up, visible to the last detail, with all before it blank and all after it blank, for miles and miles?

"Is it a boat? Is it a cork?" she would say, Lily repeated, turning back, reluctantly again, to her canvas. Heaven be praised for it, the problem of space remained, she thought, taking up her brush again. It glared at her. The whole mass of the picture was poised upon that weight. Beautiful and bright it should be on the surface, feathery and evanescent, one colour melting into another like the colours on a butterfly's wing; but beneath the fabric must be clamped together with bolts of iron. It was to be a thing you could ruffle with your breath; and a thing you could not dislodge with a team of horses. And she began to lay on a red, a grey, and she began to model her way into the hollow there. At the same time, she seemed to be sitting beside Mrs. Ramsay on the beach.

"Is it a boat? Is it a cask?" Mrs. Ramsay said. And she began hunting round for her spectacles. And she sat, having found them, silent, looking out to sea. And Lily, painting steadily, felt as if a door had opened, and one went in and stood gazing silently about in a high cathedral-like place, very dark, very solemn. Shouts came from a world far away. Steamers vanished in stalks of smoke on the horizon. Charles threw stones and sent them skipping.

Mrs. Ramsay sat silent. She was glad, Lily thought, to rest in silence, uncommunicative; to rest in the extreme obscurity of human relationships. Who knows what we are, what we feel? Who knows even at the moment of intimacy, This is knowledge? Aren't things spoilt then, Mrs. Ramsay may have asked (it seemed to have happened so often, this silence by her side) by saying them? Aren't we more expressive thus? The moment at least seemed extraordinarily fertile. She rammed a little hole in the sand and covered it up, by way of burying in it the perfection of the moment. It was like a drop of silver in which one dipped and illumined the darkness of the past.

Lily stepped back to get her canvas—so—into perspective. It was an odd road to be walking, this of painting. Out and out one went, further and further, until at last one seemed to be on a narrow plank, perfectly alone, over the sea. And as she dipped into the blue paint, she dipped too into the past there. Now Mrs. Ramsay got up, she remembered. It was time to go back to the house—time for luncheon. And they all walked up from the beach together, she walking behind with William Bankes, and there was Minta in front of them with a hole in her stocking. How that little round hole of pink heel seemed to flaunt itself before them! How William Bankes deplored it, without, so far as she could remember, saying anything about it! It meant to him the annihilation of womanhood, and dirt and disorder, and servants leaving and beds not made at mid-day—all the things he

most abhorred. He had a way of shuddering and spreading his
fingers out as if to cover an unsightly object which he did
now—holding his hand in front of him. And Minta walked on
ahead, and presumably Paul met her and she went off with Paul
in the garden.

The Rayleys, thought Lily Briscoe, squeezing her tube of
green paint. She collected her impressions of the Rayleys. Their
lives appeared to her in a series of scenes; one, on the staircase
at dawn. Paul had come in and gone to bed early; Minta was late.
There was Minta, wreathed, tinted, garish on the stairs about
three o'clock in the morning. Paul came out in his pyjamas carrying a poker in case of burglars. Minta was eating a sandwich,
standing half-way up by a window, in the cadaverous early
morning light, and the carpet had a hole in it. But what did they
say? Lily asked herself, as if by looking she could hear them.
Minta went on eating her sandwich, annoyingly, while he spoke
something violent, abusing her, in a mutter so as not to wake
the children, the two little boys. He was withered, drawn; she
flamboyant, careless. For things had worked loose after the first
year or so; the marriage had turned out rather badly.

And this, Lily thought, taking the green paint on her brush,
this making up scenes about them, is what we call "knowing"
people, "thinking" of them, "being fond" of them! Not a word
of it was true; she had made it up; but it was what she knew
them by all the same. She went on tunnelling her way into her
picture, into the past.

Another time, Paul said he "played chess in coffee-houses."
She had built up a whole structure of imagination on that saying too. She remembered how, as he said it, she thought how he
rang up the servant, and she said, "Mrs. Rayley's out, sir," and
he decided that he would not come home either. She saw him
sitting in the corner of some lugubrious place where the smoke
attached itself to the red plush seats, and the waitresses got to

know you, and he played chess with a little man who was in the tea trade and lived at Surbiton, but that was all Paul knew about him. And then Minta was out when he came home and then there was that scene on the stairs, when he got the poker in case of burglars (no doubt to frighten her too) and spoke so bitterly, saying she had ruined his life. At any rate when she went down to see them at a cottage near Rickmansworth, things were horribly strained. Paul took her down the garden to look at the Belgian hares which he bred, and Minta followed them, singing, and put her bare arm on his shoulder, lest he should tell her anything.

Minta was bored by hares, Lily thought. But Minta never gave herself away. She never said things like that about playing chess in coffee-houses. She was far too conscious, far too wary. But to go on with their story—they had got through the dangerous stage by now. She had been staying with them last summer some time and the car broke down and Minta had to hand him his tools. He sat on the road mending the car, and it was the way she gave him the tools—business-like, straightforward, friendly—that proved it was all right now. They were "in love" no longer; no, he had taken up with another woman, a serious woman, with her hair in a plait and a case in her hand (Minta had described her gratefully, almost admiringly), who went to meetings and shared Paul's views (they had got more and more pronounced) about the taxation of land values and a capital levy. Far from breaking up the marriage, that alliance had righted it. They were excellent friends, obviously, as he sat on the road and she handed him his tools.

So that was the story of the Rayleys, Lily thought. She imagined herself telling it to Mrs. Ramsay, who would be full of curiosity to know what had become of the Rayleys. She would feel a little triumphant, telling Mrs. Ramsay that the marriage had not been a success.

But the dead, thought Lily, encountering some obstacle in her design which made her pause and ponder, stepping back a foot or so, oh, the dead! she murmured, one pitied them, one brushed them aside, one had even a little contempt for them. They are at our mercy. Mrs. Ramsay has faded and gone, she thought. We can over-ride her wishes, improve away her limited, old-fashioned ideas. She recedes further and further from us. Mockingly she seemed to see her there at the end of the corridor of years saying, of all incongruous things, "Marry, marry!" (sitting very upright early in the morning with the birds beginning to cheep in the garden outside). And one would have to say to her, It has all gone against your wishes. They're happy like that; I'm happy like this. Life has changed completely. At that all her being, even her beauty, became for a moment, dusty and out of date. For a moment Lily, standing there, with the sun hot on her back, summing up the Rayleys, triumphed over Mrs. Ramsay, who would never know how Paul went to coffeehouses and had a mistress; how he sat on the ground and Minta handed him his tools; how she stood here painting, had never married, not even William Bankes.

Mrs. Ramsay had planned it. Perhaps, had she lived, she would have compelled it. Already that summer he was "the kindest of men." He was "the first scientist of his age, my husband says." He was also "poor William—it makes me so unhappy, when I go to see him, to find nothing nice in his house—no one to arrange the flowers." So they were sent for walks together, and she was told, with that faint touch of irony that made Mrs. Ramsay slip through one's fingers, that she had a scientific mind; she liked flowers; she was so exact. What was this mania of hers for marriage? Lily wondered, stepping to and fro from her easel.

(Suddenly, as suddenly as a star slides in the sky, a reddish light seemed to burn in her mind, covering Paul Rayley, issuing from him. It rose like a fire sent up in token of some celebration by savages on a distant beach. She heard the roar and the crackle. The whole sea for miles round ran red and gold. Some winey smell mixed with it and intoxicated her, for she felt again her own headlong desire to throw herself off the cliff and be drowned looking for a pearl brooch on a beach. And the roar and the crackle repelled her with fear and disgust, as if while she saw its splendour and power she saw too how it fed on the treasure of the house, greedily, disgustingly, and she loathed it. But for a sight, for a glory it surpassed everything in her experience, and burnt year after year like a signal fire on a desert island at the edge of the sea, and one had only to say "in love" and instantly, as happened now, up rose Paul's fire again. And it sank and she said to herself, laughing, "The Rayleys"; how Paul went to coffee-houses and played chess.)

She had only escaped by the skin of her teeth though, she thought. She had been looking at the table-cloth, and it had flashed upon her that she would move the tree to the middle, and need never marry anybody, and she had felt an enormous exultation. She had felt, now she could stand up to Mrs. Ramsay—a tribute to the astonishing power that Mrs. Ramsay had over one. Do this, she said, and one did it. Even her shadow at the window with James was full of authority. She remembered how William Bankes had been shocked by her neglect of the significance of mother and son. Did she not admire their beauty? he said. But William, she remembered, had listened to her with his wise child's eyes when she explained how it was not irreverence: how a light there needed a shadow there and so on. She did not intend to disparage a subject which, they agreed, Raphael had treated divinely. She was not cynical. Quite the contrary. Thanks to his scientific mind he understood—a proof of disinterested intelligence which had pleased her and comforted her enormously. One could talk of painting then seriously to a man.

Indeed, his friendship had been one of the pleasures of her life. She loved William Bankes.

They went to Hampton Court and he always left her, like the perfect gentleman he was, plenty of time to wash her hands, while he strolled by the river. That was typical of their relationship. Many things were left unsaid. Then they strolled through the courtyards, and admired, summer after summer, the proportions and the flowers, and he would tell her things, about perspective, about architecture, as they walked, and he would stop to look at a tree, or the view over the lake, and admire a child— (it was his great grief—he had no daughter) in the vague aloof way that was natural to a man who spent so much time in laboratories that the world when he came out seemed to dazzle him, so that he walked slowly, lifted his hand to screen his eyes and paused, with his head thrown back, merely to breathe the air. Then he would tell her how his housekeeper was on her holiday; he must buy a new carpet for the staircase. Perhaps she would go with him to buy a new carpet for the staircase. And once something led him to talk about the Ramsays and he had said how when he first saw her she had been wearing a grey hat; she was not more than nineteen or twenty. She was astonishingly beautiful. There he stood looking down the avenue at Hampton Court as if he could see her there among the fountains.

She looked now at the drawing-room step. She saw, through William's eyes, the shape of a woman, peaceful and silent, with downcast eyes. She sat musing, pondering (she was in grey that day, Lily thought). Her eyes were bent. She would never lift them. Yes, thought Lily, looking intently, I must have seen her look like that, but not in grey; nor so still, nor so young, nor so peaceful. The figure came readily enough. She was astonishingly beautiful, as William said. But beauty was not everything. Beauty had this penalty—it came too readily, came too completely. It stilled life—froze it. One forgot the little agitations; the flush, the pallor, some queer distortion, some light or shadow, which made the face unrecognisable for a moment and yet added a quality one saw for ever after. It was simpler to smooth that all out under the cover of beauty. But what was the look she had, Lily wondered, when she clapped her deer-stalker's hat on her head, or ran across the grass, or scolded Kennedy, the gardener? Who could tell her? Who could help her?

Against her will she had come to the surface, and found herself half out of the picture, looking, a little dazedly, as if at unreal things, at Mr. Carmichael. He lay on his chair with his hands clasped above his paunch not reading, or sleeping, but basking like a creature gorged with existence. His book had fallen on to the grass.

She wanted to go straight up to him and say, "Mr. Carmichael!" Then he would look up benevolently as always, from his smoky vague green eyes. But one only woke people if one knew what one wanted to say to them. And she wanted to say not one thing, but everything. Little words that broke up the thought and dismembered it said nothing. "About life, about death; about Mrs. Ramsay"—no, she thought, one could say nothing to nobody. The urgency of the moment always missed its mark. Words fluttered sideways and struck the object inches too low. Then one gave it up; then the idea sunk back again; then one became like most middle-aged people, cautious, furtive, with wrinkles between the eyes and a look of perpetual apprehension. For how could one express in words these emotions of the body? express that emptiness there? (She was looking at the drawing-room steps; they looked extraordinarily empty.) It was one's body feeling, not one's mind. The physical sensations that went with the bare look of the steps had become suddenly extremely unpleasant. To want and not to have, sent all up her body a hardness, a hollowness, a strain. And then to want and not to have—to want and want—how that wrung the heart, and wrung it again and again! Oh, Mrs. Ramsay! she called out silently, to that essence which sat by the boat, that abstract one made of her, that woman in grey, as if to abuse her for having gone, and then having gone, come back again. It had seemed so safe, thinking of her. Ghost, air, nothingness, a thing you could play with easily and safely at any time of day or night, she had been that, and then suddenly she put her hand out and wrung the heart thus. Suddenly, the empty drawing-room steps, the frill of the chair inside, the puppy tumbling on the terrace, the whole wave and whisper of the garden became like curves and arabesques flourishing round a centre of complete emptiness.

"What does it mean? How do you explain it all?" she wanted to say, turning to Mr. Carmichael again. For the whole world seemed to have dissolved in this early morning hour into a pool of thought, a deep basin of reality, and one could almost fancy that had Mr. Carmichael spoken, for instance, a little tear would have rent the surface pool. And then? Something would emerge. A hand would be shoved up, a blade would be flashed. It was nonsense of course.

A curious notion came to her that he did after all hear the things she could not say. He was an inscrutable old man, with the yellow stain on his beard, and his poetry, and his puzzles, sailing serenely through a world which satisfied all his wants, so that she thought he had only to put down his hand where he lay on the lawn to fish up anything he wanted. She looked at her picture. That would have been his answer, presumably—how "you" and "I" and "she" pass and vanish; nothing stays; all changes; but not words, not paint. Yet it would be hung in the attics, she thought; it would be rolled up and flung under a sofa; yet even so, even of a picture like that, it was true. One might say, even of this scrawl, not of that actual picture, perhaps, but of what it attempted, that it "remained for ever," she was going to say, or, for the words spoken sounded even to herself, too boastful, to hint, wordlessly; when, looking at the picture, she was surprised to find that she could not see it. Her eyes were full of a hot liquid (she did not think of tears at first) which, without disturbing the firmness of her lips, made the air thick, rolled down her cheeks. She had perfect control of herself— Oh, yes!—in every other way. Was she crying then for Mrs. Ramsay, without being aware of any unhappiness? She addressed old Mr. Carmichael again. What was it then? What did it mean? Could things thrust their hands up and grip one; could the blade cut; the fist grasp? Was there no safety? No learning by heart of the ways of the world? No guide, no shelter, but all was miracle, and leaping from the pinnacle of a tower into the air? Could it be, even for elderly people, that this was life?— startling, unexpected, unknown? For one moment she felt that if they both got up, here, now on the lawn, and demanded an explanation, why was it so short, why was it so inexplicable, said it with violence, as two fully equipped human beings from whom nothing should be hid might speak, then, beauty would roll itself up; the space would fill; those empty flourishes would form into shape; if they shouted loud enough Mrs. Ramsay would return. "Mrs. Ramsay!" she said aloud, "Mrs. Ramsay!" The tears ran down her face.

VI

[MACALISTER'S BOY took one of the fish and cut a square out of its side to bait his hook with. The mutilated body (it was alive still) was thrown back into the sea.]

VII

"MRS. RAMSAY!" Lily cried, "Mrs. Ramsay!" But nothing happened. The pain increased. That anguish could reduce one to such a pitch of imbecility, she thought! Anyhow the old man had not heard her. He remained benignant, calm—if one chose to think it, sublime. Heaven be praised, no one had heard her cry that ignominious cry, stop pain, stop! She had not obviously taken leave of her senses. No one had seen her step off her strip of board into the waters of annihilation. She remained a skimpy old maid, holding a paint-brush.

And now slowly the pain of the want, and the bitter anger (to be called back, just as she thought she would never feel sorrow for Mrs. Ramsay again. Had she missed her among the coffee cups at breakfast? not in the least) lessened; and of their anguish left, as antidote, a relief that was balm in itself, and also, but more mysteriously, a sense of some one there, of Mrs. Ramsay, relieved for a moment of the weight that the world had put on her, staying lightly by her side and then (for this was Mrs. Ramsay in all her beauty) raising to her forehead a wreath of white flowers with which she went. Lily squeezed her tubes again. She attacked that problem of the hedge. It was strange how clearly she saw her, stepping with her usual quickness across fields among whose folds, purplish and soft, among whose flowers, hyacinths or lilies, she vanished. It was some trick of the painter's eye. For days after she had heard of her death she had seen her thus, putting her wreath to her forehead and going unquestioningly with her companion, a shade across the fields. The sight, the phrase, had its power to console. Wherever she happened to be, painting, here, in the country or in London, the vision would come to her, and her eyes, half closing, sought something to base her vision on. She looked down the railway carriage, the omnibus; took a line from shoulder or cheek; looked at the windows opposite; at Piccadilly, lamp-strung in the evening. All had been part of the fields of death. But always something—it might be a face, a voice, a paper boy crying *Standard, News*—thrust through, snubbed her, waked her, required and got in the end an effort of attention, so that the vision must be perpetually remade. Now again, moved as she was by some instinctive need of distance and blue, she looked at the bay beneath her, making hillocks of the blue bars of the waves, and stony fields of the purpler spaces, again she was roused as usual by something incongruous. There was a brown spot in the middle of the bay. It was a boat. Yes, she realised that after a second. But whose boat? Mr. Ramsay's boat, she replied. Mr. Ramsay; the man who had marched past her, with his hand raised, aloof, at the head of a procession, in his beautiful boots, asking her for sympathy, which she had refused. The boat was now half-way across the bay.

So fine was the morning except for a streak of wind here and there that the sea and sky looked all one fabric, as if sails were stuck high up in the sky, or the clouds had dropped down into the sea. A steamer far out at sea had drawn in the air a great scroll of smoke which stayed there curving and circling decoratively, as if the air were a fine gauze which held things and kept them softly in its mesh, only gently swaying them this way and that. And as happens sometimes when the weather is very fine, the cliffs looked as if they were conscious of the ships, and the ships looked as if they were conscious of the cliffs, as if they signalled to each other some message of their own. For sometimes quite close to the shore, the Lighthouse looked this morning in the haze an enormous distance away.

"Where are they now?" Lily thought, looking out to sea. Where was he, that very old man who had gone past her silently, holding a brown paper parcel under his arm? The boat was in the middle of the bay.

VIII

THEY DON'T feel a thing there, Cam thought, looking at the shore, which, rising and falling, became steadily more distant and more peaceful. Her hand cut a trail in the sea, as her mind made the green swirls and streaks into patterns and, numbed and shrouded, wandered in imagination in that underworld of waters where the pearls stuck in clusters to white sprays, where in the green light a change came over one's entire mind and one's body shone half transparent enveloped in a green cloak.

Then the eddy slackened round her hand. The rush of the water ceased; the world became full of little creaking and squeaking sounds. One heard the waves breaking and flapping against the side of the boat as if they were anchored in harbour. Everything became very close to one. For the sail, upon which James had his eyes fixed until it had become to him like a person whom he knew, sagged entirely; there they came to a stop, flapping about waiting for a breeze, in the hot sun, miles from shore, miles from the Lighthouse. Everything in the whole world seemed to stand still. The Lighthouse became immovable, and the line of the distant shore became fixed. The sun grew hotter and everybody seemed to come very close together and to feel each other's presence, which they had almost forgotten. Macalister's fishing line went plumb down into the sea. But Mr. Ramsay went on reading with his legs curled under him.

He was reading a little shiny book with covers mottled like a plover's egg. Now and again, as they hung about in that horrid calm, he turned a page. And James felt that each page was turned with a peculiar gesture aimed at him: now assertively, now commandingly; now with the intention of making people pity him; and all the time, as his father read and turned one after another of those little pages, James kept dreading the moment when he would look up and speak sharply to him about something or other. Why were they lagging about here? he would demand, or something quite unreasonable like that. And if he does, James thought, then I shall take a knife and strike him to the heart.

He had always kept this old symbol of taking a knife and striking his father to the heart. Only now, as he grew older, and sat staring at his father in an impotent rage, it was not him, that old man reading, whom he wanted to kill, but it was the thing that descended on him—without his knowing it perhaps: that fierce sudden black-winged harpy, with its talons and its beak all cold and hard, that struck and struck at you (he could feel the beak on his bare legs, where it had struck when he was a child) and then made off, and there he was again, an old man, very sad, reading his book. That he would kill, that he would strike to the heart. Whatever he did—(and he might do anything, he felt, looking at the Lighthouse and the distant shore) whether he was in a business, in a bank, a barrister, a man at the head of some enterprise, that he would fight, that he would track down and stamp out—tyranny, despotism, he called it—making people do what they did not want to do, cutting off their right to speak. How could any of them say, But I won't, when he said, Come to the Lighthouse. Do this. Fetch me that. The black wings spread, and the hard beak tore. And then next moment, there he sat reading his book; and he might look up—one never knew—quite reasonably. He might talk to the Macalisters. He might be pressing a sovereign into some frozen old woman's hand in the street, James thought, and he might be shouting out at some fisherman's sports; he might be waving his arms in the air with excitement. Or he might sit at the head of the table dead silent from one end of dinner to the other. Yes, thought James, while the boat slapped and dawdled there in the hot sun; there was a waste of snow and rock very lonely and austere; and there he had come to feel, quite often lately, when his father said something or did something which surprised the others, there were two pairs of footprints only; his own and his father's. They alone knew each other. What then was this terror, this hatred? Turning back among the many leaves which the past had folded in him, peering into the heart of that forest where light and shade so chequer each other that all shape is distorted, and one blunders, now with the sun in one's eyes, now with a dark shadow, he sought an image to cool and detach and round off his feeling in a concrete shape. Suppose then that as a child sitting helpless in a perambulator, or on some one's knee, he had seen a waggon crush ignorantly and innocently, some one's foot? Suppose he had seen the foot first, in the grass, smooth, and whole; then the wheel; and the same foot, purple, crushed. But the wheel was innocent. So now, when his father came striding down the passage knocking them up early in the morning to go to the Lighthouse down it came over his foot, over Cam's foot, over anybody's foot. One sat and watched it.

But whose foot was he thinking of, and in what garden did all this happen? For one had settings for these scenes; trees that grew there; flowers; a certain light; a few figures. Everything tended to set itself in a garden where there was none of this gloom. None of this throwing of hands about; people spoke in an ordinary tone of voice. They went in and out all day long. There was an old woman gossiping in the kitchen; and the blinds were sucked in and out by the breeze; all was blowing, all was growing; and over all those plates and bowls and tall brandishing red and yellow flowers a very thin yellow veil would be drawn, like a vine leaf, at night. Things became stiller and darker at night. But the leaf-like veil was so fine, that lights lifted it, voices crinkled it; he could see through it a figure stooping, hear, coming close, going away, some dress rustling, some chain tinkling.

It was in this world that the wheel went over the person's foot. Something, he remembered, stayed and darkened over him; would not move; something flourished up in the air, something arid and sharp descended even there, like a blade, a scimitar, smiting through the leaves and flowers even of that happy world and making it shrivel and fall.

"It will rain," he remembered his father saying. "You won't be able to go to the Lighthouse."

The Lighthouse was then a silvery, misty-looking tower with a yellow eye, that opened suddenly, and softly in the evening. Now—

James looked at the Lighthouse. He could see the whitewashed rocks; the tower, stark and straight; he could see that it was barred with black and white; he could see windows in it; he could even see washing spread on the rocks to dry. So that was the Lighthouse, was it?

No, the other was also the Lighthouse. For nothing was simply one thing. The other Lighthouse was true too. It was sometimes hardly to be seen across the bay. In the evening one looked up and saw the eye opening and shutting and the light seemed to reach them in that airy sunny garden where they sat.

But he pulled himself up. Whenever he said "they" or "a person," and then began hearing the rustle of some one coming, the tinkle of some one going, he became extremely sensitive to the presence of whoever might be in the room. It was his father now. The strain was acute. For in one moment if there was no breeze, his father would slap the covers of his book together, and say: "What's happening now? What are we dawdling about here for, eh?" as, once before he had brought his blade down among them on the terrace and she had gone stiff all over, and if there had been an axe handy, a knife, or anything with a sharp point he would have seized it and struck his father through the heart. She had gone stiff all over, and then, her arm slackening, so that he felt she listened to him no longer, she had risen somehow and gone away and left him there, impotent, ridiculous, sitting on the floor grasping a pair of scissors.

Not a breath of wind blew. The water chuckled and gurgled in the bottom of the boat where three or four mackerel beat their tails up and down in a pool of water not deep enough to cover them. At any moment Mr. Ramsay (he scarcely dared look at him) might rouse himself, shut his book, and say something sharp; but for the moment he was reading, so that James stealthily, as if he were stealing downstairs on bare feet, afraid of waking a watchdog by a creaking board, went on thinking what was she like, where did she go that day? He began following her from room to room and at last they came to a room where in a blue light, as if the reflection came from many china dishes, she talked to somebody; he listened to her talking. She talked to a servant, saying simply whatever came into her head. She alone spoke the truth; to her alone could he speak it. That was the source of her everlasting attraction for him, perhaps; she was a person to whom one could say what came into one's head. But all the time he thought of her, he was conscious of his father following his thought, surveying it, making it shiver and falter. At last he ceased to think.

There he sat with his hand on the tiller in the sun, staring at the Lighthouse, powerless to move, powerless to flick off these grains of misery which settled on his mind one after another. A rope seemed to bind him there, and his father had knotted it and he could only escape by taking a knife and plunging it. . . . But at that moment the sail swung slowly round, filled slowly out, the boat seemed to shake herself, and then to move off half conscious in her sleep, and then she woke and shot through the waves. The relief was extraordinary. They all seemed to fall away from each other again and to be at their ease, and the fishing-lines slanted taut across the side of the boat. But his father did not rouse himself. He only raised his right hand mysteriously high in the air, and let it fall upon his knee again as if he were conducting some secret symphony.

IX

(THE SEA without a stain on it, thought Lily Briscoe, still standing and looking out over the bay. The sea stretched like silk across the bay. Distance had an extraordinary power; they had been swallowed up in it, she felt, they were gone for ever, they had become part of the nature of things. It was so calm; it was so quiet. The steamer itself had vanished, but the great scroll of smoke still hung in the air and drooped like a flag mournfully in valediction.)

X

IT WAS LIKE that then, the island, thought Cam, once more drawing her fingers through the waves. She had never seen it from out at sea before. It lay like that on the sea, did it, with a dent in the middle and two sharp crags, and the sea swept in there, and spread away for miles and miles on either side of the island. It was very small; shaped something like a leaf stood on end. So we took a little boat, she thought, beginning to tell herself a story of adventure about escaping from a sinking ship. But with the sea streaming through her fingers, a spray of seaweed vanishing behind them, she did not want to tell herself seriously a story; it was the sense of adventure and escape that she wanted,

for she was thinking, as the boat sailed on, how her father's
anger about the points of the compass, James's obstinacy about
the compact, and her own anguish, all had slipped, all had
passed, all had streamed away. What then came next? Where
were they going? From her hand, ice cold, held deep in the sea,
there spurted up a fountain of joy at the change, at the escape,
at the adventure (that she should be alive, that she should be
there). And the drops falling from this sudden and unthinking
fountain of joy fell here and there on the dark, the slumbrous
shapes in her mind; shapes of a world not realised but turning
in their darkness, catching here and there, a spark of light;
Greece, Rome, Constantinople. Small as it was, and shaped
something like a leaf stood on its end with the gold-sprinkled
waters flowing in and about it, it had, she supposed, a place in
the universe—even that little island? The old gentlemen in the
study she thought could have told her. Sometimes she strayed
in from the garden purposely to catch them at it. There they
were (it might be Mr. Carmichael or Mr. Bankes who was sitting with her father) sitting opposite each other in their low
arm-chairs. They were crackling in front of them the pages of
The Times, when she came in from the garden, all in a muddle,
about something some one had said about Christ, or hearing
that a mammoth had been dug up in a London street, or wondering what Napoleon was like. Then they took all this with
their clean hands (they wore grey-coloured clothes; they smelt
of heather) and they brushed the scraps together, turning the
paper, crossing their knees, and said something now and then
very brief. Just to please herself she would take a book from the
shelf and stand there, watching her father write, so equally, so
neatly from one side of the page to another, with a little cough
now and then, or something said briefly to the other old gentleman opposite. And she thought, standing there with her book
open, one could let whatever one thought expand here like a

leaf in water; and if it did well here, among the old gentlemen smoking and *The Times* crackling then it was right. And watching her father as he wrote in his study, she thought (now sitting in the boat) he was not vain, nor a tyrant and did not wish to make you pity him. Indeed, if he saw she was there, reading a book, he would ask her, as gently as any one could, Was there nothing he could give her?

Lest this should be wrong, she looked at him reading the little book with the shiny cover mottled like a plover's egg. No; it was right. Look at him now, she wanted to say aloud to James. (But James had his eye on the sail.) He is a sarcastic brute, James would say. He brings the talk round to himself and his books, James would say. He is intolerably egotistical. Worst of all, he is a tyrant. But look! she said, looking at him. Look at him now. She looked at him reading the little book with his legs curled; the little book whose yellowish pages she knew, without knowing what was written on them. It was small; it was closely printed; on the fly-leaf, she knew, he had written that he had spent fifteen francs on dinner; the wine had been so much; he had given so much to the waiter; all was added up neatly at the bottom of the page. But what might be written in the book which had rounded its edges off in his pocket, she did not know. What he thought they none of them knew. But he was absorbed in it, so that when he looked up, as he did now for an instant, it was not to see anything; it was to pin down some thought more exactly. That done, his mind flew back again and he plunged into his reading. He read, she thought, as if he were guiding something, or wheedling a large flock of sheep, or pushing his way up and up a single narrow path; and sometimes he went fast and straight, and broke his way through the bramble, and sometimes it seemed a branch struck at him, a bramble blinded him, but he was not going to let himself be beaten by that; on he went, tossing over page after page. And she went on telling herself a story about escaping from a sinking ship, for she was safe, while he sat there; safe, as she felt herself when she crept in from the garden, and took a book down, and the old gentleman, lowering the paper suddenly, said something very brief over the top of it about the character of Napoleon.

She gazed back over the sea, at the island. But the leaf was losing its sharpness. It was very small; it was very distant. The sea was more important now than the shore. Waves were all round them, tossing and sinking, with a log wallowing down one wave; a gull riding on another. About here, she thought, dabbling her fingers in the water, a ship had sunk, and she murmured, dreamily half asleep, how we perished, each alone.

XI

SO MUCH depends then, thought Lily Briscoe, looking at the sea which had scarcely a stain on it, which was so soft that the sails and the clouds seemed set in its blue, so much depends, she thought, upon distance: whether people are near us or far from us; for her feeling for Mr. Ramsay changed as he sailed further and further across the bay. It seemed to be elongated, stretched out; he seemed to become more and more remote. He and his children seemed to be swallowed up in that blue, that distance; but here, on the lawn, close at hand, Mr. Carmichael suddenly grunted. She laughed. He clawed his book up from the grass. He settled into his chair again puffing and blowing like some sea monster. That was different altogether, because he was so near. And now again all was quiet. They must be out of bed by this time, she supposed, looking at the house, but nothing appeared there. But then, she remembered, they had always made off directly a meal was over, on business of their own. It was all in keeping with this silence, this emptiness, and the unreality of the early morning hour. It was a way things had sometimes, she thought, lingering for a moment and looking at the long glittering windows and the plume of blue smoke: they became unreal. So coming back from a journey, or after an illness, before habits had spun themselves across the surface, one felt that same unreality, which was so startling; felt something emerge. Life was most vivid then. One could be at one's ease. Mercifully one need not say, very briskly, crossing the lawn to greet old Mrs. Beckwith, who would be coming out to find a corner to sit in, "Oh, good-morning, Mrs. Beckwith! What a lovely day! Are you going to be so bold as to sit in the sun? Jasper's hidden the chairs. Do let me find you one!" and all the rest of the usual chatter. One need not speak at all. One glided, one shook one's sails (there was a good deal of movement in the bay, boats were starting off) between things, beyond things. Empty it was not, but full to the brim. She seemed to be standing up to the lips in some substance, to move and float and sink in it, yes, for these waters were unfathomably deep. Into them had spilled so many lives. The Ramsays'; the children's; and all sorts of waifs and strays of things besides. A washer-woman with her basket; a rook, a red-hot poker; the purples and grey-greens of flowers: some common feeling which held the whole.

It was some such feeling of completeness perhaps which, ten years ago, standing almost where she stood now, had made her say that she must be in love with the place. Love had a thousand shapes. There might be lovers whose gift it was to choose out the elements of things and place them together and so, giving them a wholeness not theirs in life, make of some scene, or meeting of people (all now gone and separate), one of those globed compacted things over which thought lingers, and love plays.

Her eyes rested on the brown speck of Mr. Ramsay's sailing boat. They would be at the Lighthouse by lunch time she supposed. But the wind had freshened, and, as the sky changed slightly and the sea changed slightly and the boats altered their positions, the view, which a moment before had seemed miraculously fixed, was now unsatisfactory. The wind had blown the trail of smoke about; there was something displeasing about the placing of the ships.

The disproportion there seemed to upset some harmony in her own mind. She felt an obscure distress. It was confirmed when she turned to her picture. She had been wasting her morning. For whatever reason she could not achieve that razor edge of balance between two opposite forces; Mr. Ramsay and the picture; which was necessary. There was something perhaps wrong with the design? Was it, she wondered, that the line of the wall wanted breaking, was it that the mass of the trees was too heavy? She smiled ironically; for had she not thought, when she began, that she had solved her problem?

What was the problem then? She must try to get hold of something that evaded her. It evaded her when she thought of Mrs. Ramsay; it evaded her now when she thought of her picture. Phrases came. Visions came. Beautiful pictures. Beautiful phrases. But what she wished to get hold of was that very jar on the nerves, the thing itself before it has been made anything. Get that and start afresh; get that and start afresh; she said desperately, pitching herself firmly again before her easel. It was a miserable machine, an inefficient machine, she thought, the human apparatus for painting or for feeling; it always broke down at the critical moment; heroically, one must force it on. She stared, frowning. There was the hedge, sure enough. But one got nothing by soliciting urgently. One got only a glare in the eye from looking at the line of the wall, or from thinking—she wore a grey hat. She was astonishingly beautiful. Let it come, she thought, if it will come. For there are moments when one can neither think nor feel. And if one can neither think nor feel, she thought, where is one?

Here on the grass, on the ground, she thought, sitting down, and examining with her brush a little colony of plantains. For the lawn was very rough. Here sitting on the world, she thought, for she could not shake herself free from the sense that everything this morning was happening for the first time, perhaps for the last time, as a traveller, even though he is half asleep, knows, looking out of the train window, that he must look now, for he will never see that town, or that mule-cart, or that woman at work in the fields, again. The lawn was the world; they were up here together, on this exalted station, she thought, looking at old Mr. Carmichael, who seemed (though they had not said a word all this time) to share her thoughts. And she would never see him again perhaps. He was growing old. Also, she remembered, smiling at the slipper that dangled from his foot, he was growing famous. People said that his poetry was "so beautiful." They went and published things he had written forty years ago. There was a famous man now called Carmichael, she smiled, thinking how many shapes one person might wear, how he was that in the newspapers, but here the same as he had always been. He looked the same — greyer, rather. Yes, he looked the same, but somebody had said, she recalled, that when he had heard of Andrew Ramsay's death (he was killed in a second by a shell; he should have been a great mathematician) Mr. Carmichael had "lost all interest in life." What did it mean — that? she wondered. Had he marched through Trafalgar Square grasping a big stick? Had he turned pages over and over, without reading them, sitting in his room in St. John's Wood alone? She did not know what he had done, when he heard that Andrew was killed, but she felt it in him all the same. They only mumbled at each other on staircases; they looked up at the sky and said it will be fine or it won't be fine. But this was one way of knowing people, she thought: to know the outline, not the detail, to sit in one's garden and look at the slopes of a hill running purple down into the distant heather. She knew him in that way. She knew that he had changed somehow. She had never read a line of his poetry. She thought that she knew how it went though, slowly and sonorously. It was seasoned and mellow. It was about the desert and the camel. It was about the palm tree and the sunset. It was extremely impersonal; it said something about death; it said very little about love. There was an impersonality about him. He wanted very little of other people. Had he not always lurched rather awkwardly past the drawing-room window with some newspaper under his arm, trying to avoid Mrs. Ramsay whom for some reason he did not much like? On that account, of course, she would always try to make him stop. He would bow to her. He would halt unwillingly and bow profoundly. Annoyed that he did not want anything of her, Mrs. Ramsay would ask him (Lily could hear her) wouldn't he like a coat, a rug, a newspaper? No, he wanted nothing. (Here he bowed.) There was some quality in her which he did not much like. It was perhaps her masterfulness, her positiveness, something matter-of-fact in her. She was so direct.

(A noise drew her attention to the drawing-room window— the squeak of a hinge. The light breeze was toying with the window.)

There must have been people who disliked her very much, Lily thought (Yes; she realised that the drawing-room step was empty, but it had no effect on her whatever. She did not want Mrs. Ramsay now.)—People who thought her too sure, too drastic. Also her beauty offended people probably. How monotonous, they would say, and the same always! They preferred another type—the dark, the vivacious. Then she was weak with her husband. She let him make those scenes. Then she was reserved. Nobody knew exactly what had happened to her. And (to go back to Mr. Carmichael and his dislike) one could not imagine Mrs. Ramsay standing painting, lying reading, a whole morning on the lawn. It was unthinkable. Without saying a word, the only token of her errand a basket on her arm, she went off to the town, to the poor, to sit in some stuffy little bedroom. Often and often Lily had seen her go silently in the midst of some game, some discussion, with her basket on her arm, very upright. She had noted her return. She had thought, half laughing (she was so methodical with the tea cups), half moved (her beauty took one's breath away), eyes that are closing in pain have looked on you. You have been with them there.

And then Mrs. Ramsay would be annoyed because somebody was late, or the butter not fresh, or the teapot chipped. And all the time she was saying that the butter was not fresh one would be thinking of Greek temples, and how beauty had been with them there in that stuffy little room. She never talked of it—she went, punctually, directly. It was her instinct to go, an instinct like the swallows for the south, the artichokes for the sun, turning her infallibly to the human race, making her nest in its heart. And this, like all instincts, was a little distressing to people who did not share it; to Mr. Carmichael perhaps, to herself certainly. Some notion was in both of them about the ineffectiveness of action, the supremacy of thought. Her going was a reproach to them, gave a different twist to the world, so that they were led to protest, seeing their own prepossessions disappear, and clutch at them vanishing. Charles Tansley did that too: it was part of the reason why one disliked him. He upset the proportions of one's world. And what had happened to him, she wondered, idly stirring the plantains with her brush. He had got his fellowship. He had married; he lived at Golder's Green.

She had gone one day into a Hall and heard him speaking during the war. He was denouncing something: he was condemning somebody. He was preaching brotherly love. And all she felt was how could he love his kind who did not know one picture from another, who had stood behind her smoking shag ("fivepence an ounce, Miss Briscoe") and making it his business to tell her women can't write, women can't paint, not so much that he believed it, as that for some odd reason he wished it? There he was lean and red and raucous, preaching love from a platform (there were ants crawling about among the plantains which she disturbed with her brush—red, energetic, shiny ants, rather like Charles Tansley). She had looked at him ironically from her seat in the half-empty hall, pumping love into that chilly space, and suddenly, there was the old cask or whatever it was bobbing up and down among the waves and Mrs. Ramsay looking for her spectacle case among the pebbles. "Oh, dear! What a nuisance! Lost again. Don't bother, Mr. Tansley. I lose thousands every summer," at which he pressed his chin back against his collar, as if afraid to sanction such exaggeration, but could stand it in her whom he liked, and smiled very charmingly. He must have confided in her on one of those long expeditions when people got separated and walked back alone. He was educating his little sister, Mrs. Ramsay had told her. It was immensely to his credit. Her own idea of him was grotesque, Lily knew well, stirring the plantains with her brush. Half one's notions of other people were, after all, grotesque. They served private purposes of one's own. He did for her instead of a whipping-boy. She found herself flagellating his lean flanks when she was out of temper. If she wanted to be serious about him she had to help herself to Mrs. Ramsay's sayings, to look at him through her eyes.

She raised a little mountain for the ants to climb over. She reduced them to a frenzy of indecision by this interference in their cosmogony. Some ran this way, others that.

One wanted fifty pairs of eyes to see with, she reflected. Fifty pairs of eyes were not enough to get round that one woman with, she thought. Among them, must be one that was stone blind to her beauty. One wanted most some secret sense, fine as air, with which to steal through keyholes and surround her where she sat knitting, talking, sitting silent in the window alone; which took to itself and treasured up like the air which held the smoke of the steamer, her thoughts, her imaginations, her desires. What did the hedge mean to her, what did the garden mean to her, what did it mean to her when a wave broke? (Lily looked up, as she had seen Mrs. Ramsay look up; she too heard a wave falling on the beach.) And then what stirred and trembled in her mind when the children cried, "How's that? How's that?" cricketing? She would stop knitting for a second. She would look intent. Then she would lapse again, and suddenly Mr. Ramsay stopped dead in his pacing in front of her and some curious shock passed through her and seemed to rock her in profound agitation on its breast when stopping there he stood over her and looked down at her. Lily could see him.

He stretched out his hand and raised her from her chair. It seemed somehow as if he had done it before; as if he had once bent in the same way and raised her from a boat which, lying a few inches off some island, had required that the ladies should thus be helped on shore by the gentlemen. An old-fashioned scene that was, which required, very nearly, crinolines and peg-top trousers. Letting herself be helped by him, Mrs. Ramsay had thought (Lily supposed) the time has come now. Yes, she would say it now. Yes, she would marry him. And she stepped slowly, quietly on shore. Probably she said one word only, letting her hand rest still in his. I will marry you, she might have said, with her hand in his; but no more. Time after time the same thrill had passed between them—obviously it had, Lily thought, smoothing a way for her ants. She was not inventing;

she was only trying to smooth out something she had been given years ago folded up; something she had seen. For in the rough and tumble of daily life, with all those children about, all those visitors, one had constantly a sense of repetition—of one thing falling where another had fallen, and so setting up an echo which chimed in the air and made it full of vibrations.

But it would be a mistake, she thought, thinking how they walked off together, arm in arm, past the greenhouse, to simplify their relationship. It was no monotony of bliss—she with her impulses and quicknesses; he with his shudders and glooms. Oh, no. The bedroom door would slam violently early in the morning. He would start from the table in a temper. He would whizz his plate through the window. Then all through the house there would be a sense of doors slamming and blinds fluttering, as if a gusty wind were blowing and people scudded about trying in a hasty way to fasten hatches and make things shipshape. She had met Paul Rayley like that one day on the stairs. It had been an earwig, apparently. Other people might find centipedes. They had laughed and laughed.

But it tired Mrs. Ramsay, it cowed her a little—the plates whizzing and the doors slamming. And there would fall between them sometimes long rigid silences, when, in a state of mind which annoyed Lily in her, half plaintive, half resentful, she seemed unable to surmount the tempest calmly, or to laugh as they laughed, but in her weariness perhaps concealed something. She brooded and sat silent. After a time he would hang stealthily about the places where she was—roaming under the window where she sat writing letters or talking, for she would take care to be busy when he passed, and evade him, and pretend not to see him. Then he would turn smooth as silk, affable, urbane, and try to win her so. Still she would hold off, and now she would assert for a brief season some of those prides and airs the due of her beauty which she was generally utterly without;

would turn her head; would look so, over her shoulder, always
with some Minta, Paul, or William Bankes at her side. At length,
standing outside the group the very figure of a famished
wolfhound (Lily got up off the grass and stood looking at the
steps, at the window, where she had seen him), he would say her
name, once only, for all the world like a wolf barking in the
snow, but still she held back; and he would say it once more, and
this time something in the tone would rouse her, and she would
go to him, leaving them all of a sudden, and they would walk
off together among the pear trees, the cabbages, and the rasp-
berry beds. They would have it out together. But with what attitudes and with what words? Such a dignity was theirs in this
relationship that, turning away, she and Paul and Minta would
hide their curiosity and their discomfort, and begin picking
flowers, throwing balls, chattering, until it was time for dinner,
and there they were, he at one end of the table, she at the other,
as usual.

"Why don't some of you take up botany? . . . With all those
legs and arms why doesn't one of you . . . ?" So they would talk
as usual, laughing, among the children. All would be as usual,
save only for some quiver, as of a blade in the air, which came
and went between them as if the usual sight of the children sitting round their soup plates had freshened itself in their eyes
after that hour among the pears and the cabbages. Especially,
Lily thought, Mrs. Ramsay would glance at Prue. She sat in
the middle between brothers and sisters, always occupied, it
seemed, seeing that nothing went wrong so that she scarcely
spoke herself. How Prue must have blamed herself for that earwig in the milk! How white she had gone when Mr. Ramsay
threw his plate through the window! How she drooped under
those long silences between them! Anyhow, her mother now
would seem to be making it up to her; assuring her that everything was well; promising her that one of these days that same

happiness would be hers. She had enjoyed it for less than a year, however.

She had let the flowers fall from her basket, Lily thought, screwing up her eyes and standing back as if to look at her picture, which she was not touching, however, with all her faculties in a trance, frozen over superficially but moving underneath with extreme speed.

She let her flowers fall from her basket, scattered and tumbled them on to the grass and, reluctantly and hesitatingly, but without question or complaint—had she not the faculty of obedience to perfection?—went too. Down fields, across valleys, white, flower-strewn—that was how she would have painted it. The hills were austere. It was rocky; it was steep. The waves sounded hoarse on the stones beneath. They went, the three of them together, Mrs. Ramsay walking rather fast in front, as if she expected to meet some one round the corner.

Suddenly the window at which she was looking was whitened by some light stuff behind it. At last then somebody had come into the drawing-room; somebody was sitting in the chair. For Heaven's sake, she prayed, let them sit still there and not come floundering out to talk to her. Mercifully, whoever it was stayed still inside; had settled by some stroke of luck so as to throw an odd-shaped triangular shadow over the step. It altered the composition of the picture a little. It was interesting. It might be useful. Her mood was coming back to her. One must keep on looking without for a second relaxing the intensity of emotion, the determination not to be put off, not to be bamboozled. One must hold the scene—so—in a vise and let nothing come in and spoil it. One wanted, she thought, dipping her brush deliberately, to be on a level with ordinary experience, to feel simply that's a chair, that's a table, and yet at the same time, It's a miracle, it's an ecstasy. The problem might be solved after all. Ah, but what had happened? Some wave of white went over the window pane. The air must have stirred some flounce in the room. Her heart leapt at her and seized her and tortured her.

"Mrs. Ramsay! Mrs. Ramsay!" she cried, feeling the old horror come back—to want and want and not to have. Could she inflict that still? And then, quietly, as if she refrained, that too became part of ordinary experience, was on a level with the chair, with the table. Mrs. Ramsay—it was part of her perfect goodness—sat there quite simply, in the chair, flicked her needles to and fro, knitted her reddish-brown stocking, cast her shadow on the step. There she sat.

And as if she had something she must share, yet could hardly leave her easel, so full her mind was of what she was thinking, of what she was seeing, Lily went past Mr. Carmichael holding her brush to the edge of the lawn. Where was that boat now? And Mr. Ramsay? She wanted him.

XII

MR. RAMSAY had almost done reading. One hand hovered over the page as if to be in readiness to turn it the very instant he had finished it. He sat there bareheaded with the wind blowing his hair about, extraordinarily exposed to everything. He looked very old. He looked, James thought, getting his head now against the Lighthouse, now against the waste of waters running away into the open, like some old stone lying on the sand; he looked as if he had become physically what was always at the back of both of their minds—that loneliness which was for both of them the truth about things.

He was reading very quickly, as if he were eager to get to the end. Indeed they were very close to the Lighthouse now. There it loomed up, stark and straight, glaring white and black, and one could see the waves breaking in white splinters like smashed glass upon the rocks. One could see lines and creases in the rocks. One could see the windows clearly; a dab of white on one of them, and a little tuft of green on the rock. A man had come out and looked at them through a glass and gone in again. So it was like that, James thought, the Lighthouse one had seen across the bay all these years; it was a stark tower on a bare rock. It satisfied him. It confirmed some obscure feeling of his about his own character. The old ladies, he thought, thinking of the garden at home, went dragging their chairs about on the lawn. Old Mrs. Beckwith, for example, was always saying how nice it was and how sweet it was and how they ought to be so proud and they ought to be so happy, but as a matter of fact, James thought, looking at the Lighthouse stood there on its rock, it's like that. He looked at his father reading fiercely with his legs curled tight. They shared that knowledge. "We are driving before a gale—we must sink," he began saying to himself, half aloud, exactly as his father said it.

Nobody seemed to have spoken for an age. Cam was tired of looking at the sea. Little bits of black cork had floated past; the fish were dead in the bottom of the boat. Still her father read, and James looked at him and she looked at him, and they vowed that they would fight tyranny to the death, and he went on reading quite unconscious of what they thought. It was thus that he escaped, she thought. Yes, with his great forehead and his great nose, holding his little mottled book firmly in front of him, he escaped. You might try to lay hands on him, but then like a bird, he spread his wings, he floated off to settle out of your reach somewhere far away on some desolate stump. She gazed at the immense expanse of the sea. The island had grown so small that it scarcely looked like a leaf any longer. It looked like the top of a rock which some wave bigger than the rest would cover. Yet in its frailty were all those paths, those terraces, those bedrooms—all those innumerable things. But as, just before sleep, things simplify themselves so that only one of all the myriad details has power to assert itself; so, she felt, looking drowsily at the island, all those paths and terraces and bedrooms were fading and disappearing, and nothing was left but a pale blue censer swinging rhythmically this way and that across her mind. It was a hanging garden; it was a valley, full of birds, and flowers, and antelopes. . . . She was falling asleep.

"Come now," said Mr. Ramsay, suddenly shutting his book.

Come where? To what extraordinary adventure? She woke with a start. To land somewhere, to climb somewhere? Where was he leading them? For after his immense silence the words startled them. But it was absurd. He was hungry, he said. It was time for lunch. Besides, look, he said. "There's the Lighthouse. We're almost there."

"He's doing very well," said Macalister, praising James. "He's keeping her very steady."

But his father never praised him, James thought grimly.

Mr. Ramsay opened the parcel and shared out the sandwiches among them. Now he was happy, eating bread and cheese with these fishermen. He would have liked to live in a cottage and lounge about in the harbour spitting with the other old men, James thought, watching him slice his cheese into thin yellow sheets with his penknife.

This is right, this is it, Cam kept feeling, as she peeled her hard-boiled egg. Now she felt as she did in the study when the old men were reading *The Times*. Now I can go on thinking whatever I like, and I shan't fall over a precipice or be drowned, for there he is, keeping his eye on me, she thought.

At the same time they were sailing so fast along by the rocks that it was very exciting—it seemed as if they were doing two things at once; they were eating their lunch here in the sun and they were also making for safety in a great storm after a shipwreck. Would the water last? Would the provisions last? she asked herself, telling herself a story but knowing at the same time what was the truth.

They would soon be out of it, Mr. Ramsay was saying to old Macalister; but their children would see some strange things. Macalister said he was seventy-five last March; Mr. Ramsay was seventy-one. Macalister said he had never seen a doctor; he had never lost a tooth. And that's the way I'd like my children to live—Cam was sure that her father was thinking that, for he stopped her throwing a sandwich into the sea and told her, as if he were thinking of the fishermen and how they lived, that if she did not want it she should put it back in the parcel. She should not waste it. He said it so wisely, as if he knew so well all the things that happened in the world that she put it back at once, and then he gave her, from his own parcel, a gingerbread nut, as if he were a great Spanish gentleman, she thought, hand-ing a flower to a lady at a window (so courteous his manner was). He was shabby, and simple, eating bread and cheese; and yet he was leading them on a great expedition where, for all she knew, they would be drowned.

"That was where she sunk," said Macalister's boy suddenly.

Three men were drowned where we are now, the old man said. He had seen them clinging to the mast himself. And Mr. Ramsay taking a look at the spot was about, James and Cam were afraid, to burst out:

But I beneath a rougher sea,

and if he did, they could not bear it; they would shriek aloud; they could not endure another explosion of the passion that boiled in him; but to their surprise all he said was "Ah" as if he thought to himself, But why make a fuss about that? Naturally men are drowned in a storm, but it is a perfectly straightforward affair, and the depths of the sea (he sprinkled the crumbs from his sandwich paper over them) are only water after all. Then having lighted his pipe he took out his watch. He looked at it attentively; he made, perhaps, some mathematical calculation. At last he said, triumphantly:

"Well done!" James had steered them like a born sailor.

There! Cam thought, addressing herself silently to James. You've got it at last. For she knew that this was what James had been wanting, and she knew that now he had got it he was so pleased that he would not look at her or at his father or at any one. There he sat with his hand on the tiller sitting bolt upright, looking rather sulky and frowning slightly. He was so pleased that he was not going to let anybody share a grain of his pleasure. His father had praised him. They must think that he was perfectly indifferent. But you've got it now, Cam thought.

They had tacked, and they were sailing swiftly, buoyantly on long rocking waves which handed them on from one to another with an extraordinary lilt and exhilaration beside the reef. On the left a row of rocks showed brown through the water which thinned and became greener and on one, a higher rock, a wave incessantly broke and spurted a little column of drops which fell down in a shower. One could hear the slap of the water and the patter of falling drops and a kind of hushing and hissing sound from the waves rolling and gambolling and slapping the rocks as if they were wild creatures who were perfectly free and tossed and tumbled and sported like this for ever.

Now they could see two men on the Lighthouse, watching them and making ready to meet them.

Mr. Ramsay buttoned his coat, and turned up his trousers. He took the large, badly packed, brown paper parcel which Nancy had got ready and sat with it on his knee. Thus in complete readiness to land he sat looking back at the island. With his long-sighted eyes perhaps he could see the dwindled leaf-like shape standing on end on a plate of gold quite clearly. What

could he see? Cam wondered. It was all a blur to her. What was
he thinking now? she wondered. What was it he sought, so
fixedly, so intently, so silently? They watched him, both of them,
sitting bareheaded with his parcel on his knee staring and staring at the frail blue shape which seemed like the vapour of
something that had burnt itself away. What do you want? they
both wanted to ask. They both wanted to say, Ask us anything
and we will give it you. But he did not ask them anything. He
sat and looked at the island and he might be thinking, We perished, each alone, or he might be thinking, I have reached it. I
have found it; but he said nothing.

Then he put on his hat.

"Bring those parcels," he said, nodding his head at the
things Nancy had done up for them to take to the Lighthouse.
"The parcels for the Lighthouse men," he said. He rose and
stood in the bow of the boat, very straight and tall, for all the
world, James thought, as if he were saying, "There is no God,"
and Cam thought, as if he were leaping into space, and they
both rose to follow him as he sprang, lightly like a young man,
holding his parcel, on to the rock.

XIII

"HE MUST have reached it," said Lily Briscoe aloud, feeling
suddenly completely tired out. For the Lighthouse had become
almost invisible, had melted away into a blue haze, and the effort of looking at it and the effort of thinking of him landing
there, which both seemed to be one and the same effort, had
stretched her body and mind to the utmost. Ah, but she was relieved. Whatever she had wanted to give him, when he left her
that morning, she had given him at last.

"He has landed," she said aloud. "It is finished." Then, surging up, puffing slightly, old Mr. Carmichael stood beside her, looking like an old pagan god, shaggy, with weeds in his hair and the trident (it was only a French novel) in his hand. He stood by her on the edge of the lawn, swaying a little in his bulk and said, shading his eyes with his hand: "They will have landed," and she felt that she had been right. They had not needed to speak. They had been thinking the same things and he had answered her without her asking him anything. He stood there as if he were spreading his hands over all the weakness and suffering of mankind; she thought he was surveying, tolerantly and compassionately, their final destiny. Now he has crowned the occasion, she thought, when his hand slowly fell, as if she had seen him let fall from his great height a wreath of violets and asphodels which, fluttering slowly, lay at length upon the earth.

Quickly, as if she were recalled by something over there, she turned to her canvas. There it was—her picture. Yes, with all its greens and blues, its lines running up and across, its attempt at something. It would be hung in the attics, she thought; it would be destroyed. But what did that matter? she asked herself, taking up her brush again. She looked at the steps; they were empty; she looked at her canvas; it was blurred. With a sudden intensity, as if she saw it clear for a second, she drew a line there, in the centre. It was done; it was finished. Yes, she thought, laying down her brush in extreme fatigue, I have had my vision.

Notes to *To the Lighthouse*

Two other editions of *To the Lighthouse* are referred to in these notes: *To the Lighthouse,* edited by Susan Dick (Oxford: Blackwell/ Shakespeare Head Press, 1992) ("Dick"); *To the Lighthouse,* text edited by Stella McNichol, with an introduction and notes by Hermione Lee (London: Penguin, 1992) ("English edition"). Details of other works referred to will be found in the list of works cited in the introduction or in the suggestions for further reading.

Ramsay [7]   In August 1899, Woolf wrote in her diary about the history of a town near Cambridge called St. Ives, famous for its bridge with six arches "erected by the Abbots of Ramsey" (*Passionate Apprentice* 150). She also wrote about "Ramsey (or Ram's Island) a market town on the borders of the Fens" (ibid. 140).

James Ramsay [7]   Presumably named after Mrs. Ramsay's uncle James (83). Woolf's younger brother, Adrian, has usually been taken as the model for James. On reading the novel in 1927, Vanessa Bell wrote to Woolf, "I wonder how Adrian will like James! Perhaps you'll finish his psycho-analysis for him. I shouldn't be surprised" (Bell, *Letters* 318). Leonard Woolf wrote to Adrian's daughter Ann in 1964 that some of her father's troubled and complicated childhood "is used in James" (*Letters of Leonard Woolf,* edited by Frederic Spotts, 531 [San Diego: Harcourt, 1989]).

Army and Navy Stores [7]   Founded in 1872, initially to serve officers, the Stores were on Victoria Street in London. By the 1920s they were open to the public.

tuberculous hip [8]   The boy is probably suffering from mesenteric disease, a swelling of the abdominal lymph glands caused by drinking milk from tuberculosis-infected cows.

Hebrides [9]   A group of about fifty mostly uninhabited, small islands off the coast of Scotland. The "Outer Hebrides" has long signified extreme remoteness in English vernacular.

Bank of England [10]   The government's bank, and note-issuing authority, it stands at the center of the British banking system and is similar to the U.S. Federal Reserve.

Indian Empire [10]   British involvement in Indian affairs dates back to the fifteenth century. The English East India Company, established in 1600 to facilitate the spice trade, became increasingly involved in Indian politics. In the mid-nineteenth century, following the "Indian Mutiny," the British government took direct control of the country, dissolving the East India Company. During the time in which Part I takes place, there was increasing agitation for self-government by the native Indian population.

ringed fingers and lace [10]   Most likely an allusion to Queen Victoria.

Isles of Skye [11]   The Isle of Skye is the largest of the islands of the Inner Hebrides. Woolf mistakenly added an "s" to the proof for the American edition of her novel. Dick suggests Woolf might have been thinking of the Isles of Scilly, off the west coast of Cornwall (xxxv).

Balliol [11]   A college of Oxford University.

Bristol [11]   Founded in 1876, University College, Bristol was the first to admit women on the same basis as men. Bristol is a city in the west of England.

Bedford [11]   A town about fifty miles north of London. Bedford School, founded in 1552, is one of England's oldest "public" schools. There was also a Bedford College for Women in London, founded in 1849.

Prolegomena [11]   Most common in philosophy, a preface or introductory section to a book of observations.

Reform Bill [12]   Three Reform Bills were passed in the nineteenth century, restructuring the electorate and extending the franchise, in 1832, 1867, and 1884. They greatly diminished the power of the aristocracy. However, given that Part I takes place about 1909, it makes more sense that the children are discussing what was known as the "People's Budget" proposed by Chancellor of the Exchequer Lloyd George in that year. The House of Lords rejected the budget and the December 1910 election was widely regarded as a referendum on Prime Minister Asquith's challenge to the power of the Lords.

Grisons [12]   The largest canton of Switzerland, an area of Alpine peaks and fertile valleys.

half grudgingly, half respect [12]   The English edition of the novel reads "receiving from her, half grudging, some respect" which makes better sense. In proof, the passage read: "the great in birth coming to her mind now and then, half grudgingly, half respectfully, for" (Dick 193).

yellow cat's eyes . . . vivid streak of canary-yellow [13–14]   Mr. Carmichael apparently uses laudanum, a tincture of opium that has a yellow color (see Lilienfeld, *Reading* 207–14).

chemist [15]   Equivalent to a U.S. druggist.

shag [15]   A strong tobacco cut into fine shreds (OED).

Ibsen [16]   Henrik Ibsen (1828–1906) was a Norwegian playwright known for his radical social dramas, such as *A Doll's House* and *Hedda Gabler*.

Panama hat [16]   Woven from the straw of the toquilla plant in Ecuador, and so named when workers constructing the Panama Canal (1880–1914) wore them as protection against the fierce sun.

Mr. Paunceforte [17]   An invention of Woolf's, but representative of the fact that St. Ives (the inspiration for the novel's location) became a popular destination for painters at the end of the nineteenth century.

tea-caddies [17]   Containers for tea leaves, often decorated.

the blue ribbon of the Garter [17–18]   The Order of the Garter is the highest order of chivalry in Britain, dating back to the fourteenth century. The Order is limited to the Sovereign and no more than twenty-five knights. Its insignia is a blue garter inscribed *"Honi Soit Qui Mal Y Pense"* (Evil to him who thinks this evil).

cyclamen [18]   A member of the primrose family with strikingly beautiful flowers.

Stormed at with shot and shell [20]   A line from Alfred, Lord Tennyson's poem "The Charge of the Light Brigade," commemorating an ill-fated charge by the British Light Cavalry Brigade against Russian troops at Balaklava during the Crimean War on October 25, 1854. At various times, Mr. Ramsay recites lines from the second and third stanzas:

'Forward the Light Brigade!'
Was there a man dismay'd?

> Not though the soldier knew
> Some one had blundered:
> Their's not to make reply,
> Their's not to reason why,
> Their's but to do and die:
> Into the valley of Death
> Rode the six hundred.
>
> Cannon to the right of them,
> Cannon to the left of them,
> Cannon in front of them
> Volley'd and thunder'd;
> Stormed at with shot and shell,
> Boldly they rode and well,
> Into the jaws of Death,
> Into the mouth of Hell
> Rode the six hundred.

little Chinese eyes [21]   "Lily's 'Chinese eyes' suggest not the Empire's foraging glance toward the distant lands of China and India for trade and gain, but the new aesthetic voyaging in the East during the modernist period" (Patricia Laurence, *Lily Briscoe's Chinese Eyes: Bloomsbury, Modernism, and China,* 10 [Columbia: South Carolina University Press, 2003]). In *Mrs. Dalloway,* Elizabeth Dalloway is also described as having "Chinese eyes."

Boldly we rode and well [21]   A slightly misquoted line, substituting "we" for "they," from Tennyson's "Charge of the Light Brigade."

jacmanna [21]   A flower, purple clematis, more properly called jackmanii.

"Some one had blundered" [22]   A line from Tennyson's "Charge of the Light Brigade."

Brompton Road [23]   In the early twentieth century, a quiet suburban road near the Knightsbridge neighborhood of London.

pampas grass [23]   A giant grass introduced as ornament to European gardens from its native South America in 1843.

red-hot pokers [23]   Nickname of the kniphofia, or torch lily. A plant native to South Africa, it was first brought to England in the early eighteenth century and became a popular garden plant in the mid-nineteenth.

Westmorland [24]   A county in the Lake District of England (now part of Cumbria).

Cam [25]   Presumably the youngest daughter is named after Mrs. Ramsay's aunt Camilla (70). This is also the name of a character closely based on Virginia Woolf in her husband's 1914 novel, *The Wise Virgins.* In Virgil's *Aeneid,* Book 11, Camilla is a warrior celebrated for her speed who dies fighting against Aeneas.

Sweet Alice [25]   Sweet alyssum, or sea alyssum, is a flowering herb that grows near the sea.

Vesuvius [26]   Europe's only active volcano, on the shore of the Bay of Naples in Italy.

Subject and object . . . [26]   In his *History of English Thought in the Eighteenth Century* (1876), Leslie Stephen wrote: "The whole history of philosophical thought is but a history of attempts to separate the object and the subject."

heather-mixture stocking [30]   Mrs. Ramsay is knitting with heather-colored yarn.

twopence halfpenny [30]   In English currency at the time, twelve pennies (or pence) made one shilling, and twenty shillings made one pound.

"For her whose wishes must be obeyed" [30]   An allusion to the great
Queen Ayesha in H. Rider Haggard's popular 1887 novel *She*.
Ayesha was known as "she-who-must-be-obeyed."

"The happier Helen..." [30]   Alludes to Helen of Troy, renowned
for her beauty.

Croom on the Mind [30]   George Croom Robertson was editor of
the philosophical journal *Mind* and a friend of Leslie Stephen,
Woolf's father.

Bates on the Savage Customs [30]   Dick suggests Woolf may here be
conflating two naturalists, Henry Walter Bates (1825–1892) and
Alfred Russel Wallace (1823–1913), who accompanied Bates on
a trip to the Amazon in 1848.

The Graces [32]   Thalia, Euphrosyne, and Aglaia, three goddesses
in Greek mythology who personified (respectively) grace or
flowering, joy, and beauty.

asphodel [33]   A flower of the lily genus, often planted on graves.
Poets (e.g., Homer) have described it as an immortal flower covering the Elysian fields. The white asphodel, or king's spear, is
very common in the Apulia region of Italy.

authenticated masterpiece by Michael Angelo [33]   I.e., a reproduction
of a work by the celebrated painter of the Sistine Chapel's ceiling, Michelangelo Buonarotti (1475–1564).

valley of death... volleyed and thundered [34]   Fragments from Tennyson's "Charge of the Light Brigade."

"in June he gets out of tune" [36]   An old rhyme refers to the cuckoo's
time in Britain:

> In April I open my bill
> In May I sing night and day

In June I change my tune
In July far far I fly
In August away I must

the letter Q. . . . If Q then is Q— [37]   In characterizing Mr. Ramsay's intellectual struggle in this way, Woolf is displaying her knowledge of conventional notation of the philosophical issue of the syllogism. In Alfred N. Whitehead and Bertrand Russell's *Principia Mathematica* (1910–13), they used the following conventionalized notation of the syllogism to discuss its form:

All P are Q
R is P
Therefore R is Q.

the icy solitudes of the Polar region [38]   Stories of the heroic polar expeditions of the early years of the twentieth century were well-known. The Norwegian Roald Amundsen (1872-1928) was first to reach the South Pole, in 1911, followed a month later by the Englishman Robert Falcon Scott (1868–1912). Scott and his four companions died attempting to return to their base, beset by frostbite, lack of food, and blizzards, and their story was widely publicized as an epic of exploration. Adding to this polar lore were the accounts of the American Robert Edwin Peary's (1856–1920) attempts to reach the North Pole, which he did in 1909, and those of the Anglo-Irish Sir Ernest Henry Shackleton (1874–1922), who made a tremendous overland journey in the Antarctic after his ship was crushed by ice in 1915.

Grimm's fairy story [42]   Mrs. Ramsay is reading the Grimm Brothers' tale "The Fisherman and His Wife" to James. This tale concerns a magic flounder that grants wishes to a fisherman and his wife. As the wife's wishes become increasingly grandiose, the sea becomes rougher, the sky darker. Eventually the wife wishes to be god. In Woolf's draft of the novel, Mrs. Ramsay first reads

"The Three Dwarfs" to James, and then "The Three Bears." Only in the published version is the story she is reading "The Fisherman and His Wife."

St. John's Wood [44]   A residential neighborhood of London, populated before the First World War by many artists.

half-a-crown? eighteenpence? [44]   Two shillings and sixpence, and one shilling and sixpence, respectively.

Does the progress of civilisation depend upon great men? [46]   Possibly an allusion to Thomas Carlyle's "The history of the world is but the biography of great men" (*On Heroes, Hero-Worship and the Heroic in History*, 1841); the question is also raised by Jacob Flanders in Woolf's novel *Jacob's Room*.

liftman in the Tube [46]   Several stations on the London Underground railway have elevators between the platforms and the street.

Cardiff [46]   The capital city of Wales; its university was founded in 1883.

Locke, Hume, Berkeley [48]   English philosopher John Locke (1632–1704) was the founder of British empiricism and author of *An Essay Concerning Human Understanding* (1690). David Hume (1711–1776) was a Scottish philosopher who built on the work of Locke in his *Enquiry Concerning Human Understanding* (1748). Bishop George Berkeley (1685-1753) was an Anglo-Irish philosopher who famously argued that there is no existence of things independent of perception. Leslie Stephen wrote about all three in the *History of English Thought in the Eighteenth Century* (1876).

Swansea, Cardiff, Exeter, Southampton, Kidderminster [48]   With the exception of Kidderminster, which is known for carpet-making, university colleges were founded in these cities in the late nineteenth or early twentieth century. The first two are in south Wales; Exeter is in southwest England; Southampton is a port city on the south coast; and Kidderminster is in the Severn Valley, in Worcestershire.

Carlyle [49]   Thomas Carlyle (1795–1881) was an influential and somewhat eccentric historian and philosopher whose works had a profound effect on many Victorian intellectuals. Woolf's father, Leslie Stephen, knew him, and her great-aunt, Julia Margaret Cameron, photographed him.

light of a butterfly's wing... [51]   Lily's thoughts about her painting (recalled in very similar terms in Part III, p. 174) closely echo an April 1925 comment in Woolf's diary about Marcel Proust: "He searches out these butterfly shades to the last grain. He is as tough as catgut & as evanescent as a butterfly's bloom" (*Diary* 3: 7).

treasures in the tombs of kings [54]   Most likely an anachronistic allusion to the discovery of the tomb of Tutankhamen in late 1922.

Kennet [56]   A tributary of the River Thames, flowing from Wiltshire to Berkshire.

"Next morning the wife awoke..." [58]   Mrs. Ramsay continues to read Grimms' "The Fisherman and His Wife" to James.

It was more true about hospitals... [61]   Woolf's mother worked among the poor and ill in both London and St. Ives. She established a subscription to raise funds for a nurse in St. Ives, and in "A Sketch of the Past," Woolf notes that after her death this became the Julia Prinsep Stephen Nursing Association (131).

Hume [67]   See note to page 48. Leslie Stephen included the anecdote in the *Dictionary of National Biography* entry on Hume.

Best and brightest come away! [73]   From Percy B. Shelley's "To Jane: The Invitation," the first stanza of which reads:

> Best and brightest, come away!
> Fairer far than this fair Day,
> Which, like thee to those in sorrow,
> Comes to bid a sweet good-morrow
> To the rough Year just awake
> In its cradle on the brake.

Amsterdam . . . the Rembrandts [74]   The works of Rembrandt van Rijn (1606–1669) can be seen in the Dutch city of Amsterdam's Rijksmuseum and also in the Rembrandt Museum, the painter's former house.

Prado [74]   A museum in Madrid, Spain, with one of the world's largest art collections.

Sistine Chapel [74]   Part of the Vatican in Rome, and most famous for Michelangelo's paintings.

Padua . . . Giottos [74]   The Scrovegni (Arena) Chapel in the Italian city of Padua is famous for its frescoes by Giotto di Bondone (c. 1267–1337).

Titian [75]   Tiziano Vecellio (1488–1576), a leading Renaissance painter from Venice.

Darwin [75]   Charles Darwin (1809–1882), author of *Origin of Species*.

Tube [75]   London's underground rail system is the oldest in the world, its first section having opened in 1863.

Constantinople . . . Santa Sofia [76]   Woolf had been struck by the beauty of Constantinople (now Istanbul) when she visited it in 1906, and references to the city abound in her work. Santa Sofia, the cathedral built by Justinian the Great in the sixth century, became a mosque after the Turkish conquest of Constantinople in the fifteenth century. (See Julia Briggs, "Constantinople: Virginia Woolf at the Crossroads of the Imagination," in *Woolf Across Cultures,* edited by Natalya Reinhold, 179–89. New York: Pace University Press, 2003.)

Golden Horn [76]   A freshwater estuary that separates the old and new parts of Istanbul.

Damn your eyes [77]   Last line of the traditional ballad "Samuel Hall," the first two stanzas of which are:

> Well, my name it is Sam Hall, Sam Hall.
> Yes, my name it is Sam Hall; it is Sam Hall.
> My name it is Sam Hall an' I hate you, one and all.
> An' I hate you, one and all:
> Damn your eyes.
>
> I killed a man, they said; so they said.
> I killed a man, they said; so they said.
> I killed a man, they said an' I smashed in his head.
> An' I left him layin' dead,
> Damn his eyes.

Pope's Nose [78]   A slang term for the rump of a chicken or turkey, here probably describing the shape of a geographical feature.

Boeuf en Daube [82]   Beef stew cooked slowly in a *daubière,* an earthenware pot from Provence.

no-man's land [86]   Levenback (94) points out that readers in 1927 would not have missed this anachronistic use of a term made familiar by the First World War.

flower in pattern [87]   The second English edition, published in 1938 by Dent for the Everyman Library, has "flower in the pattern," which might make better sense. However, both the U.S.

and British first editions have the line as given here; the article was probably inserted by Dent's copyeditor.

dress clothes [88]   The Ramsays and their guests have put on formal evening dress for dinner.

Marlow [89]   A town on the River Thames, about thirty miles west of London.

bear garden [92]   Originally a venue for bear-baiting, the term in the late nineteenth century colloquially expressed an idea of rough discourse and rowdy behavior.

dished himself [92]   Slang for being completely defeated or "done for."

X-ray photograph [93]   X rays were discovered by William Röntgen in 1895.

That the fishing season was bad [96]   Fishing was an important industry in Scotland in the nineteenth century (as it remains today), but the work was seasonal and dependent on the catch. Thousands of men and women would follow the herring migration on foot, often living in insanitary and crowded accommodations while the men worked the boats and the women cleaned the fish.

Neptune [99]   Roman god of the sea.

Bacchus [99]   Roman god of wine. Sir Lawrence Alma-Tadema's painting *A Dedication to Bacchus* (1889) displays some of the traditional elements associated with the god mentioned here. Another famous Bacchus painting is that of Caravaggio (1597), which has a bowl of fruit in the foreground.

George Eliot . . . Middlemarch [100]   Eliot's novel *Middlemarch* was published in 1871–72. Woolf described it as "one of the few English novels written for grown-up people" in her essay "George Eliot" in *The Common Reader.*

and thought, This [102]   In all U.S. editions prior to this, the word "thought" has been followed by a period, which gave an odd sense to the line. The corrected proof shows that this error was likely introduced by an American editor (misled by the upper case T of "This"?).

Mile End Road [105]   A broad thoroughfare in the East End of London.

vail her crest [105]   "Vail" means to lower a banner or weapon as a sign of submission. In the first and all subsequent U.S. editions, the phrase reads "veil her crest," but the English edition and Dick, which is based on the corrected proof of the first U.S. edition, have "vail." It is almost certain that a U.S. copyeditor made the change for the first edition, thinking "vail" was a typo.

dismount her batteries [105]   Continuing the military metaphor, a battery is a platform on which artillery is mounted.

Voltaire [107]   The pen name of François Marie Arouet (1694–1778), author of *Candide* and many other works expressing his contempt for authority and institutions.

Madame de Staël [107]   1766–1817, an important figure in the French Revolution who wrote on politics and literature.

Napoleon [107]   1769–1821, French emperor.

French system of land tenure [107]   The manner in which property in land is held has long been crucially important in law. The French Revolution caused dramatic changes in land tenure.

Lord Rosebery [107]   1847–1929, a British politician appointed by Queen Victoria to be prime minister in 1894 but forced to resign a year later due to opposition from his own Liberal party.

Creevey's memoirs [107]   Thomas Creevey (1768–1838), a Whig politician whose *Creevey Papers* (1903) gave a gossipy account of Georgian social life.

Waverley novels [108]   The series of novels by Sir Walter Scott (1771–1832) that concern the Waverley family. Among them is *The Antiquary* (1816), which Mr. Ramsay reads after dinner. Scott was Leslie Stephen's favorite author and intimately connected for Woolf with memories of her father. Set in Scotland, *The Antiquary* also includes the image of a lighthouse. Woolf published an essay on the novel in the *Nation & Athenaeum,* November 1924; a revised version is in *The Moment and Other Essays.*

poor Sir Walter [108]   Sir Walter Scott, the novelist.

Jane Austen [108]   English novelist (1775–1817), author of *Pride and Prejudice, Emma, Sense and Sensibility, Persuasion,* and other works.

Tolstoi [110]   Leo Nikolayevich Tolstoy or Tolstoi (1828–1910), Russian author of *Anna Karenina, War and Peace,* and many other works. His novels were introduced to English-speaking readers in the translations of Constance Garnett.

Vronsky [110]   The lover of Anna Karenina in Tolstoy's novel.

Come out and climb the garden path ... Luriana, Lurilee [112–13]   All the lines quoted here are from "Luriana, Lurilee," a poem by Charles Elton (1839–1900) that was first published in *Another World Than This ...,* a collection edited by Vita Sackville-West and her husband, Harold Nicolson, in 1945. Woolf knew the poem from Lytton Strachey, who was related to Elton:

> Come out and climb the garden path
>   Luriana, Lurilee.
> The China rose is all abloom
> And buzzing with the yellow bee.

We'll swing you on the cedar bough,
　　Luriana, Lurilee.

I wonder if it seems to you,
　　Luriana, Lurilee,
That all the lives we ever lived
And all the lives to be,
Are full of trees and changing leaves,
　　Luriana, Lurilee.

How long it seems since you and I,
　　Luriana, Lurilee,
Roamed in the forest where our kind
Had just begun to be,
And laughed and chattered in the flowers,
　　Luriana, Lurilee.

How long since you and I went out,
　　Luriana, Lurilee,
To see the kings go riding by
Over lawn and daisy lea,
With their palm leaves and cedar sheaves,
　　Luriana, Lurilee.

Swing, swing, swing on a bough,
　　Luriana, Lurilee,
Till you sleep in a humble heap
Or under a gloomy churchyard tree,
And then fly back to swing on a bough,
　　Luriana, Lurilee.

Labour Party [114]   Founded in 1900, a collective of various independent and union organizations with the aim of representing
the working class in Parliament.

wash-leather [119]   A soft kind of leather, usually made of split sheepskin, in imitation of chamois leather.

one of old Sir Walter's [119]   Mr. Ramsay begins reading chapter XXXI from Walter Scott's *The Antiquary*, in which a drowned fisherman, Steenie, is mourned.

the China rose is all abloom [120]   Mrs. Ramsay recalls the lines from "Luriana, Lurilee" that her husband and Mr. Carmichael recited after dinner.

Steer, hither steer your winged pines [121]   The opening of "The Sirens' Song," part of "The Inner Temple Masque" by William Browne (1591–1643).

Mucklebackit's cottage [122]   Mr. Ramsay is thinking about the scene in *The Antiquary* describing the grief over Mucklebackit's son Steenie's death by drowning.

Balzac [123]   Honoré de Balzac (1799–1850), French author of a number of romances collectively known as *La Comédie humaine*.

Nor praise the deep vermilion in the rose [123]   The tenth line of Shakespeare's Sonnet 98 ("From you have I been absent in the spring").

Yet seem'd it winter still . . . [123]   The concluding couplet of Shakespeare's Sonnet 98.

"Yes, you were right . . ." [126]   The last paragraph of Part I in the English edition is different: " 'Yes, you were right. It's going to be wet to-morrow.' She had not said it, but he knew it. And she looked at him smiling. For she had triumphed again."

One by one the lamps . . . [129]   On the eve of the First World War, Lord Grey of Fallodon, the British foreign secretary, famously remarked, "The lamps are going out all over Europe; we shall not see them lit again in our lifetime." Woolf heard Lord Grey speak at a large public meeting of the League of Nations Union in October 1918; a copy of Grey's memoir *Twenty-Five Years, 1892–1916* (1925) was in the Woolfs' library.

Virgil [129]   Roman poet (70–19 B.C.), author of the *Aeneid,* the *Georgics,* and the *Eclogues.*

[Mr. Ramsay, stumbling along a passage . . .] [132]   Perhaps an indication of the profound trauma in Woolf's life this passage recalls (the death of her mother), it appears with variations in several different editions of the novel. The English edition follows the "Uniform Edition" published by the Hogarth Press in 1930: "[Mr. Ramsay stumbling along a passage stretched his arms out one dark morning, but, Mrs. Ramsay having died rather suddenly the night before, he stretched his arms out. They remained empty.]." In "A Sketch of the Past," Woolf wrote that when her mother died, "My father staggered from the bedroom as we came. I stretched out my arms to stop him, but he brushed past me, crying out something I could not catch; distraught" (91). See also Dick 201.

base-born [135]   Born out of wedlock.

[Prue Ramsay, leaning on her father's arm . . .] [135]   In the English edition, this sentence reads, "Prue Ramsay, leaning on her father's arm, was given in marriage that May."

[Prue Ramsay died that summer . . .] [136]   Woolf's half sister Stella Duckworth died in July 1897, three months after her marriage. She was pregnant, and although the usual explanation of her death is that it was due to peritonitis, some have also suggested her death was connected to her pregnancy. The English edition reads slightly differently: ". . . which was indeed a tragedy, people said. They said nobody deserved happiness more.]"

blows of hammers [137]   The sound of heavy artillery from the war in France.

blown up in France [137]   Most of Britain's fighting in the First World War was at the Western Front, a system of trenches running from the coast of Belgium through France to the German border.

Michaelmas [139]   The Christian Feast of Saint Michael is celebrated on September 29.

dorbeetle [145]   Common beetle that flies after sunset.

(Lily Briscoe had her bag…) [145]   English edition has an additional sentence and encloses this passage in brackets: "[Lily Briscoe had her bag carried up to the house late one evening in September. Mr. Carmichael came by the same train.]"

peace had come [145]   The armistice ending the First World War was signed on November 11, 1918.

"Alone" she heard him say, "Perished" [151]   Mr. Ramsay is reciting lines from the last stanza of William Cowper's poem "The Castaway," written in 1799, which reads:

> No voice divine the storm allayed,
>   No light propitious shone;
> When, snatched from all effectual aid,
>   We perished, each alone;
> But I beneath a rougher sea,
> And whelmed in deeper gulfs than he.

waistcoat [157]   Vest.

that was the question at what point… [161]   In the English edition there is a semicolon after "question," which sense demands: "that was the question; at what point…" (Dick 191 notes that on the proof, Woolf deleted a comma after "question" but put nothing in its place.)

ducks and drakes [163]   Skimming flat stones on the water's surface to see how many times they skip before sinking.

when ten ships . . . [167–68]   At the end of this paragraph, Mr. Ramsay is questioning Macalister about *eleven* ships. The second English edition, published in 1938 by Dent, corrected this to "ten," but other editions retain what seems to be Woolf's error.

Rickmansworth [177]   A town in Hertfordshire, just outside London.

a plait [177]   A braid.

Raphael had treated divinely [179]   A master painter of the Italian Renaissance, Raphael (Raffaello Sanzio, 1483–1520) is known for his many paintings of the Madonna and Child (Mary, with the infant Jesus).

Hampton Court [180]   The center of government in the time of King William III (reigned 1689–1702), this palace in London on the River Thames is famous for its architecture and gardens, including a maze.

omnibus [185]   In the nineteenth century, the French gave this name to new, long passenger coaches, the origin of our modern "bus." In 1925 Woolf wrote to the daughter of a friend that she wrote the word in full (in *Mrs. Dalloway*) "because 'busses' sounds to me like 'booses', and not 'busses'" (*Letters* 3: 184).

Piccadilly [185]   A major thoroughfare in the West End of London, incorporating Piccadilly Circus, and the location of several large hotels and theaters.

Standard, News [185]   Two of London's evening newspapers.

(The sea without a stain . . .) [191]   The English edition encloses this section in brackets.

shapes of a world not realised [192]   Echoes line 145 from William Wordsworth's "Ode: Intimations of Immortality from Recollections of Early Childhood" (1802–04):

> Blank misgivings of a Creature
> Moving about in worlds not realised,

Trafalgar Square [197]   In central London, site of Nelson's column celebrating the victories over the French and Spanish of Britain's greatest naval hero, Admiral Horatio Nelson (1758–1805).

Golder's Green [199]   A suburb of London.

how could he love his kind [200]   In Woolf's short story "The Man Who Loved His Kind," the socially awkward character Prickett Ellis seems to foreshadow Tansley.

How's that? [201]   In cricket, the appeal of the fielders to the umpire when they believe a batsman to be out.

crinolines [201]   Stiff petticoats.

peg-top trousers [201]   A form of trousers very wide in the hips and narrow in the ankles, in fashion circa 1858–65 (OED).

It is finished [211]   The last words of Christ on the cross (John 19:30).

old pagan god . . . trident [211]   Identifies Mr. Carmichael with Poseidon/Neptune.

Suggestions for Further Reading: *Virginia Woolf*

Editions

The Complete Shorter Fiction. Edited by Susan Dick. 2nd ed. San Diego: Harcourt, 1989.

The Diary of Virginia Woolf. Edited by Anne Olivier Bell. 5 vols. New York: Harcourt, 1977–84.

The Essays of Virginia Woolf. Edited by Andrew McNeillie. 6 vols. [in progress]. San Diego: Harcourt Brace Jovanovich, 1986–.

The Letters of Virginia Woolf. Edited by Nigel Nicolson and Joanne Trautmann. 6 vols. New York: Harcourt Brace Jovanovich, 1975–80.

Moments of Being. Edited by Jeanne Schulkind. San Diego: Harcourt, 1985.

A Passionate Apprentice: The Early Journals, 1897–1909. Edited by Mitchell A. Leaska. San Diego: Harcourt, 1990.

Biographies and Reference Works

Briggs, Julia. *Virginia Woolf: An Inner Life*. San Diego: Harcourt, 2005.

Hussey, Mark. *Virginia Woolf A to Z: A Comprehensive Reference for Students, Teachers, and Common Readers to Her Life, Works, and Critical Reception*. New York: Facts on File, 1995.

Kirkpatrick, B. J., and Stuart N. Clarke. *A Bibliography of Virginia Woolf*. 4th ed. Oxford: Clarendon, 1997.

Lee, Hermione. *Virginia Woolf*. New York: Knopf, 1996.

Marder, Herbert. *The Measure of Life: Virginia Woolf's Last Years.* Ithaca, NY: Cornell University Press, 2000.

Poole, Roger. *The Unknown Virginia Woolf.* 4th ed. Cambridge: Cambridge University Press, 1995.

Reid, Panthea. *Art and Affection: A Life of Virginia Woolf.* New York: Oxford University Press, 1996.

General Criticism

Abel, Elizabeth. *Virginia Woolf and the Fictions of Psychoanalysis.* Chicago: University of Chicago Press, 1989.

Bazin, Nancy Topping. *Virginia Woolf and the Androgynous Vision.* New Brunswick, NJ: Rutgers University Press, 1973.

Beer, Gillian. *Virginia Woolf: The Common Ground.* Ann Arbor: University of Michigan Press, 1996.

Cuddy-Keane, Melba. *Virginia Woolf, the Intellectual, and the Public Sphere.* Cambridge: Cambridge University Press, 2003.

DiBattista, Maria. *Virginia Woolf's Major Novels: The Fables of Anon.* New Haven, CT: Yale University Press, 1980.

Fleishman, Avrom. *Virginia Woolf: A Critical Reading.* Baltimore: Johns Hopkins University Press, 1975.

Froula, Christine. *Virginia Woolf and the Bloomsbury Avant-Garde: War, Civilization, Modernity.* New York: Columbia University Press, 2005.

Guiguet, Jean. *Virginia Woolf and Her Works.* New York: Harcourt Brace Jovanovich, 1965.

Harper, Howard. *Between Language and Silence: The Novels of Virginia Woolf.* Baton Rouge: Louisiana State University Press, 1982.

Hussey, Mark. *The Singing of the Real World: The Philosophy of Virginia Woolf's Fiction.* Columbus: Ohio State University Press, 1986.

———, ed. *Virginia Woolf and War: Fiction, Reality and Myth.* Syracuse, NY: Syracuse University Press, 1991.

Majumdar, Robin, and Allen McLaurin, eds. *Virginia Woolf: The Critical Heritage*. Boston: Routledge, 1975.

Marcus, Jane. *Art and Anger: Reading Like a Woman*. Columbus: Ohio State University Press, 1988.

———, ed. *New Feminist Essays on Virginia Woolf*. Lincoln: University of Nebraska Press, 1981.

———, ed. *Virginia Woolf: A Feminist Slant*. Lincoln: University of Nebraska Press, 1983.

———, ed. *Virginia Woolf and Bloomsbury: A Centenary Celebration*. Bloomington: Indiana University Press, 1987.

———. *Virginia Woolf and the Languages of Patriarchy*. Bloomington: Indiana University Press, 1987.

McLaurin, Allen. *Virginia Woolf: The Echoes Enslaved*. Cambridge: Cambridge University Press, 1973.

McNees, Eleanor, ed. *Virginia Woolf: Critical Assessments*. 4 vols. New York: Routledge, 1994.

Minow-Pinkney, Makiko. *Virginia Woolf and the Problem of the Subject: Feminine Writing in the Major Novels*. New Brunswick, NJ: Rutgers University Press, 1987.

Phillips, Kathy J. *Virginia Woolf Against Empire*. Knoxville: University of Tennessee Press, 1994.

Roe, Sue, and Susan Sellers, eds. *The Cambridge Companion to Virginia Woolf*. Cambridge: Cambridge University Press, 2000.

Ruotolo, Lucio. *The Interrupted Moment: A View of Virginia Woolf's Novels*. Stanford, CA: Stanford University Press, 1986.

Silver, Brenda R. *Virginia Woolf Icon*. Chicago: University of Chicago Press, 1999.

Zwerdling, Alex. *Virginia Woolf and the Real World*. Berkeley: University of California Press, 1986.

Suggestions for Further Reading:
To the Lighthouse
(in addition to the works cited in the introduction)

Abel, Elizabeth. "*To the Lighthouse*: James and Cam" and "Spatial Relations: Lily Briscoe's Painting." In *Virginia Woolf and the Fictions of Psychoanalysis*. Chicago: University of Chicago Press, 1989.

Annan, Noel. *Leslie Stephen: The Godless Victorian*. New York: Random House, 1984.

Banfield, Ann. "Tragic Time: The Problem of the Future in Cambridge Philosophy and *To the Lighthouse*." *Modernism/Modernity* 7.1 (2000): 43–75.

Beer, Gillian. "Hume, Stephen, and Elegy in *To the Lighthouse*." In *The Common Ground: Essays by Gillian Beer*. Ann Arbor: University of Michigan Press, 1996.

———. "The Island and the Aeroplane: The Case of Virginia Woolf." In *Nation and Narration*. Edited by Homi K. Bhabha, 265–90. New York: Routledge, 1990.

Bicknell, John. "Mr Ramsay was Young Once." In *Virginia Woolf and Bloomsbury*. Edited by Jane Marcus, 52–67. Bloomington: Indiana University Press, 1987.

Cameron, Julia Margaret. *Victorian Photographs of Famous Men & Fair Women*. London: Hogarth Press, 1973.

Clark, Miriam Marty. "Consciousness, Stream, and Quanta in *To the Lighthouse*." *Studies in the Novel* 21 (Winter 1989): 413–23.

Corsa, Helen Storm. "*To the Lighthouse*: Death, Mourning, and Transfiguration." *Literature and Psychology* 21.3 (1971): 115–31.

Daugherty, Beth Rigel, and Mary Beth Pringle, eds. *Approaches to Teaching Woolf's* To the Lighthouse. New York: Modern Language Association of America, 2001.

Emery, Mary Lou. " 'Robbed of Meaning': The Work at the Center of *To the Lighthouse*." *Modern Fiction Studies* 38 (1992): 217–34.

Esch, Deborah. " 'Think of a Kitchen Table': Hume, Woolf, and the Translation of Example." In *Literature as Philosophy/Philosophy as Literature*. Edited by Donald G. Marshall, 262–76. Iowa City: University of Iowa Press, 1987.

Fisher, Jane. "The Seduction of the Father: Virginia Woolf and Leslie Stephen." *Women's Studies* 18 (1990): 31–48.

Flint, Kate. "Virginia Woolf and the General Strike." *Essays in Criticism* 36 (1986): 319–34.

Gabler, Hans Walter. "A Tale of Two Texts: Or, How One Might Edit Virginia Woolf's *To the Lighthouse*." *Woolf Studies Annual* 10 (2004): 1–29.

Hankins, Leslie. "A Splice of Reel Life in Virginia Woolf's 'Time Passes': Censorship, Cinema, and 'the Usual Battlefield of Emotions.' " *Criticism* 35 (1993): 91–114.

Haule, James M. "*To the Lighthouse* and the Great War: The Evidence of Virginia Woolf's Revisions of 'Time Passes.' " In *Virginia Woolf and War*. Edited by Mark Hussey, 164–79. Syracuse, NY: Syracuse University Press, 1991.

Hill, Katherine. "Virginia Woolf and Leslie Stephen: History and Literary Revolution." *PMLA* 96 (1981): 351–62. (And see "Forum," for letters in response from Louise DeSalvo and Alice Fox. *PMLA* 97.2 [March 1982]: 103–06.)

Hoffman, Anne. "Demeter and Poseidon: Fusion and Distance in *To the Lighthouse*." *Studies in the Novel* 16 (1984): 182–96.

Homans, Margaret. "Postscript: Mothers and Daughters in Virginia Woolf's Victorian Novel." In *Bearing the Word: Language and Female Experience in Nineteenth-Century Women's Writing*, 277–319. Chicago: University of Chicago Press, 1986.

Lavin, J. A. "The First Editions of Virginia Woolf's *To the Lighthouse*." In *Proof: The Yearbook of American Bibliographical and Textual Studies*. Edited by Joseph Katz, 185–211. Columbia: University of South Carolina Press, 1972.

Leaska, Mitchell A. *Virginia Woolf's Lighthouse: A Study in Critical Method*. New York: Columbia University Press, 1970.

Levenback, Karen L. "The Language of Memory as Time Passes." In *Virginia Woolf and the Great War*. Syracuse, NY: Syracuse University Press, 1999.

Lilienfeld, Jane. " 'The Deceptiveness of Beauty': Mother Love and Mother Hate in *To the Lighthouse*." *Twentieth Century Literature* 23 (October 1977): 345–76.

———. " 'The Horrors of Family Life': A Feminist Interrogation of the Politics of Codependence in *To the Lighthouse*." In *Reading Alcoholisms*, 159–231. New York: St. Martin's, 1999.

———. " 'Like a Lion Seeking Whom He Could Devour': Domestic Violence in *To the Lighthouse*." In *Virginia Woolf Miscellanies*. Edited by Mark Hussey and Vara Neverow-Turk, 154–64. New York: Pace University Press, 1992.

Matro, Thomas G. "Only Relations: Vision and Achievement in *To the Lighthouse*." *PMLA* 99 (1984): 212–24.

Paul, Janis. *The Victorian Heritage of Virginia Woolf: The External World in Her Novels*. Norman, OK: Pilgrim, 1985.

Reid, Su. To the Lighthouse: *An Introduction to the Variety of Criticism*. London: Macmillan, 1991.

Rosenbaum, S. P. "Railing Against Realism: Philosophy and *To the Lighthouse*." *Philosophy and Literature* 7.1 (April 1983): 89–91.

Rubenstein, Roberta. "Yearning and Nostalgia: Fiction and Autobiographical Writings of Virginia Woolf and Doris Lessing." In *Home Matters: Longing and Belonging, Nostalgia and Mourning in Women's Fiction*. New York: Palgrave, 2001.

Vanita, Ruth. "Bringing Buried Things to Light: Homoerotic Alliances in *To the Lighthouse*." In *Virginia Woolf: Lesbian Readings*.

Edited by Eileen Barrett and Patricia Cramer, 165–79. New York: New York University Press, 1997.

Winston, Janet. "'Something Out of Harmony': *To the Lighthouse* and the Subject(s) of Empire." *Woolf Studies Annual* 2 (1996): 39–70.

Zwerdling, Alex. "The Domestic Politics of *To the Lighthouse*." In *Virginia Woolf and the Real World.* Berkeley: University of California Press, 1986.

Virginia Woolf Annotated Editions

Top Woolf scholars provide valuable introductions, notes, suggestions for further reading, and critical analysis in this paperback series. Students reading these books will have the resources at hand to help them understand the text as well as the reasons and methods behind Woolf's writing.

Between the Acts
Annotated and with an introduction by Melba Cuddy-Keane
978-0-15-603473-9 • 0-15-603473-5

Jacob's Room
Annotated and with an introduction by Vara Neverow
978-0-15-603479-1 • 0-15-603479-4

Mrs. Dalloway
Annotated and with an introduction by Bonnie Kime Scott
978-0-15-603035-9 • 0-15-603035-7

Orlando: A Biography
Annotated and with an introduction by Maria DiBattista
978-0-15-603151-6 • 0-15-603151-5

A Room of One's Own
Annotated and with an introduction by Susan Gubar
978-0-15-603041-0 • 0-15-603041-1

Three Guineas
Annotated and with an introduction by Jane Marcus
978-0-15-603163-9 • 0-15-603163-9

To the Lighthouse
Annotated and with an introduction by Mark Hussey
978-0-15-603047-2 • 0-15-603047-0

The Waves
Annotated and with an introduction by Molly Hite
978-0-15-603157-8 • 0-15-603157-4

The Years
Annotated and with an introduction by Eleanor McNees
978-0-15-603485-2 • 0-15-603485-9

Each volume includes a preface by Mark Hussey, professor of English and women's and gender studies at Pace University, and editor of *Woolf Studies Annual*.

⬛Harcourt | HARVEST BOOKS
www.HarcourtBooks.com